Dedication

This book is dedicated to my mother, Angelina, my guidance and strength, and to my late father, Enrique, for showing me the power of humility and the beauty of simplicity. And last to my son, Manny, you're my life...I love you so much!

Acknowledgment

This book is a product of love, determination, and pure stubbornness. Against all obstacles, I was adamant not to be denied in writing it. The way this story was spawned in my mind; how it drove me, and haunted me could have been a book of its own. A semi-autobiographical fiction mixed with the craziness we all writers have, that uncontrollable urge to have our voices be heard through our words. It was first self-published in 2006 and after deep contemplation, I removed it from circulation to tweak it a bit more. After the release of "When Angels Fall" by Aignos Publishing and the great reviews the book received, we decided to re-publish this book. What was once titled "Josefa's Curse"—to give it a new life and a fresh beginning—we decided to change the title to the "Battle for a Soul"; and in actuality, the book itself was a battle for my own soul to be satisfied.

There are many people in my corner, always cheering me on, and for that I consider myself very fortunate. The first person I want to thank is my mother Angelina Veléz, for her love and her remedies to chase the willies away. Manny Meléndez, my son and best friend, my daughter-in-law Erica and the two most incredible angels, Eva and Nikolas, my grandchildren. Furthermore, big hugs to my sisters, Carmen Feliberty and Lydia Cabassa, and their husbands Martin Feliberty and Oscar Cabassa and my brother Jose Meléndez, I thank you for your support. Always kudos to my nieces, Jennifer and Stephanie and their lovely daughters, Skyleen and Izabella, and my nephew Phil, you guys fill me with pride. To Mary Lofaro for your understanding my crazy motto, 'it's all about me', and to Dolores, Hudson, Hunter and Juliet, you guys rock!

Additionally, a big shout to Jonathan Marcantoni for your friendship, Zachary M. Oliver for your guidance and putting everything together, and Carlos Aleman, man, your artistic masterpiece of the book cover is worth the price of the book.

There's no way a person could stumble, nor fail, when surrounded by an awesome team of wonderful human beings! I thank you all!

And last, I thank You God, for this gift you gave me of putting words together, sentences into paragraphs, pages into chapters, and stories into worlds that I create under Your watchful eyes…for You will always be my first reader!

PROLOGUE: PUERTO RICO 1956

Agapito could still hear his wife's screams as he ran past his neighbor's farm. In the silence of the dying night, the screams climbed and lifted themselves high above the darkened mountains. The screams disturbed him, rattled his brain, yet they pushed him and drove him into a mad dash across the uneven dirt road. He tumbled through gashed ditches and raised roots from old mango trees while shadowed branches ambushed him. Knotted pains squeezed his stomach forcing him to stop and to reclaim the breath his lungs had released in painful gasps. A dried metallic taste coated the inside of his mouth, and he swallowed the last drops of his dense saliva. He could feel his heart pounding, rattling convulsively inside his chest.

Around him, armies of crickets shrieked in monotonous sounds and unseen coquis—tree frogs—joined the chorus. A gentle breeze covered his perspired face with cool kisses. The exhaustion during the day began to weigh down on his shoulders with frustrated thoughts. Thin blue lines threatened to slice the sky's darkness, throwing hints of a morning ready to spread its new brilliant colors.

His eyes—deprived of sleep—began to close, as he leaned for a second or two upon the trunk of a tree to rest his fatigued body. He heard snores deep within the cavity of his throat welcoming oblivion. His wife's screams, which once echoed in his ears, were now distant and no longer important. Slowly, he felt himself succumbing to the soothing touch of sleep; a touch that hunched his shoulders and buckled his knees. He plummeted to the ground hard, a pain exploding through his body snapping the sleepiness away. He jumped back on his feet, the old tree aiding him in finding strength. For a few seconds, he felt disorientated while he pushed away from the tree in unsteady steps. Above him, leaves rustled in murmuring whispers while more strips of blue streaked the velvet, navy sky. Somewhere a rooster croaked at the unfolding dawn.

Once again, his wife's screams tore through the air, awakening the reason of his mad race through the country hills. His wife was in labor and there was something terribly wrong, which he couldn't understand. It seemed the child inside was forcing itself from the womb before the pregnancy had reached its nine-month term. Throughout the evening, he'd tried everything to soothe her pain, it all failed—so he decided to seek the only person able to help; Doña Lola, the midwife. Leaving his wife alone kept gnawing at him in small annoying bites. He was relieved that he had taken their other children to his sister's house the second his wife's conditions had worsened; they were too young to witness their mother's sufferings. He was not far from the midwife's house and for that he was grateful. He took a deep breath and started to run again. He stopped short on a hill where he could make out the shape of the shack where the midwife lived; it looked like a black smear on the canvas of an amateur artist. He dashed down the knoll, his feet scrambling to keep his balance. Scrawny dogs ran at him from underneath the shack with snarling, angry barks. But, they ran by his side when his smell was registered as familiar and as someone who belonged among them. As he came closer, the hut's door was flung open and an old brown-skinned woman appeared like a ghost. A ragged shawl covered her bony shoulders, protecting her from the coldness of the early aurora. Against her chest, she held a bundle, which she quickly shoved into Agapito's arms. She went around him, and with the help of a stick, she moved toward the screams. Agapito followed her, struggling to keep up with her hurried steps. Doña Lola's agility and strength defied her old body.

"Why didn't you come sooner?" she asked in a scolding fashion.

"I didn't think that it was time for the baby to come out. This is only the beginning of her eighth month. I just thought it was nothing more than bad indigestion from dinner."

"What did she have for dinner?" The old woman maneuvered her makeshift cane through the rugged path.

"She didn't eat that much…just a few spoonfuls of noodle soup. She didn't have much appetite," he was puffing hard, his words coming out in halting spurges.

The old woman remained silent; the only sound came from her walking stick as it hit pebbles on the road and slashed at branches that had grown too close to the dirt path.

As they rushed the screams ceased, and Agapito hoped that his wife had finally fallen asleep and that all the pain was truly caused by what he'd thought—indigestion—and nothing as serious as the baby being born premature. He could see his house now, a wooden shack with a zinc patched roof, which stood a bit slanted on top of four stilts. His two old dogs peeked at them from underneath the house; a slow cough of a bark was all they could muster. The midwife entered the shack, and he followed, afraid of what lay before him. Overhead, the sky was illuminated with more light, as slivers of blue and yellow stroked the radiant pale blue space.

An intense suffocating heat mixed with a stench of unearthly sweat which greeted them. Agapito looked at his wife as she wiggled and took deep breaths on the sweat-soaked cot, he was traumatized to see that she didn't have any resemblance to his wife of nine years. She had been swollen to twice her weight, and her face was streaked with a mixture of tears and sweat. Her hair was plastered against her skin; her puffed face was pale, red blotches appeared all around her body like a rash. She opened and closed her mouth with the desperate action of a fish thrown upon the sand to die. Her screams were now reduced to an irritating whimper. Her drenched body lifted itself from the cot, writhing with every painful contractions. Her pupils, covered with a deathly white film, seemed to stare blankly at the inside of her head.

Agapito stood there paralyzed, until a strong push from the midwife snapped him out of it. In a domineering voice, she instructed him to bring her water and without looking at him, she began to undo the bundle and spread on a table small glass jars containing an assortment of dried herbs and different color lotions.

"For the love of the Almighty, what's taking you so long? Either be alert or get out of the way," the midwife raised her voice without anger, but with an authoritative tone. This was clearly not the first time she had been in a situation this grave. Doña Lola had been delivering babies all over the area for over fifty years, something she had learned from her mother when she was barely the age of conceiving. She was never baffled by the process of birth.

Many sick newborns had been restored to health by her after the local hospitals had given up hope to the poor illiterate jíbaros—hicks—from the hills. In all her sixty-plus years of midwifery, only ten had passed away. A small margin to the hundreds that had grown up to adulthood. And now she was delivering their offspring as well.

Agapito walked clumsily inside the partitioned area that formed their bedroom as water from a tin bucket, which he carried, spilled all over his feet as he held a porcelain basin under his arm. Doña Lola seized the basin and placed it next to her opened bundle. "Fill the basin halfway and go and get me a clean blanket and a few towels."

When he came back, she grabbed a towel and submerged it in the water. She squeezed the excess water, afterwards smeared a brownish lotion on the center of the cloth and massaged the mixture on the woman's temple and next rubbed the rest on the woman's belly; her soothing touches bringing sudden relief to the laboring mother. Doña Lola lowered her body and with the morning light, she could see part of the baby's head. She massaged the woman's stomach as she felt for the body of the struggling child. She guided her slender experienced hands around the woman's vagina, her fingers becoming her eyes. The mother hissed with soundless yells while her nails ripped the thin soiled mattress beneath her.

Agapito caressed his wife's forehead with trembling hands. His lips twisted into a sneer of fright. He had never felt such a helplessness in his whole life, and he prayed to God for a miracle. He watched his wife's body contort on the cot; her lips chapped and bleeding by her clenched teeth. He pulled his eyes away from her and stared at a large cross that hung on the wall by the head of the cot. *Sweet Jesus,* he found himself silently praying. *Don't let her die; please, don't let her die.*

In gradual moving actions, Agapito watched as the old woman's hands disappeared inside his wife. Her eyes closed as she followed her slender fingers. His wife jumped in pain, and quickly he began to recite prayers in his head, prayers he'd abandoned many years ago.

"Wait outside," Doña Lola's stern instructions startled him, her clear brown eyes focusing on his blood-shot eyes.

He began to protest, but her controlled anger chilled the marrow in his bones.

"Go outside I said. When it's over you can come back, but for now, you would be more helpful if you stand outside with the dogs. Make me some coffee. When I'm finished, a hot black cup will be much appreciated."

"But—"

"Please Agapito, don't let me waste precious time by arguing with you. Get out!"

He glanced apprehensively at his wife, with hesitated steps, Agapito went outside. The harsh morning sun attacked him as soon as he exited the shack as colorful birds and wild red parrots flew above, oblivious of his pain. He climbed down the wooden planks that served as stairs and stepped on the reddish dirt. His eyes wandered through the peaceful countryside, yet he could not shake the fearsome image of his wife out of his head.

He feared for their new baby, but he was willing to accept the death of the child over hers. His beautiful wife Josefa, without her existence, life would be a frivolous laughable concept. His whole life was entrusted into the hands of Doña Lola. What other choices did he have? The sophisticated medicine and complicated apparatus that the hospital possessed were not invented for people like himself or his wife. He trusted the old woman; everyone in the whole area did. Didn't she deliver his other four children? Didn't she deliver him and his wife as well? His wife was in good hands; he consoled himself, and with God on their side, very soon there will be another mouth to feed.

His two old smelly dogs dragged themselves from underneath the house, their matted sickening coats showing patches of missing fur. Agapito looked at them, and then glanced around disorientated, as if he were noticing his whereabouts for the first time. He sat on a rock next to a large barrel where the rainwater was collected, and squeezed his face between his rough callused hands. He looked down and began to pray again.

Besides a few soft moans and large sighs from Doña Lola, everything was calm and peaceful. He thought of his mother and what she taught him about the beauty and love of God. However, now he questioned the reality of those aspects. He felt betrayed by his beliefs, and even though he prayed for the safety of his wife, deep within he was cursing at everything associated with God. He was beginning to accept the child's death, thinking it would be a blessing instead of a tragedy. He closed his eyes, and the fatigue began to creep and consume his bones; sleep was not far behind.

The first shout that startled him was his wife's, and even though the yell was weak and laced with pain, it was a good sign. The dogs barked and howled in unison terror and like terrified vermin, they ran underneath the house. A second cry was alien and small. A third scream belonged to Doña Lola and that revelation disturbed Agapito and seized his heart with horror. He jumped to his feet and stood staring at the door; his body tensed and paralyzed. Like a mad symphony, the three different cries melted and fused into each other.

"Agapito!" Doña Lola called in an almost childish shriek.

"Agapito!" she called again, this time the urgency was alarming.

He took a few steps toward the shack, but Doña Lola came out;

her eyes glowing with awe and disbelief. Her hands were no longer brown, but were a rich loud red. Her clothes were splattered with bloody droplets, and tears streaked her bloodstained face.

"Agapito," she repeated his name again in desperation. The old midwife took one step forward—a single step—that she missed completely. She fell hard on top of the bushes of roses by the side of the house. Thorns slashed her thin wrinkled skin with perfect red lines. Agapito ran to her, confused at the old woman's behavior and the sudden screams that seemed to rush at him from the depth of the house. From under the shack, the two dogs howled, their sagging necks quivering and squeezing the wails into pathetic yelps.

Agapito lifted Doña Lola from the bushes, her skeleton-like body weightless and limp. He carried her into a hammock that hung between the avocado and mango trees. He placed her down gently, smelling the aroma of herbs and lotion all around her along with the foul smell of fresh blood. Doña Lola's breaths were short; many pauses separating each breath. Her large brown eyes opened up, leaping from her sunken face. Her arms flailed in a desperate effort to keep invisible hands from touching her. Her paper-thin fist grabbed Agapito by his collar and brought him closer to her trembling lips.

"He wants him," she whispered, before she died.

Chapter One

A dry bitter cold came from the East River chased by a turbulent gust that grew in force and nastiness. A dirty-gray sky cast a gloom over the old dilapidated tenements of East Harlem, N.Y.—El Barrio. Josefa felt the hard freezing slaps of the merciless wind and needle-sharp pains of hail slamming on to her face. Her breath came out of her mouth in white spinning vapors. She placed the two shopping bags she had been carrying, for four blocks, on the cracked sidewalk and tightened the scarf around her neck; hoping that the tightness would bring more warmth and protection from the severe weather.

Her gloveless hands were frigid, and the skin over her knuckles was stretched and white. The rests of her hands were blotchy and dry. The marks of the shopping bag handles were traced like carved reddish scars on her palms. She cursed at her forgetfulness for leaving her gloves at work. She sneezed hard, and it was followed by a hacking cough that scraped her throat, she knew that the cough was going to nag her all night long. Two young children came out from the candy store on the corner and ran past her, their small hands packed with candy and comic books. Their laughter reminded her of her own children, who by now were probably anticipating her arrival.

She scooped the shopping bags, not welcoming the discomfort they brought to her hands, and hurried her steps. There were two more blocks separating her from home. She approached the elevated Metro-

North tracks where speeding trains escaped the city for the suburbs of upstate New York—a place she had seen only a few times and reminded her of Puerto Rico, with its open fields, towering trees and small houses. Unlike this dump, she called home with its dying trees, filthy concrete and the lifeless buildings that stood like solemn stoned robots.

She crossed the street and before entering the underpass of the brick structure that split Park Avenue, she slowed down and looked around. She was always afraid of this spot and very seldom did she use the small pedestrian underpass, usually walking through the large one designed for the cars. Everyone in the neighborhood knew that the dim claustrophobic underpass was the place where muggers made their living.

Howling angry winds roared from the bared branches from the trees in nearby Central Park, meeting in the middle of Madison Avenue, the savage blast spawned by the East River. Both forces combined ripped at her coat and push her aside with vicious shoves. Her wool red cap loosened its grip from the hairpins, and the raw ferocious cold threatened her with arctic embraces. A snow flurry danced over the ground, attaching to her coat like a bad case of dandruff. She shivered, and already she could see the flakes piggy-backing on one another, the beginning of a white blanket that nature was weaving.

She let out a heavy sigh, grateful that she was finally climbing the four steps of her building's stoop. With her hunched shoulders, she pushed the door open and the dimness of the long hallway enveloped her. She could smell tomato sauce seeping through Mrs. Pepenelli's apartment; the last Italian family left from the old days when East Harlem was predominately an Italian section. Josefa dragged herself up the creaking stairs. She was hoping the landlord would keep his promise and allow her to switch places when the next apartment became available on the lower floors. Her apartment was on the last floor and the constant traffic of junkies going up and down to the roof, not only kept her awake most of the night, but she also was afraid when she left for work. The steady fear of some strung-out dope fiend breaking in her apartment was something that always kept her uneasy.

It was no secret throughout the neighborhood that her husband worked two jobs and was mostly away from his family, placing her as the easiest candidate to become a statistic on the police blotters, and if not her, one of her children who ranged from ages of ten to sixteen. The oldest was Felix, followed by Migdalia, Gisela, Norma, and the baby of the house, Eddie. The young thugs of the area were already defiantly looking at her daughters with their slimy up and down disrespectful stares. How many times did she want to gorge their eyes out and spit at their leery faces? Nevertheless, for the safety of her children, she always ignored the parasites that slithered at all hours during the day and night.

She cursed the day that she fell for the promises that her husband, Agapito, placed in front of her. He had left Puerto Rico when Eddie was barely three years old to seek a better life in New York. "I can't live like this anymore," he had told her one night as a treacherous rain crashed and shook their little shack. Agapito had family living in the mainland, and stories about the opportunities available were too enticing to be ignored. After a flurry of letter exchanges with his cousin Enrique, Agapito stuffed a few items of clothing in a suitcase and boarded a plane that flew him into the so-called 'arms of riches and success'. He had found work in a factory where Enrique had been employed for the past five years, and soon a bit of money began to arrive weekly to Puerto Rico.

After years of struggling, he decided that it was best for the whole family to meet him in New York, a move that she was not thrilled in making. Even so, being a loyal wife, she gathered their children and left Puerto Rico. She believed in her husband, and thought too many years passed since her children had a father. Besides, he boasted about the great schools and the excellent housing in New York. The opportunities were endless, and more available than in Puerto Rico, he had argued, "our kids could become doctors and lawyers, instead of sugarcane cutters and housewives."

However, now that they were together for almost a year, the novelty and greatness of this new golden land became the biggest lie of them all. Her husband was working two jobs, killing himself for a small salary, and her job at the button factory was great financial help. Even so, regardless how much they worked there was never enough to give them peace of mind. It seemed that their mailbox was always filled with bills.

She missed the warm sunny days of her Puerto Rico, and the cool evenings fanned by palm trees that swayed at the command of the wind. The thought of returning to her homeland and forgetting the notion of re-creating her life in this heartless slab of cement were thoughts that came to her mind often. The same way she had packed her belongings and those of her children to venture to New York, was the identical way she could pack and go back to the land where birds serenaded you with melodic songs in the morning, not garbage cans being thrown on still dirty sidewalks. The land where small tree frogs sing lullabies that snuggle you into a comfortable sleep, and where you don't need clumsy looking coats and ugly barbarian snow boots.

Josefa placed the bags in front of her apartment door and began to rummage through her pocketbook for the keys.

Through the dark, paint-peeling door, she could hear the music blaring from inside. An up-tempo beat of The Beatles yelling some garbage that she couldn't understand, music that to her will never be as romantic as her Puerto Rican tunes. Just less than a year in America and already her kids were listening to American music and complaining loudly whenever she played her Spanish sounds. The boleros and the plenas to her children were now hick music that they began to disassociate from. She definitely had to get away from this land before it completely removed the pride of being jibaros—country people from the island.

Josefa opened the door, and the music attacked her with its screeching electric guitar wails. Her three daughters sat in a semi-circle—Apache style—around the small record player. Their .45 vinyl records littered the floor, each girl trying to mouth the lyrics that screamed out from the tiny vibrating speakers.

"¡Baja eso, por favor!" Josefa shouted without penetrating the high decibels that her daughters' ears were been bombarded with.

"Lower that now!"

She finally got their attention as all three snapped their necks back in perfect synchronized unison. Migdalia, the oldest and the leader of the three turned the knob as The Beatles faded into a muffled yelp. All three jumped, again timed with precision, and surrounded Josefa showering her with kisses and hugs. Gisela grabbed one of the shopping bags and Norma the other, while Migdalia helped her mother with her coat.

"Ay Dios mio," Josefa shook her head while rubbing her hands together and blowing on them at the same time. "It's cold out there, and now it's beginning to snow. How the hell can any human being get used to these conditions? Neither human being nor animal belongs in the cold unless you are an Eskimo or a polar bear. Where are your brothers?" Josefa glanced around.

"Eddie is in the room reading one of his stupid comic books," Migdalia reported like a general. She always took the initiative to give a complete summary of what went on during the day. Who cursed, who farted, who refused to help with the chores, and who had the audacity to question her commands.

"Where's Felix?"

"He went out," Norma blurted, receiving a disapproving stare from Migdalia. Gisela gasped, knowing that Norma was going to get a hair pulling from Migdalia for her boldness.

"What do you mean out?" Josefa shot a stern look at Norma as she walked into the kitchen as the three girls followed. Gisela and Norma busied themselves with putting away the groceries from the shopping bags while Migdalia sat upon a chair and watched as her mother ran cold water on her frozen hands.

"Does that really work?" Migdalia asked while she glared every other second at Norma.

"Si hija," Josefa let out a low hurtful sigh. "Your Tia Carmen always said that when your fingers are frozen from the cold not to let neither hot, nor warm water runs through them. The first thing you must do is let cold water run on them, and then add a bit of hot water."

"How come?" Migdalia like always looking for more answers.

"I don't know, if it works, the reason behind it does not matter. But forget about my hands, I want to know where did your brother go?"

"He just left," Migdalia, responded again glancing at Norma to remind her who was in command, regardless if their mother was home or not.

"So Felix left, just like that?" Josefa didn't hide her annoyance while her hands were warming. "Did he say where he was going? How many times have I told him not to leave you kids alone?"

"Ay mami, you know how he is," Norma defied Migdalia. "He thinks that he's the man around the house. He just took his coat and left and only mumbled that he was coming back."

Josefa dried her hands on a towel that hung from the handle of the refrigerator and sat down next to Migdalia and started to remove her boots. She stretched her toes and wiggled them from under the thick sweat socks that belonged to her husband.

"Mami, you want some coffee?" Gisela asked timidly, from all the children, she was the most sensitive and was always trying to please everyone.

"Ay, God bless you, nena," Josefa blew her daughter a kiss while she massaged her feet hoping for blood circulation in her toes to return.

Eddie came crashing through the kitchen, with a comic book flailing in one hand and a lollipop in the other. He ransacked the refrigerator to see what delights his mother brought. Josefa reached out and grabbed his arm pulling him to her. She gave him a kiss and a tight hug. "You don't love your mother anymore? All you care is what I bring home on Fridays, right?"

Eddie wiggled himself from his mother's arms and plopped into the chair facing her. The syrup of the lollipop glazed his lips with a reddish sparkling color.

Gisela placed a cup of coffee carefully in front of her mother, accepting the smile from her and the gentle squeeze on her arm. She then leaned proudly against the kitchen sink as her mother took a sip and savored the warmth of the strong coffee. All the children watched in silence as their mother finished her coffee, her eyes misty and far away.

"I think Felix is in love," Eddie broke the silence, his small hands twisting the lollipop inside his cherry-colored mouth. "He took a bath, got dressed and splashed his neck with the Avon cologne that you gave him for his birthday."

Josefa laughed, and her children laughed with her. Eddie was pleased, and he laughed the hardest, happy with himself and with his comment.

"Tu eres un bochinchero," Josefa smirked. "You are such a gossiper. Now, does anybody know where Felix really went?"

They stared blankly at each other, shrugging because in actuality none of them knew.

The phone rang, and they all jumped startled at the intrusion. Migdalia as always, leaped and snatched the receiver and then looked around to remind her sisters that she was still in command.

"Hello," Migdalia answered. Her eyes squinted, and her eyebrows crunched into a frown. She listened carefully at the voice on the other end, everyone's eyes on her, making her more important and special; she loved that, every bit of it.

"One second, please," Migdalia struggled with her English. She held the phone close to her chest and turned to her mother.

"Mami is for you, es una Americana."

Josefa took the phone as her children listened at their mother's halting bad English. A few minutes later, she placed the phone down, feeling her children's eyes burrowing into her. Patiently, they waited to hear the context of her conversation. They knew that it was important, because the caller was an American woman, with their fast speech and sharp 'S' sounding syllables.

"Who was that mami?" Norma couldn't control her curiosity, again receiving a neck-whiplash stare from Migdalia.

"Why are you so nosy?" Josefa asked her daughter playfully.

"Yeah, right, you are so nosy," Migdalia couldn't contain herself and was also a discreet warning to Norma for the outburst. And to remind her that as soon as their mother was not around, there would be consequences for Norma to pay.

"What about you?" Norma said as she turned and confronted Migdalia, her large brown eyes fierce. "You want to know as much as I do sángana."

"Don't call your sister stupid," Josefa reprimanded Norma as Migdalia took a few steps forward, but staying close to her mother.

"You are the sángana, idiot," Migdalia tried to show her superiority to the others, but knowing that lately she was losing her air of power and all because of Norma and her combative self.

"¡Por favor niñas ya basta!" Josefa raised her voice silencing them quickly. "You kids are always fighting; anyone will think that you came from different fathers."

"I'm not fighting," Eddie pleaded his innocence from behind the cover of a Green Lantern comic book.

"I didn't say anything, mami," Gisela added; her voice was timid and low. She didn't want to say anything but felt that she had to be part of the conversation.

Josefa sat back down, tilted her head backward as her hair cascaded like a brown waterfall over the chair. She closed her eyes and twisted her neck from side to side, feeling the knots bunched on top of her shoulders. "Go and watch television, I need five minutes of rest before dinner," Josefa whispered through chapped lips, the last bit of her lipstick after the long hard day, still boasting reddish shades. "And please keep it down; I just need five minutes to recuperate from this brutal week."

One by one they marched without uttering protests or questions of whom or what the telephone call was about. Eddie was the last one to leave, but not before planting a soft kiss on his mother's cheek and a quick caress from his small hand across her forehead. "I love you, nene," Josefa murmured with a smile.

She felt herself drifting into a euphoric calmness. Her breathing, the slow lifting and descending of her chest, relaxed her. The warmness of the kitchen cocooned her weary body while the sounds of her children were distant lullabies of comfort. She just wanted to stay like this forever, liberated of problems and released of worries. But most of all, free from all the ugliness and the constant dead-end streets that somehow became her private hellish highway. She hated to be away from her children, but when bills started to pile up, there were few choices to select from.

The call had been from a woman, a rich white woman on Park Avenue, calling to confirm that Josefa was coming to clean her apartment in the morning. It wasn't this hard in Puerto Rico; it seemed that everyone was much happier than now, at least in her small-town, La Trocha in Vega Baja. Josefa rubbed her forehead hoping to remove all the madness that was exploding inside her mind. She heard the steam hiss from the radiators, and she knew that soon those hot pipes would be as cold as the air outside. Damn bastard, she almost shouted out loud, same little game every night.

After a certain hour, the heat was turned off until the following morning, and soon the banging on pipes was going to begin. Frustrated tenants released their anger by grabbing the first solid object and liberating their rage on the radiators as they were convinced that, by hitting the heat pipes with hammers and pots, the heat was going to come on. Who the hell came up with that nonsense about hitting the pipes and radiators to get heat? She wondered smiling. Then she remembered Enrique, Agapito's cousin, explaining how the custom began.

At one time, the supers live in the basement, and when there was no heat, the banging on the pipes by enraged cold tenants, not only kept the super from sleeping, but also assured everyone that soon the heat was going to be turned on. Those were old habits that refused to die. Everyone knew that supers were becoming as extinct as the toasty warmth that everyone desired in the winter. Landlords, always greedy and ready to cut expenses so that their little fat grubby hands could keep every possible penny, got rid of supers. Now the banging on pipes was just annoying frustrated music by tenants with nothing better to do to keep warm.

Josefa stretched her arms and allowed a deep yawn to escape her. She got up slowly and started to remove from the refrigerator what they were going to have for dinner, as her children returned to the kitchen; each taking their assigned jobs for dinner preparation. As the canned laughter filtered from the television set, she began to move as her daughters avoided one another. Eddie was the only one that sat in a chair waiting for the goodies to be placed before him.

Friday was always the special dinner night. Unlike the other nights during the week, which they ate a diet that consisted of mostly rice, beans, and meat; on Friday, they had what Eddie baptized as 'American Night', based on the commercials he saw in the television. It was hamburgers and French fries, pizza, or everyone's favorite; cold cut sandwiches with milk shakes. Migdalia took the task of preparing the sandwiches. Carefully, she spread mayonnaise on sliced bread after that she added ham, bologna, olive loaf, and cheese to complete the sandwich. As the sandwiches were made, Josefa scooped vanilla ice cream inside a pitcher, then poured soda and mixed it until the shake was frothy, cold, and delicious.

Gathering in the living room, they were bathed by the hypnotizing light of the small second-hand black-and-white television set. They munched on their fun dinner trying to figure out what was so funny that made the unseen crowd on the screen laugh hysterically. Unless the comedy was physical, the things that were said were lost because of their lack of knowledge of the English language. Josefa would have preferred the Spanish channel. Yet, she realized that they had to learn English and watching television was probably the best way possible. Besides they all loved *'I Love Lucy'*, especially delighted whenever Desi Arnaz went ballistic with his rapid Cuban Spanish. She was beginning to hear the kids' everyday conversation laced with English words; the most often used were 'alright', 'because', and 'maybe'.

Agapito forbade them to speak English in the house. He felt very strongly about his children not ending up like many of his friends' kids who only knew English and Spanish was less and less spoken. "Not in his house." Agapito was quick to yell. "You are Puerto Ricans and in my house, you speak Spanish or get the hell out and move in with one of those white bastards." With that type of attitude, the children were glad that he worked late on Fridays, because he refused to eat for dinner what he called 'American pigeon scraps.' You are supposed to eat that crap for lunch because time does not allow for a nice plate of rice with pork chops, he would yell out. In his mind for dinner if there weren't any rice and beans on that plate, then what you were eating was garbage; not a proper Puerto Rican dinner.

As the sitcoms intertwined with more corny sitcoms, one by one, Josefa's children began to file into the bedrooms, and soon only Eddie remained. His eyes fighting from closing, until he crumbled like a small stuffed bear by the arm of the plastic covered sofa. Gently, Josefa helped her little son to bed and then returned to the living room and made herself comfortable on the couch. Changing the dial on the television to the Spanish channel, Josefa watched, through half-closed eyes, as the over-acted novellas unfolded its predictable plot.

It was past eleven when Josefa was brought out from her sleep by keys scratching the front door. Felix swung the door open, delicately hitting the love seat that sat next to the door in the crammed apartment.

Josefa followed her son with tired eyes; now that he was home her worries were turning into anger. She sat up, registering every movement he made as her mind rehearsed the speech she was about to give him. There was no way she was going to accept this type of behavior. She refused to ignore it as some 'ritual of a boy becoming a man' nonsense. He was only sixteen; regardless of the fuzzy hair growing from his chin and under his nose, he was still her first little boy. She could neither tolerate, nor allow him to think that he could go out or come home whenever he pleased. When she was not home, she expected him to stay with his younger siblings, not to leave them alone while he gallivanted around town doing God knows what.

Felix closed the door and threw his coat on the love seat. With uneasy steps, he walked up to his mother, bent over and kissed her cheek. His lips were cold and his breath smelled like a whole pack of gum, yet there was a faint aroma of cigarette.

"Bendicion," Felix said, asking for the customary blessings.

"Dios te acompañe," Josefa responded, blessing her son through straight lips that refused to smile.

Felix sat next to her and began unlacing his hi-top sneakers. He felt his mother's eyes piercing right through him, like laser rays from a futuristic gun straight out of Eddies' comic-books. In his mother's mind, he had disobeyed her. He knew that she was angry and disappointed, but her silence was deafening. He hated when she gave him the silent treatment, the same way she did with his father whenever he came home drunk after a night of unwinding with friends.

Felix preferred if she scream and carried on like a maniac or even slapped him a few times. He was ready for anything, but the accusing silence that she had mastered; was something he couldn't take. He felt her eyes, red-hot steel pokes penetrating his skin. He wanted to move away from her, to go inside the bedroom and leave her there with her burning eyes. If anything had to be said, let those words be spoken on the morning when a goodnight's sleep would have calmed his mother's nerves and her over-reacting bullshit.

The ticking of the clock from the kitchen counted the minutes as both mother and son remained quiet, no one ready to make the first move. Felix's anxieties were beginning to smother him, and he couldn't take any more of this abusive silent treatment. Thoughts of leaping to his feet and screaming from the top of his lungs were increasing in his mind. He wanted to yell for the two of them. "Scream at me, mom," he wanted to shout at her, "hit me, anything, but please, your silent lips are killing me." The young man felt a growing moistness popping under his nose and a streaking drop slicing the middle of his back. Felix didn't dare to look at her, but just kept his eyes downward on the worn-out linoleum floor under his socked feet.

Josefa knew that she was losing him; it was as simple as that. No warnings, no easing slowly before entering the highway of reality, just hit the gas pedal and fly to the arms of the unknown. *My God,* she thought, *he is merely sixteen.* He's still a little boy with fuzz on his face that looks more like mascara-painted hair which he used to wear when he was dressed-up as a pirate for Halloween only a few years ago. She didn't want to suppress his independence like most mothers do, but when do you let go? When is a mother supposed to give them that gentle push out of the nest and allow them to fly and fend for themselves? Is there any timetable that suggests the best time to let them take their solo flight? Why do they have to grow-up so fast?

Josefa's heart grew heavy, and she wondered if heart attacks began with these symptoms. Her desire to explode was so great she had to bite her lower lip and allow the words to come out slowly. She felt like an actress stumbling through over-dramatized lines. "Do you know what time it is?" she asked knowing that she had to start somewhere, and that question was the best starting point, even if it sounded like a cliché. She noticed Felix fidgeted on the couch; his shoulders were slouched, and his brown hair fell over his forehead, he needed a haircut. Josefa thought to herself; *my very first baby is now becoming my very first grown man, where did the years go? My God, it was only yesterday that he fed from my breast.*

Felix lifted his eyes from the floor and pushed them into his mother's face. "I just went out," he mumbled with dull syllables admitting his guilt.

"Out? What do you mean out?" Josefa fought hard to maintain her composure. "Do you realize the time? You know, forget about that now, what I'm really angry about is that you left your sisters and little brother alone, you know that your job is to stay with them. You are the oldest and, when your father and I are not here, we expect you to watch over them."

"I'm sorry, mami," Felix whispered. "But some friends invited me to their house to listen to records. It was not far from here, besides Migdalia could take care of them. She always does, even when I'm nearby; she still bosses everybody around."

"Migdalia es una niña—she's only a girl."

"Yeah, but she behaves like she owns the place when you're not here."

"Mira Felix, we are not here to discuss Migdalia or no one else but you. Now, who are these friends and where do they live?"

"Some kids from school and it's not far from here."

"Do they have names, and what kind of parents allow other children to stay at their home so late?"

"Mami is only a bit after eleven. That's not late."

"You don't tell me what's late and what's not!" Josefa didn't want her frustration to fog her words. She took a deep breath and held it inside her lungs. She saw Felix raising his shoulders slightly, perhaps trying to test his newfound manhood. Josefa released the trapped air from her mouth slowly, calmness soothing her temper. She wanted to avoid building a wall between herself and Felix. A small clock on top of the television kept the time for them as it displayed that it was ten minutes into the next day, and another hour for Agapito to come home. It was best to deal with this now, rather than with her husband's quick temper.

Josefa gazed at her son, and the rage she once had was no longer there, just love. "Mira hijo," her voice was serene. "I know that lately we are going through a lot, too many changes twisting our lives. I know that you need to go out and lead your own life, Felix, I know that—yo lo sé—but you also have to understand that I need your help now more than ever. Yes, you tell me that Migdalia tends to overdue her charges in the house, I know that very well. If I'm not careful, very soon she'll be scolding me and probably sending me to my room without supper."

Felix chuckled placing a smile on his mother's face. A dark uncomfortable cloud detached itself from her shoulders. Josefa moved closer to her son and rubbed the back of his neck and then slid her hand across his growing broad shoulders. He accepted his mother' love; it felt like a warm comfortable soft blanket in the middle of a wet cold night.

"Ay, nene, I know that it's hard, and I applaud you for doing everything with no complaints," Josefa told her son while her hands stroked his back and brought him closer to her. "Understand that the last thing I want to do is treat you like a newborn, the way your Tia Claudia babies your cousin Luis. I don't want to raise you like that, always depending on me to do everything for you. All I'm asking from you is not to keep me in the dark. If you're going out, then let me know; and, if it's getting late, then pick-up the phone and call me. I'm your mother, so I do worry when you are not here, especially if I have no idea where you're at.

Yo no te pido mucho—I'm not asking for much, and you have to remember that this is not Puerto Rico—aqui nadie te conose—nobody knows you here; everyone is a stranger. I have enough to worry with your sisters and the thugs from outside and let's not forget your little brother with his conditions; I shouldn't have to worry about you. ¿Tu me entiendes?"

"Si mami," Felix answered her, the little boy in him coming out. "I'm sorry...perdon."

Josefa leaned forward and held his youthful face that was slowly chiseling into adulthood features. She kissed him gently on his forehead and brought him into her with a tight hug. There were no more words to be said; no more motherly wisdom to be shared. Embraced in each other's arms they remained, mother and child until the sound of keys broke their privacy and their mutual good-bye to Felix's childhood. Agapito was home, tired and very angry. He had lost one of his jobs.

Chapter Two

Staring at the cracks in the ceiling, Felix saw each line twisting and spreading like rivers on an African school map. Within the cracks and lumps and the way the warped shadows settled on the ceiling, Felix could make out faces and shapes of animals. It was something he never mentioned to anyone. Sometimes, he wondered if this was some type of hidden gift or talent that he possessed.

Along the wall above the closet, he could see the large body of a bear with its fangs protruding from its wide-open mouth. Right above his head, he made out the perfect profile of a dog, and if he turned his head to a certain angle, then the dog transformed into the face of a skinny old woman. Around the light fixture, he saw birds and leaping zebras. He had no idea why he saw them as zebras rather than just plain horses, but something convinced him that they were zebras. Perhaps it was because of the two thin curves that bubbled from a bad plaster job.

His little brother, Eddie, slept a few inches away from him on a small cot that every night was unfolded and placed next to the twin bed his mother had purchased from a neighbor who was moving. For a little kid of only ten years old, his brother Eddie snored like an old man with bronchitis. He reached out and slapped his brother on the shoulder, just to make him shift, which unfortunately caused him to snore even louder. Felix gave up, took his pillow, and held it tight against his ears in an attempt to dull out the snores. After a few uncomfortable minutes, he abandoned the idea and slipped the pillow under his head. He smacked Eddie again and, this time, his brother's grunts and heavy breathing subsided to a more humanly sound.

From the room behind him, he could hear the softer snores of his sisters. His sisters' room was the largest one in their railroad apartment. Felix remembered the first time that he heard the term 'railroad apartment'. He marveled at the idea of a building constructed by using old trains. It wasn't until his father explained to him the real reason behind such an interesting name. The apartments were designed like a typical passenger train car; a narrow hallway ran from the front of the building to the back on one side, while all the rooms were positioned along the opposite side. There was not much privacy beyond the curtains on each threshold to separate each room.

His sisters shared the last room, which was the only room that faced the front of the building and had a door for privacy. From the windows of that room, they spent hours looking at the people from the neighborhood and the passing cars, learning about a new exciting place which was so unlike their Puerto Rico.

He and Eddie slept in the middle room followed by the smallest room and the one closest to the front door belonged to his parents'. The first time they entered the apartment, his father automatically declared that room was his. 'If any bastard breaks into my home, I want them to confront me first'. Felix recalled his father proclaiming with his thumb pointing at his puffed-out chest and his mother's worried look expecting thugs to come crashing through the door. Maybe that's why she insisted in adding another lock to accompany the already two existing ones plus the steel police bar, which was a bar fastened to the door which extended into a hole on the floor.

His father always thought of the family first, and Felix respected him for that. He wasn't close to his father; the love was there, but not as strong as a father-and-sons' love should be. Felix was only nine when he saw his father depart Puerto Rico to venture into the mythic golden streets of America. Once a year he would visit them, but for only one week, and this was too quick for a father and son to bond with one another. Besides, he, being the oldest, was usually the errand boy while his father spent time with his sisters and his sickly little brother.

Felix always felt like an afterthought. He often came last after everything was taken care of. When there were not enough gifts for everyone during any special occasion, he was supposed to understand because, 'you're the oldest one and the youngest ones come first'. Thank God for his mother and her hidden small gift that she would give him when everyone was asleep, otherwise he would have spent his whole life unloved, undesired.

For the most part, he still cared for his father, although their conversations were almost non-existent. His mother, on the other hand, he loved immensely. He admired her for her strength and her pride towards her country, making sure not one of her children would forget about Puerto Rico.

When they arrived in New York less than a year ago, during an intensely hot summer in 1967, everyone advised her that she should go straight to the Department of Welfare and claim that she didn't have a husband. Many family members informed her that with five children and a bullshit story about an estranged husband she would be taken care of like a queen. Regardless of the 'advice' given to her, Felix's mother did not want any part of what she considered to be degrading panhandling.

She saw how welfare strips people of their self-pride. It wasted lives motivating people to do nothing more than getting involved in everyone's affairs and count the days until their precious checks were delivered. His mother refused to fall under that demeaning syndrome. And, ignoring the snickering of the neighbors, she went out and sought a way to help her husband support the household. She slaved in a dirty, loud, hot factory making buttons and on Saturdays, she scrubbed and cleaned the apartments of Park Avenue's rich white families to pay the bills.

Behind her back the women in the block laughed and mockingly called her stupid, called her 'La Reina'—the queen—because in their minds, his mother carried herself with empty dignity. They all felt that it was beneath them to clean the white man's toilet. "Mejor coger a willie, que limpiar la mierda de los blancos," they all said—*it's better to accept a welfare check than clean up the-white-man's shit.*

"Foolish people," Felix always shook his head. "Whatever happened to the hardworking, prideful Puerto Ricans that he grew up with in Puerto Rico? Did they suddenly become lazy the second they surrounded themselves with roaches, rats and garbage? All those negative things that spilled over from ghettoes the Italians, Irish, Germans, and Jews left behind?" He shook his head uncomfortably as he continued to ask himself if what he was doing was another form of disrespect toward his Puerto Rican upbringing.

Felix tossed and turned in his bed, feeling the worn springs of the mattress dig into his back. He felt the dollar bills in his pocket, and he dreaded the idea of telling his mother what he was really doing tonight. He knew it was not the smartest idea, but what could he do? Especially with the bombshell his father came home with. There was no way; he couldn't sit around baby-sitting those that needed no watchful eyes, when he could be out there making money to help with the bills that kept stacking up on the kitchen table. In a matter of months, his parents had aged years, and that didn't sit too well with him.

He was going to be seventeen in a few months, and no one could force him into attending school if he didn't feel like going. Besides, he was sick and tired of being the butt of every cruel joke in school. The Puerto Rican kids born in New York ridiculed him at his halting hard to understand English. They called him 'pato jibaro', or 'hillbilly faggot'.

Even worse, teachers didn't make it any easier for him. The week before school closed for Christmas vacation, the English teacher made him read aloud from the storybook they were reading. He hadn't ever felt so humiliated, never felt so useless and dumb in his life before that painful moment. It was a moment that left him with a sour taste, almost impossible to spit out. This was the type of ugly memory which would follow a person the rest of their life, constantly reminding that he didn't belong, that he would always be a foreigner.

He still remembered the humiliation as he read the sentences, foreign words that contorted his tongue and flooded his face with bright-red embarrassment. All around him, he heard the snickering comments, the laughter degrading him. Most importantly, he remembered the teacher not coming to his rescue. He read two pages; two pages that seemed to last forever. His lips trembled; tears gathered behind his eyelids. Adding insult to injury, the teacher asked another student, a fluent English speaker to re-read the pages while he sat feeling the hot blood on his face, and the stares from the giggling students silently calling him 'the hillbilly faggot.'

In the darkness of his room, while his brother Eddie continued with his wall-shaking snores, Felix decided what he was going to do. It was going to break his mother's heart if she ever found out, but he realized that he must do what he thinks is right for him and for his family. He shut his eyes and begged for sleep, yet it refused to give him the comfort he sought. After a while, he slid out of the bed and went toward the window in the kitchen. He stared out at the sky that was still dark, as black as the depth of the sink's drain. He hated New York. There weren't even stars in this goddamn place.

Chapter Three

The window shook, and Gisela feared the glass was going to explode into pieces. She opened her eyes and stared at the window and shivered. She was not used to these cold, strong, wintry winds. She glanced across the room, the low hissing of the radiators announcing that finally the heat was coming up. Holding the blanket close, she did not want to let her body heat escape. She could hear her sisters still sleeping and, from the depth of the house, the movements of her father getting ready to work. The strong smell of coffee brewing told her that her mother was preparing breakfast.

There was light already seeping through the small opening between the curtains. Lifting her head, Gisela saw that it was a few minutes after six. She was an early bird, something that for some crazy reason bothered her sisters. She could have easily understood if she was the type that caused enough commotion to wake them up, but she wasn't; she was considerate about their love of sleeping late. Most of the time, she slid out of bed quietly and went to the kitchen where she would either read or write in the notebook she kept hidden from everyone.

Gisela enjoyed the quiet of the morning, the slowness of that time of day that allowed her to pretend that she was not in the middle of a ghetto, but rather in the middle of paradise where fairy tales were born. It was also the time when her imagination seemed to flow with great ideas— causing her to fill pages and pages with poetry and short stories, where everything always started and ended in magical laughter and radiant expectations of life.

Sometimes, she wondered why she was so different from her sisters, who were volatile, and had attitudes that seemed to be the perfect way to survive the hallways of the New York City schools. Gisela was calm, shy to a fault. She was glad that Norma and Migdalia went to the same school; otherwise she would have been eaten alive by the bullies who preyed on students like her. In the past few months, Norma had gotten into enough fights to allow Gisela the freedom to walk around school without being picked on. Norma was a natural when it came to duking it out with anyone who picked on Gisela.

Migdalia, on the other hand, befriended the girls who walked in groups always sharing make-up they secretly bought at Woolworth's. The makeup, which was applied before entering the school, was always removed before returning home. Gisela only had a few friends, girls mostly like her, shy and afraid of their own shadows. They were the patsies, easily targeted by the predators. Yet, thanks to Norma and Migdalia, Gisela usually was left alone.

Gisela slowly removed the wool blanket away from her and quietly swung out of the bed. The floor was cold and she quickly snuggled her feet inside her slippers and snatched her flannel robe from a chair next to the bed, wrapping it around herself. She stood up and after taking her composition notebook from underneath the mattress, she walked out of the bedroom, looking back once to make sure that both her sisters were still asleep. She would have died if any of her sisters discovered her notebook and read what was inside.

They would have made her life as miserable as possible, ridiculing her about her stories of frail maidens and brawny heroes that came to their rescue. If they read her poems, that would be worse. Through poetry, Gisela overcame her shyness and allowed her voice to speak loudly, as passionately as she wanted it to do in real life.

Once outside the room, she breathed a bit easier. As she stood inside the room where her brothers slept, she paused for a second. Felix was tightly rolled up in his blanket; his face was not even exposed, but Eddie was sprawled on his back, like a sun worshiper soaking up sun on the beach. His blanket was thrown across the floor where he had kicked it off; his sleeping position looked very uncomfortable within the coldness of the room. She reached down and took the blanket off the floor and covered him. But, before she crossed the room, he swiftly kicked the blanket unto the floor again. She shrugged and pushed the curtain that separated their room from her parents' room and went in.

Walking straight through to the living room, she could hear her parents' voices clearly. She could smell the fresh scent of soap that escaped the bathroom after her father's shower. She went inside the kitchen, and the warmth throughout the room made her feel alive and fully awake.

"Bendición," she kissed her mother, then her father. There was something wrong, she could feel the friction between her parents, and knew they had been arguing, something that was becoming a frequent thing.

Feeling like a trespasser and weird about walking into their privacy; so, she turned and went inside the bathroom. She couldn't understand that lately whenever her mother and father spoke; it was always in uptight sentences that ended in silence. She knew it was because of the accumulation of the bills; something that she didn't remember being an issue when they were in Puerto Rico, but then again, she was too young then to notice.

Perhaps they did have money problems in Puerto Rico, wasn't that the reason her father left them and came to New York? She wanted to escape, throw herself into the pages of her imagination and find solace in the words that were fused between her mind and the pages from her notebook. She turned the water on and let it run as she sat upon the edge of the bathtub and opened her notebook. She flipped through the filled pages until she stopped at a clean sheet. She stared at the thin blue lines on the paper and concentrated, trying to will her mind to come up with something to write about. From the outside, she heard her father shout something that was incoherent through the splashing from the water inside the sink.

She slammed the notebook and pressed it against her forehead shutting her eyes tight. "Oh God," she begged, "please let them stop...please let them stop." She placed the notebook down and sat on the toilet bowl to relieve herself, once done, she then washed up and brushed her hair with one hundred strokes. It was something she saw Migdalia do every night and after learning that it was supposed to add body and shine to your hair, she did it too, but in the privacy of the bathroom. Gisela knew that, if Migdalia found out she was brushing her hair the same way, then she would not only be angry with her, but would probably threaten her to stop.

Gisela came out of the bathroom and found her mother sitting alone in the kitchen, a cup of coffee warming her hands. To Gisela, her mother looked older, and it seems all the weight of the whole world was sagging down her shoulders. Her father was already out of the house; it didn't matter what day it was—weekday or weekend—he was always doing some type of work, odd jobs that he found through buddies. He managed to get moving jobs, painting apartments, or light construction. Her father's presence became rare and when he was home, it was always the same routine, eat and straight to bed. He was becoming more like a passing shadow that smelled of hard work, even if he was just getting up in the morning.

"Where's papi?" Gisela asked just to say something.

Her mother looked up. There was a distant look in her eyes. She gave Gisela a smile and then took a sip from the coffee and nodded. "You know your father; he's working with some men from his job. Something about knocking down walls in a store, I don't know, just another one of his many jobs that doesn't add too much."

"Why does papi work so hard?" Gisela took the cereal box from the cabinet above the sink and grabbed a bowl and a spoon from the dish rack, and the milk container from the refrigerator. She sat down across from her mother. "You and Papi, all you do is work and work. Why?"

"Nena, you are too young to understand," Josefa said, and she reached across the table and squeezed Gisela's hand for a second. "Everything costs money; it's not like we could snap our fingers, and all the money that we need is going to appear from thin air."

"Titi Esperanza doesn't work and Tio Juan only works one job," Gisela said as she poured milk over her cereal listening to the soft crackles that the cereal made. "And there are more children living there. How come they don't work as hard?"

"Ay nena, why are you always so curious?" Josefa shook her head in amusement. "Your aunt receives help from the government."

"You mean welfare?" Gisela took a spoonful of the crunchy and cold cereal.

"Yes...welfare—the government pays for her rent, food, clothes...practically everything."

"So, why don't we have the government pay for our stuff also, like that: you could stay home and Papi could only get one job, instead of all these jobs he has."

"Ay mi hija, you are so innocent," Josefa took another sip from the cup and pushed it aside. "Number one, I did not come into this country to be a beggar, or a liar. I have enough pride, that as long as I have health, I'll carry my own share. Your father is the same way too. I can't answer for other people, but taking welfare and lying about your conditions just to have the government give you that help is something that I would never allow myself to do. Your aunt has to lie that your uncle does not live with them, and that she has no idea where he is at. Like that the government sends her a check twice a month for all her needs and your cousins' as well."

"Did the government also give them money to buy the car that they have?" Gisela picked up the bowl and slurped the milk and the last bits of the cereal grains.

"No. That's why they have to lie about your uncle. With the money, he gets from his job; he can buy those extra things that are luxury for most poor people."

"So, they should also be able to afford good stuff in the house, like a big console record player and maybe a color television," Gisela wiped her mouth with a napkin she took from the napkin holder that was always in the middle of the kitchen table. "How come they live like they have no money?"

Josefa laughed and shook her head again. She knew that Gisela was going to be someone important in life, the girl always wanted to know all the answers to everything. "Because they have investigators making surprise visits to those families that claim they need help. If they go to a house and find expensive things they would know that somebody is lying, and they could get in trouble. That's the reason why they live worse than us, even though they always have money to spend on things that aren't important. Your cousins wear sneakers that cost more than ten dollars each," Josefa sighed. "With ten dollars I buy sneakers for you and your sisters and still have enough money to buy a whole pizza pie."

Gisela nodded understanding a bit more of what New York was all about. Now, she had an idea why most of the kids at school had parents who were always around, and most of them wore better clothes than she and her siblings. She thought that it was not fair that her parents had to work so hard while it seemed everyone was getting everything for free. She always felt like a poor sap when the families used to get together, even her cousins used to put them down about their cheap clothes, and their cheap sneakers, that all the kids used to call 'skips'.

Josefa stared at her daughter, absolving the naiveté of the child and knowing that, in her answer, she would hopefully make Gisela understand the difference. "Number one, to live within a lie is not the right way to live. We might be poor, but it is no reason to give up and expect people to do what our responsibilities dictate us to do. As long as we have a roof over our head and something warm to put in our stomachs, and the love of our family, the rest is just material baggage that we don't need. All of us could use a heavier coat, a better dress or a pair of shoes, but if we have to lie to get those things...is it worth it?"

Josefa reached and took Gisela's hands and locked her eyes into those of her daughter's. "Always remember, that if you can't hold your head up high with pride, then you have nothing in life. Dignity and pride of a person are worth more than any amount of fancy televisions or console record players. Always remember that—mi hija—to be poor is not an excuse to lower yourself into the gutters with the liars and thieves of the world."

Gisela smiled. She loved her mother, more than ever. She understood so well. She wanted to stay here for the entire day and speak to her mother like this. Their personal secrecy, their private bonding that was special, and only they could share it with each other. From the rooms, she heard the bickering between Migdalia and Norma, and she knew that this magical moment was finished, and she wondered if they could ever rekindle it again. For a second, she hated her sisters; she would have to share her mother with them and with the rest of the parasites that keep taking chunks of her mother's life.

Norma came running into the bathroom slamming the door just as Migdalia came after her with fire in her eyes. "Mami, do you see what I have to deal with when you are not here?" Migdalia screamed. "She thinks she owns this whole house. Tell her something because she's going to keep doing it until I slap her."

"You are not slapping anybody here," Josefa stood up from the table and put her hands on her hips. "Can you two live like sisters for once? What's going on now?"

Migdalia shot a hateful glare at Gisela annoyed that her sister was already up. *God knows,* she thought, *what she was telling mom about me!* But, she said out loud, "Norma was snooping around my drawers when she thought I was still sleeping."

"Norma," Josefa called out. "Come out of that bathroom right this minute."

"Wait mami," Norma yelled behind the closed the door. "I'm peeing...I was just looking for a pair of socks Migdalia took from me."

"I did not," Migdalia defended herself as she rolled her eyes. "Why do I want to use her socks? They smell like sweat—like boy's socks—you dumb tomboy."

Norma came out and squared in front of Migdalia, her nose flaring, the way it always did when she was angry. She hated to be called a tomboy, to her that was Migdalia's way of calling her a pata, a lesbian. "You call me a tomboy again, and I'll pull your eyebrows so you don't have to pluck them with your stupid friends at school."

"You are just jealous," Migdalia tried to retaliate; trying not to show the fear she was beginning to have of Norma.

"Jealous of what?" Norma smiled, and that seemed to infuriate Migdalia even more. "Don't make me tell mami what else I found inside the drawer."

"Okay, enough," Josefa raised her voice to quiet her bickering daughters. "The two of you better shut up. It's too early for you two to be arguing like cats over a bowl of milk. Norma you respect your sister's privacy. I don't want to hear about you looking around places where you don't belong."

Migdalia stuck her tongue out feeling victorious, but it was a feeling that didn't last long.

"And you," Josefa addressed Migdalia. "These name callings are going to stop right now, and don't think I haven't noticed about you plucking your eyebrows. You are too young to be doing that, and I better not see you wearing make-up in school or anywhere else for that matter. I might show up in your school one day without you knowing it, to see if my daughter is parading around painted like a clown. Now go and wash up and have some breakfast, there's a lot to be done around this house. I have to go to work in about one hour so let's move it."

Migdalia stood there aghast for a second, wondering how her mother found out about her make-up, and suddenly she knew. It had to be Gisela; that's why she was here whispering so early with her mother. She gave Gisela another dirty look and walked angrily into the bathroom slamming the door behind her.

Gisela stood up, took the bowl and spoon to the kitchen sink and put away the milk and cereal box. It was Saturday morning, and she wished her mother could stay home today. She didn't know why, but of all days this was one that she wanted so much for her mother to be here with them. From the inside of the bedrooms she heard Felix cough, and very soon the beautiful morning she woke up to, would be transformed into a day that would forever change their lives.

Chapter Four

Eddie kept his eyes fixed on what appeared to be a drab mist drooping from the ceiling. The shape elongated at times, and then in a sudden movement; it would shrink to the size of a dime. He was in his room enjoying the serenity of being alone, surrounded only by the latest adventures of his comic book heroes. He enjoyed Saturday more than any other day. It seemed it was the only day everyone in the house had something important to do, and he could spend most of the day in his room.

His mother was at her Saturday cleaning job in some fancy apartment where the streets were garbage-free and men in starched uniforms with big gold buttons running down the center of their jackets, stood behind shiny glass doors, which according to his mother was more beautiful than any place she had ever seen. 'Un palacio'—a palace—was how his mother described the buildings.

Moreover—with Felix out of the house—it was the single time he could pretend he had his own room, just like the kids on television. Eddie was not sure where Felix was going, but he knew that Gisela and Migdalia were heading to the library. Although he was convinced that Gisela was the only one planning to go to the library. He was no fool, and he had realized at a very early age; few people gave him enough credit for what he knew or what he observed. He was always ignored as if he had no idea as to what was going on. Sometimes he would hear Migdalia talking on the phone to her friends, unconscious that he was only a few feet away from her. She didn't put much mind about his presence; he guessed that it was because his siblings always saw him with a comic book. They all felt he was unaware of everything that was happening around him. Little did they know: he was aware of everything.

He knew about Migdalia and that, on this particular Saturday, she was going to see a boy from school. He also knew that Gisela had no other choice but to cover for her; otherwise, she was going to be in big trouble. Gisela was not like Norma, and because of her shyness, his poor sister had to go along with whatever Migdalia decided to do. However, Norma was different. She was a fighter and out of all his siblings, she was the one that took care of him. It wasn't that she babied him or treated him like an invalid—no; she was more like his protector. And right now, she was the only one with him in the apartment, blasting music and having a grand old time.

Eddie leisurely stretched across the bed and stared into the mist. Soon he knew he would feel the familiar tinkling sensation he always received when a visitor was going to appear. He wondered who it was going to be this time. Eddie closed the Fantastic Four book and neatly placed it with the others on a small table, and took a deep breath. The apparition began to take shape, and the best way he could describe it, if he ever had to tell anyone, was like watching a fuzzy picture at the movies finally put into focus. And only then, was when you could see its lines and the fine details that formed the picture. It was a man, a man Eddie had never seen before.

Eddie knew that what he was seeing was a spirit. Instead of being afraid, he was fascinated and intrigued with the phenomena. His earliest memories of whom he called visitors were traced back to his early days in

Puerto Rico, when he was only an infant. He remembered that there was a nice man with a peculiar smile that visited him at nights when everyone was asleep. He vividly recalled the odd smile of the stranger, because instead of the lips turning upward in a perfect smiling curve, the lips took a distorted, sourpuss look. However, crooked smile and all, hours were spent playing and being caressed until sleep took Eddie away from the nightly visitor.

Since then, all the apparitions that had come to him were kept a secret. Eddie never revealed his unique talent to anyone, not even his parents. He, at one time, asked the man with the deformed smile if it was a good idea to share his gift with his family. To Eddie's surprise, the man quickly became angry and in stuttered words forbade Eddie from telling anyone. This was their little secret—a secret that no one should be allowed to know. People would not understand, and they would accuse Eddie of being a liar or a troublemaker.

They would, the apparition said, even lock Eddie up inside an insane asylum where he would rot to death. Eddie listened to the warnings of the man. Trusting his new friend, from that moment, he decided to keep his uniqueness bottled up inside, safe from others. He did not want to be held in the clutches of a crazy hospital and become the shame to his family.

As the new visitor sat at the edge of Felix's bed, Eddie waited for the spirit to introduce himself. He understood very well their make-up; he became a pro at dealing with these ghosts. Sometimes, they came to him and spoke to him freely and other times they just traveled from one wall through another wall without acknowledging his presence. This time the visitor stared at Eddie with hollowed eyes; there was distrust that poured from those dead sockets. For the first time, it sent shivers down Eddie's back. The ghost floated straight to the ceiling, transforming itself from a colorless mist into the disfigured form of a rotting cadaver.

Then, it descended slowly, all the time with a black stare that never left Eddie's eyes. The ghoul came closer to Eddie and slid next to him on the bed; the eyes were no longer dark, but reddish holes revealing the opening of an alien and evil place. Eddie wanted to shout and run away from him, but he couldn't move. Every muscle of his body was paralyzed into a disturbing stiffness he couldn't break. With long fingers and dirt-caked crooked nails, the spirit traced the face of the frightened boy as a conniving smile slithered across his face.

"He is using you," a raspy, gargling voice came out of the spirit. "He uses everybody…he doesn't want you—he just wants what you have." With those strange words, the ghost disappeared in an odorless mist.

A desperate apprehension took hold of Eddie, and the boy began to gasp. He couldn't breathe. He startled to struggle, and cold sweat coated his chest and face. Eddie took deep breaths in wild attempts to release himself from such a paralyzing nightmare. Then, slowly, he felt the comfort of slight movements in his body. Gradually, he began to make out the sounds of the neighborhood, the common sounds from the apartment, familiar sounds, yet they were mixed with other strange sounds.

From somewhere a roaring explosion rattled his brain, and it pressed hard into his eardrums, bringing deep menacing echoes in his skull. The sounds increased in volume until he was embraced by the whispers of dead people that suffocated him and mocked his mortality. He felt hundreds of cold hands pulling and pinching him, until his body went limp.

With a dull crash, Eddie's body collapsed violently onto the floor.

Tightness clinched into his lungs—depleting them—until he was no longer able to breath. Eddie began to panic. He struggled, trying to climb back onto his feet, but his empty lungs held him hostage against the cold linoleum floor. In a seizure of terror, he twitched on the floor, his arms flailing and banging against the floor with incredible force. He was losing consciousness and feared that he would die all alone with just the colorful drawn heroes from his comic books to witness his death.

He tried to scream, but the only thing that came out was a whimper that was drowned by the loud shrieks of Norma's music. Darkness began to enclose him inside a lifeless cocoon that he had no desire to be part of. Yet the more he battled, the tighter the invisible cocoon of darkness tightened around him. He felt strong unseen hands squeezing his upper body, and all circulations from his heart were stymied, while his collapsed lungs choked his brain into a quick delirium. He was dying; he knew it. The last thought he had was that it was not fair, that he was still a child.

He was a child who had already cheated death once, and at this moment, the moment when he felt the darkness of death wrapping around him its tight grip, he prayed that he could cheat death once again.

His eyes flipped inside his head in rapid motion, and his body convulsed uncontrollably. Eddie opened his mouth and, this time, his yell ripped violently through his body and out of his mouth, breaking through the loud music that held the apartment walls captive. For one second, he opened his eyes, but before he could feel happiness for such minor accomplishment, his body tumbled aimlessly into unconsciousness. He thought he screamed again, but he wasn't sure if those screams were his or the shrieks of the dead welcoming him into their world.

Chapter Five

The streets of Manhattan flew unnoticed by the taxi window. Agapito's worried eyes were fixated on the road ahead. He wanted to shout to the driver to go faster, but he controlled himself. All Agapito could do was sit back and pray for the best. The worst was over, his cousin, Enrique, had informed him of this from the hospital. Josefa was already there and the doctors were working on his son. His hands trembled as he stared angrily at the city flashing by. The yellow cab jumped to the right lane avoiding a truck from crashing into them, Agapito was jolted from one side to the other, while the cab driver stuck his head out the window and began shouting every curse known to mankind while his middle finger was up in the air.

"Goddamn motherfuckers!" the driver was still fuming. "I'll tell ya'…some of those bastards should be shot in front of the motor vehicle center, a message to any asshole that doesn't know how to drive to rip their license application and take the goddamn train…goddamn bastards!"

The battered cab swung around a slow-moving-Volkswagen and settled in the middle lane, blowing his horn at anyone who dared attempt to jump in front of him. He slammed on the brakes and cranked up the speed almost at the same time. Agapito positioned himself in the middle of the seat just in case the fool got into an accident so he would, hopefully, survive the impact. The taxi screeched to a standstill as cars crossing Third Avenue towards the Queensboro Bridge ran past them at the encouragement of an overzealous traffic cop waving them through.

Agapito wanted to just jump out of the cab and take the train.

During the commotion, he began to wonder why he ever thought that taking a cab would be quicker than taking the train. When was he going to learn that the trains were faster and cheaper? But, it was too late now. Hopefully, the higher the numbers went on the blocks, the less traffic they were going to face. Who the hell goes to Spanish Harlem anyway?

With tires spinning on the dry road, the cab leaped forward and soon thereafter was leading the pack of cars that filled the streets of New York. The cab driver was fast and agile in a way which could easily challenge the best Indy 500 drivers. Agapito leaned back on the torn backseat, and watched the fine expensive boutiques from the downtown streets turn quickly into bars, bodegas, and bargain stores.

"Mi hijo," he wanted so much to yell out the window, "what type of curse was his son born with?"

Agapito remembered the face of his son when the child was born, which now seemed like such a long time ago. There was something about his eyes, which to this day fascinated him and at the same time bothered him. Eddie's eyes possessed a piercing look that lacked the innocence of a child, as if his eyes had seen more than their share of life and death combined. How could Agapito ever forget the morning after his son's birth? In desperation, Agapito had gone to get the priest, for surely the child needed to be baptized before dying. Coming back with holy water and instructions from the priest, when he made the sign of the cross on his son's forehead, Eddie had looked at him with a stare that chill his bones, it was a stare of contempt.

The taxi came to a sudden full stop in front of Mount Sinai

Hospital, its rusted, dented fender showing the battle scars of being a New York City cab. Agapito climbed out not knowing if the relief he felt was from finally arriving at the hospital, or from surviving with that crazy man behind the wheel. He put a few crumbled bills into the outstretched hand of the cabby and hurried his steps toward the Emergency-Room entrance. Before reaching the glass doors, Enrique was coming out to meet him.

"No te preocupes, Agapo," Enrique almost shouted before both men were close enough. "Everything is under control, so don't worry; the kid is going to be okay."

"But what happened?" Agapito ran past Enrique pushing the doors wide open and rushing inside.

"They said it was a seizure; the bad thing was that it took a long time for him to receive medical help. The only one that was in the house when it happened was Norma, and by the time she heard him scream...well...you know—"

"No, I don't know!" Agapito's mind was racing, trying to figure out why the two youngest children were alone in the house. "Where the hell was Felix? ¡Coño! What about Migdalia?"

"Hermano no sé, after Norma called the police she called me...when I got there, she had already called Josefa and was kneeling next to Eddie trying to console him. Thank God that I was there before the cops, in this country they don't take too kindly at kids under age left alone."

"Damn! How many times have we told Felix not to leave them alone? I'll kill that fuckin' kid if it's the last thing I'll do."

"Cojelo suave, hombre," Enrique put his arm on Agapito's shoulders and forced him to stop. "Oye esto...the last thing that we need now is anger. So relax and let's concentrate on Eddie getting better, then after that we can find out what really went on."

Agapito stared at Enrique's eyes trying to find the calmness that his cousin always seemed to have. He tried to push away from Enrique's hold, but his cousin refused to release him. Agapito looked away and glanced at the guard who was paying attention to the commotion, then he stared back at Enrique blowing the angry air out of his lungs. He shook his head in agreement with his cousin. "Okay, let's go. I want to see my son," he finally said.

They rode the elevator to the second floor and exited into a long corridor surrounded by the smells of sickness and death. Empty stretchers lined up along the twisting maze, like taxis waiting to brisk someone to their final resting place. Agapito hated hospitals, and the way doctors made him feel, stupid and useless. He followed Enrique as he avoided looking into the opened doorways that led into deep darkened rooms. The thought about his son being part of this sick freak show made him shiver.

At a distance, he saw Josefa, standing all alone and her worried face seemed to reach down to the floor. He felt the anger slithering back into his heart. A stretcher appeared before him and Josefa ran to it. He knew that the small body beneath the blanket with tubes snaking out of a pale face was his little boy, Eddie. His knees buckled, threatening to plunge him onto the tiled floor. Enrique read the stuttered steps of his cousin and quickly wrapped his steady arms around Agapito's waist. Stabilizing himself with this welcome support, Agapito walked slowly toward Josefa and Eddie's side. Josefa ran up to him. Her eyes streaked with tears, and threw her arms around his neck almost knocking him to the ground. He pushed her away gently and approached the gurney, which was beginning to wheel his son to another place where the father's powers were not needed. Agapito felt useless.

Behind the oxygen mask, Eddie gave a slight moan acknowledging him, and Agapito lowered his face and kissed his son's cheek. It was clammy and cold. He felt tears gather behind his eyelids, and he fought hard to keep them there. Josefa came to him. Once again, he ignored her and for that he felt awful, but someone had to bear his anger and that someone was her. He let go of the stretcher as an orderly rolled his son through the corridors. He began to follow but was stopped by Enrique's grip.

"Agapo," Enrique whispered into his ears. "Let them take care of him, stay here with your wife. She needs you now more than ever."

"No...I'm going with my son." Agapito tried to free himself, but Enrique refused to give in.

"Coño hombre, what the hell did I tell you before? You better relax 'cause you're not helping the situation with this nonsense. Now settle down and attend to your wife and stop acting like a brat."

"You don't understand—"

"And neither do you!" Enrique snapped. "So let those that understand do their job, while we do ours...and that's to wait and trust God and the doctors."

Agapito turned away from his cousin, disturbed and angry with what was coming at him too fast for his mind to digest. He looked at a nurse walking towards them. She carried a friendly caring smile, but to Agapito, it was a gesture that he'd love to wipe off her face. There was nothing to smile about when his son has been taken to a strange place. "Mr. and Mrs. Santiago," the nurse said. "Please follow me; the doctor would like to speak with you."

They followed the nurse through the halls that echoed with every single step they took, and every so often their steps squeaked on the waxed floors. They were led inside a small office, with an entrance that was hidden by a metal cart filled with plastic trays of discarded, half-eaten lunches. In front of a mahogany desk, two chairs were neatly placed. Josefa sat in one of them, and Agapito ignoring her gesture to sit, stood next to the chair balancing his weight from heel to toes. After a few seconds of anxious rocking, Enrique pleaded with Agapito to sit down. Staring at his cousin, Agapito finally gave in and sat down.

Enrique leaned nonchalantly on the wall paying keen attention to stay away from anything that looked important or priceless. A gentle sob slipped from Josefa's lips, a sob that reached out to her husband, but Agapito only offered her coldness. She felt her lips tremble and absentmindedly brought her hand to her lips to stop the quivering from becoming a scream. Agapito narrowed his eyes on the wall, his thoughts boiling into a rage, which he had no idea how to release.

The doctor came in, and sat down behind the desk. To Josefa, his wrinkled face portrayed an assurance of knowledge, wisdom, and authority. However, to Agapito, he represented the arrogance of wealth.

"Hello, my name is Doctor Whitcom," he said as he looked at them and then glanced quickly at the chart he was holding. "Your son suffered a minor seizure, but it's still too early to determine if there are any serious effects to the brain. We are conducting a few examinations, which consist of blood tests, CT and MRI's that will help us determine if he's suffered from any trauma to the brain from this seizure. You may see him later, and please when you do, don't be alarmed if he's asleep. We have him under heavy medications that will keep him unconscious for the tests we are running on him," he cleared his throat as he studied their faces.

Wondering if they understood his words as clear as he had said them, the doctor started again. "Since he is so young, it's better that we keep him asleep for the tests." He looked over the chart again as Josefa wrung her hands, her eyes never leaving his. The doctor leaned forward and sighed. "I need some information on your son's medical records. Has he suffered seizures in the past? And if he has, is he taking any medication for it?"

He waited for their responses, instead got their blank stares. Finally the man who stood behind the child's parent said something in Spanish, then turned his face toward him and answered. "This was the first time, but he was always a sick boy."

"What type of sickness?"

Enrique leaned down, then straightened his back again. He took liberty in answering all of the doctor's questions, and why shouldn't he? Everyone in the immediate family knew about Eddie's health history. "He was born sick; that's why he is smaller than other kids his age."

"He was born sick?" Dr. Whitcom shifted in his chair; his elbows propped on top Eddie's folder.

"Yes," Enrique answered, no longer consulting with his cousin or Josefa. He took it upon himself to be their authoritative voice. He began to explain to the doctor how Eddie was born prematurely, detailing about the internal bleeding suffered by Eddie during when he was born. He told him how the doctors in Puerto Rico had given up hope for the child to survive—since the umbilical cord was wrapped around Eddie's neck blocking the first crucial moments of air to flow into the brain of the newborn. Finally, Enrique told the doctor that, "little Eddie was brought back to health by a midwife's herbs and lotions."

Agapito looked at his cousin, envious of his knowledge of a language that seemed to elude him. He shrugged as he tried to concentrate on the three-way conversation that went from the doctor to him and his wife, with Enrique as their voice, and back to the doctor. He tried to look less anxious through the exchange of questions, answers and detailed explanations. Through all the confusion, he could only grasp that his youngest son had suffered what seemed to be an epileptic attack. Agapito frowned at the information, wondering how a child becomes cursed with such a dreadful illness without any warning. Behind all the strange sounding names, Agapito listened, concerned about the seriousness of his son's problem, but one thing he was more concerned with: how was he was going to pay for all this? He didn't have any health insurance. As the conversation circled around him, he worried how the hell he was going to pay for all the medication, the testing, and the hospital stay. After a while, he lowered his face into his cupped hands and wished to be anywhere but here, anywhere, even in hell.

Chapter Six

Eddie couldn't identify the familiar, yet nostalgic odor right away. He heard a voice from a distance that he faintly recognized. He wanted to go to him...was it a he? It must be; Eddie was sure of that. Then, it became clear; the voice was the same one that many nights kept him company and watched over him as he slept during his early days of childhood. Eddie opened his eyes, though they felt like they remained closed. The darkness that surrounded him was thick and there was a feeling of danger. He felt cold and he sensed something in the blackness, something evil and rotten waiting patiently before it devoured him with its blood-dripping fangs. He didn't like this place. With his arms spread in front of him, Eddie began to take small steps and each stride that he took; he expected the worst.

"No tengas miedo, muchacho." The voice came at him in booming echoes, assuring him there was nothing to fear. "Vente conmigo." Come with me. Eddie stopped, no longer sure if his steps were taking him to the voice, and if they were...was that a good idea? He turned around feeling disoriented. Hearing the voice again, this time closer, Eddie felt the urge to run as far away from it as possible. The darkness began to disappear slowly, dissolving finally to show Eddie what was in front of him: a sickly thin man who shuffled his steps as he walked along an uneven porch.

The man held a cup of, what Eddie knew for sure, was coffee. Eddie noticed the careful steps the man took in order not to spill any of the coffee that filled the tin mug to the brim. Despite his diligence, two heavy drops fell on the top of the man's right shoe. Between his clenched teeth, he held on to a piece of bread layered with visible chunks of butter. With great care, the man placed the cup on the top edge of the porch railing as he removed the bread from his mouth, after taking a huge bite. He chewed in exaggerated bites and then chased it down with a gulp of the black coffee.

Eddie watched the man settle into a rocking chair that once belonged to the man's mother. Quickly, Eddie wondered how he knew that. He didn't quite know the answer, or how to explain what was happening; still, Eddie also knew that the previous owner of that rocking chair was dead. There was a peculiar way the man admired the rocking chair with the same fervor a collector would cherish something as priceless as a renaissance masterpiece. Back and forth, the ill-looking man rocked himself slowly, stopping only to sip the coffee and take a bite of bread.

Crumbs fell gingerly on his patched-up brown shirt, which was buttoned all the way up to his scrawny, chicken-like neck. Eddie noticed the early morning sun washing over the landscape which revealed itself from behind thick leaves of a tall tree next to the house. Above him, red parrots chattered loudly and chased each other off the branches of a mango tree. As they sought refuge from one another, the parrots landed forcefully causing the over-ripe mangoes to fall and explode onto the grass.

What is this place?

Eddie sensed the familiarity of the shapes of the trees, from the green moss-covered mountains on the horizon, to the boisterous array of birds flying around and descending on tree branches all around him. It also felt as foreign as the tall dark buildings that he saw for the first time in New York City.

"Maybe this is Puerto Rico," Eddie answered himself out loud. But, this was a Puerto Rico that he was never aware of. He saw the man jump to his feet, causing the rocking chair to come to a sudden stop. There was someone approaching the house; Eddie could see it was flustering the man enough to make him abandon his coffee, forcing him to run and hide within the shadows of the shack.

Eddie strained his neck to see a young girl coming around the bend of the road. Her face reminded him of someone, but he couldn't figure out whom. Even as the girl was a few feet away from the house, Eddie noticed her mannerisms and they seemed so familiar. With interest, he peeked at the man, who now stared at the girl from his safe place.

A slight tremble hunched the man's shoulders. Watching closely, Eddie saw how the man pressed his body against the inner wall of the shack, as if he wanted to embed himself into the wooden planks. The old man's breathing was hard, coming out of his chest in a dragged wheeze. It made Eddie sad for him.

Not being able to explain the connection to the sick man, Eddie followed the girl as she approached the shack until he finally realized that the girl resembled his sister, Gisela. Eddie wondered why this girl was causing such fear in this man.

Does she hold a secret, a dark intimate secret and her mere presence is enough to drive the man insane?

A commotion erupted from behind the man, and he quickly peeled himself from the shadowed wall and hesitantly went back to the porch, with his eyes glued to the ground.

Two girls were chatting with one another, as they passed by the house; inexplicably, Eddie knew they were the man's sisters. They ran to meet the girl who waited for them with her books tucked underneath her arm. Then, all three girls, giggling and joking, walked into the bright sunlight and were soon lost in the thick vegetation. Eddie wondered if he had just witnessed a mirage.

Do I know that girl?

"Hush your mouth, boy," an annoyed voice intruded upon his thoughts. "How in the world are you going to learn if you insist on wasting your time asking questions too early to be asked? Sit tight; let me tell you my story. If you are as smart as you think you are, then there would be no questions left in that stupid head of yours."

Eddie jumped, and a fear rose through him. How could another voice other than his own invade his thoughts? Was this possible? Nothing was making any sense, and he was beginning to wonder—to really wonder—what was going on. He was frightened, and all these new experiences were too far-fetched to comprehend. Was this a reality meshing with something non-existent? Was this a world that he created to avoid death? Maybe, he was already dead, and this was just a twisted waiting room that he was shoved in before God decided where his soul really belonged.

Eddie remembered everything at the hospital in fine detail. He remembered his mother's face and the pain behind her eyes. And, his father's anger…why was his father furious? Was he angry with him for getting sick?

Eddie felt the presence of the voice, and he wondered who it was inside him—was this man a savior or a demon waiting to claim his young life?

"Your head is filled with too much nonsense. It must be from all that junk you're always reading," the voice snapped with a nastiness that brought tears to Eddie's eyes. "You are going to drive yourself into a fever of madness, boy. Is that what you want? 'Cause if those are your wishes, then let me know at this moment, and save me from wasting my time. Suck those girly tears back where they came from and behave like you are supposed to behave…a strong man like me."

Eddie wanted to run from those harsh words, words that sliced through him with the precision of a scalpel. He didn't want to be with this man anymore. The man walked slowly to the end of the porch and gazed through the trees and bushes that surrounded him. Eddie saw the man peek with sadness toward the direction where the girl and his two sisters had hurried through. Only the green vegetation of the countryside was visible.

"Someday, she'll be my bride," the man sighed. "Have you ever been in love?" the man asked, but quickly answered his own question. "But of course not," he chuckled. "You are just a mere child not yet able to wipe your own ass correctly."

Eddie heard the man's quiet laughter, this time it was no longer in his head. The laughter was ancient and all around him, mingling with the stirring of the wind through the tall trees.

"Come here, boy; let me show you something."

Eddie looked up at the man, and then he looked around. He didn't know how or when, but found himself standing a few feet away from the man on the porch. He didn't remember when he climbed up, and he took two steps backward. There was something here that he didn't trust. The man stared at him with a cold look, and then he smiled.

"Come on, I'm your friend, have you forgotten already? Come on, I want to show you something," he said as he led Eddie inside the house. The first thing that hit Eddie as he entered was the smell of old sweat and tropical heat protruding from the uneven cracked planks that made up the walls. They stood in the middle of a large room that, if it weren't for a small table with two crooked chairs, it would have been bare. The man went through a doorway, and Eddie followed feeling an eerie awareness that the dark house was coming to life and was reaching out for him.

They entered a small room where the heat was more intense; it was a struggle for Eddie to take a deep breath. There was a soiled cot pushed against the wall. It was the only piece of furniture in the place. The man sat on the cot, while Eddie stood in front of the threshold. "Don't be a shy boy; come inside and sit next to me. I have something to show you. You could say I'm going to share with you a secret, and if you tell anyone I'll sure as kill you as sure as the rooster croaks in the morning." The sick man laughed, his laugh sounding old and forced. Placing his hand under the thin mattress, the man pulled out a notebook. It reminded Eddie of the notebook that Gisela kept hidden under her mattress, and that thought made him feel homesick and ashamed that he had secretly read Gisela's poems and stories.

He rubbed his eyes trying to remove the sadness of the images in his mind. The man looked up and his excited face quickly twisted into a scowl when he saw Eddie still standing near the doorway. He brushed the side next to him and motioned Eddie to sit. "Come on boy, you're not royalty, so don't expect a special invitation...now come on and sit beside me and stop acting like a retarded hick."

In the ailing man's hands, he held a notebook wrapped with rubber bands. Eddie couldn't help noticing the whiteness—no—but the paleness of the man's skinny hairy arms. It seemed his complexion was immune to the hot Caribbean sun. Eddie tried to peel his eyes from the sickly sight, but the further he averted his eyes, the closer they were drawn the man's long black hair on his arms. They seemed to have been neatly combed on the chalky skin and dandruff-like flakes flew every time he moved. Visions of vampires and dead things conjured in Eddie's mind, and he quickly dropped his eyes and kept them focused on his own two feet.

Carefully, the man removed the rubber bands off the notebook and then looked at Eddie with a toothy smile.

With peek curiosity, Eddie saw the man opened the notebook and reveal its content. Small, almost childish print was scrawled in every possible space of the lined composition sheets. There was no formation or style in the writing; just continuous words that followed without punctuations and no space between the words.

In a pensive mood, the man flipped the pages one by one, creating a soft whisper between the turned pages. Lost in the black written symbols, the man's eyes twinkled with a certain pride of accomplishment.

Eddie got closer, inhaling the powerful scent of old sweat and stale medication that seeped through the pores of those awful looking arms. The closer Eddie looked at the writing, the less he understood it, and the more it resembled scribbles. That didn't stop the man from admiring his precious work. The man turned his head slowly away from the printed messages and looked strangely at the boy with watery eyes.

"Do you know what this is?" the man lifted the notebook. "In this book I hold the most powerful thing that man would ever hold. This is my soul."

Eddie stared at the notebook and for what it was supposed to be…a soul. To him, it still resembled an ordinary notebook ready for the trash can. "What's your name?" Eddie asked not entirely ignoring the notebook, but there was a sudden urge to know the man's name.

The man placed the notebook across his knees, looking at Eddie and debating if he should be angry at the boy for his lack of respect or just ignore the question as a sign of idiocy of a child who knows no better. With raised eyebrows, he leaned closer to the boy. "Is a name that important when I'm telling you the secrets of life?"

"I don't know," Eddie shrunk back, fear sliding down his back. "My name is Eddie." He put his hand out like he saw his father do many times when introducing himself to another man. Not that he was thrilled in wanting to feel the pale skin of the man, but it was something that he saw men do, part of what he understood to be the etiquette of being a grown up.

The man took the small hand and squeezed hard. The boy winced, but to his credit didn't flinch, and that pleased the older man. "Nice to meet you Eddie, my name is Eduardo," the man said, a smile spreading his lips and revealing yellowish teeth.

Eddie glanced up at Eduardo, a surprised look upon his face. The man was still holding his hand, and the smile was fading as quickly as it appeared. Eddie pulled his hand and to his relief, Eduardo let go. The man's hand felt cold and clammy, like touching a dead fish buried in ice at the market. "Eduardo is my name too," Eddie said pointing to his chest. "But they call me Eddie ever since we came to Nueva York."

"I know," Eduardo lifted the notebook and pressed it against his chest. "You were named after me." Eduardo opened the notebook again, and mists of vapor ascended up towards the sky.

Chapter Seven

The words were frozen, as frozen as the statues that her youngest child, Eddie loved so much in Central Park. They are words with sharp edges that sliced through the internal veins of her heart, horrible words that hung in the air like defying ghosts challenging anyone to try to exorcise them.

"It can't be," Josefa kept repeating herself, wondering if her mind had finally snapped. 'He slipped into a coma,' the doctor said the words with such normalcy, as if he was ordering a ham sandwich for lunch.

'Slip?'

At first she didn't understand the meaning of the simple sounding word. Slip? Like a slip that you wear under your dress? And at the end of the day if the elastic stretched out, and someone might say, 'hey your slip is showing'. Slip? Like slipping on a banana peel? Slip?

"¿Pero que carajo es slip?"

What the hell is he saying, Enrique?

"Me no speaky tu much inglish, doctor, wha' deed jew sae to me? Sleep? I know, tanku berry moch, me son ez sleepin' jes." *Please somebody, anybody, please translate what the doctor is saying. What is wrong with my son? Why is the doctor looking at me as if I have two heads…or maybe my slip is actually showing?* She thought to herself in desperation before bursting into tears, tears that scorched her face and refused to stop flowing. The people around her tried consoling her in vain. A nurse handed her some water in a tiny paper cup and a handful of Kleenex tissues. Enrique put his arm around her, holding her tightly in an attempt to stop the trembles from her body. While the doctor, bit his lower lip, and waited for her to control herself, Agapito raised his head toward the ceiling with closed eyes, pleading to the heavens where his curses would find a home.

'Slip into a coma', to Josefa this was a hell of a term for the doctor to use. She began to wonder if her son would spend the rest of his life hooked to cables and plastic tubes. Would he ever read another adventure of Batman and Robin with his beautiful puppy-brown eyes?

"NOOOO!" She screamed, refusing to accept there was nothing they could do for their son, but to just wait for God's hands to take charge of the situation. She was dragged out from the room while fast moving nurses and men too young to be doctors attended her lovely Eddie. She fought hard, wrestling the strong grasp of Agapito, as she tried to free herself and take her little boy back where he belonged, her home among his comic books and pack of M&M's and cherry Charms lollipops.

If only she had been home, where mothers were supposed to be on Saturdays; cleaning her own house, collecting her own dust from her own television set, cooking her own lunch for her own children rather than doing all that for white strangers who behave like she has no right to be a mother. Then again, a real mother would be home now on Saturday with her own, not slaving herself for a lousy twenty bucks and a few empty bottles of Coke that she could exchange for a nickel per bottle.

At night, Josefa lay awake in bed while her husband snored comfortably. She could identify the soft snores of all of her children throughout the dark apartment, and it pained her that between all the deep breathing, there was one missing, and that thought filled her eyes with tears again. She didn't know how many tears a human being had inside, one thing she did know, was that her supply of tears seemed to be endless. Parts of her wanted to ask God, no—not ask—demand answers. She wanted to know the reason why, her son, her baby, was being punished. It seemed as if he'd suffered since the first day of his life, when his underdeveloped lungs struggled to take that precious first breath of air.

She battled with herself when she began to question the powers of God and His reasons. She hugged the comic book that she had picked from the floor, most likely the last thing he was reading before the seizure, and now the colorful book became her talisman, the closest link between her and her lovely little boy. Between the covers of the comic book was Eddie's soul, neither trapped nor imprisoned, but waiting patiently for him. Until then, she would become the keeper of his soul—the protector—just like the red and blue character that adorned the glossy cover on the book. When she finally found sleep, it was early morning and the sunlight filled the room with golden streaks. She closed her eyes again, and her consciousness slipped smoothly into a dream. There were birds perched high atop tree branches, chirping happily as Eddie stood in front of her.

"Mami, I'm ok," Eddie reassured her; his lips smeared with the stickiness of the cherry lollipop that he held between his fingers ready to put it back in his mouth. "It's fun in here, don't worry. Your friend is nearby with me, and he promised that nothing is going to happen to me. He just feels lonely and wanted me to keep him company for a little while.

He is teaching me all kinds of neat tricks; the best that I like is how to fly over the trees and through the clouds. It's fun, mami; I'm having a good time."

Josefa reached out for him, but before she could touch him, a pair of hands pulled him away from her. "Come here Eddie," she ran after him, but the more she ran toward him, the harder the unseen hands pulled him away from her. "Stay still, Eddie! Stay still and come here now."

"But mami, it's okay…I want to stay here a little bit longer, please mami, please. Can I stay and play a little bit more?"

"Eduardo Angel Santiago, you come here to your mother this instant!"

"But mami," he was almost in tears. "Don't be mad at me, your friend said that you wouldn't mind. Please mami don't be angry with me. I just want to play a little more. Please don't yell at me, I promise I'll be a good boy when I come back. Bendición."

Josefa lunged at him, her fingers scratching the fabric of his white T-shirt, but not able to grasp her son. She lay sprawled across the floor, defeated as the dark clouds that now enveloped the entire area where Eddie once stood, swallowed him up. She jumped back on her feet and threw herself inside the mist. Engulfed by the thick gray fog, she felt a frigid feeling clamp on to her bones bringing a fear of her childhood nightmares. Josefa screamed, and screamed until her own frightful sounds brought her back to reality, to the tormenting waking world that she wanted so badly to escape.

"God bless you my baby, God bless you," Josefa whispered at the fading image of Eddie. She somehow knew that her son was not in danger, but for how long? For how long was he going to be safe? And how much more did she have to wait until he'd be back by her side?

Waking up abruptly, she looked around the room, confused, not only about the time, but also the day of the week. The bed sheet was soaked underneath, and she was surprised to find that she had slept in the same clothes that she left the house in. There was a tomb-like quietness around her house, haunted only by the faint sounds of traffic from the street below that announced the existence of humanity. She slid out of bed and walked around the crammed apartment, disorientated and puzzled about her family's whereabouts. Was this some type of a cruel joke? To first lose her son, and now her entire family? Was she losing her sanity in this sewer of a city? Her hands began to shake, and she curled her fingers and formed tight fists. Josefa bit down on her lips hard enough to break the blood vessels around her lower lip. Her heart bounced in her chest like a rattling engine, and she doubled over with pain that jammed inside her guts.

The room spun wildly, her eyes losing the focus of reality and her bones became weak and brittle. She collapsed on the linoleum floor with a heavy thump. She gasped for air, her mouth contorted in a grin and a scream eager to burst out from her lungs. She struggled to her knees, supporting herself with the armrest of the sofa. She buried her perspired face into the plastic that covered the thick furniture fabric allowing herself to sob quietly, and with each sigh, a piece of her sanity was restored. She remained in that position until her eyes could register, and her breathing was no longer coming out choppy and laced with fear.

She lifted herself from the floor, and sat down on the edge of the sofa and stared at the black empty screen of the television set. The wall clock clicked its arms to the one-thirty mark as the streets outside were enveloped by the serenity of a cold Sunday. Only the patchy conversations and Christmas carols seeping through from other apartments, let her know that she wasn't the last person in the world. Still, Josefa felt alone and vulnerable. With the strong feeling that someone was watching her, Josefa kept looking around the apartment the same way a frightened child would as it was trying to avoid the wrath of a schoolyard bully.

She jumped at the sound of the phone ringing. Her heart once again racing out of control, and a shriek touched her lips gently, but died before it left her mouth. The telephone continued to ring. Each ring like a panic scream, until she finally, snapped out from her paralysis, ran toward it and yanked the receiver off its cradle and dropped it right on the floor. She snatched it from the floor, and her fears began to whisper the worst news that she could imagine.

"Josefa, ay Dios, Josefa," a distressed voice shouted. It was Marta, her aunt who only called when situations were grave or when she needed a receptive ear to unload her complaints and history of her phantom illness. "Josefa, pero nena, are you there?"

"Si Tia, I'm here," Josefa said, surprised at the strength in her own voice.

"Oh my God, I just heard about the baby," Marta punctuated on 'baby', with an over-dramatic tone. "Dios mio, that poor child and all his sufferings." Then the water works began, and the exasperation increasing in volume.

The last thing that Josefa needed was her aunt Marta to add to her own anxieties. She listened to her aunt, as she began to compose herself.

"Ay, pero hija, tell me…how is he doing? I just cannot believe the bad news when I heard them from Enrique. Thank God that he was home, if not God forgive what would've happened. Is there anything that I could do? Anything. Por favor hija, whatever you need, just call me and let me know."

"Thank you, Tia," Josefa frowned, feeling a dull pain pinch the bridge of her nose. She wanted to believe in the sincerity of her Tia Marta, but the whole family had traveled this road too many times before. She found herself hating her aunt, especially at a time like this. "There's not much that anyone could do now, but just pray and hope for the best."

"Si, I already said a rosary in his name and lit a candle at church. That poor boy, Josefa, I don't know, but there's something there. I sense evil. Listen, I know a good man in the Bronx that, if you want: I could take him to you. If your son was cursed, he's the only person that could get rid of that evil eye that someone has placed on him."

A twinge of anger rose slowly over Josefa. Her aunt meant well, but her beliefs were always centered on evil spells. If anything happened out of the ordinary, her aunt constantly felt it must be the work of a bad spirit's brew. Tia Marta believed that nothing could be the cause of sickness; dark witchcraft and spirits were the true culprits. Josefa sighed, annoyed by the intrusion, even if she welcomed the voice on the other side of the receiver as a testament that she wasn't alone in the world. She listened disparagingly at the nonsense that spilled out of Tia Marta's superstitious mind. After listening to her aunt's rants for ten minutes, Josefa decided to end the one-way conversation and get on with her life. She politely excused herself and returned the receiver to its cradle.

The phone rang again and she answered on the second ring, hoping that it was not her aunt. To her relief, it was Agapito; he had taken everyone to church, and the news didn't please her at all. For Agapito to enter a church, things had to be very serious. Josefa panicked—had someone from the hospital called while she was asleep and gave her husband the bad news. She tried to push away those negative thoughts invading her brain. She put the phone on its cradle and sat on the couch; she cried and as the tears ran down her; she wished to be the last person on Earth.

Chapter Eight

A white crystal star on the window shone a bright steady light. Around it, lines of red, blue, yellow, and green tiny bulbs shaped as a Christmas tree blinked rapidly like fireflies chasing each other. Around the glass, fake snow spelled out 'Merry X-Mas'. Two silk red Christmas balls hung on the latch of the window, giving it a festive touch.

Gisela admired her handiwork, mesmerized by the lights not only on her window, but also the other windows from the buildings throughout the neighborhood, Christmas brightness overwhelming the hard streets of El Barrio. Gisela decided to decorate the windows, not wanting to let the ornaments she and her mother bought at Woolworth's to go to waste. It was their first Christmas in New York, and Gisela knew that it had to be a special and memorable one. Her mother spent the little money she earned to buy the colorful holiday lights; wanting for her children to feel some of the Christmas spirit and the excitement of new customs.

As Gisela sat in the room lit by only the bright colors of Christmas lights that tinted her face, she realized the magic of the holidays had taken a dark turn that no one could have anticipated. It was Christmas Eve, and Eddie was still in the hospital with no changes in his recovery. His sudden sickness and the conditions that followed were taking a heavy toll on everyone. Tempers were quick to be rise; silence was met with more silence and the way Eddie's name was spoken was with the same reservation is if he had died and buried in the quiet of the night. Gisela refused to continue thinking along those lines, repeating to herself that Eddie was going to be okay, she was certain of it, just as certain that Gisela was her name. There was closeness she felt with Eddie, something more special than with her other siblings. She felt a positive sensation, or perhaps it was a message that Eddie was sending to her. That's why she kept on with the decorations, to make sure that at least one person in the house was going to welcome Christmas. Most importantly, she wanted Eddie to see the blinking lights and the beautiful guiding star when he returned home.

She heard her mother call from the kitchen, and she quickly put the scotch tape and scissors away along with the spray can of fake snow that she was going to use to decorate the back windows. Her mother called again with an edge of annoyance in her voice, and Gisela called back to acknowledge that she was on her way. She just wanted to take another quick look at her creation, and was pleased at how the room was transformed into a magical, multicolored place; a smile appeared softly on her thin lips.

"Are you deaf?" her mother walked inside the living room and glared at Gisela. "You girls better stop listening to that music so loud; your ear drums are going to explode one of these days."

"Ay mami, who's listening to music now?" Norma came from the room; not fond with her mother's crankiness.

Josefa twirled rapidly and frown at Norma. "Señorita, may I

remind you who's the mother here and who's not. Lately, you have been talking a bit too much, and I appreciate if you get rid of your little attitudes. ¿Entiendes? Now go and help Migdalia set the table…and you…" she addressed Gisela. "Go and wake up your father. It's Christmas Eve, and the least thing we could do is have dinner as a family."

Josefa walked back to the kitchen and opened the oven and peeked inside. Satisfied with what she saw, she turned off the oven and removed the hot pan carefully, placing it on top of the stove. Grabbing the tip of the aluminum paper, as she peeled it open, aromatic smoke flew past her, further toasting her already warm face. She winced and pinched off a bit of meat from the pork roast to taste. It was delicious as the crispy skin glistened in its golden color, and the well-cooked meat crumbled at the mere touch of her fork. She removed the aluminum paper completely and set the pan aside so it could cool off before cutting it. She lifted the cover from a large pot and stirred the rice with pigeon peas that was ready to complement the pork.

How much she would have loved to make pasteles, but with the constant vigils at the hospital, she was lucky that she had enough time to make this. She sighed and looked at the time; something she was doing almost every other second wondering where was Felix. She prayed for his return before Agapito sat on the table, and began demanding to know where the hell Felix was. 'Someone better remind that lazy boy', Josefa could already hear her husband. 'As long as he lives in this house he'd better abide by my rules and if not, he can get the hell out'. Josefa shuddered at the thought of the encounter. It was another disaster she had to avoid, if at all possible, especially on Christmas Eve.

The heart-to-heart talk she had with Felix seemed to have been more of a show than anything else, her oldest son was still coming home at all hours of the night. And now with most of her free time consumed with Eddie and hospital visits, Felix became more defiant in his comings and goings from the apartment.

From the front door, Josefa heard the clicks of locks opening and, in a silent prayer, thanked God that Felix was finally home. He entered quietly and walked into the kitchen to greet her. She could smell the powdery gum on his breath and another alien, something like a stale herbal smell, when he lowered his head to kiss her cheek and to ask for her blessings. She wanted to scold him and demand an explanation of his whereabouts, but the sound of steps coming from the bedroom forced her to hold that conversation for another time. Under the circumstances, it was best avoiding any explosive situations. Josefa wished to salvage the bit of happiness they were still able to squeeze in their gloom.

Josefa glimpsed at the table, the plates sitting side by side with the forks, knives and neatly folded napkins. In the middle of the table she placed a platter of yellow rice with pigeon peas, its white vapors climbing to the ceiling. Right next to it, she placed the pork and both spicy-smelling scents mingled to create a mouth-watering aroma. Agapito stumbled toward the kitchen, his unshaven face and tousled hair contradicting the holiday essence exhibited on the table. He plopped into the chair at the head of the table with indifference, like a king waiting to be served without a single pleasant comment about the Christmas feast in front of him. It seemed that for him, tonight was just another night and most likely after dinner he was heading back to bed.

Josefa ignored his brutish behavior and began to prepare a green salad; still her thoughts on Eddie and the awful dream that kept recurring every night ever since. She arranged the plate on the table and sat down across from Agapito. To her left was Gisela, to her right was Migdalia, next to Migdalia was Norma and to Agapito's right sat Felix, fidgeting and showing his discomfort of being too close to his father. Josefa looked around and instead of blissfulness, she felt sadness, their humble dinner table was missing her youngest child. Without any warning, Josefa began to cry. Her shoulders sagged into her chest, and her lips trembled as tears flowed down her cheeks. Josefa felt the gentle touches of Gisela rubbing her arm, and Migdalia quickly stood by her side massaging her neck and brushing the hair away from her forehead. Feeling humiliated and angry with herself, Josefa kept reminding herself she needed to be strong, regardless of the severity of the situation.

Josefa felt she needed to maintain at least a shred of strength and composure for the rest of her children. She had shed enough tears in the early part of the day as she kissed and held Eddie's hands in the hospital. She didn't want to leave his side; she would rather coil up next to him and spent the rest of her life as close to him as possible, her poor little child. Ever since God gave him life, He had been trying to reclaim it. Nevertheless, now with her tears brightly displayed she felt like she was ruining everybody's happiness. Through wet eyelids, she saw the bloodshot eyes of Agapito, probably hating her for giving him a weak, sickly son. She saw the discomfort in Felix's eyes, and the way he stared through her. She saw the anger in Norma's eyes, a fire that burned steadily, not for her, but for everything around her, she could not control, a situation that she knew her daughter could defeat someday.

Josefa felt an urge to run out of the kitchen, away from all the problems and the curses that seemed to be accumulating on top of her.

"How long, my sweet God? When will it be enough for You to stop the torment that You keep placing in our path?" she wondered within. The caresses of her daughters both comforted and shamed her. Josefa dried her tears and patted the arms of both Gisela and Migdalia assuring them that she was okay. As if with that simple gesture, she was telling her daughters her outburst was nothing more than just the foolishness of a mother wanting her entire family together for Christmas Eve supper.

She composed herself, and as she attempted to forget her emotions, she began filling plates and handing them out to outstretch hands. As soon as everyone had a plate, Josefa stood up and with her eyes motioned for the rest of the family to do the same. In a hushed voice, she prayed, thanking God for their riches, for their happiness, and for their misfortunes and yes even though it was painful, her trust and love towards Him to give them strength and to understand His ways. Solemnly, they crossed themselves, sat down and in a stony silence, ate their dinner. And, after they were done, chairs were pushed away, and, once again, the family dispersed to their own private worlds. Norma went to the television set and decided for everyone the programs to be watched. Migdalia went into her bedroom and swayed at the memories of Victor's hands finding hers as they walked out of the library, toward the benches along the East River. Felix went into his bedroom and digested the food while planning his departure. Agapito went inside the closet and took a swig from the hidden bottle of rum; Gisela stayed with her mother and helped her clean up the mess and put away all the leftovers that would surely be eaten for the rest of the week.

"Everything is going to be okay, mami," Gisela told her mother while adjusting the water temperature and lathering the dishrag. "That's why I decorated the windows; I'm sure he's going to love the lights and how they blink on and off."

"Thank you, nena. I wish that I was as optimistic as you," Josefa fought hard not to let grief overcome her again. "I hope to God that your brother would come out of that sleep and return home before the holidays are over. But I don't know if that's going to be possible."

"Why can't I go and visit him?"

"You will soon, but now it's not a good idea…they are still doing other tests."

"Do you think that he's able to hear even though he's in a coma?" Gisela asked as she began to wash the dishes.

Josefa emptied the rice into a large plastic bowl, the rice cascading like a yellow rocky waterfall, some rice finding the table and then bouncing off the floor. Josefa marveled at the term 'coma', a word that just days ago was not part of their vocabulary, and now it was thrown in almost every sentence. How could she answer Gisela with an honest response when she had no idea to what was the true answer? "I want to believe that he will," she finally responded. Yet, deep in her heart, she didn't believe what she just said.

"You have to teach me how to season the pernil like you do mami. It was delicious," Gisela changed the uneasy subject.

Josefa glanced at her daughter and gave her a weak smile; she appreciated what her daughter was trying to do. Everyone was walking on eggshells around her. No one wanted to be the one to cause her sadness to come pouring out. "The next time I'll let you do all the work," Josefa promised, forcing her lips to smile and putting a phony gayness to her voice.

"When are you planning to make another one?" Gisela sprinkled Ajax on the blackened pot and began scraping it clean. "I thought that Tio Enrique was coming over for dinner. Maybe we could have a party for New Year's Day. We could invite the whole family, and then I could cook the pernil. They could all become my guinea pigs." Gisela giggled at the idea, and for the first time, in a long time, Josefa joined the quiet laughter and that made Gisela feel great about herself.

Chapter Nine

"I think it's raining," Eddie said stretching his hand out and looking into the sky. There was a big blue sky that looked down at him, as the old timers used to proclaim, 'with not a rain cloud in the sky'. Eddie put his hand down while stealing questionable glances at the sky. "My face is wet," Eddie insisted on the rain theory, not convinced that the wetness on his cheek was anything other than water from the skies.

"That's not rain, boy," Eduardo informed him calmly, his body rocking back and forth on the old rocking chair. Perfect midday sun rays framed the porch and the countryside in blazing colors of yellow and green.

"Those are tears."

Eddie frowned and looked strangely at the sick man. He searched around him; still baffled about his surroundings. He shifted his small body on the edge of the first step of the porch and stuck his arm out again into the cool drizzle. It was weird that although the sky was blue, and the sun was shining; a warm rain was falling.

Eduardo saw the queries written all over the child's face, and that amused him. He liked the boy a lot; the kid made him feel smart and useful. "Yep, those are tears that fell upon your cheeks. Go on, don't believe me if you don't want, but I'll tell you those tears are from Heaven."

"Who's crying up there?" Eddie wanted to believe him, but somehow the absurdity of tears from Heaven was a bit too far-fetched. He peeked closely at the hammered edges, which lined the zinc roof; maybe some water from the last rainfall was finally spilling over, he thought to himself. His eyes followed the canoe-like edges and all he saw were spider webs and dead insects waving on the easy breeze.

"God is crying," Eduardo stopped rocking and stood up. With shuffled steps, he walked to the front of the porch.

"Why is God crying?" Eddie admired the rocking chair that Eduardo no longer occupied. He eyed the chair like a forbidden fruit. He went closer to it, his hands itching to pass his fingers around the smooth, wooden armrest that gleamed with strips of gold from the sun.

"You ask too many questions, boy. Why is that?" Eduardo leaned forward, and the hot sun reminded him quickly why it was better to stay covered by the roof.

"It's the only way to learn things," Eddie touched the back of the chair; the gentle stroke brought on the rocking motion. "If you don't ask questions about things that you don't know, you'll always stay dumb and end up working in a job that no one wants."

"Is that a fact?" Eduardo turned to face the child, wondering if there was an insult hidden in the boy's statement. *There better not be*, he said to himself—the last thing he wanted was a snot-nosed pip-squeak hanging around him showing off his superiority. It was enough to hear his sisters mock his simplicity, which they mistook for stupidity, but no way in this crummy, backward world was he going to allow it from this boy. "Do you think that I'm dumb?" Eduardo asked, having to satisfy his curiosity.

"I don't know. I'm just a little kid, and you are a grown-up. How can I tell if you are dumb or not when I'm only learning things myself?" Eddie circled the chair like Indians surrounding the wagons of cowboys before the attack. "But I still don't believe that those were tears."

"I see, so now you're calling me a liar?" Eduardo straightened his back to his full height of three inches short of six feet. It was an assertiveness of his stature of a grown-up, way of showing the kid who was really running the show. "Didn't your parents teach you any manners, boy?"

Eddie glanced upward, realizing for the first time that this was a man old enough to be his own father. The boy stopped walking around the rocker and now stood in front of it, waiting for a friendly push to deliver his skinny body onto the slumped wicker seat. He was getting bored with the whole conversation and the only thought in his mind that really mattered was feeling the rocking sensation of the chair. He wanted to yell to the man, that yes his parents taught him good manners; otherwise, he would have jumped on this stupid beat-up rocker a long time ago. Instead, like a proper well-behaved boy, he knew that you never sat on anybody's chair until the host gives permission.

Eduardo studied the boy. It appeared the poor boy was madly in love with his mother's rocking chair. He had been watching the gleam in the kid's eyes ever since he had gotten up from it. He wanted to tell the boy that it was okay for him to take a little ride on the rocker, but it was more amusing to see the changes that the kid was going through. The poor boy did practically everything to the rocker but mount it. Eduardo chuckled dryly, and for that senile laugh, he received a look of concern from his small guest. He was about to tell the boy to go ahead and sit down, but at the end he neglected the idea. It was better to maintain the power that he had over the ownership of the rocking chair, and let the boy continue to drool over it.

Eddie left the side of the rocking chair and sat on the wooden steps that led to a strip of baked reddish dirt. It was littered with pebbles, dried fruits and worms that burrowed in and out of the unusually colored ground. Along the side on the dirt road, twisting blades of thick grass grew along a few wild yellow and purple flowers, while mangoes that had fallen from the trees, littered the area as they began to rot. Fallen from grace, Eddie thought about the mangoes, and that brought a wicked smile on his lips, which broke into a hearty laughter.

"What's so funny, boy?" Eduardo's annoyance was clearly noticeable. He didn't enjoy hearing the sound of giggles; especially when in his opinion, there was nothing funny to laugh at. It made him feel the laughter was because of him and this he could not tolerate. "Are you mocking me?"

"I'm laughing at the mangoes spread all over the grass," Eddie stepped on the wet dirt and grabbed a small rock. It shone like a precious gem. The rain stopped, and the wetness of the ground and vegetation was quickly drying under the hot, bright sun.

"What is so funny about mangoes? Boy, I think that you are dumber than the mule that carries the bananas and pineapples to the town's market. Better yet, maybe a mule kicked you on your head a few times."

"It's not that I'm dumb; I just feel that mangoes remind me of people, and that makes it funny."

Eddie threw the rock at the tree, missing the tree trunk completely. It bounced and skipped along the tall grass and then struck something hollow. Two grasshoppers leaped into the air joined by a yellow and brown butterfly and a miniature bluish bird jetted by with blinding speed.

From the tall branches on the tree that surrounded the shack, a hot breeze whistled through Eddie's ears. The high sun above felt comfortable to Eddie, and its rich golden rays were injecting him with all the vitamins that he needed to survive. He felt like a big mango himself.

He walked away from the porch and went closer to the old mango tree that stood forgotten, with its offerings neglected. A sweet putrid scent of the toppled fruits tickled the inside of his nose. He searched on the ground, turning a few mangoes with his foot, before finding one that had just recently fallen from the tree branches. He picked it up and brought it to his mouth. It felt soft and juicy as he sunk his teeth breaking the smooth skin and slurping the sticky juices. He tasted the full sweetness of the yellow meat of the mango and felt as if he had never eaten anything more delicious in his life.

He licked his forearms as the nectar traveled down to his elbows and when he felt that it was an impossibility to keep his forearms clean, he gnawed on the mango until all that was left was the large pit. He hungered for another one and when he reached out, Eduardo was calling him from the shaded porch. "One is enough, boy, unless you want to end up shitting all day long."

Eddie stared at him, not certain what Eduardo was talking about, but nevertheless, he began to walk back to the shack while the sticky sweetness began to dry in twisted raised lines on his arms. "I have eaten more than one mango before," the child protested. "I'm not going to get sick."

"Why are you such a stubborn boy?" Eduardo glared at the kid with the syrupy smear glistening all over his face and arms. "You don't even know how to eat a mango the right way. Look at yourself, there's more of the fruit on your face and arms than inside your stomach. Go and clean yourself before the insects and the bees confuse you with a big stupid flower with a lot of honey to give."

"Flowers don't give honey," he corrected the man, not out of malice but with a matter-of-fact attitude, the same way he corrects his parents and siblings when he wanted to show off his intelligence.

Two burning eyes flared at Eddie, the man's cheeks turning a feverish color of red. Eduardo held the banister of the porch tight, his knuckles popping and turning white. "I ought to drag you by the hair and beat you with a stick. How dare you to disrespect me, when I'm going out of my way to help you in every which way possible? Come here boy!"

"I have to wash myself," Eddie meekly backed away.

"I said to come here now if you know what's best for you." Eduardo climbed the wooden steps, his walk weak and uncertain.

Eddie stood there and gawked at the man. "Why are you so angry at me? What have I done to upset you?" Eddie shrieked in bewilderment.

"Do you still mock me?" Eduardo made a fist and shook it in the air. "What makes you better than me? What gives you the right to laugh at me, to my face?"

"I haven't done anything…I just said that flowers did not give honey, but the bees make the honey from the nectar of the flowers. That's not making fun of you…honest…I don't even know you, to feel comfortable in joking with you." In Eddie's eyes, a doubt fell over them, and suddenly he realized something that before had gone unnoticed. He raised his head and glimpsed around him. A cold nightmarish fear slithered the linen of his belly and right then he got the urge to vomit the mango that he had just devoured. "Who are you?" he finally asked. His gulps of air were rough and hard, like swallowing meat without chewing.

"Where am I?"

Eduardo's anger disappeared rapidly. He knew beforehand that leading the boy into his home was not going to be easy. He had been forbidden to make any contact with the child, even when the child's life was in peril, but he had to disobey. He felt he had to continue to deceive the boy; otherwise, all his planning, all his conniving would be wasted, and punishment for his disobedience will be painful. The sick man turned and started to climb the steps to the porch, but before he could reach it, Eddie ran past him and jumped on the porch.

Positioning himself on the edge of the porch, while Eduardo still stood on the steps, Eddie was now eye-to-eye with the man whose mystery intrigued him. There were too many questions bouncing inside his young head, questions that he felt demanded answers, and all those answers must come from Eduardo's mouth. "What is this place?" Eddie was stern. "Who are you? Where are my parents? I want to go home now; you're not a nice man."

Eduardo bowed his head, the sun baking the back of his neck. His arms dangled heavily on his side. It was his take-pity-of-me stance, one that he had used whenever he needed the sympathy from his mother, a stance that always worked, but only with her, never with anyone else. He prayed that it would work on the innocence of the boy. "Don't be mad at me," Eduardo's voice was weak, yet manipulating.

"Who are you?"

"I'm your friend," he kept his head down looking at his worn-out boots, just as a child whose in trouble would.

"If you are my friend, then tell me what this place is and how I got here," Eddie was not falling for the man's antics; he knew exactly what Eduardo was doing. He almost laughed when he recognized the exact same tactics he had used on his own mother whenever he wanted another comic book or a piece of candy before dinner. It was uncanny; Eddie thought. There were so many similarities between Eduardo and himself.

"This place is where I was born and the only place I know…it's home," Eduardo stressed an accent of loneliness to his carefully soft-spoken words.

"But how did I get here? I'm supposed to be in a place that's cold with falling snow with my family, but I'm in a place that's hot and mangoes all around. I feel that I'm back in Puerto Rico, but that's impossible. So tell me, am I dead?"

Eddie's voice choked in desperation; the unseen tears made Eduardo lookup and cast aside his little game of pity. He watched the boy with caring eyes, with genuine love that could only be shared between father and son. Once, he longed to father this boy. Many years; many hurtful years even though the child's mother never knew or even suspected the love he possessed for her. Still, he never gave up; no love is too strong to be shattered by mere inconvenience of time and space. Nothing could keep him away from the child's mother, his single desire for her love, his only passion that blinded his soul.

Oh, mother, what can I do?

Eduardo implored to his own mother within the silence of his heart. Help me to do what is best for us; I need your guidance now more than ever. A soothing calmness fell over him as a voiceless entity answered him. He smiled at the boy with the assurance that everything was going to be okay, now and forever. Eduardo walked up to the boy and gently put his arm around Eddie's skinny shoulders. The boy quickly rejected the gesture and stepped away almost falling on top of the rocking chair.

"Don't be afraid of me, I am here to help you and nothing else."

"Am I dead?" Eddie was confused, and felt scared for the first time. Perhaps the man standing before him knew the answer, and this frightened Eddie. He felt wetness on his face again, and he knew that they could not be his tears because he held them inside. Once more, he began to study the hammered edges of the zinc roof, there was no rain, yet he felt the drops falling on his face, and he wondered if it was true that those were the tears of God.

"You're getting wet again?" Eduardo leaned against the rail of the porch and folded his hands on his sunken chest. "Now you believe me that those are tears? Maybe they belong to someone other than God."

Eddie didn't know what to think anymore. He felt his entire being in orbit, beyond the planets that he had learned about in school. He felt plucked from all reality, and now he was left in limbo, in a nameless place. He didn't know what to believe, and if this man was somehow part of his life, can he be trusted? Eddie stared at Eduardo and suddenly he remembered Eduardo's face; he was the man who had come to him in his early days of his childhood. He was friendlier then, and the voice of reason. Eduardo had become his mentor and his inner voice that filled his mind with knowledge and allowed him to peek into a world beyond his own. This voice saved him from long, lonely days when he was sick.

Eddie wanted to know all about Eduardo; but, most importantly, Eddie wanted to know if he was dead or not. He began to question everything. Eddie wondered if, in fact, he wasn't dead, then why was a ghost part of his life? Now, Eddie remembered so well. Eduardo was the first spirit he saw when he spent hours sick in bed; he also remembered that it had been Eduardo, who had entered his bedroom through the wall. He never was startled or frightened, by his apparition. In his mind back then, Eduardo was his friend. The jester who made him laugh during those long-ago nights, by staying with half his body in, the other half out; pretending to be stuck in the wall. Eduardo was the clown in Eddie's private circus. His pranks caused Eddie to laugh uncontrollably, and Eddie's mother would rush to his room to investigate. She would stand there bewildered seeing there was nothing there to warrant such rambunctious behavior.

Now, as he stood here in the place Eduardo called home, he thought he had to be dead. Otherwise, why was he in this strange world? There was too much to grasp, so the confused child crumbled on the dirty uneven planks of the porch and for the first time since arriving there—he cried.

Eduardo watched in silence; watching Eddie cry made him feel sad—the little kid he had befriended for the wrong reasons, was now completely vulnerable and broken down. Eduardo knew that because of his selfish desires, this child would pay the hefty price. He wondered how many others will also pay as he took a few steps toward the child; wanting to comfort him, but an unexpected screeching voice rammed a command through his head. Eduardo's lips shivered and his knees buckled, almost sending him plummeting to the ground.

"Eduardo!" the voice screamed; an ancient wrath covered the syllables of the simple name.

"Si mami," Eduardo responded with the weakness of a child.

"Come here boy, come here now," the voice ordered and that demand, not only frightened Eduardo, but Eddie as well. There was a rustling inside the house that sounded like feet dragging on old beat-up slippers. Eddie wanted to run as far away from the shack as possible, but when he tried a shadow came over him and froze him where he stood. Her scent was old and stale, like the smell of a dust-covered piece of wooden furniture abandoned centuries ago.

She came to him; and he saw something black and evil in her hateful, cataract-ridden eyes. It was a woman, a very old woman who smiled down at him with a toothless grin. "Yo soy tu abuela," she said. "I'm your grandmother." And that's when Eddie screamed for the safety of his mother' embrace.

Chapter Ten

Felix lifted his collar to protect his neck against the dark cold sky. The air rushed through freezing every breath as it raised goose bumps all over his body. A rain mixed with ice began to fall, and soon it increased into a downpour. It was the cleansing of the soul of a city that refused to be scrubbed. Felix hunched in the doorway of a condemned building and peeked through the rain, wondering if his lateness caused his friends to leave without him. A breath escaped his nostrils leaving a white trail of smoke behind, and he dug his hands deep inside his pants pocket seeking warmth.

He sneezed with a trembling force and then tried to sniff back the mucous and water that trickled from his red, numb nose. The hole in his sneaker kept his toes frozen and wet. Felix adjusted his collar once more, while the rain continued to splash around him, and the wind howled like mourning wolves throughout the city. The ice began to fall with more intensity, as little frozen pellets crashed and stung Felix's exposed skin. Trying to protect himself from the burning impact of the small ice, Felix shook his head thinking that no matter how hard he tried to adjust to this crazy climate, he just couldn't get used to it. *There was no way in hell that I'm staying here*, he repeated in his mind for the millionth time.

He mumbled to himself in frustration, "the second I get the chance, I'm going back to where I belong, Puerto Rico. To hell with the snow, the cold bitter wind, the ice cubes from the sky and the tongue twisting language." He continued to complain to himself as he tried his best to warm his hands, while shaking the water out from inside his shoe.

As he stood there waiting for the rain to stop, Felix saw a station-wagon spin for a slight second on the slippery road, regain control and resumed its course.

As he watched it drive slowly, almost too slow to even be moving and the first thing that came to Felix's mind was—la policia—the cops. He backed up, deeper inside the boarded-up entrance and held his breath, afraid that the vapors from his mouth would reveal him as clearly as a red flag in a mountain of snow. He felt the heart-stopping coldness of fear grab his testicles and press hard; his knees knocked with a nervous beat and the desire to take a shit right here caused him to shudder.

The car pulled over and settled two buildings away from where he stood. The urge to leap from his hideaway and run back home was very inviting at this moment. He began to plan his escape, taking deep breaths. At the precise moment when Felix was going to push himself away from the building, someone on the passenger seat opened the door and let himself out. The wind whipped the man's coat, as if wanting to rip it off his shoulders. Felix's heart began to race, and he wondered what charges the cops could pin on him. What type of an explanation could he give that would sound reasonable? How would he be able to explain, why a sixteen-year-old Puerto Rican boy was standing on the steps of a condemned building in the middle of a storm and of all nights, Christmas Eve?

"Puñeta," he cursed with a sandpaper-tongue that felt sluggish and bloated. He kept his eyes transfixed on the figure that was now standing in the middle of the street looking from building to building. The driver said something, but to Felix's ears, it sounded muffled and foreign, yet the man outside nodded agreeing to whatever was said. Another shape came from the back seat, this one puffing on a cigarette and talking much louder than the others, and for the first time Felix relaxed. His breath jumped out of his lungs with a thrust that made him cough, announcing his presence.

"What the fuck you doin', bro?" the smoker came to the building his arms raised to the sky. "Are we playing hide and seek? Come on bro, stop fuckin' around and let's go. We don't have all night you know!"

Felix climbed down the stairs and joined Papo, the tough guy from the bunch and the one that let his mouth come to life before his brain was even awake. He scowled at Felix, and his lips twisted into a sneer that threatens to clip the cigarette in half. Whenever he spoke, the words seemed to squeeze themselves out from the tight corners of his mouth, and seldom did he show the camaraderie the others did. He took pride in his life with hoodlums and bragged more than he had a reason to. Behind Papo, Lefty appeared and strolled next to Felix; his small stature lost in his long over-sized coat; it was the coat that had previously belonged to his father. The same coat that Lefty's father wore when he plunged onto a cold sidewalk as he suffered a massive heart attack, induced by the alcohol in his veins and the nicotine that poisoned his lungs.

Lefty was the typical follower who tried to make up his tiny size with fake bravado thugs are obsessed with. Deep inside he was harmless and with a good heart. He was the butt of almost every joke in the group until Felix came along, and then most of the jokes were targeted at Felix. Perhaps, being the target of jokes, and the mocking of the other guys, was the reason why their friendship developed much faster and stronger than the rest of the group. Perhaps misery did really love company.

"Hey, Felix, what were you doing? Are you hiding from us?" Lefty playfully punched Felix on the chest, another habit that Lefty had, one of many.

"Yo creia que ustedes eran la policia," Felix was able to say through frozen lips and trembling knees.

"Yo', hick, this is America," Papo hissed through a cloud of cigarette smoke. "We speak English here…ok…what is it? No speaky inglishhh."

"Come on Papo, leave him alone. He just came from the island; he can't help it; cut him some slack, man," Lefty came to Felix's rescue. "He thought we were the cops. I don't blame him for hiding."

"Great, that's what we need, another pussy afraid of la jara," Papo looked at Felix up and down, an invitation to show your manhood in street talk. Felix ignored him, refusing to take the bait. The last thing he wanted to do was to be labeled as a troublemaker; there was a time for everything, including showing Papo that he had more balls than any asshole in the group.

"Never mind this pendejo," Lefty grabbed Felix's elbow and began walking towards the idling car. "Let's go inside the car, 'cause coño, is cold out here and this fuckin' rain is going right through my coat."

"Yo' asshole," Papo blocked their path. "Who the fuck you callin' a pendejo?"

"Come on Papo," Lefty stared at the car, avoiding Papo's flare. "Are we going to do this job without any hassle or what?"

"Just remember one thing," Papo poked his finger on Lefty's chest. "Next time you call me a pendejo, I'll stab your ass. You got that, maricón? And that goes also for your jibaro faggot of a friend."

"I'm no faggot." Felix spat, his heavy accent coming out thicker than ever, something that Papo found extremely hilarious. He roared with sarcastic laughter while mimicking the way Felix had pronounced 'faggot' as 'fagut'.

"Hey guys are you coming or are you going to stay out there laughing like a bunch of strung-out tecatos?" An impatient voice came slashing out from the darkness of the station wagon; a voice that to Lefty was a savior, God knows what was going to follow. He dragged Felix and pushed him into the back seat of the car, and then he slid next to him, leaving the front seat for Papo. Best to keep these two apart for a while, he didn't like how Felix tensed up when Papo was making fun of him.

Lefty felt that somehow he had just saved Papo from a serious beating, and who knows maybe even worse. Felix was a quiet person. Maybe he felt intimidated by the way they spoke English with ease. Something else kept his lips tight most of the time; it was a saying Lefty remembered his father constantly repeated— 'los callados tienen la musica por adentro'—'the quiet ones have the music inside'; therefore, be warned and most-of-all, be careful when dealing with them.

The car pulled away from the curb and maneuvered to the middle of the road, the traction of the wheels digging into the icy surface and carefully, as Ralphy, the driver and already an ex-con at the ripe old age of twenty-two, navigated through the dark empty streets of Spanish Harlem. He combed the wet city with the sharp eyes of a vulture in search of a rotten carcass. He couldn't believe he allowed Rubio to talk to him into this escapade. Knowing for sure that if he gets busted one more time, especially while still on parole, he would end up back in prison. And that mere thought of going back to jail sent shivers down his back. Being locked up in a cell was not for him, not one bit.

Here on the streets he was respected and feared among his

neighborhood peers. Anyone who has done time in the big house was considered deadly, someone to keep your distance from. If they only knew that just because you served time does not exactly make you a tough son-of-a-bitch to fear. Ralphy heard all the stories, but in actuality, they were as badly informed as he was. Rumors were that once he walked through the metal gates of Rikers Island, he became the baddest motherfucker. How wrong were they, if only they knew that the big, bad-ass Ralphy they all feared, peed on himself the second, he heard that BANG. Yeah, the big-bang, the echoing, haunting sound that huge steel door made when you finally realized you were locked away from civilization.

Ralphy shifted the long station wagon to his left and like a concerned law-abiding citizen, stopped at the red light and waited patiently for the green. The last thing he wanted was to be harassed by the cops. Shit, even a misdemeanor like driving a vehicle without a license would guarantee him a nice stay in Rikers Island. Throw in a stolen car and now you're talking that, for the next few years, you're someone's sweetheart. And that someone is not going to be a soft, curvaceous woman who smells like lavender and vanilla.

"Coño Ralphy," Rubio complained from behind. "I know blind grandmothers that drive faster than this. Damn bro', if you want to do some sightseeing, do it on your own time."

Through the rear-view mirror, both friends exchanged glances. "Are you going to do my time if the cops jump on my ass?" Ralphy stared at Rubio.

"Bro', the way you're driving they're going to stop us even faster; you're practically crawling, man."

"Rubio," Ralphy was getting edgy; the stupid nonsense of the job was getting to him. "Don't you fuckin' see that it's hailing? If you want I could go faster, and the least of our worries is going to be the cops, 'cause, then our only worries is how the hell we're going to remove car parts from our ass when we crash against a goddamn lamp post."

"Coño, bro'," Rubio threw his hands up in the air in frustration, ending the argument before it got uglier. "Okay, you are Captain Kirk. I'll stay back here and play Mr. Spock."

"You can't do that, Rubio," Papo twisted his body to face Rubio in the back seat. "I'm sitting next to Ralphy, so that makes me Mr. Spock."

Rubio shook his head and turned toward Lefty. "Do you believe this shit?" Then addressing Papo, "don't you know that Mr. Spock always watches Kirk's back, the one that sat next to him was the black chick or the little faggot Russian guy. So that makes you either a Commie or a bitch."

There were chuckles in the car. Rubio, not only was the pretty boy, the lady's man, but also the insult-machine-comedian of the group.

"You think you're funny?" Papo settled back on his seat.

"Wow, that's a great comeback Papo. Remind me to write it so I won't forget such a great put down line."

"Fuck you," Papo growled.

"Another great comeback. Damn bro', you're really cooking tonight."

"Do you think that she gave any tail to Kirk?" Lefty intervened before it escalated into something more serious.

"What the hell are you talking about, Lefty?" Papo found Lefty a better opponent in giving and taking.

"You know the black babe on Star Trek," Lefty explained. "Do you think that she got down with Captain Kirk?"

Papo rolled his eyes in disbelief. "Who the fuck cares?"

"I do; I mean…Captain Kirk used to jump even on the purple aliens."

"How do you know that they were purple?" Papo barked without looking back, but keeping his eyes on the passing sidewalks. "The only way you have seen a color TV is when your mom takes the plastic wrap from the Valencia cake and tapes it to the screen."

"Shut up pendejo, at least we have a television. You don't even own a damn transistor radio."

"What did I tell you before about calling me a pendejo?" Papo turned around and half kneeling was almost on top of Lefty, his hot alcohol breath intoxicating the air. Lefty leaned back, the springs of the car threatening to push him straight into Papo and without a warning, he felt Papo's punch cave into his scrawny chest. He threw a punch back, but more to keep face than to actually hurt Papo.

Ralphy slammed on the brakes, a mistake that he realized the second he jammed his foot on the pedal. The station wagon spun in a complete circle, the tires seeking the traction that the slippery street did not have. The car ricocheted off a parked delivery truck and miraculously settled pointing the wrong way of the one-way street.

"Will you motherfuckers stop this shit!" Ralphy bellowed, his hands sweaty and holding the steering wheel with a tight grip. "Goddamnit, if you bunch of clowns cannot behave, do me a favor and get the fuck outta the car and let's forget about this job!"

He straightened the car first, afterwards swiftly turned it to the right direction, and drove it to the curb. He killed the engine and in silence removed a cigarette from a pack in his shirt pocket and took a long drag. "Now what?" he asked to no one in particular. "This job is supposed to be a one, two, three bullshit. If everything goes right, we should be outta there in less than an hour, now all that I'm asking, are you assholes up to this or would you rather keep acting like little faggots in the schoolyard?"

He squashed the cigarette on the dashboard and threw the butt on the floor. He glanced at the back of the car and took his time staring first at Rubio's eyes; even in the dark shadows of the car, Rubio's blonde hair shone like a saint's halo, his blue eyes blinking and a painted smile on his lips that hid the fear. Next to Rubio sat Felix, his eyes staring back with a look that made Ralphy feel uncomfortable, and he quickly threw his eyes at Lefty. He then turned and wondered if Papo was the asshole of the bunch that would undoubtedly bring them all straight to the jailhouse.

"Papo, listen up," Ralphy knew that he had to put a leash on him. "I don't know what the hell is wrong with you, but every time we are together you seem to be always in the middle of the shit. Why is that?"

Papo cracked his knuckles and shifted his body against the door, not once looking at Ralphy, but deciding that the mirrored reflection of his face on the window was more important. "Because I'm surrounded by maricones," Papo said from clenched teeth.

Ralphy ignited the car and started driving again, the car spinning for a second and then settling on the dangerous terrain. "I'll tell you one thing Papo," Ralphy was not finished. "You have two choices; either be one of the maricones or get the fuck outta the car right now. Your choice, bro', you decide 'cause if I have to decide for you, bro' I swear," Ralphy kissed his thumb to emphasize the swearing. "I'll throw your ass outta the car, and if you get bad I'll make sure that you'll never see another shitty sun go up. So what is it, bro'? How are we going to play it?"

"Okay, bro', I'm cool," Papo was not thrilled to be singled out and be made to look like a fool. The rage within Papo continued to burn; it was a rage that seldom burned out. He knew the damn score very well; Ralphy was playing the bad-ass again. That was cool; let him have his glory days; Papo reasoned, as he began scheming to a grander scale. His future agenda was going to knock a few pendejos off their pedestal and dump them where they belong. If only the rest of this bunch of assholes knew how their hero, Ralphy, had acted in prison, they wouldn't be so quick in kissing his ass.

They drove in a silence broken only by the ice pebbles that bounced off the hood on the car. Felix had remained quiet during the whole melee, not taking sides, not even laughing when everyone laughed at Rubio's put downs. Felix glanced at the passing streets through the car's window, wondering to himself at what the hell was he doing. This was not who he was; he was not a cheap hoodlum, like the clowns around him. So why the hell was he sitting here sandwiched between two losers who most likely would end up behind bars?

He befriended Lefty and Rubio in school; they were the only ones that actually tried to help him whenever he felt defeated or disturbed by the antics of his classmates. Lefty was the first one to come to his rescue one day when the entire English class thought it was hilarious that he mispronounced a word. Which word was it? It didn't matter; every word was difficult to pronounce. Lefty almost got into a fight with a fat pimpled-face boy on that day and for that, Felix was grateful. A friendship developed and soon Rubio joined them whenever he went to school, which was practically never.

They stopped in front of a school and as the car idled, Ralphy smoked another cigarette. When he was finished, he opened the window and flicked it out. A sudden freezing gust rushed through the window stealing all the heat from inside the car. Ralphy put the car in motion again and drove around, circling the school building, glancing from top to bottom as they drove. Satisfied, he parked the car by a fire hydrant, and took a deep breath. He spoke to Lefty through the rear-view mirror. "Okay, Lefty, remember…the window by the yard should be easy to open and is big enough for you to get through. Felix, you go with him, in case he needs someone to boost him up and then wait by the door, when Lefty opens the door come out and let us know. Simple shit, now let's not mess up."

Lefty and Felix slid from the car seat; their bodies tensing against the brutal cold that wrapped around them. They walked slowly, on crunchy sounding steps as the hail puncture their faces like dull needles. They squeezed themselves through a hole of the chain-link fence and cut through the yard, disturbing a layer of virgin, crystallized snow. As they approached the side to the school, slipping and sliding like a pair of drunks, they saw the window was slightly ajar and long shiny icicle, hung from the edges. Felix positioned himself beneath the window and interlacing his fingers creating a perfect lift for Lefty to climb up. Lefty lifted his left foot on the exposed palms and pushed his body up to the window.

As he balanced himself, Lefty pried the window with a strong push, smoothly gliding it on its track rail. He grabbed the windowsill and pulled himself up until his stomach lay on the cold metal ledge, and he could see inside. Forcing his eyes to adjust quickly to the darkness, Lefty looked inside the small room that was lit only by the weak glow from the street light. Holding onto the side against the cinder-block wall, he raised his legs, one at a time until he sat on the ledge. He scanned the room, searching for a way he could descend to the floor without breaking his neck. Not far from the window, he spotted a table pushed against the wall, littered with books and boxes. He twisted his body carefully, and slowly lowered himself.

Extending his foot as far as he could, he touched the surface of the table with his toes. With his hands grappling onto the ledge, he placed his other foot on top of a box and with a prayer on his lips; he pushed away from the safety of the window. For a second, he kept one foot planted on the edge of the table, and the other foot buried inside the box. He moved his arms wildly trying to maintain his balance, at that moment Lefty wondered if this had been the best thing to do. He reached out for something to grab on, but to his distress, found only air. He went crashing against the floor, as boxes, books, and mimeographed papers rained down upon him. A flagpole smacked him right between the eyes, causing him to let out a small yelp from the mountain of paper.

As he lay on the floor, his breath expanded his mouth into an elongated 'O', while he rubbed the bridge of his nose. He felt the blood bubbling a few inches above his right eye, pushing the box away from his stomach; he sat up and moaned like a wounded animal. The blood trickled down his open mouth, sliding slowly to his neck. He raised himself from the floor with wobbling legs; Lefty's first few steps were as clumsy as those of an infant learning to walk. He walked to the door hoping that there were not going to be any more surprises. He stepped into a dark hallway and glanced around to familiarize himself with the layout of the building.

He visualized where the car was parked, where the schoolyard was, and where Felix was waiting and most likely freezing to death.

Poor bastard, Lefty thought, *was wearing a jacket that was not even warm enough for the late days of autumn.* Lefty remembered there was an extra coat that belonged to his father taking up space in the closet. Perhaps Felix could use it instead of letting it collect mold and dust in the already jammed closet.

With his hand against the wall for guidance, he looked for the door. He figured it was closer to the yard, and after turning a corner, he found it. He ran to it, aware that the sooner the door was opened the faster they could burglarize the place and get the hell out. There was something deep in his guts that didn't seem right; perhaps it was his nerves sending bad vibes about the whole scheme. Maybe he didn't feel secure around Papo, whatever it was he couldn't wait to be back in his house, nice and warm and eating Christmas Eve leftover.

Christmas Eve, the word just made him stop as he thought, *what the hell am I doing on a night like tonight? I should be with my family; spending time with my little brothers.* A tightness swelled in his throat as Lefty stopped before opening the door. He took a deep breath and pushed that emotion far down within...where it could never get out. Then he took a handkerchief from one of the coat pockets and removed the blood on his face.

******

Mike, the school janitor, leaned forward on the chair and lifted his head at what he thought was a sound that came from the first floor. He reached out and turned the volume down low of the black-and-white-television with the grainy picture and the wire hanger for antenna. He listened closely, holding his breath to concentrate. Nothing. Not a sound. *It must be the weather outside,* Mike convinced himself, before settling back in the chair but not before raising the volume again. It had taken him a while to get used to the eerily strange sounds that haunted empty schools during the hours of the night. He was the head custodian in this school for the past ten years, and after been kicked out of his apartment by a nagging wife, he settled inside a small room in the basement, hidden by dark corridors and old discarded furniture. At first, he planned to spend a few nights, save some money for a new apartment. One month turned into another month, before he knew it, a year had gone by. And now that he was going on his third year; he found no reason to leave the premises. It was the perfect bachelor pad. No bills to pay, and the lunchroom was always stocked with everything he wanted to eat and drink, except during the summer months. He took a strong, long swig from the cheap booze and followed James Stewart running through snow-covered streets of a small-town shouting like a lunatic. Another sound was heard, this time louder. Mike turned the television off this time and lifted his head sideways in attempts to bring his ear closer to the ceiling of the small structure. He swore it was the distinct sound of a door slamming shut, and his first thought was to just ignore it and hide.

As he contemplated the benefits of remaining comfortably safe, the sounds were becoming bolder, menacing. He stood there, bottle in hand, contemplating his next steps. Mike placed the bottle of whisky down, went across the room and wrapped his swollen fingers through the neck of a baseball bat; the piece of wood fortified him with newfound bravery. Before he went through the door, he took a swig of liquid courage to be able to face head on the menace above.

******

Rubio looked around the hallway of the darkened school and turned to the others around him. "Now what? It would have been better if Ralphy was actually here, instead of just telling us where to find the stuff."

"We don't need that punk," Papo almost shouted, saliva drooling from the side of his mouth. "You assholes think that the fuckin' world orbits around Ralphy, but you see; he rather stayed inside the nice, warm car, while we come out and do the job."

"Come on Papo, we knew the plan before we even agreed to it," Rubio defended Ralphy's action. "And the plan was that he was going to stay inside the car not only as a lookout but to keep the car ready to go when we came out with the shit."

Papo stared at Rubio, his wet short hair standing up resembling a dead porcupine. "Whatever you want to think Rubio, but I tell you, this is the last time that I'm taking orders from Ralphy. Just because he came out of jail, that doesn't make him a hot shot. If you ask me that only makes him an asshole that got his ass caught, and who knows what the hell happened inside the joint. You people have heard about dudes getting pop in the ass by the other prisoners. Maybe Ralphy was somebody's bitch inside the joint and now here he comes as mister bad-ass when he probably turned faggot in jail."

"You know Papo," Rubio turned around to face him. Next to Ralphy, Rubio was the other member of the group that saw Papo as what he really was, a punk with a loud mouth. "How come you don't say those things to the man's face? Let's see what he has to say about it."

"Maybe I will," Papo shook the wetness off his coat, avoiding the accusing eyes of Rubio.

Rubio didn't like Papo at all, and he wondered why Ralphy always insisted on counting him in every time something was going to go down. Rubio shrugged and ended the conversation between them as he stared down the long hallway lined with bright inspirational bulletin boards. He studied the piece of paper where Ralphy had drawn a crude floor plan that zeroed in on the spot where the goodies to be stolen were. With confident strides, he began walking toward the mark.

Felix sneezed hard and his body shuddered, agitating him with uncontrollable shivers. He waited for what seemed a long time outside until finally Lefty opened the door. He had been ankle-deep in freezing snow, and braving the icy hail, and savage winds gusts that tore through his thin jacket unto his skin. He sneezed again and doubled over in pain, and his face felt hot and sickly.

"Carajo bro', you look like shit," Lefty touched Felix's arm with a genuine concerned gesture. "Man it's winter, what the hell are you still wearing that jacket? You don't have a warmer coat?"

Felix sneezed again and wiped his nose on the old wet sleeve of his jacket. He nodded and sniffed hard. Lefty took off his coat and threw it over Felix's trembling shoulders. "Look man, go over there by the radiator and warm yourself up with my coat."

"It's okay," Felix protested trying to remove the warm coat from his shoulders. He didn't want to seem like a charity case.

"Mira Felix," Rubio came to him. "Lefty is right. Just stay there and warm up. When we find the room with the stuff, we'll come and get you. The way you're sneezing and shaking you won't be any help anyway, not right now."

"Hey ladies, what the hell is all that whispering about," Papo turned around quickly, annoyed at the tight bond that the other three were developing. "Am I the only dummy that's going to do some work around here?

******

Mike was sure that he heard the distant sounds of people talking. The echoes were traveling through the corridors, although, he couldn't pinpoint the exact spot where those sounds were coming from, he was more than certain that what he was hearing were voices. *What if the voices belong to someone from the school board that came to investigate a complaint? Or, perhaps it was a noisy neighbor?* He began to wonder. 'Damn,' he whispered under his breath. Immediately, he began to think about the trouble he would be in if any school official found him. He wasn't supposed to live there—clean the place: yes, keep it running: yes, but not claim the whole damn building as his home. He began to think that maybe it was best to go back to his little hole in the wall, turn off the lamp, and remain quiet, until whoever was there left.

He stood at the corridor that led to the stairs, and feeling his drunkenness evaporate as quickly as it had come. *What if they are robbers? Then what? They could have guns, and obviously; a gun always wins over a baseball bat*, he thought while shaking his head. They could also be vagrants looking for a warm dry place to sleep. And if they are vagrants, they could easily out-muscle him and not only give him a good beating, but also rob him. The millions of possibilities of the scenario Mike was about to walk into crippled him against the wall as his thick fingers gripped tighter around the neck of the wooden bat.

There was a crash, and Mike jumped and screamed like a teenage girl watching a horror movie. He ran back to his hidden area and turned off the lamp. In the darkness, he could hear the rapid pulse of his heart drumming intensely against his ear canals. He held on to the wall for support, the baseball bat hitting the cylinder blocks softly as he tilted his head sideways, his ear extending upward, in a vague attempt to clearly hear the commotion one floor above him. There were no sounds, and the weak bravery began to surface. He forced a pathetic smile; almost admitting how stupid he was to behave so cowardly. Mike took a few steps forward and listened. He took a few more steps and then climbed the stairs, one by one, his body leaning sideways should he needed to jump and run back to his hiding place.

He now stood by the double doors that lead to the hallway. Through the glass opening at the center of the door, he peeked through the darkness. He pushed the door quietly, and cautiously entered the hallway. He kept the bat parallel to his right leg while his left hand dragged itself and guided him through the corridors of the school. In the middle of the hallway he stopped, sniffed the air for no reason and that delighted and relaxed him all at once. He felt at ease and lessened the grip on the bat. A nervous whistle came out of his lips, and he was satisfied that what he heard was probably the wind from outside. He spun happily on his heels and headed back to his room. Then, a loud blast exploded, and Mike jumped in fright. He crouched quickly to the floor, panic erupting within, and he wanted to run; he wanted to yell, but all he could do was stay frozen on the ground.

******

"Goddamnit!" Papo cursed, his face beet-red and drenched with sweat. "Fuckin' door is locked. Can someone go out and tell our goddamn leader that his dumb one-two-three bullshit isn't working out." Papo backed away from the door and for the third time placed a hard kick on the lock. The door only moved slightly, and all that Papo received for his effort was a cramp on his calf and sore ankles. He limped away angry, throwing up his arms in disgust. "The hell with this shit, goddamn ass hole is out there nice and warm listening to fuckin' Bing Crosby while we are here like pendejos trying to open a steel door with only our dicks in our hands. Fuck it, I'm out of this shit!"

"Hey guys," Lefty waved from a door that divided the large room by a bulletin board still decorated with crude drawings of Santa Claus and big colorful snowflakes. "This door is open and it goes to the same room."

They shuffled inside, and the first thing that they saw was the neat pile of boxes looking like forgotten Christmas gift. They started to open the boxes and like bright-eyed innocent children, they found brand new typewriters, their metallic bodies giving off a nice oily fresh smell. In other boxes, they discovered school supplies, pens, pencils, and a round globe with raised brown, green, and white mountains all around its countries, mounted on an elegant wooden stand. With their greedy excited hands, they marveled at their new-found treasures, imagining the solid cash they were going to make for such loot.

"Coño," Rubio whistled through thrilled grinning lips. "Hermanos, Santa Clo made a special stop just for us."

"You ain't kidding bro'," Lefty grabbed a box and began walking towards the opened door. "So let's get our gifts and get the hell outta here."

"Wait assholes, wait one second," Papo jumped in front of Lefty; his hands held high. "There must be a hand-truck or something to carry this stuff; I doubt that they brought in one box at a time."

The three of them glanced around, considering the logical observation. "It makes sense Papo," Rubio said as he started lifting boxes and moving chairs and desk while he searched. "These city workers are so lazy the last thing they would do is break their back if they could use something."

"I'm on a roll guys," Lefty shouted from the side next to the row of windows. He was standing next to two red candy-apple-hand-trucks; the price labels still glued to the handles. "You know how much we could get for these two babies from any store down Third Avenue. Man we just scored big time."

They piled the boxes onto the hand-trucks and began filing out of the room. Papo and Rubio rolled the boxes while Lefty followed holding on to the globe. They walked through the corridors laughing and singing and acting like the best of buddies. They approached Felix, who was huddled by the heat, Lefty's coat covering him like a blanket. From a distance, he resembled a homeless man on the stairs of a subway. He saw them and he quickly held the door open, sniffling and happy that at least the sneezing stopped. He was still shivering, and the cold air slapped him hard the second he pushed to open the door. The hail had turned into snow, and the sidewalks and streets were now more slippery. Felix felt a wave of nervousness take over, and began to wonder if someone or something was warning him about a forthcoming disaster. He watched as the three hoodlums went past him, Papo eyeing him, thankfully he didn't say any of his trademark wise-cracks. As soon as they all exited the building, Felix closed the door and got near the radiator while pulling the heavy wool coat tighter around his shivering shoulders.

An unexpected whisper in his ear startled him, like the fluttering of the wings of a butterfly. He turned around; fear suddenly consuming his bones and now Felix wondered if he was perhaps delirious. He touched his forehead, but his hands were too cold to tell if he was feverish or not. The whisper came again, and now Felix stood looking around expecting to find one of the guys next to him, but all he saw was his own reflection on the black windows as Lefty's coat fell on his feet. He circled the spot where he kept vigil, listening for the whisper to come again—but mostly praying that the hushed tones were just a combination of the sickness that his body felt and the howling of the cold night.

To his comfort, the rest of the guys came back and with them, the frigid merciless claws of winter seeped through the doors as they walked in the school. They stopped and stared at him; a strange look sparkled in their eyes, Felix began to wonder why all the attention and noticed Lefty looking down at the fallen coat on the floor. Felix noticed the hurt in Lefty's eyes before he quickly stooped down and handed the coat back to Lefty. "Thanks Lefty, sorry it just fell off," Felix said with a weak voice. Uncomfortable with the three of them standing still and watching his every move, he spoke, not before clearing his throat. "I feel better now…what can I do to help?"

"Here," Papo pushed the hand-truck toward him, the wheels doing a little dance. "You could start with moving some of the boxes to the car."

Felix caught the handles of the hand-truck and stood looking at them, not knowing where he was supposed to go and at the same time afraid of what lay hidden inside the darkness. Although he felt both silly and frightened, he couldn't help but feel a bit stronger. In the distance, Felix felt the strong and eerie sensation of eyes watching him, watching closely his every move. Before the feelings could sink further in and paralyze him, Rubio wheeled the other hand-truck, and Felix followed him, relieved that he was walking and although there was a weakness in his bones and a hot fever burning his cheeks, he was to do something other than standing there alone. It was better to be around them, rather than staying alone in the dark with whispers infiltrating his mind.

******

Mike counted four of them—four young punks—and he tightened his grip around the bat. A strong bitter taste of the whisky lined his inside with bravery or a sense of blind stupidity, whatever it was. As he stood behind the hallway door, he got a better view of the punks having the time of their lives, but not for long—not if Mike could help it. He fought with the best back in his country, against actual soldiers, with real weapons, no comparison with four juveniles looting his school.

"Four goddamn spics," he whispered. *All those bastards were alike; they were born with robbing and killing in their minds, goddamn bloody bastards,* he thought as he lowered his body, with old knees that sounded like rusty hinges. He tried to calculate his next move, trying to figure out how his attack was going to take place. As far as he could see none of the Puerto Rican sons-of-bitches were carrying any weapon, and that put the odds in his favor. He'll wait until at least two of them, most likely the two with the hand-trucks, left the building, and then he could surprise the other with a nice swing of the wooden bat. He could hear them arguing in the gutter way of their devil's dialect, half English and half Spanish.

Goddamn punks were so dumb they couldn't even speak correctly in one language at the same time, Mike thought as he continued watching them. One of them was coughing and sneezing, and he sounded like he just caught the worse bloody cold in the country. At least that one was not going to be too much of a nuisance; then again, he heard that these hoodlums were as cowardly as they come. He raised himself from his knees, and opened the door slowly the adrenaline inside him began washing away the fear that once overpowered him. He stepped inside the corridor, staying low and against the wall. One of the kids came out, balancing about four to five boxes on one of the red hand-trucks that the school had purchased after years of begging the Board of Education for funds.

Mike watched him closely. The punk's confident walk was swaggering from side to side even as he pushed the loaded hand-truck. He heard mumbles coming from the room, and then shuffled steps and finally; a blond-haired boy appeared pushing the other hand-truck while a smaller kid wearing a huge coat trailed behind holding one box. Mike waited, his nervousness sending droplets of sweat down his back. His wheezing breath escaping his mouth in halting pauses. He started walking quietly towards the room; the old baseball bat rested on his shoulder ready to jump into action. He could hear the kid sneeze, and pity ran through him, pity that made him think of his own son.

He entered the room quietly, keeping the bat high above his head. And his eyes transfixed on the shaking back of the kid with the nasty bronchial cough. *I'll show everyone*, Mike fantasized, *let them see that I am a fearless hero who not only confronted four deranged cold-blooded spics, but also saved the school from being robbed of precious supplies.*

******

Felix looked inside the last remaining box and saw the top of a shiny brand new overhead projector. He calculated how many boxes they had already taken out to the station wagon, and he was sure it was at least fifteen, including the raised-map globe that he knew was going to end up in Lefty's possession. That was a sizable piece of loot that was going to bring in a nice sum of sweet cold cash. He coughed inside his fist and sniffed hard. For a moment, he thought he was going to plummet to the floor, and grabbing the back of a chair, he steadied himself, taking deep breaths and convincing himself to hold on a little longer. He tried to persuade himself that they were on their way out of this place and that soon money would be filling their pockets. He picked up the box to feel its weight, convinced that if he didn't start to do some work, he might end up with nothing to show for this excursion, but a nasty pneumonia. The muscles on his back, hunched and aching, trembled at the heaviness of the box; *damn*, he thought, *how could a projector be so heavy?* He placed the box back down as a coughing fit sunk on his chest and sent stiffening pain around the lower part of his back. He tasted the bitter sickness in his mouth and the idea of forgetting the whole deal and just head back home was enticing. He leaned forward on the chair, his hands holding him up, as the fever seemed to boil into a hot fire. Felix started to sit down, to rest his feverish body that just threw in the towel like a boxer who had stayed in the ring twenty punches too late.

He was startled by a voice that rang in his head. He looked straight ahead, the darkened window reflecting the room and the shape of a man standing behind him. He almost screamed out of fear; he was certain that what standing behind him was a ghost, a ghost with a baseball bat ready to crack his skull in half. Again, the voice shouted at him, snapping him out of his fear as he turned around with barely enough time to jump sideways to escape the bat that whistled close to his head. This was no ghost; Felix realized, but a man of flesh and bones. He snatched a chair and shielded himself. The man came at in a crouched, bow-legged stance. Felix jumped over a desk and watched splinters from the desk fly through the air. The fever and the aches in his body were slowing him down, but thankfully, the man was drunk, by the way his breath smelled like a brewery; otherwise, he would have felt the crushing blows of the bat many swings ago. Felix threw the chair at his attacker, buying enough time to run across the room and closer to the door.

Noticing Felix's plan, Mike crisscrossed his lumbering steps and reached the front of the room faster than he thought possible. Felix was coughing hard and dry, his body begging for mercy and a place to rest. Mike also coughed, bringing up old phlegm from wasted days and nights of cheap booze and chain-smoking.

"You goddamn bloody bastard," Mike spat at Felix, his chest heaving and wheezing like a dying old dog. "I'm gonna split your spic head in half. What's wrong with you sons-of-bitches? You think you could just take whatever you bloody please?"

Felix kept his eyes fixed at the taunting, twisted face of the man in front of him. The words were coming out distorted and the drunk's heavy strange accent contorted the sounds into phrases difficult to understand. Despite the inability to comprehend him, Felix knew damn well that the man was not there to tell him sweet stories. Heavy sweat poured out of the man's deep red face, and Felix stared at the baseball bat that rested on top of one of the desks. He had to find a way to wrestle that bat away from him. If not, he had to figure out a better escape plan away from this lunatic.

The outside metal door swung open, the metal squeaking from the hand-truck's wheels rumbled throughout the empty school. Mike shot a quick nervous stare at the direction of the approaching hoodlums, and his body stiffened. Felix saw the slight hesitation in Mike's actions and without neither plan nor idea; he leaped on top of the man, taking both onto the floor. The bat hit the ground first, with a solid bang. They were both sprawled on the tiled floor, as both reached for the bat. Mike got to it first and quickly wrapped his fat fingers around the wide barrel, while Felix yanked the handle. They both pulled and pushed; a tug of war for the bat.

With a final desperate snatch, Felix ripped the bat from Mike's grip and in a flowing, motion scrambled to his feet, a tightness across his chest filling his eyes with blue and white dancing dots. Mike made it to his knees, his coarse breathing tightening his lungs and rushing the beat inside his fatty heart. Felix was afraid, more afraid than he ever knew was possible. He had never crossed this strange almost surreal threshold in his whole life. As he looked down at the panting man, he prayed that he would never have to cross it again.

Mike swung his meaty fist at Felix's midsection, the fist landing solidly and halting the air in the boy's wheezing lungs. Felix's knees buckled, but he quickly recovered, and he leaped away from Mike's fist. Mike sneered with the passion and the confidence of a conqueror overpowering those weaker than him. Felix could hear the boisterous laughter from the others in the hallway. As panic rose in him, he wondered what was taking them so long to come inside the room and help him escape from this maniac. Felix felt Mike's strong grip clenched him tight and pull him closer. Felix swung his elbow, poking at the unshaved chin of the custodian and then dug his knee into the man's groin. Mike released his hold, and his groan was violent. Felix backed away quickly.

Desks, chairs and boxes blocked his path and pushed him back to the place he was trying to escape from. In the midst of the turmoil and the confusion of how he got into the situation to begin with, his mind was muddled. Felix saw the shiny silver cutting edge of the switchblade in Mike's hand. Felix's heart stopped in desperation, and a cold fear announced to him that he was in a real fight, not the push and slap fight in your basic schoolyard tussle. This was an actual fight, with a man, old enough to have seen and been involved in more than his fair share of battles. This was a real fight where punches were no longer needed because baseball bats and shiny deadly knives would lay down the rules.

Mike thrust forward awkwardly, and Felix knew this was not the first time the man had held a knife during a fight. With eyes wide open in panic and horror, Felix watched the blade cut through the air in a dance that mystified and mesmerized him all at once. He maintained his stare, for he knew that just one blink would be enough time for this crazed man to plunge the blade into his heart. Without a warning, Mike made his first deadly move; the knife speared through the space that divided both opponents and slashed Felix's thin jacket and found some skin. Felix jumped back; a chair that had been placed on top of a desk crashed loudly to the floor and jammed a desk trapping Felix within a semi circle. He had no room to escape the slashing blade that grew deadlier with each plunge. Mike was toying with him now, and that brought great pleasure to Mike. He was going to show these punks that they crossed the wrong man. He was convinced that the second the others would see this bastard with his guts hanging out; their toughness would melt away and show what they really were...grease-eating punks.

He moved the knife from side to side, switching hands and keeping the poor coughing teenager off balance, and at his mercy. Let the punk stare at death, and let him know before he died that nobody messed with bloody bad ass Mike!

Mike saw the shadow of a moving arch coming down. He was too slow to react or even realized what it was. When it landed on top of his head, making a sickening hollow sound, it was hard to comprehend what was taking place. He felt something sticky flow down freely from the top of his skull; still he was not able to register what was actually happening. Again, he saw the moving arch, and once more; the dull hollow sound rebounded through his head. Just then, when his mouth was filled with red rich blood, Mike registered the message that his mind was relaying. The fucking kid was hitting him with his own fucking bloody baseball bat. Cracking his skull and all he could do was stand there and do absolutely nothing, but bleed like a fool.

Felix watched the drama unfold as if he was part of an audience. In front of him, the main character, the main attraction of the show, was doing a funny skip and dance routine that it bordered on the obscene. The man's eyes, which at one time were bloodshot and wild, were now blank and dull. The blood poured from the top of the drunk's head, and it occurred to Felix that if it didn't stop soon, this crazy bastard was going to bleed to death. Felix still held the bat, bloody and with a crack curving through the middle of the barrel; it was above his head ready to smash the old drunk again.

Mike was still holding onto the knife, but the dance that it once was gifted with was gone and all it could do was droop lifelessly, and scraping the floor. Mike was looking up at the kid with the bat, and he felt his knees bend forward and sideways, his head spinning and losing the strength to stand up. He dropped on one knee; the pain swelling from his head was now an agonized screaming echo that could not be silenced. Mike tried to move his hand upward; the one with the knife, but all he could muster was the twitching of his cold fingers, as the knife fell down on the floor. His body screamed commands to get up and slice the throat of the punk that cracked his head wide-open. All attempts and inner battles to try to get back on his feet and fight were futile, washed away by the throbbing pain that overpowered his motor skills. With a whimper, he rolled to his side and kicking his legs a few times with involuntary reflexes; he welcomed his death.

"Holy shit, jibaro…what the fuck have you done?" Papo's head bopped from the bleeding man on the floor to Felix that still held on to the bat dripping with blood. "What the fuck you doing?"

Lefty came around Papo, and his hand flew over his opened mouth the second he saw the twitching, dying man. Rubio plopped down on top of a desk and brushed his wet hair from his forehead, his eyes frozen in fright at the kid whom he thought couldn't even step on a fly.

Papo came to Felix, this time talking softly, and a bit afraid. He reached out for the bat and at first Felix turned towards him with the bat flinching in the air. It took a few seconds, but Felix's mind came to, and he recognized Papo, and allowed him to take the bat away from his trembling hands. He was no longer coughing or sneezing, and the fever and the cold chills that shook him before were now gone. In its place, a sense of surrealism—a dream-like state—took residence instead.

He let himself be led away from the room and inside the hallway, where the air was cleaner and a bit colder, and it did not have the suffocating iron scent of blood. The three of them circled around him, but not too close. What had just occurred in the room behind them put Felix in a different light. The cat had shown his claws, and they were razor-sharp and deadly. Lefty couldn't help remembering for the second-time tonight his late father's words about being careful around a quiet man with the music inside. Papo contemplated about what he wanted to say to Felix, a new-found respect mixed with increasing fear began to brew inside toward the kid, who not too long ago he was calling a 'hick faggot'.

Rubio kept staring at the open door and peeking inside the room. Though all he could see from that angle was upturned chairs and battered boxes and desks, his mind could not let go of the frightful image of a real person dying. A real man bleeding, twitching, slipping into the cold embrace of death, and all of that was too much for him to handle at that moment. It was one thing to see death in the movies, but it was quite another thing to see it in real life. Real-life death came with its own soundtrack and nasty, sickening smells.

They all watched as Felix, eyes blank and staring straight, started walking away from them. He was as silent as the death that came and stayed inside the room. He went down the hallway with steps that seemed to be barely touching the tiled floor, gliding like an apparition that manifested in front of them. They watched as he eased through the opened door that led to the cold, black of the night. All three hoodlums discovered that night; they were not as tough as they thought they were.

"We better get the fuck outta here," Papo whispered, his voice hoarse and the hard edge that always coated his words was now replaced by the voice of scare little boy. "I don't want to be blamed for the death of that man…robbery is one thing murder is another. Come on, I think Ralphy would understand."

Lefty and Rubio followed Papo like lost sheep. Papo shook his head; still trying to convince himself at what they all witnessed. Before leaving, he stole one last glance at the room in total disarray that had become the musty dark tomb of a lonely man. "Jesus," Papo murmured to no one in particular. Perhaps it was supposed to stay in his mind, but everyone heard it. "Goddamn Felix, a fuckin' jibaro Al Capone."

Chapter Eleven

"You are losing them one by one and you better start fighting back, or you're going to suffer the rest of your life," the old lady said while lifting the cup of coffee to her painted lips. "What's happening in your life, nena, it's not normal."

Josefa looked at her aunt through the smoke that swirled out of her own cup of coffee. Tia Marta arrived into the apartment in one of her unannounced visits. It was a habit that the old woman had, dropping by unexpectedly on family members, especially if there was drama involved. She meant well—everyone knew that—but her annoying habit of always trying to force her advice onto people aggravated those she was *'trying'* to help. She would volunteer unwelcome advice until the other person, just to get rid of her, ended up agreeing with anything that came out of her mouth.

"Mira esto," Tia Marta continued, oblivious of Josefa's gesture for her to stop talking. "There's something evil that surrounds you and your whole family, and unless you get the proper help, mi'ja, you will always wear the color of suffering. Escuchame bien, there's a man in the Bronx that is gifted. Te digo nena, this man would be able to help you get rid of the spirit that's causing you all the problems you've been having since the day you got married."

Josefa wanted to tell her aunt to shut up, finish her coffee and go home, especially when she had things to do before rushing out to the hospital. In a polite silence, Josefa listened to her aunt's superstitious babbling. The elderly woman's head was filled with old beliefs of an

African religion, Santeria, where there are more gods and sinful lords than in any horror story. It was always the same, if someone was clumsy and fell down a flight of stairs; there was an evil spell on you. If anyone was taken to the hospital in need of an operation, then obviously there were snakes or some other deadly parasites growing in the person's stomach, the result of voodoo conjured up to eliminate that person. From the smallest things to the larger serious cases, to Tia Marta the reasons for such misfortune were always twisted in black magic. Therefore, you had to seek the help from a gifted person—who for a few dollar bills—would give you candles, herbs, and concoctions to bathe yourself in, burn in the house or dispense around the corners of the house. By then your troubles would be gone, unless the spell was too strong and evil; in which case now required more visits, more candles, more slaughtered chickens and more chants.

Tia Marta sensed her niece's uneasiness, she observed the fidgeting with the cup, the quick glances at nothing, in particular; those were all behavioral signs that confirmed to Marta that what she was saying was correct, there was something evil controlling this family. She could feel it, and at whatever cost; they needed to protect themselves from the evil she knew was here. Even if it meant that she had to go alone and bring something that belongs not only to Eddie, but to Josefa as well. And then, she would be able to educate them, to convince them her suspicions were not stupid fragments from a foolish woman.

She didn't care if they accuse her of meddling in their affairs— affairs that according to them didn't concern her. When the truth revealed itself, they would realize that she was right all along, and afterwards would respect her and seek out her wisdom advice.

"Are you okay?" she asked her niece, trying to make her open up. "You've been sitting there without even taking a sip of your coffee. It must be cold by now. Talk to me…I could help you in many ways, if you only let me."

"Tia, gracias," Josefa was convinced that the old woman was thick-headed. "There's not much that you or anyone, for that matter, can do right now."

"Yes there is," Tia Marta protested her voice snarling louder as coffee trickled to the corners of her tightened lips. "This man could help you more than all the doctors in that hospital where that poor child is wasting away. Those doctors and their medicine do not have a damn chance in finding the cure for Eddie. They are just going to let him lay there in some dark room, away from everybody he loves until he dies, and you know what? With all their fancy instruments and all their needles and pills, they'll see that it's not going to have any effect on that little boy and, when they finally realized that, your son will be dead. His illness comes from something bigger and deadlier than any germ in the world. Por favor niña, believe in me and stop being so stubborn, the quicker we start fighting back this evil, the sooner your son will be back home. Por favor…what do you have to lose?"

"My son," Josefa said softly, hiding the anger that was slowly surfacing. "Are we supposed to take Eddie away from the hospital and have some voodoo man come and treat him, all because you feel that there's a spirit controlling our lives? Por favor, Tia, my son is in a coma because he suffered an epilepsy attack not because someone is putting pins on a rag doll."

Tia Marta crossed herself and put the cup down, a bit harder than she expected, spilling coffee onto the table. "Go ahead, hija, make all the fun you want. But I tell you that your stubbornness is robbing that child from precious time…time that we can't afford. Do I have to remind you the things that happened when he was born? You almost died because he was born not only pre-mature, but he was also on the brink of dying himself. Even the doctors gave up on him, do you remember? The same medicine that now you are trusting so blindly, that same medicine was willing to give up on you and your poor baby back then. Open your eyes woman and see beyond what's in front of you. Answer this, what was it that saved your child's life back then? Tell me, what really saved his life?"

"Ay Tia, por favor," Josefa felt tension tightened her back. "I don't want to be disrespectful, but enough is enough. This is America, and we are not going to compare the advance of medicine now than what it was ten years ago especially in a hick town from the mountains of Puerto Rico."

The old woman glared at her niece, then closed her eyes and moved her head from side to side. She knew the conversation was over. No matter what she said at this point, Josefa had shut her mind from anything that involves rituals. Tia Marta sighed heavily and forced her mouth to stretch into a smile, hoping that the gesture would convince her niece that she was willing to abide by her wishes.

"Pues entonces," she tapped her forehead with a napkin. "Pues mira Josefa, I'm always here for you and your family. If there's anything that I could do just give me a call, ok? And if I disturbed you, all I could say is I'm sorry, but I'm just trying to help you as much as possible. Forgive the meddling of an old stupid woman." Tia Marta, pushing the porcelain cup further away from her, stood up, straightened out the sweater over her large belly. She adjusted the belt of her pantsuit and waited for Josefa to respond, hoping that she at least sounded convincing enough to inspire guilt in her niece.

"Tia," Josefa stood up as well, relieved that her aunt was finally leaving, but like always the old woman's guilt game was in full force. She was willing to play the game, as long as her aunt just left and let her go on with her business. "I know that you mean well, and if I hurt you in any way, I'm sorry too. But in my heart, I know that what I'm doing is the right thing to do. I have faith that God is going to bring Eddie back with the help from the doctors."

Adding the 'old-I'm-so-ashamed-look' to her repertoire of her quilt dance, Tia Marta lowered her eyes. "Bueno hija, I just want the best for my sister's daughter, nothing more. I will light up a candle and recite a rosary in honor of that poor child." Then on cue, like a well-trained actress, the old woman began to cry. Heavy, clumsy tears began to pour from the sides of her eyes, running wildly through the thick layered rouge that smeared her chubby cheeks. Her broad shoulders trembled, adding the perfect touch of despair. She watched Josefa come to her, and wrap her arm around her and deep within her mind; Marta felt a bit victorious. 'When everything fails, bring out the tears and just sit back and score the points,' was her motto.

Josefa knew exactly what her aunt was doing and just to get rid of her; she surrendered to the idiocy of this stupid role.

"Ay Tia," Josefa wanted her aunt to leave, before she lost her temper and exposed the charade. "It's okay, don't worry…maybe you are right. Maybe, there is something out there bigger, more powerful than mere medicine could cure him, but for now let's see what happens with the doctors, but I promise the second that I see no improvements I'll call you up, and we'll talk with this man. So please, calm down, there's no need for you to be upset with yourself, you must be careful…remember your heart is very weak."

"Gracias nena," Tia Marta clutched on to Josefa. "Don't worry about me. I'm okay, and my heart is stronger than anyone thinks it is. But as you know, I don't have much, the little that I have I'm willing to share it with you. That's all I'm doing, nena; I just want the best for you and your family. Ay Dios mio," she sobbed as she raised her head toward the ceiling. "May God protect that beautiful child."

Both women embraced, and then Tia Marta gently stepped away from Josefa, sniffled hard and strolled to the bathroom. She mumbled about composing herself as she closed the door.

Inside the bathroom, Tia Marta searched around, while letting the water run to camouflage any noises that would expose her snooping. She opened the hamper and peeked inside, choosing two garments that she knew belonged to Eddie and Josefa. It was a small T-shirt with a cartoon character jumping over a star, and a yellow sweater with tiny pink flowers printed across the bottom. She could still smell the talc powder identifying it as Josefa's, plus she had seen her wear the sweater many times. She removed the jacket of her pantsuit and her heavy sweater with huge, red rose pattern. She was about to stretch the collar of Josefa's sweater through her head, and then suddenly stopped.

What the hell am I doing? She reminded herself. *The garments of Josefa and Eddie must be as true to their owner as possible.* The second she wears Josefa's sweater, her own perfume and sweat would contaminate it. All that Josefa had left entrapped in the fabric would be lost. The same rules applied to Eddie's shirt, and with those thoughts stopping her, Tia Marta sat down on the toilet and contemplated her next move.

She poked around, underneath the sink, above a shelf by the door where the toilet paper was stashed with laundry detergent, and wrinkled old boxes. The shelf was high, too high for her five-foot frame to reach without making any questionable noises. She peeked through the toilet paper and the big box of detergent, and under some boxes, she saw the zigzag edges of folded brown bags. She reached high stepping on the tips of her toes, but only barely scratched the bottom part of the wooden shelf. Giving up for a second, she sat back down on the toilet and collected herself.

She looked at the bathtub and measured the distance between the shelf and the tub. She walked to the bathtub, touched the edge and then looked up at the shelf. She lifted her leg and carefully placed her right foot on the edge of the tub. Holding on to the wall with her left hand; she raised herself. Her face was above the shelf, and she could peek inside, all the way where you could see part of the wall at the end. She felt sweat running down the side of her face, and she cursed herself for not turning on the cold water, instead of the hot water that was filling the small room with steam.

Hesitantly, she raised her right arm, feeling her leg tremble slightly on top of the bathtub edge, as her other leg swung underneath her to keep her balance. She touched the bags, a feeling of accomplishment sending a powerful surge throughout her. Tia Marta started to pull one bag slowly, not wanting to disturb the other objects around them. Half way through, the bag held, stuck from coming all the way out, and she yanked to dislodge it from whatever it was keeping from coming loose. She tugged a bit harder, lifting the bag upwards and sideways, until it finally jumped out at her.

The bag slapped Tia Marta's face scattering what seemed to be dead insects and dust all over her. She pressed her lips hard to squelch the scream of her repulsion. As she squirmed trying to shake off the flaky remains of insects, her roundish body slammed against the wall and peeled the nail off her right index finger. She tumbled to the floor as she squeezed her hand, the pain sending shivers throughout her hand as the blood spilled on the floor and covered her knuckles in red. She ran to the sink and without thinking shoved her bleeding finger under the running water.

"AHHHHHHHHH!!!!!!!" Her scream ripped through the confinement of the bathroom, and tears exploded from her eyes. The hot boiling water splashing from the hot faucet burned her hand, and the pain, the white-burning pain blinded her as she jerked away.

Josefa banged against the door from the outside, as she frantically turned the doorknob. The door was locked and feeling a slimy coldness rush through the small of her back; Josefa began to yell.

"Tia, Tia, open the door, Dios mio, what's going on in there? Open the door, Tia, open this door, por favor."

She could hear mumbling, and gibberish moans coming from her aunt and those incoherent sounds drove her onto a deeper hysteria. Josefa braced her shoulders and slammed against the door with all her might. The cheaply made latch easily gave in with no protest from Josefa's slamming. The door swung inward colliding with Tia Marta's plump body, which was sprawled across the floor. Horrified, Josefa saw the woman's back and what she saw made her shrink away for a second. On her aunt's back, she could see red blisters clustered in patches like tiny, inflamed abscesses.

Josefa waved her arm as thick clouds of gray vapor swirled around her, the intense heat plastering her clothes to her body. She squinted her eyes at the hot water splashing out from the faucet that was open at full blast. She covered her mouth and coughed into her hands, her eyes watery and her throat raspy as she gasped for air. Her mind began to shout in frantically and finally, Josefa jumped into action. She grabbed the hot-water knob—feeling the heat on her palm—as she turned the water off. There was a loud hiss, almost human, escaped from the pipes.

Josefa looked around as the vapors slowly reached up toward the ceiling and began to disperse. She turned toward her aunt and putting her arm around the woman's waist, she helped her to her feet. Struggling under her aunt's larger body, Josefa dragged her Tia Marta out of the bathroom and into the kitchen. She sat her aunt on one of the chairs and sighed with relief that they were both out of the bathroom. Under the bright light from the kitchen, Josefa could get a better look at the blisters on her aunt's back. They looked like tiny ruptured volcanoes with white thick pus oozing out from each fissure. She wanted to look away, even run far from her aunt and hide somewhere until she could overcome her fear.

Come on, Josefa, she coaxed herself, *push those fears aside.* She had to maintain her cool in order to help her poor aunt; her safety was in her hands. Josefa took a deep breath and tried to comfort the old woman. Tia Marta's eyes were closed tightly, and her mouth was twisted in visible pain that ravaged through her body. Every so often, her body shook like someone suffering a seizure. Josefa put her arms around her aunt and felt the woman's shakes slowly subside. "Tia, can you hear me?" Josefa asked as she rubbed the top of her aunt's head. "Talk to me, please talk to me." Only groans escaped her aunt as she kept her eyes tightly closed. "Listen," Josefa gently lifted her aunt's face, and she was glad that the woman opened her eyes and forced a weak smile. "Tia, I'll be back very soon. I'm going to get some ointment from the medicine cabinet for the burns on your back."

Tia Marta grabbed Josefa's arm in a silent plea not to leave her alone. Josefa gently pried her aunt's hand and kissed her forehead. "It will be okay; you need something on those blisters."

It was only a short walk toward the bathroom, but a fear took hold of Josefa, and she hesitated for a second. Was she putting herself in danger? Was something or someone waiting for her behind the door? Waiting to jump on top of her the second she set foot inside? Josefa tried to dismiss the fear and convince herself that there was nothing to fear.

There's nothing inside, she shouted to her terrified self, *there is nothing inside that bathroom that's going to harm me!* All that happened inside the bathroom was her aunt turning the hot water on at full blast, then she slipped on the wet floor, and the scorching water splashed all over her back. That's all that really happened, the clumsiness of an old woman and nothing more. But why did her aunt took off her sweater? *Damn!* Josefa cursed herself and forced her steps to hurry inside the bathroom. Once inside, she peeked quickly behind the door, nothing but a towel hanging from a nail. She began to regain her composure, yet she could not help feeling like an idiot.

"Pendeja," she cursed at herself as she looked around the narrow pink-painted bathroom. The shower curtain with its bent rod was on the wet floor and although that was puzzling to her, she reasoned that her aunt had grabbed on to the curtain as she was falling. Josefa opened the cabinet and rummaged through the aspirin bottles, deodorant and cough syrup until she came with a bottle of Caladryl lotion and a bag of cotton balls. She closed the cabinet taking quick nervous glances around her. She was jumpy and ran out of the bathroom. She returned into the kitchen and found her aunt leaning forward, her elbows propped on top of the table with her face resting on her hands.

Her aunt's face was covered with an ocean of sweat. The blisters were now huge red welts oozing a clear thick slime, and by the silence of her aunt, Josefa wondered if they were as painful as they looked. She soaked the cotton balls with the healing ointment and began dabbing the blisters with light gentle dabs. Tia Marta winced a bit, but soon seemed to feel relief from the softness of the cotton and coolness of the Caladryl lotion.

"Tia," Josefa asked softly, curiosity of wanting to know what occurred inside the bathroom was killing her. "What happened in there?"

Tia Marta shrugged and sighed. She tilted her head sideways and stared at Josefa, then shook her head without saying anything. There was something that frightened her, and at the moment it seemed that the old woman had decided not to discuss it. Josefa saw the struggle in her aunt's face, a face that instead of having its normal tan complexion was pale and wet. Josefa finished covering the blisters with the pinkish lotion and after throwing the used cotton balls away she sat in front of her aunt. She wanted to know in detail what went on inside the bathroom. She was not going to let her aunt remain silent even if it meant that both would sit in front of each other for the rest of the day. Her body language spoke in high volume, and it was not lost on her aunt as the old woman took a deep breath and began to speak, and Josefa wished that she never had.

"Hija, there's something evil in here, something so evil it wants to make sure you don't find a way to fight it."

Josefa raised an eyebrow and part of her wanted to wave off her aunt's wild superstitious talk, but the old woman nodded her head, crossed herself and continued. Her voice was just a mere whisper. "I was attacked inside that bathroom because I took steps in helping you. Do you think I'm that stupid to turn on the hot water at full blast? And I don't know how my back looks, but the way it feels I know that no hot water could cause the pain and those awful sounds that are popping all over my back. Open your eyes Josefa; have you ever seen hot water from the tap, do that to skin? Don't think that I'm a crazy old woman...I saw the fear in your eyes when you came out of that bathroom. You sense something, and don't lie to me...I know damn well that you felt its presence too. Mira hija, please listen to me," she grabbed Josefa's arm tight. "I'm telling you, you have to see this man in the Bronx; he is the best in situations like this. I know you don't want to believe in Santeria, and I don't care if you believe it or not...evil does exist. The same way there's goodness on this earth, there's also evil, and the more you ignore it the stronger it becomes...like now."

Tia Marta closed her eyes and heaved a loud sigh. "You want to know what I was doing inside that bathroom. I'll tell you what I was doing in the bathroom; I was gathering some of your clothes and Eddie's, so I could take them to him. But this evil thing knew, somehow knew, what I was doing and tried to stop me. It tried to kill me and now that he lost this time; this wicked thing is going to come back with more malice, more anger to make sure that whatever he wants he's going to get. Please hija, you have to trust me on this; you have to go and see this man as soon as possible. This evil spirit could be defeated, but only if you are willing to believe and seek the proper help."

Josefa didn't want to believe what she was hearing, but the more she listened to her aunt's argument, the less convinced she was that the hot water actually caused those blisters. She felt uneasy about what her aunt was saying, yet she couldn't deny the fright she felt inside the bathroom. Wasn't she a devout Catholic? All this Santeria mumble-jumble was not something encouraged by her beliefs. What Tia Marta was talking about was evil spirits; things associated in the work of dark forces. She wanted to place her hands over her ears like a child trying not to listen to the scolding of a parent. Her aunt's words were no longer believable, and now Josefa wanted to tell her to keep her mouth shut, to keep her comments to herself.

Reaching out and taking both of Josefa's arms, Tia Marta forced her to look at her—straight in the eye. "Your son is in a very grave situation that no amount of doctors or modern medicine could cure him. Your son is being controlled by a power that is not from this world. Por favor niña, trust in me, believe in me, and I'll promise you that your son will be returned to you again."

Josefa exhaled deeply. She felt the exhaustion of the day weighted down on her making it impossible to breathe and think. She would do anything to bring her Eddie back home healthy and out of danger. But how can one trust in something that sounds influenced by evil? Josefa pulled away from her aunt, determined not to risk Eddie's welfare on some dark religion. Even so, as she began to put an end the conversation of evil spirits, she saw her aunt wince and close her eyes in pain. The old woman's whimpers turned into screams as she straightened her back while the boils began to pop. Pop, pop, pop, they sounded like a toy gun firing off caps.

Her aunt convulsed on the chair, writhing like a captured animal in the claws of a metal trap. Her back stiffened; and in every blister that popped red-like coal fire appeared as thin swirling lines of smoke spiraled to the ceiling. Although Josefa refused to believe that something strange, something blasphemous was going on, the smoking boils on her aunt's back were too alarming to ignore. This was not common, for a human back to pop so loudly and to smell as if an entire box of matches was lit up, just from hot water from the tap? Josefa's thoughts rattled her brain, was it normal for a bathroom to come alive with one single purpose, and that was to harm an old woman? *DAMN IT!* That was not normal. A horrible feeling overwhelmed her, choking her and settling in the middle of her stomach, like a tumor ready to burst.

Josefa looked around desperately wanting to wake up from this awful nightmare. But this was no nightmare, much less a practical joke. This was real, as real as the humming sound of the refrigerator. Josefa wanted to scream, release the holler, lodged in her throat. She swallowed hard, dissolving the scream with her saliva, and she took the flailing arms of her aunt and felt the old woman's nails dig painfully in her palms. Josefa looked and was alarmed to see one of her aunt's nails ripped from her finger. Blood seeped down in bubbling wavy lines. "Dios mio, hija pray with me—por favor—pray with me," Tia Marta begged as her voice quivered and her eyes stared out in fright. "The evil is all around us; it came back, and I feel its anger as black and cold as the bottom of a murderer's heart."

Tia Marta pushed herself out of the chair and dropped down hard on her knees and began mumbling the Lords' Prayers. "Our Father who art in Heaven hallowed be thy name…" the boils popped louder and the smoke from each fissure grew dark and foul. "…thy will be done on Earth as it is in Heaven…" the boils began to disappear. Josefa stared hypnotized by what she was witnessing, and she also dropped onto her knees next to her aunt and joined the prayer. "Forgive our trespasses as we forgive those that trespass against us…" Both women closed their eyes tight and were deep in prayer as the stench of sulfur ran into their noses like burning rods. The bathroom door slammed shut and then opened up crashing hard against the wall. Something crashed loudly onto the floor. And stomping running steps filled the apartment as somewhere inside one of the rooms something fell hard, crashing thunderously on the floor. Both women continued their prayers their hands sweaty and shaking, clenching to each other. "…lead us not in temptation and deliver us from evil…" There was a high-pitched shriek that scratched the walls of the apartment, and a thrust of violent air tried to break the women's stronghold. Josefa and her aunt, their bodies trembling with fear, felt something rushing through them, and they began praying again, their voices quivering, but loud.

Then, a tomb-like silence fell over the apartment, and both women stared at each other, sweat running down their faces. Josefa glanced at Tia Marta's back, and she shrunk away; her aunt's back was smooth. There were no signs of boils; no redness or the presence of smoke…even the nail on her finger was back on. "Get dressed Tia," Josefa said rushing to the bedroom to get her coat. "I need to see this man."

Chapter Twelve

From the green valleys on the island, a scorching heat climbed and quickly dipped until it hung on the air with discomforting thickness. Eduardo jumped out of his trance-like sleep startled and confused. He banged his fist against his thigh and let out a loud curse, and then he buried his head in his hands in defeat. Slowly, he lifted his head up and his infuriated glare fell on Eddie as the child sat by the steps on the shaded side on the porch. A bright yellow sun shone down and it seemed its burning rays did not let up for at least fifteen hours during each day, even when the sky was full of rain.

"Why is she doing this to me?" Eduardo asked as his eyes searched the sky. "I offered her my love. The little bit that I had I was willing to give to her. She refused to look past my handicap and chose to push me aside like a filthy dog. She ignored my offers of love and happiness." He shook his head almost in tears and clearing his throat, he spat on the ground with disgust. "I still love her, the wretched witch that she is, but I still love her," he looked away from the child and spat again. "The years of happiness she denied me...those will be the same years I'll take away from her life. I'll make sure that when happiness comes knocking at her door, it would go unannounced and any man who comes near to her love, to find the taste of honey on her lips; I'll make sure they will find the taste of vinegar instead. No man will ever be happy, as long as they are close to her bosom."

Eduardo glowered at the child. The boy was a reminder of his failures and disillusions. He walked to the other side on the porch and spit once more into the wind, licking the remaining saliva from his lips. He turned and stared at Eddie with malice. "She loves you very much. Do you know that child? But of course, you must; you are her little weakling— her sick puppy whom she wants to smother back to health. I could have been her puppy, if she let me. She's a capricious selfish bitch!"

He walked the length of the porch and sat down hard on the rocking chair. "They said that there's nothing more vengeful than a woman scorned, well, they never tasted the scorn of a bitter man whose love was trashed by a heartless woman."

"Why do you hate her so much?" Eddie asked as he walked down to where the steps and the grass met. Eddie had no idea the identity of this woman. All he knew was that while Eduardo slept, he thrashed from side to side on the rocking chair, and cried in hysterical sobs that led to cursing in a savage rage.

Eduardo looked at the child with malicious envy, wishing that he could also be able to touch the grass, but knowing that such an action was impossible. "I don't hate her, on the contrary, the reason that I want her to suffer is because I love her with a passion, deeper than any love any person had for another. Maybe all I always wanted was to teach her a lesson, a lesson of humility."

Eduardo waited to see if the boy would respond.

"Bah," Eduardo waved his hands dismissing Eddie. "You are still too young to understand the world of adults, a world of webs of delusions and deceptions...and of course, webs of prejudice and mockery toward those lesser than them."

A warm breeze framed their silence as they both watched in deep concentration at a dragonfly hovering above a stream. It dipped quickly into the still water immediately coming up and then flying away. A butterfly landed on the porch, its wings showing its delicate silky colors, and just like the dragonfly, it became lost in the green vegetation with a simple flutter of its wings. Eddie touched the grass blades that grew almost as high as him and then switched his attention, fascinated with a colony of reddish ants that scurried in and out from a raised anthill.

He didn't understand what Eduardo was saying, but he understood that each word was sour and filled with hate. He didn't want to be around this man anymore, and decided it was the perfect moment to walk and explore more of his surroundings. He was still puzzled over the situation he was in, but rather than sulk, he decided to accept what was happening to him. There was no other choice, so instead of welcoming a pity parade whenever he began to feel sadness over the consistent confusion of not knowing what was happening, he brushed it aside. In his mind, he was willing to accept the fact that he was either dead or perhaps in a deep almost-realistic dream, which he would be awakened from in the safety of his room in no time soon. Eddie leaped from the last few steps off the porch and into the dirt path.

Concern with the boy's actions, Eduardo called out for his return, ignoring the man's shouts; Eddie strolled until the shouting ceased. It was good to walk far from the house and as always, whenever he took his little strolls, the further away from the shack he walked, a dark cloud seemed to be lifted off his shoulders. It was a weird sensation, which at first he didn't pay much attention to, but now it was something he always expected to feel. It was like seeing the first beautiful light from the morning sky when the dark night had been a roller coaster of bad dreams.

After a while, he knew that he was far from the house, but it didn't bother him to see how far; all he wanted to do now was to feel the hot sun bake his head and enjoy the path that took him through the sweet-smelling countryside. In front of him, about eighty yards away, he noticed a huge mango tree, which he had seen on one of his previous walks. It was a great tree, the size of those huge trees he had seen in books about a famous park somewhere in California. If he remembered correctly they were called Redwoods. He reached the tree and now Eddie could see the actual size of it. It was an enormous sight, taller than any tree he had ever seen and when he lifted his neck to follow the massive trunk, it seemed that it climbed and climbed beyond the sky.

Its colossal branches stretched out like the muscled arms of giants, twisting and crisscrossing from the immense trunk, its leaves swayed and waved the heat away. Eddie looked up at the fruits that hung from the branches, amazed at the size of the mangoes. Never in his life had he seen such large mangoes, he thought as they swung teasingly—like golden forbidden fruits of Eden. As he stood beneath the tree, a cool shaded circular area beckoned him to sit and stay around a while. Within the confinements of the tree, Eddie wiggled his toes into the moist softness of the grass. It was as plush as the thick carpet that his mother spoke about when coming from one of her cleaning jobs on Park Avenue.

The air surrounding him was a pleasurable draft; it felt as if he was standing in front of and opened refrigerator in the middle of an August heat wave. He sat down and leaned his back against the trunk; the knobs on the tree bark like fingers massaging him into submission. Snuggled within the tree's embrace, he looked out at the open field, and it felt like he was sitting inside a cave, a primitive cave where everything around the outside of the tree's shade was awash in soothing yellow color. He squinted his eyes, and he could see Eduardo's house and from this distance, it resembled a miniature dollhouse; and the thought, the ugly thought to be there raised a dark cloud over his new sunny disposition. He didn't like being there. The entire place was dark and old. Eduardo was a cranky miserable man, and his mother frightened him. The old woman smelled like the inside of a stuffy cellar filled with dust and dead rats—what Eddie imagined a witch from a fairy tale would smell like. Eddie didn't want to go back. He would rather stay there, safe under the protective branches of the giant tree. He wanted to be with his family again, in the tiny bedroom he shared with his brooding brother, Felix.

Eddie began to cry, and now he discovered what being homesick felt like. He wanted his mother more than anything, his sweet mother who scratched his head and kissed him before he went to bed, leaving an imprint of red lipstick on his cheek. He lowered his head and pulled his knees to his chest. Wrapping his arms around his legs, he rested his head on top of his knees; closing his eyes. Eddie let tears slide down his chin, as he quietly cried.

He could hear Eduardo calling his name again with a frantic pitch in his voice. Eddie looked up and turned his body around as he put his skinny little arms around the huge tree. He could smell the richness of the bark, and he felt the life of the tree vibrate through his heart. There was comfort in that smell and hearing the soft heartbeat of the mango tree. It helped Eddie to concentrate on the gentle sounds around him. He celebrated in the sounds of gliding birds above the clouds and the haunting songs whistling through the sugar cane field. Eddie closed his eyes, and a comforting slumber carried him into dreams with familiar smells, his mother's cooking; his father's aftershave, the soft synthetic perfume of

Migdalia and Felix's chewing gum. He could smell Norma's asphalt-scented sweat after playing in the schoolyard and the ballpoint ink from Gisela's hidden notebook. He also smelled the pulp of the thin pages of his colorful comic books. Most of all, he could smell the sweetness of home, and that granted him, the safeguard and the necessary strength to continue his journey home. With those wonderful aromas, Eddie found sleep…the most refreshing sleep he had for such a long time.

In a slow rocking motion, he awoke; feeling refreshed, and the first thing that he noticed was the heat and the brightness of the sun had been replaced by the coolness of the early evening. The nocturnal sounds around were lovely, they had the feeling of another dream, and Eddie opened his eyes slowly and glimpsed at the sky. There were millions and millions of stars, like jewels that fell from God's pockets. They sparkled, twinkled, danced and dipped against the backdrop of a peaceful purple sky. He had never witnessed such a beautiful sight in his life. Looking at such beauty—such majesty—Eddie's fear disappeared, in its place, happiness, and a strong sense of safety wrapped around him like a warm blanket. He imagined that all those brilliant stars were galloping medieval knights sent from a faraway kingdom to escort him to safety. Eddie lay down and followed the flight of the stars, and he could fall sleep again and dream that one day he will be with the people that he loved. All ugliness would soon be nothing but a bad memory that with time, he could easily erase from his mind forever.

Eduardo searched through the blackness of the night; he wasn't able to see the boy. It was the first time that the boy had done such a thing, and that was very disturbing. He was too close for anything to come between him and his goal. He entered the house and went to where his mother waited for him.

"The boy is not back in the house," Eduardo said to his mother. "This is the first time he has wandered and not returned. Are we losing him?"

"Don't worry. He's still here, isn't he? There are more fish in this woman's ocean to complete our meal, if not him for now, we have the others."

"But no mother, I want Eddie and nobody else."

"Eduardo, enough with your childish behavior, if not the boy we could use the whole family instead."

"But mother, Eddie is my soul," Eduardo grumbled and left his mother's room.

The old woman shuffled weakly to the entrance to the porch, her cataract-ridden eyes searching around for the boy. The sacrifices a mother had to endure for her children, she thought. She lifted her tattered shawl and covered her head; she was cold and the last thing she wanted to do was venture into the brisk air that surrounded the porch, but she stepped into it anyway. *How long would they stay in here trapped with other souls like themselves?* She wondered. Her husband had left them a long time ago, refusing to be part of a scheme that he found abhorrent.

"This is evil thinking," he had shouted while raising his fist at them with anger splitting his lips. His pleas for her to come with him were ignored, she had to stay and comfort Eduardo, as the poor child was still madly in love with that awful woman. That woman had scorned her only son, and didn't even give him the satisfaction of at least a conversation or a gentle innocent caress. Her miserable child, her poor sickly Eduardo died in her arms and the last word he left in the world of the living was the name of that evil selfish wretch...Josefa.

Eduardo's mother wrapped her scrawny arms around her bony self, her eyes still piercing the thick darkness of the night wondering where the child went. *He can hide as much as he wants,* she thought as she smiled contentedly, *but no matter what, he can never leave this place...there's no place to go but here.* Captive within their little paradise of their own private purgatory, she sat on the rocking chair and began to rock. And, she smiled, laughter rising from deep within her, a laughter that was gravelly and ancient.

"You hurt my son, Josefa," the old woman whispered. "And for that I will never be able to forgive you. My hands will always be around the throat of your life. Your husband will learn to hate you, your oldest son will be shamed by his deeds, and your younger son will only return to your arms if he's reborn with my own son's soul in his little heart. Oh you mad horrible woman; you don't know the powers of a mother's love."

Chapter Thirteen

"What the hell was I thinking?" Josefa wanted to shout the question loud enough so she could hear it herself, and snap back into rational behavior. As she sat in what seemed to be a living room converted into a makeshift waiting room, the idea about seeing a witch doctor was not as appealing as it had been in her apartment. The entire atmosphere just spooked the hell out of her. She tried to slow down the pounding inside her heart, keep it steady and smooth, but no matter what she did her heart now had a mind of its own. She closed her eyes for a second wondering if her heart didn't settle down, would she die of a heart attack inside that scary place?

She glanced at her Tia Marta and what she saw made her want to laugh out loud and run out of this place. Her aunt had a stern, no-nonsense look on her face. She had never seen her aunt look that serious for all the years she had known her.

Josefa straightened her back against the metal chair and smoothed her skirt. She had to do something to occupy her mind and distract her from the experience. Josefa looked around to keep herself from laughing. She set her sights on the two women in the *waiting room* a few feet from where they sat; two bundles of humanity, guarding their own privacy as they spoke to each other in soft whispers. When she and her aunt arrived there were eight people, and now it was down to the four of them. "Well," Josefa turned toward her aunt also using the same whispered tone. "Does he know we are here? We just came in sat down, and nobody has acknowledged our arrival. All I see is people go in and out of that other room," she pointed with her chin to an entrance to another room veiled by a heavy white-curtain.

Tia Marta shot a quick embarrassed look at Josefa. "Dios mio, Josefa you are worse than a child. He never comes out, when the person he is seeing is finished, whoever was here first goes in. What's so hard about that? What were you expecting? Someone to give you a form to fill out like they do in the clinics?"

"Okay...okay," Josefa raised her hand to her aunt to calm down. "You don't have to scold me. I'm not a child. It's not like I come to places like this every day, you know."

Tia Marta feigned a smile and patted Josefa on her knee. "Sorry nena, but what happened inside that bathroom still have my nerves shot. Ay, I felt the presence of something evil when I tried to get those clothes out of there. Thank God that you believe me now."

Josefa became apprehensive with just the mention of what had occurred in the bathroom. It brought back the fear she felt when she went to fetch the ointment for her aunt's back. She felt uncomfortable with the intense level of fear her own house produced in her; it made her feel uneasy. She felt a cold perspiration dotting the middle of her upper lip and again; her heart seemed to beat rapidly as if any minute it could jump out of her chest. A knot tightening in her gut, and she exhaled quickly.

Josefa glimpsed at the other two women in the room and nodding she smiled at them with the friendliest smile she could muster. They both had been looking at her, and Josefa wondered how long they were going to keep staring and why. *Was she acting so silly that among these experienced followers of this strange religion, she stood out like some bumbling idiot?* Both ladies returned her smile and shrugged with indifference. For a second, Josefa thought that they were about to start a conversation with her, but their smiles disappeared after a few moments, and they returned to their previous hushed conversation.

There was a rustle from the other room. After a moment, the white curtain parted, and a woman emerged and on her face, Josefa saw peace...a tranquility which was almost holy. The woman gathered her coat and hat that were piled on one of the fold out chairs in the waiting room, and without looking at anyone she began to bundle up and quickly left. Then, the two ladies still sharing their whispered talk stood up and walked into the adjoining room pushing aside the curtain. Josefa and Tia Marta were now sitting in the waiting room by themselves.

Being alone with only her aunt, seemed to relax Josefa, giving her more freedom to behave like herself, and even Tia Marta seemed to loosen up.

"Are you coming with me when it's my turn?" Josefa asked in the same low tone of voice that she used when the other two ladies were present.

"I'd rather not, sometimes the consultations are too private...is better for only the person seeking answers to go in by themselves. It's like going to the doctor for a physical, the difference, here is that he's examining your soul rather than your mortal self."

"So why then did those two go in together," Josefa pointed at the curtain that separated the waiting room and whatever was behind the white thick cloth.

"Dios mio, Josefa...how in the world am I supposed to know why?"

"Well because you are the expert here," Josefa laughed a little, and it felt normal and somehow put her at ease for the first time inside this strange apartment.

Tia Marta shot her an annoying look. "Mira Josefa, if you are not going to take this serious we might as well leave right now. He won't be able to help you unless you want to believe in him. So let's stop the clowning around 'cause this is no fooling matters...¿entiendes?"

"Ok, ok...si Tia, I'm sorry," Josefa stood up and looked across the room. It still gave her an uncomfortable feeling seeing statues of saints in a different light. "It's that I have heard about places like this many times, but this is the first time I'm inside one of them...and not only that, but I'm the next person in line, and that's making me feel a bit uneasy. You have to understand all this is new to me."

Tia Marta nodded her head in agreement. "Just remember not to be afraid. Tell him everything and don't be shy. That man in there is one of the most powerful babalawo in the whole country. We are very lucky that he could see us on such short notice; there are times that people wait for weeks...even months."

"Why do you think we are so lucky? And what in the world is a babalawo?" Josefa asked still feeling a bit reluctant about expecting a total stranger to know more about her life than herself.

Tia Marta raised her head and stared bug-eyed at the ceiling, clearly exasperated. "Ay Dios mio," she stared at her niece. "You wanted to know why we are so lucky. I'll tell you why, sometimes this man is aware of things that we could never be able to understand or even see. He is one of the most powerful priests in the practice of Santeria and getting a meeting with him on such short notice is something more than a miracle, something that you shouldn't be joking about. I wouldn't be surprised if he saw the evilness around you...that curse which has become part of your life and your entire family. You have to respect the things that you don't know anything about. I'm telling you this, not because you are my sister's daughter, but because your well-being is all that matters to me. There is something awful...very awful that wants to harm you and all your loved ones and only this man will be able to find out. But remember, as long as you believe...so don't you dare to go inside and waste his time and put Eddie and your family in more dangers."

"And, for your information," Tia Marta huffed; it seemed talking this much was exhausting her. "The title babalawo is the name given only to a very gifted man whom even other Santeria priests come to him for advice," she added as she crossed her arms and looked straight ahead at the wall in front of her.

"Is he like the pope or something?" Josefa tried to joke, but her humor was like a slap to Marta's face, and she promptly glanced at the white curtain to avoid the annoyed look of Tia Marta. Josefa then walked around the small room feeling a flutter in her heart, and as she stared at the threshold that separated the great babalawo from them, there was an urge to put on her coat and walk out. She grabbed her scarf from the pile of the coats and sweaters that she and her aunt had bunched on the chair next to them and threw the scarf around her neck. She touched the sleeve of her coat wanting so much to snatch it up and run out.

There was a nervous female laughter that floated from the other room. Josefa knew that laughter very well; it was the type of laughter when someone is too embarrassed to cry. She sat down again, the desire to leave the place of the babalawo still gnawing at her. Even so, with all her desires to leave, there was something deeper, something stronger, which was convincing her to stick around a bit longer. She heard shuffled steps coming from behind the heavy curtain; the floor creaked and then the curtain parted, and the two ladies stepped out from the darkness into the waiting room area, as if they've been birthed into the light. They were silent and Josefa tried to read their emotions. They were solemn, yet calm. They seemed to be faced with a difficult situation, but they were ready for the challenge because they were forewarned. Josefa didn't bother to look at her aunt, and slowly walked into the room. Before entering she took a deep breath and hesitantly pushed the curtain aside, as the whiff of cigar smoke and candles smothered her.

To her surprise, the room was empty and for a second, she thought about turning around and high-tailing it out of there. But there was something in her that made her stop, and taking a few steps inside the room; she forced herself to relax and trust what was going on around her. Coldness clinched into her, as if a draft seeped through the floor and right through her. She shivered and rubbed her arms. She could feel her lower lip quivering as she looked around the room. If this was a regular apartment—where a real family once lived—she assumed that the room could have been the room of a child. The walls were painted in a glossy white color, and pushed against the wall was a small kitchen table with two chairs facing one another. And there was something about the table that was inviting, as if it were welcoming for two people to enjoy a good chat. Josefa sat on one of the chairs, and she noticed on the center of the table, there was a glass of water, and next to the glass was an ashtray where half of an unlit cigar laid. The whiff of the cigar climbed into her nose invading her nostrils with the smooth spice scent of its tobacco. There was also a black-and-white composition notebook; the kind her children used for school. Seeing it brought tears to her eyes. She turned away from the notebook and dropped her eyes to the floor. She felt wetness dampen her armpits and the twitch on the corner of her lower lip became more pronounced.

"What the hell am I doing here?" she asked herself.

As she fought the urge to run out of there, her thoughts turned of needing to be in the hospital, instead of this place. She should be holding her little boy's hand and willing him to wake up. *Oh God,* she lowered her head to start the prayer. She wanted so bad to take him to the candy store and buy him every comic book on the revolving rack on the back of the store he always looked at.

From the doorway that led to another hidden place of the room, Josefa heard footsteps approaching her. She stared at the doorway and watched as an older man walked in, dressed all in white. He even wore a white cap covering tight curls of white hair cropped closely to his head. His smile was the most beautiful thing she had ever seen. It was wide, and it brightened his entire face, and wrinkles curved increasing the comfort in his eyes. With the ease that this man smiled, was as if he often did so, and there was something about him that sent a wave of calmness through her body. He sat down across from her, and the fear that overwhelmed Josefa was replaced with tranquility. She had pictured the babalawo to be someone frightening and hideous. A walking nightmare, instead he was one of the most welcoming people she'd seen in a while, and she felt safe. He was the image of someone's favorite grandfather.

Unexpectedly, her nervousness, and the insecurity of being in a place like that, dissipated. His friendly demeanor made it all seem normal. When he greeted her, he felt as a family member you hadn't seen for a long time. His voice was easy and soft. "Brrrrr," he rubbed his arms up and down trying to warm them up. "It looks that this winter is going to make everyone wish they never left Puerto Rico," he said in a soft voice. He leaned across the table and placed both hands neatly in front of him, and then he folded them. "I just heard over the radio that in Puerto Rico, it's about eighty five degrees under a sunny sky and look," he pointed to the window where huge snowflakes bounced off the glass. "Here, if we want to go outside we have to wear more than ten pounds of clothing to protect us from that mess. Pero, que se va a hacer...what are we going to do?" he asked this time staring into Josefa's eyes with concern and understanding. The babalawo shook his head, shrugged, and then he laughed. His laughter was contagious in another time and place, but all Josefa could do was smiled weakly.

Sensing her fear and her self-doubts, he reached across the table, and touched her hand briefly. "Bueno mi'ja, how are you?" he asked trying to put her at ease.

Josefa shrugged, then realizing how childish her actions could have been understood; she sighed and stiffened her back. "Not that great," she found herself declaring. To her that was the most underestimated statement of the day. "That's why I'm here," she added.

"Bueno," he slid one hand over the notebook and brought it closer. "Let's see what we can find out together and what can we do about it." He opened the notebook and leafed through it until he found a clean page. He folded the front cover of the notebook backward and closed his eyes, and took a deep breath and went into a relaxation mode. His breathing was steady and when he opened his eyes and looked at Josefa, it was like seeing a different man.

Josefa felt her eyes growing wide; she had no idea how these things worked. She was under the impression that all she had to do was sit and like magic this man was going to tell her everything that was going wrong in her life. Isn't that the way they do it in the movies? Didn't every fortuneteller look into a crystal ball and in minutes everything was solved? Her apprehension began to creep slowly back into her, sensing her increasing discomfort the babalawo reached out and patted her hand with assurance. She smiled and bit the inside of her lower lip.

"I'm sorry señor," she apologized.

"No...no...There's no reason to apologize. Just take a deep breathe and relax, and I'm sorry for my manners. Sometimes I think I'm becoming senile; I have forgotten what my mother taught me a long time ago, that when you meet someone for the first time, introduce yourself...you can call me Francisco...and you?"

"Josefa," she said and just that bit of ordinary conversation made her loosen up.

"Muy bien," Francisco exclaimed. "Josefa...that was my grandmother's name...may she rest in peace. She used to love to pull my ears when I was bad," he said as he touched his ears. "Now you know why my ears are so big." He laughed, a carefree and effortless laughter, to which Josefa found herself joining.

Josefa laughed again and her outlook changed, and she felt confident that this man, this kind man, was going to help her and her little son. She knew he was someone she could trust. It was all falling in place; everything seemed to be arranging itself, and it was up to her to get the ball rolling.

"Bueno..."

Josefa leaned a bit forward and placed her hands on the edge of the table. "My son is very sick. Suddenly, he went into a coma, and the doctors have done everything possible, yet there he lies on a hospital bed," she felt her eyes welling up, but she refused to cry. "Now today in my house my aunt was attacked by...I don't know...something. I'm afraid, and to be honest with you; I have never been a believer of Santeria, but right now I'm desperate for my son...for my family, I'm willing to try anything that could help us."

"This something that you said attacked your aunt. Did you see what it was?"

Josefa shook her head and placed her right hand close to her collar. "No, but it left boils all over her back, boils that were smoking—Dios mio—they were like tiny volcanoes throughout her back. Then, they all disappear the second we started praying. I have, at no time seen anything like that in my life; I hope I won't ever again. It was awful and when I went inside the bathroom, I felt something inside. I knew that I wasn't alone. I felt the presence of someone watching me...waiting to do something bad if I stayed inside the bathroom a bit longer."

Josefa took a deep breath and closed her eyes tight, now more than ever, she felt helpless. Reliving what had happened just a few hours ago made her feel defeated. "Everything seems to be falling apart, my family...my life. If there's something out there that's trying to harm us, something that is responsible for my baby's sickness...I want to know. If there's anything you could do, I beg you señor, please help me, help us." She lowered her face into her opened hands, and she let the tears come out, allowed her heart to bring forth the pain that she had held for so long.

"I don't know what to believe anymore. My aunt told me that there may be something evil causing all this awful luck. I didn't want to believe my aunt's superstitious nonsense; to her even the simplest fall from a clumsy step is an act of a black-hearted spirit or an evil spell. I believe that everybody has problems, that's part of life...even more so if you are poor like us. I believe and trust in God to take care of me, but I was never one to believe that by killing a chicken or bathing yourself with strange plants was the way to battle some silly evil eye," she rubbed her forehead. "But sometimes your beliefs change, especially when I see my son...my baby...closer to death than life. What I saw today in my own house with my own eyes made me believe and you, señor, somehow I know that I could trust in you. I know just the same way that I know my son is not really sick, but held captive by something evil that wants him." Josefa dropped her hands on her lap and straightened her back. "And I'm going to do whatever possible to bring my baby boy where he belongs...home." Josefa sobbed quietly after offloading all her problems with one breath.

Francisco allowed her to express her grief; it was best to let her cleanse her soul with her tears. He reached out and placed his hand on the top of her head and after a few minutes, she lifted her face and stared at him with eyes, which were no longer sad, but eyes that were hopeful.

As Josefa spoke, Francisco listened quietly not wanting to interrupt her. He served as a psychologist or therapist for the much-needed moment of emotional cleansing Josefa needed. His new client continued to pour her feelings out, while Francisco was confident that his work would succeed where modern medicine would fail. There are things all around us, that he knew...things as old as the earth itself. And at times only the powers of the Santeria religion, was the single thing to battle such evil.

Santeria was a Yorùbá religion which roots originated in the deep jungles of Nigeria and brought and cultured to the New World by West Africans. Their beliefs were a combination of communicating with their ancestors, and their gods through trances, animal sacrifices and sacred drumming and dancing. The Yorùbá people after being captured, chained, and transported to the New World by slave traders; were soon scattered throughout every sugar cane plantation throughout the Caribbean. Surrounded by unknown environment, different customs, the unusual ideas and their masters' religious beliefs—which were forced into their lives—influenced their personal African practices. The slaves were forbidden to practice their own religion, which was seen by the Spaniards as pagan worshiping. In order to hide the African faith, the Yorùbá people camouflaged their own deities by identifying them with the saints of the Catholic Church. It was the beginning of two religions fusing into one—*Santeria*—which means 'the worship of saints'. It combines the magic rites of the Yorùbá and some of the traditions of the Catholic Church.

It's an earth religion that has its roots embedded in nature and natural forces where many deities are worship. It is a known fact that there are more than one hundred million practitioners of the religion in Latin America, and the United States and one of those practitioners was Francisco. He was a babalawo; the highest priest of the religion and it was not strange that other lesser priests consulted him about situations that were extremely difficult.

Francisco was glad that this young woman with deep wrinkles of worries throughout her face was sitting in front of him. He doubted that someone with less knowledge, fewer understanding would have been able to help her. His years of experience gave him the confidence to believe he was one of the few people that could help this woman, perhaps the only one to be capable to do so. He saw that as a sign from the gods. He knew they had guided her to him, which led him to believe that something evil, something dangerous was going on in her life. He felt that all the pain she was unloading on his table wasn't the result of a simple spell cast by an amateur pushed by jealousy or hatred. This was something more serious. He sensed the foulness surrounding her the second she entered his home. Even while she waited outside, as he conducted his other consultations, he had felt her presence and more precisely her troubles and anguish.

Too many charlatans saw Santeria as a magic concoction that could cure all ailments of the soul. Many thought that marriage problems could easily be resolved by burning candles, bathing in plants or have magical powder sprinkled under the mattress where their soon to be ex-spouse slept. On many occasions, those marriage failures were not the result of some twisted evil spell; the failure was the price paid for taking something so sacred like the love of another person for granted. It was a shame that generally, too many people didn't respect the religion as they would have a 'conventional faith.' Most people only turned to the old doctrine when everything else failed. Often times, those passing themselves as priests, were the ones who made matters worse, and those who sought help in their hands came to Francisco for his remedies. Sometimes, botched practices of a foolish Santeria priest, who sought their own gratification, would cause people to seek out Francisco for help as well.

However, this woman with the same name as his grandmother was not a person looking for the next winning numbers for the lottery. No, she was different. She didn't even want to be there. He sensed it. She walked into his home with hesitation weighing down her every step. He felt her desperation, confusion; it was palpable. Josefa was on the threshold of her own madness and for that he was pleased and thanked the saints for guiding her to him. With their guidance, he would be able to remove the black cloud from her eyes and replace it with the brightness of a new day.

"Bueno hija," Francisco tapped the clean page in front of him. "I don't want you to be scared, but there's something horrible that has attached itself to you. Pero no te preocupe, don't worry…together we are going to bring a beautiful smile to your face." He closed his eyes as his lips moved in the privacy of a prayer. It was a ritual known as moyubbar where Francisco asked for the blessing of the dead and of the Orishas, the Santeria gods. He prayed to all the Eggun, the dead, or their spirits of not only his ancestors, but also the spirits of the elder priests who were part of him. While mumbling his prayers, Francisco took what resembled a necklace, the opelé an iron chain that connected eight oval medallions that were made of coconut rinds. Each medallion had a different design on either of its two sides. By throwing the opelé on the table, he could read the message from his ancestors, depending, which side the eight medallions fall. He took the opelé and touched Josefa's forehead and inquired if it was okay to ask the permission of her guardian angel to start the consultation.

Josefa nodded her approval, her lower lip quivering at the sudden 'willies' she was feeling. While holding the chain by the center, Francisco threw the opelé three times to determine the principal letter or message that would lead him to the answers and advise the gods would place before him. The old babalawo threw the opelé again, each time the medallions falling in different combinations. On a clean sheet of paper, he began to write rapidly, but only using the numbers 1 and 0. The combination of those two numbers represented the concept of something—the number 1, combined with nothing—which was the 0. This is how ancient faiths saw the universe, as a combination of nothing and something. It was a system that dates back to the old Egyptian civilizations. It was the best and simplest form. All information and knowledge are stored between the one and the zero.

In awe, Josefa—like a wide-eyed child—watched Francisco. It was like observing a magician performing his act. At first, she was afraid, especially how the once easy smile on the old man's face slowly morphed into a masquerade of mystery and secrecy. When his lips moved, a barely audible whisper came out, and Josefa leaned closer to the table until she realized that his words were not for her, but were directed at something or someone else. It was amazing. Josefa felt as if she was in the center of some well-kept secret that was slowly being unraveled to only a few. She tried at first to listen closely, but the words sounded strange. Josefa studied his face, hoping to be able to understand some of the words, but it was like trying to understand a foreign language. Nothing made any sense and the more she stared at Francisco the less she understood. His eyelids fluttered in rapid motion, and she could catch quick glimpses of his dark pupils, which seemed to float in and out from his eyes.

He exhaled heavily, relief that he had finished the long and tedious task. He stopped writing and pinched the bridge of his nose. He pushed the notebook to his right side; from his left he slid a plate in front of him. Inside the plate were a small seashell and a tiny stone. Francisco took them and gave them to Josefa instructing her to rub them between her hands and without choosing to hold each one in each hand and then close her hands and present them to him. Josefa, confused and wondering exactly what she was doing, did as she was told. Francisco threw down the opelé again.

It was the way for him to determine which hand he must choose. If the hand that was chosen had the stone, the oracle was surrounded with good luck, which was known in the Santeria words as iré. If it was the seashell, then it was osogbo or bad luck. He studied the medallions' position at how they had fallen; he touched Josefa's right hand, when she loosened her fingers, it revealed the seashell. Her oracle was filled with bad luck.

Francisco placed the opelé on the dish along with the stone and seashell. He pushed the plate aside and looked up at Josefa. After many years and thousands of consultations, it still troubled him to tell someone that they were justified in coming to see him. It was never easy to tell someone that there was evil around them and that evil had infected so much of their lives. He was sure he could remove that curse from her, but it was something that wouldn't be easy. It was only accomplished by the faith that the sufferer had and their willingness to fight harder than they've ever fought before in their lives.

Josefa noticed the change in the old man's face. His brow had creased into deep wrinkles and the smile that he once wore was now a thin straight line across his lips. Outside the window, the pale light of the day was beginning to succumb to the grayness of the early evening, and she wondered how long she had they been sitting there. It seemed to have stopped snowing. However, by the way the window was shaking; it was as if the winter wind had taken the moment to pick up strength. She felt a chill rush through her; maybe it was the thought of going outside and making the long trek to the hospital. She imagined Eddie, being a prisoner of something that she now was convinced wasn't of this world. She wanted to be by his side, but sitting here in front of a man whom she just met; something assured her that this was the place if she ever wanted to see Eddie return to his normal self. She heard the breathing of the old man that her aunt called babalawo, and repeating the name to herself made Josefa want to laugh. Just a few hours ago, the word was something that sounded more like the song, which Desi Arnaz used to sing as Ricky Ricardo.

As strange as it seemed she was no longer afraid, she was relaxed. It felt as some heavy weight had been lifted off her shoulders, removing hundreds of pounds of exhaustion, leaving her feeling refreshed, renewed.

"Mira, Josefa," Francisco smiled. "I'm not here to frighten you; I'm here to help you. But one thing I'm going to tell you, it may seem like brutal honesty, but it has to be done. I'm going to tell you what I see exactly the way I see it; it's the only way. If not we are going to sit here for hours trying to make you understand...so please remember that what I'm going to tell you is serious and is something you have been carrying with you for many years."

Josefa felt her heart tighten and her breathing halt. Coldness ran through her. She moistened her lips, and her eyes bore at the old man with fear. She wanted to speak, but her mind decided against it.

Francisco raised his eyebrow and leaned back on the chair and rested his arms on his thighs. "But don't worry, the saints are on your side, with faith and trust in them; we'll be able to remove this evil from you."

Coming closer to the edge of her seat, Josefa stared at Francisco. "I don't care what type of curse or whatever you want to call it that's hurting him. All I want to know is how I can bring my baby back home; nothing else matters."

"Well, that evil that's part of your life is the cause of everything that's affecting your entire family. Something around you is very selfish and greedy and doesn't want to see you happy. It doesn't want your family to prosper and worse of all; it wants any male who gets close to you, and that means your sons and your husband, to constantly fail no matter what they try to do. As long as this evil is part of you, nothing good will ever come to them and by that, your life will constantly be a living hell. Your life will be one filled with pain and suffering," Francisco said as he came close to the table cutting the distance between him and Josefa. "Your son is a very brave and smart little boy," the old man said and Josefa nodded her head with approval. "But I have to tell you he's in trouble," Francisco added.

Josefa clutched her heart and blinked hard as tears burst through her eyes. She closed her eyes and felt her insides shake with frustration.

The babalawo saw the sadness in her face and took her hands in his. "But don't worry. Your son is in a bit of trouble, but he's not in danger...not yet, and it is up to us to help him as soon as possible."

"What do you mean that he's in trouble but not in danger? What do you mean not yet?" Josefa pleaded, clutching to his hands as she opened her eyes in desperation.

Francisco saw her anxiety. "The trouble is that there's a force around him, trying to control him, trying to possess him, and it's a force that's been part of him from the first day he was conceived. Do you understand me? Not the day he was born, but the day he was conceived." Francisco released Josefa's hands and leaned once again on his chair. "There was a man in your life—in your past—that loved you very much, but that love was more like an obsession. He was blinded by his love for you, but he was too shy to confess this to you," the old man closed his eyes, seeking the information that ran freely through his mind, trying to act quickly before it vanished forever. "I see you surrounded by flowers, many different types of flowers, especially flor maga that grows wild on the hills of Puerto Rico. Did you ever find yourself smelling the aroma of flowers when there were no flowers around?"

Josefa's eyebrows bunched together and hesitantly shook her head, but something in her did not agree with her own response. "I don't know," she mumbled, still trying hard to remember if such thing ever happened in her life.

"But...this man always brought you flowers, are you sure?" he insisted. "It was his way of showing his devotion to you and to show his presence."

Josefa laughed nervously. "Señor, I'm sorry, but no man has ever brought me flowers...not even my husband on special occasions." She began to think. It was hard to ignore the passion, which Francisco kept asking about these flowers. She scrambled her mind, searching through long ago memories, wanting to give Francisco those details he needed to open the door to the mystery of all her agonies. She wanted to tell him 'yes', lie to this poor old man who perhaps behind his mumbled ancient African prayers, and his strange artifacts, he was just another visionary without a vision.

She noticed his brown old face looking at the notebook where he had scribbled during his trance state. She wondered what he was seeing. She heard him sigh, before he spoke again.

"Who is Eduardo?" Francisco asked abruptly. His question came like thunder; it made Josefa straighten up as her hand practically slapped her mouth.

"That's my son," she stuttered. "That's my little baby in the hospital."

"Are you sure?" he asked, yet he doubted her answer.

"Yes, I am sure," Josefa felt annoyance lacing her words. "That's why I'm here señor, for my son. His name is Eduardo...we call him Eddie."

"Was your son named after your husband?" Francisco glanced quickly at the notebook and back at Josefa.

"No, he was not," she said shaking her head as her hand slowly moved away from her mouth and settled on top of her chest.

"Well, I'm getting that name in a very strong way; someone is shouting it, but the name belongs to someone who's not among the living," the babalawo insisted.

His statement snapped Josefa into attention. Now everything became clear; every memory rushed violently toward her leaving her dizzy. The blood on her face drained. Her hands trembled, as they became cold and wet. "Dios mio," she gasped at the realization of what was happening to her family, to her, and began confessing to Francisco what she now knew was the cause of all this. "Oh my God...there was a young man when I was a school girl who was infatuated with me."

"He was not infatuated," Francisco corrected her. "He was madly in love with you. He was obsessed with you. He dreamt of someday marrying you and being the father of your children."

Josefa gasped, wanting so much to run away from this nice old man who seemed to know secrets and events that she had long ago forgotten. The days that she dismissed as insignificant, were the days that are at the moment haunting her; Josefa now remembered, the young man of her youth. He was the brother of her two closest friends, a sickly boy a few years older than she. He had stopped going to school because of his illness—he began having epileptic seizures more often, uncontrollable seizures that made the school officials nervous. Therefore, they encouraged his parents to keep him home. He was a loner; he never went anywhere and didn't have any friends. He spent his entire day sitting near the steps of the porch accompanied by his mother who gently rocked herself in a rocking chair. He was not allowed to venture by himself any place, and for reasons, she didn't understand, he was not allowed to walk under the hot sun, and was forced to stay protected by the roof over the porch. He had a pale gaunt look about him that not even his sisters wanted to go near him.

As Josefa now clearly remembered, there were times he gave her the creeps, the way he would hide every morning and peek at her like some sinister entity from the shadowy entrance of his home. He merely managed a quick, timid hello from his porch steps, which happened only at the end of the school day when she returned with his sisters. His sisters used to tease him about how he wanted to marry her, even ridiculing him one day when she was around. It made him blush, and he kept his eyes focused on his feet until Josefa left while his sisters giggled at his expense.

Josefa rubbed the middle of her forehead and then ran her fingers through her hair. Everything that she had forgotten, subconsciously or on purpose, now came back to her as vivid as it had occurred yesterday. She remembered the strong scent of flowers. She also remembered the frequency of those smells, especially during her pregnancy with Eddie. What did this all meant? She wanted to scream at the old man. What did some poor sickly dead boy from her past have to do with her Eddie and her life? She looked around bewildered by the sudden scent of flowers that invaded the room. It was as real as standing in the middle of a blooming garden. *Was she going mad?* She wondered at the border of hysteria. She stared at Francisco wanting to ask him if he also smelled the flowers, but the words couldn't come out.

"I smell them too," Francisco said winking. "He wants his presence to be known."

"Oh God...no...no," Josefa lifted herself from the chair and backed away from the table and the babalawo. "What the hell is going on? This can't be real. Please señor, tell me that this is some little trick that you are pulling on me."

"Please Josefa," Francisco motioned toward the chair. "Please niña...sit down. This is no trick. It's as real as that bitter cold day outside. This man is not as powerful as he thinks he is. Actually, he's pretty harmless and we should have more pity for him than fear. He is just confused and still believes that he is a part of this world."

Josefa raised her hands above her head and then rolled her fingers into fists. She tried walking towards the curtain wanting to run out of this place at once, but her feet felt like 50lbs weights, keeping her fastened to the floor. She lowered her arms and unrolled her fists into fingers that smoothed the fabric of her skirt. She looked at Francisco for answers. She heard the soft voice of the babalawo urging her to sit down. She slowly took a few steps toward the table and placed a shaking hand on the back of the chair. She needed support, and giving in to the persuasions of Francisco, she sat down, but staying away from the table.

"Your son almost died the day he was born," Francisco uttered with authority. "After he was born in your home and rushed to the hospital, the doctors felt that there was nothing they could do. They wanted you to go back home and to leave your baby with them, where you knew he would die if you left him there by himself."

"Yes," Josefa sighed as fresh tears rolled down her eyes remembering that awful day. "I knew where they were going to send him…to another hospital where only patients who were about to die were shipped…like infected cattle." Josefa came closer to the table and placed her elbow on the edge while resting her head on the back of her hand. "I refused to let my baby die by himself," she sobbed, snapping forward and grabbing the edge on the table. "I told those cold-blooded bastards that if my son was going to die, he wasn't going to die inside a cruel place like that, but he was going to die in my arms in his own home."

"You did the right thing, Josefa," Francisco nodded his head and smiled. "Now, what I'm about to tell you might alarm you, but it is something you have to know…something you need to know if you want your son back home."

Josefa cocked her head sideways trying to make her ear to extend all the way to the old man's lips, not wanting to miss a single syllable. "Go ahead, señor…what's there that's going to disturb me more? This day has turned out to be something of a nightmare; I might as well go all the way and see how all this craziness is going to end."

"When your son was born, this man, Eduardo was angry that he was not able to be the father," Francisco leaned forward gathering his fingertips together and forming what look like a church steeple. He moved his head barely touching his hands. "When he learned from his sisters that you had married and left town with your husband, he was hurt; he even considered killing himself. For some reason, he always felt that someday he was going to propose to you and like the fairy-tale, the two of you were going to live happily ever after. After years, obviously he lost touch, yet his obsession never faltered, on the contrary, it became stronger. But along with his passion for you, his health took a turn for the worse, the poor man died...in a major epileptic seizure, which he suffered while walking alone on his way to see the house where you used to live. When he died, he found himself on the other side of life and to his amazement, his sickness was something that he didn't have to worry about any longer. He felt free...free like a bird, to do as he pleased with no barriers to keep him trapped. The first thing he did with this newfound power was search for you, something, which is easily accomplished when a man becomes part of the spirit world. There are no walls, no obstacles, no time to dictate their movements, they could snap their fingers and what they seek or where they want to be is attained within seconds."

Josefa shuddered at the words of the old man; she felt like a kid listening to a corny Halloween story, but knowing that this was her own real story that she obliviously carried with her for so long. She fought the urge to ask questions, instead hunching her body slightly, and she listened intently to what the babalawo had to say.

Francisco moistened his lips as he moved closer and touched Josefa's arm leaving his hand on her forearm for a second and then putting his hand on the table. "When he found you, he sat next to you staring at you, like old lovers reunited for the first time. He studied the visible changes the years brought you; the way your eyes sparkled and the way your hair had grown. He tried to hug you, to kiss you, but realized that with this new ability, something was lost and that was the sensation of touch and feeling the warmth of another human being. He cried on your unsuspecting shoulders, while you went around cleaning and cooking thinking, you were by yourself. Then he noticed your belly, and the sound of another heart beating along with yours. That was the child you were carrying at that time—your son Eddie. He caressed your stomach and placed his ear next to it, hoping to hear the creation of life within you. He was saddened, yet pleased that another life was taking form...and at that moment, he came up with an idea, if he couldn't have you as a wife, as a lover...then he would have you as a mother. He would reincarnate as your son, the one that was growing slowly inside your belly."

Josefa let out a small cry, muting it as she brought her hand over her mouth, astonished at what she was hearing. She was surprised she was not shaking, the story the old man was revealing to her was too amazing to believe. As incredulous as the story was, she believed the babalawo was telling the truth. "My God," was all she could say as Francisco continued.

"Every day he kept you company, after your children went to school and your husband went to work. He would follow you, step by step like a little puppy wanting to play. At the end of your chores, whenever you sat down and enjoyed the breeze that came through the window, he would become part of that breeze. Then, he could slip through your hair, smell the scent of your soap, and be part of the most intimate moment to your life. At that moment, he wanted to reveal himself to you, to cry out loud the love he had for you. It made him crazy, absolutely mad that he was not even able to hold your hand and feel the tingle of your skin. It was at that moment he began bringing you flowers, flowers created in his own mind. He created these bouquets in the middle of the day, after the chores were done, and before you began to prepare dinner. But as your stomach grew and your son's birth was near; Eduardo became desperate. He knew that if he was to reincarnate as your son, he had to act quickly. But this transformation was not easy. Spirits cannot simply create rules as they see fit. He failed to realize that there are rules over the world of the living, just as there are rules over the land of the dead. The powers that dictate the spirit world forbid Eduardo to perform such a transformation. He was punished and ordered to continue his journey to the afterlife. But his love is stubborn; his love is blind. It is defiant force and will continue fighting a battle that he already lost. In his living world, he was forced to live a life with limits and depend on others because of his disabilities. Now he felt strong and powerful, and he wanted to challenge his superiors. He tried to enter your stomach, become part of your womb, and become part of the tiny heart that was growing in the embryo that was Eddie. He tried and he tried, each time growing more forceful, more determined, yet all his attempts left him standing looking at you from afar. Desperate moments cry out for desperate actions, and that was when Eduardo realized that if he could not be part of you, if he couldn't be Eddie, he would make sure to be part of your existence in some other way. He waited, for the moment, to take control; it didn't matter how long; his life now had no measure of time or space."

Francisco stroked his thin white mustache and closed his eyes, displaying his obvious exhaustion. He looked at Josefa and gave her a smile of reassurance. It was his way of telling her that everything will be fine. He cleared his throat and that simple act shook him; it was an old habit he had acquired years ago that manifested whenever he felt apprehension.

The habit first appeared when he was under the watchful eye of his padrino, or godfather in the world of Santeria. A padrino was the person that initiated an apprentice in Santeria, and his padrino was a wonderful man who he loved more than his own father. His named was Maruco Del Valle, and he noticed that every time Francisco was involved in a consultation, the clearing of his throat was as frequent as the blink of an eye. He told Francisco that it was a sign of his uneasiness during a reading, and it would be misinterpreted and cause more harm. The more he learned and the more knowledgeable he became; the nervous habit vanished, until now.

He had been involved in many cases that filled pages and pages of the unexplained, but this case seemed unique. He didn't want to lead Josefa down the wrong path, and he hoped that the poor woman would not dismiss him as some old fool and never come back. He had to trust the Orishas and most of all, trust that Josefa would realize the seriousness of the situation she was in. He reached out and touched her arm and to his delight, she smiled. He saw a new glow in her eyes, and that was what he was hoping to see. She believed, and that was what you needed for the Orishas to help your cause.

"Now this man," the old babalawo continued, wanting to tell her everything and then begin the healing. That healing was known as santigüo, the process of blessing or 'to heal by blessing', especially when a young child was the victim as it was in this case. Everything that was revealed during this consultation proved that the child was bewitched and under the spell of an evil eye. This evil eye is a poor soul, confused and was willing to do anything in his powers to obtain something that was unattainable, even when he was alive. "Every day, Eduardo waited patiently, anticipating the moment he would entwine with your unborn son, but he couldn't wait. His obsession for you and the desire to be part of you was driving him mad, and he grew inpatient. He discarded the basic concept of time, and he began to count the seconds, the minutes and the hours, just as he did when he was alive. Then, the unimaginable happened. He found a way to force himself into the consciousness of the unborn child. With this abominable act, he made your son as desperate to remove himself from your womb, just as much as Eduardo was determined to become part of it. At that time, you poor woman…your pains became unbearable. And even before the eighth month of your pregnancy, you felt contractions. You were confused at that time and vulnerable, and he used that vulnerability to his advantage. Eduardo willed your pregnancy to end prematurely, and at that precise moment, he became part of your unborn son, and your unborn son became part of him. It was not reincarnation, but it was as close as Eduardo could get to involve himself in your life by attaching himself to the soul of your unborn son."

Josefa gasped and intuitively held her stomach trying to protect the child. 'My God,' poor Eddie, her poor…poor defensive Eddie…to be trapped with this delusional man, all because he believed in a love that never existed. She grabbed her hair and pulled it with all her might, *my Sweet Lord, how can you create such evil? This was a monster that should have been buried and never given the chance to resuscitate.* She straightened her back and looked at Francisco and then dropped her gaze to the table where the composition notebook laid open. "Will that notebook help us get my baby back?"

Francisco touched the page and nodded solemnly. "Si hija, and many other things...the Orishas will help us defeat this spirit...and your son will be saved. But please Josefa, be aware that it's not going to be easy...this man has been doing his little tricks for a long time, and it's not just Eddie he wants to hurt, your husband and your eldest son are in danger as well."

Chapter Fourteen

Agapito walked to the bathroom and stood in the doorway confused. The bathroom was in disarray. The shower curtain and its rod were twisted and shoved inside the bathtub, and the floor was spotted with puddles. The clothes from the hamper were scattered and half of the cleaning bottles they kept on a shelf above the entrance door were either on the floor, or hanging off the shelf. It was as someone had tried to pull them off and was interrupted before they had finished.

The whole damn place was going to hell right before his eyes, Agapito thought as he shook his head. Lately, it seemed every time he came home from work; he didn't have the luxury to kick up his feet and enjoy a good cold one—no—there was always some type of drama or emergency waiting for him. Agapito stepped out from the bathroom, the urge to use the facilities vanished the second he saw the condition of the place.

Where in the world is everybody? He wondered, hissing between his teeth. He went inside the kitchen and stared at a bottle of the pink medicine Josefa used on the kids when insects devoured them during the summer months. He found it odd that the bottle was out in the middle of the winter.

He turned around and began to walk through the apartment, first through the room that he shared with his wife, the bed nicely made with a yellow bedspread embroidered with big colorful flowers. The edges ended in tiny fabric balls that hung in a row like unlit bulbs. He then went inside the rooms of the boys, and there he stopped and stared at Felix's bed, and flinched for a moment at the neatly stacked comic books that belonged to Eddie. His son, his small son was forced to be a fighter, a little trooper ever since he was thrown into this unforgiving world. He took a deep breath, and he wanted to scream out to God and demand answers. Wasn't it bad enough that He made him a small, sickly boy? Now this shit, this nonsense that made no damn sense at all.

Agapito walked toward the comic books and sifted through them, colorful muscle-bound superheroes jumping at him from death-defying situations. As he looked at the illustrations, he wondered if that was what Eddie wished to be, a superhero waiting for his superpowers to kick in. He put the comic books down and peeked quickly into the girls' room. He'd never felt comfortable inside their room when his daughters weren't there. He didn't want to be caught by either one of them and be accused of spying and snooping around, and invading their privacy. Besides, the last thing he wanted to see was any type of sanitary napkins, make-up, or underwear that let him know that his daughters were no longer little girls, but young ladies—señoritas—and that certainly didn't go along with his machismo way of viewing the world.

He heard the locks of the front door click open, and he ran out of the girls' room and into the living room. When the door swung opened it was Felix, looking his worst. The kid was growing fast, and Agapito noticed that his body was beginning to fill out a little. The shoulders were a bit sharper, stronger, and muscles began to define around the slim frame of the young man. *Maybe with a few more pork chops in the kid's stomach he would soon have the body of a man,* Agapito thought as he noticed that Felix also needed a haircut. Frowning, he remembered stressing to Josefa that he didn't want his sons looking like the freaking Beatles.

"Where's your mom?" Agapito asked realizing that the last time he had a real conversation with his oldest son was probably when they arrived from Puerto Rico.

Felix shrugged in response to his father's question. Felix was tired and the last thing he needed was to be interrogated by his father. "I don't know," Felix mumbled as he turned toward his room. "I just got here."

Agapito glared at his son's back noticing a tone of annoyance on the kid's answer. "Where were you?"

"Out with some friends."

"Friends?"

"Si, papi. Friends from school," Felix said over his shoulder as he went past his parents' room and began to enter his.

"Lately you have been spending a lot of times with these friends," Agapito called out irritated that his son was dismissing him the way you dismiss a servant. "Come here, Felix," he demanded putting his hands on his waist.

Felix returned to the living room and in the light, Agapito noticed shadow of a mustache appearing on his son's youthful face. Felix stared at his father wondering whatever he could possibly want at that moment. When his father didn't speak fast enough, he sat on the sofa and stared at the wall. He was tired and all he craved at that moment was to crawl under the covers of his bed and sleep for at least a month. His sleep has suffered since the night of the robbery, and every time he closes his eyes, the disturbing image of the janitor appears vividly in his mind. Felix feared someone would find the janitor when classes resumed after the Christmas holidays, but every second he still expected to hear the heavy knock on the door by rough cops looking forward to throwing him inside a jail cell for the rest of his life.

"When was the last time you went to see your brother at the hospital? He's been there for almost a month." Agapito asked. It was the only thing that came into his mind.

"I don't know," Felix leaned back and stretched his arms over his head. "Besides it's too depressing seeing him like that."

"I know it's depressing, but as a family, we have our duties. They said that even in his condition, he is still aware of what's happening around him. You should have gone with your mom today."

"I'll go tomorrow; I'll make sure to tell mom early enough so she won't run out of here by herself."

"That's a good boy," Agapito sat down on the edge of the sofa next to Felix; his body slightly turned towards his son. "Do you know if your sisters went with your mom?"

Felix nodded fighting hard to keep his eyes from closing. He yawned, deep and long, the type of yawn that freezes the jaws for a second or two. "I think they were going to the library…that was the last thing I heard before I left this morning."

"Mira hijo," Agapito leaned forward with one hand on his knee as the other one dangled slightly off his other knee. "We have to set some rules here; you are the oldest one and when I'm not home, you become the man about the house, and that means that you can't just take off and leave your mom and your sisters alone. Your job is to be here with them not out somewhere doing God knows what."

"I'm not doing anything wrong, papi," Felix straightened up hoping that this stupid chat would come to an end as quickly as it began so he could go into his room and sleep.

"I didn't say that you were doing anything wrong," Agapito pressed on ignoring the fatigue in his son's eyes. "What I'm saying is that I expect you to be around, especially with your brother's situation. Hey, I wish I could be here, but with losing my second job, now I have to do everything possible, any odd jobs that I could find to pay the bills around here. If I don't do it, who's going to pay them?"

Felix stood silent. Lately, it has been the same nonsense, like a damn broken record, every time his father opened his mouth it surely was about bills, bills, and more goddamn bills. They didn't have this many bills back in Puerto Rico.

"It takes a lot of money to support a household like this," Agapito kept on. "Do you know how much it takes to feed five people for one week? More than I make in one month. I'll tell you, I'm surprised that we are not starving by now."

"Do you want me to get a job?" Felix asked deadpanned. He was tired of his father's old speech.

"Now what is that supposed to mean?" Agapito asked with a hint of annoyance in his voice.

"Nothing," Felix shrugged and turned halfway to catch his father's image from the corner of his eye. "Hey, some kids in school have jobs. The supermarket is always looking for kids to deliver groceries."

Agapito stared at Felix, for a long time without saying a word. Just wondering if his son's statement was an insult to him and his odd jobs. "What about your school?" he finally asked, but it was not what he had in mind.

"Papi, if you have so many bills, hey, I could always get a job,"

Felix suddenly felt awake; sleep was something he no longer craved. "One of my friends worked at a supermarket in the Sixties and First Avenue; that's where all the rich white people live. He says that on Saturdays, he makes over ten dollars in tips, plus his salary for the week. I'll have enough time for my school work; besides, the way I'm doing at that school…maybe quitting wouldn't be such a bad idea. I'm not learning anything that's worth my time."

"Oh great, what kind of future do you think you're going to have delivering groceries?"

"Didn't your friend start the same way, you know, Sammy, and now he owns two bodegas?" Felix mentioned the success of the man his father was delivering groceries for. "He's doing pretty well. He even bought a building and owns a nice car, and I know he never completed high school, he can't even write his name."

"Do you think I brought you kids here so you could go and work in a supermarket?" Agapito was irritated at the suggestion of one of his children dropping out of school. "You stay in school and get yourself an education."

"Mira papi," Felix was surprised that unexpectedly his father seemed to care about him. "School right now is a place that I hate going to. I'm not learning a damn thing. All I get is teachers screaming at me because I don't know enough English to please them and the kids just laugh at me whenever I'm forced to talk in English."

"So you decided not to learn the language and quit school. When did you come up with such a brilliant plan...eh genius?"

"Ay papi...even knowing English is not going to guarantee anything. Look around, there're a lot of people out there that knows the language. I don't see them doing anything great, but sit on the stoop wasting their lives away."

"So in that case because the asshole next to you is working in a shitty job you think that's the way you're also going to end up?" Agapito's frustration with the conversation was evident. He slapped his knee and moved closer to Felix. "Is that the shit you are learning from your new friends?"

"Come on now," Felix looked up and rolled his eyes. "My friends have nothing to do with what I'm telling you. You are telling me that the family needs money and just because I volunteer to help you're getting angry about it?"

"Coño I'm not getting angry at you offering to help us," Agapito blurted. "What do you think your mother is going to say? This is the way you show your appreciation to the sacrifices, your mother and I are making, by quitting school and becoming a bum?"

"Jesus! I just mentioned it, it's not like I just went out and did it and what the hell: soon I'll be old enough to make my own decisions. And if one of those decisions is to get the hell out of school and get a job, then that's what I'm going to do."

"I'm not going to support a bum in my house...do you understand?"

"I'm not going to be a bum...I'll get a job."

"A job doing what, bagging toilet paper and delivering can of soups to rich white folks? Excellent, I brought you here from Puerto Rico so you could become the great deliverer of cat food."

"I didn't ask to be brought here from Puerto Rico," Felix squeezed his words from clenched teeth. "I was doing pretty damn well over there."

"So now you are telling me that coming to New York was a mistake?" Agapito got up from the sofa and looked down at his son. He was glad that they were alone in the house, the last thing he needed was to have his son tell him he made a mistake in front of the entire family. "What was so great in Puerto Rico? A damn house made of cheap wood and zinc ceilings!"

"For one thing I was doing well in school. Do you know how it feels to be laughed at by everyone in the class whenever the teacher makes me stand up and read from a book? In Puerto Rico, the teachers applauded me at how excellent I used to read, here I'm ridiculed; I'm the school clown in their eyes. Do you know how it feels to be serenaded by the assholes in the school with names like spic, and jibaro faggot? Do you know how it feels...eh papi? You don't have to go through that shit everyday...but I do, and for what? Tell me, for what? So I could get a diploma that's going to be as worth as a sheet of toilet paper with shit. How many great jobs do you think I'm going to get? Zero!"

Agapito watched his son's angry face and for the first, time realized that his son had his temper. He was sorry that he ever stopped his son from walking toward his room.

"Now, my son the brain, the fortune teller, knows what's in store for everyone who completes high school. He knows it's absolutely nothing, but a piece of worthless paper with shit stuck on it," Agapito said trying with all his might to stay calm. "You sit there telling me your problems...telling me how I have no idea how it feels to be called names, but I tell you one thing...you don't know shit! Do you know what I'm telling you? Shit...goddamn shit is what you know. Do you know how it feels to be called fucking Pedro all the time by the white assholes in suits?

Do you know how it feels to get cheated by a few dollars on your paycheck by those bastards with their great education because they goddamn know that you are too dumb to complain? And if you complain, you lose your job. Do you know that? Answer me 'Mister-smart-I-know-everything-guy'...how the hell do you think I lost my second job? Tell me! Do you goddamn know? I'll tell you, and this is something that not even your mom knows...I lost that job because I finally told my boss that I refused to be the all-willing-to-serve-you-spic anymore. That's why now I'm delivering groceries—a kid's job—in order to put food on the table, because I told someone with something that I don't have to take a flying fuck. Well, 'Mister-I'll-quit-school-and-become-a-delivery-boy', I found out that when you have that piece of paper, you are not the one that takes the flying fuck. Only the ass holes that do not have a diploma are the fucking assholes that take the flying fuck."

Felix was stunned; he looked at his father standing above him, spit hanging angrily on the side of his lower lip. He didn't know what to say, for the first time in a long time he was afraid of his father. He wanted to tell him how sorry he was. Tell him that he was wrong and to please forgive him. He even wanted to confess what he had done a few nights ago. He had never seen his father as a fighter, a man that took his pride seriously, because all the time he saw his father as someone that went along doing things just for the hell of it, like a programmed robot.

For the first time in his life, Felix realized that his father was a different man the second he stepped out of the house. His father was a proud hard-working man, a man who regardless of his education saw himself no less than the rest. If he didn't get the opportunity to achieve academic greatness in his life, he was going to try like hell to make sure that his children did. This revelation of character, made Felix love to get to know his father better. Felix lowered his head and stood silent, hoping that his father would leave the room, so he could soak up everything that just happened. To his relief, his father did leave the room, slamming the bathroom door shut and cursing aloud about the damn pigsty the apartment was beginning to resemble.

Felix stood up and went quickly to his room and dropped his weary self on his bed. As he sunk into the mattress, he stared into the ceiling trying to come up with answers to the many questions that kept flashing through his mind. What could he do? What would happen if the cops found out who was responsible for the robbery that led to beating, and perhaps killing, of a man? He had no idea what happened to the stuff they stole. All he knows is that this morning he received his share of the loot. Fifty lousy bucks! He shuddered to think that by accepting the money, he put a price on the life of a human being. He passed his hand over his hair afraid that if the buyer of the merchandise gets caught, he had no doubt the others will rat him out. Every traitorous finger would surely point his way; it was just a matter of time.

Could he blame them? No, when they returned it was he who they saw standing with a cracked bloody baseball bat and a man squirming on the floor. Felix rolled on his side facing the wall feeling a tear slide from the corner of his eye right to the tip of his nose. He could always run back to Puerto Rico and get lost. No one would ever find him, even if they traced the murder of that janitor here to his home, if he is gone and his parents have no idea of his whereabouts...then what? It's not like they are going to arrest his entire family for a crime that only he committed.

He knew for sure that his actions would break his mother's heart, more than it is broken now. But what could he do? Maybe the man did not die, and he could get help. The man was drunk and it was dark, there is no way he could identify him, besides; his picture is not in some big fat book at the police station. That thought made him relax and closing his eyes, he said a small prayer, hoping that God would forgive him and with God in his thoughts, Felix made a promise; he would never be caught in another stupid situation like that. He heard his father's footsteps in the living room, steps that seemed to be walking from one corner to the other, and he expected from his father to come into the room looking for him to continue the conversation.

He heard a knock at the door, and his heart froze. His father did not open the door fast enough, and the knocks echoed throughout the apartment. Felix was gagging in his fear and the vision of an army of cops; guns pulled out from their holsters, lips grimacing with anticipation of getting even with a homicidal punk. His body trembled and the urge to go smashing through the bedroom window was very appealing. His father's steps toward the door seemed unhurried. He heard the squealing of the hinges as the door slowly opened, and he could have sworn he heard the familiar strong English language of someone that was not Hispanic. The cops had arrived at his home and there was nowhere to hide; his only option was to jump out of the fifth floor window and risk breaking his legs. He could not move and there was a panicked scream stuck down his throat making it difficult for him to breathe. Then, he heard the voices again, this time more clearly, and he felt like a ton of steel had been lifted off of him, it was the chatter of his sisters. Felix exhaled. He was relieved now and, closing his eyes tightly, he forced himself to sleep.

Chapter Fifteen

Josefa stepped out from the Children's Hospital of New York, where Eddie had been moved from Mount Sinai two weeks ago. The cold night and the wind whipped the bottom of her coat against her legs. Usually, they had to pry her away from Eddie's bed; her anguish always getting the best of her. Even her other children stopped coming with her; her ordeal was too much for them to deal with. It was painful enough to see their brother in his grave conditions; the last thing they needed was to witness their mother's hysterics. Tonight, however, was different; there was hope for her youngest child.

So much had been revealed to her by Francisco that now she was a pillar of strength and, according to the old man, that strength was something that her son needed. She didn't know if it was an illusion created by her visiting Francisco, but she had sworn that Eddie seemed more at peace. He had the sweet look of someone taking a well-deserved nap, rather than his previous look of a troubled child trapped in a permanent sleep. She was pleased with what she had done today—it didn't really matter why she hadn't thought about it before—she was glad that Francisco had suggested it to her.

"Do something that he likes a lot," the old man had said. "Even in his condition he can register. Do something that reminds him of home, something that would make him fight to return to his family." With that encouragement, Josefa bought some comic books from a candy store near the hospital along with a Charms cherry lollipop, Eddie's favorite. She had rubbed the lollipop on his lips for a few seconds, and she was planning to do that every day until her little boy would wake-up and could bite into the hard candy shell like he always did.

After that, she opened the comic books, and began reading them to him. After reading each page, she showed the colorful pages to her son, holding the comic book close to his face, knowing in her heart that her baby could see the action displayed in the pages. As she read Eddie's favorite characters' adventures, she found a bridge that drew her closer to him through Superman and Spiderman. She struggled through the words in English not knowing exactly how to pronounce the tricky syllables, but not really caring if her pronunciations made any sense or not. One thing was certain; Eddie was listening and every time she saw the words that spelled out the names of his two beloved characters; she made sure to enunciate their names: "SUPERMAN! SPIDERMAN! It was her personal battle cry for him to wake up and come home.

Josefa crossed First Avenue and Sixty-Eight Street and hurried through the empty icy streets towards the subway at Lexington Avenue. She still couldn't believe all the things that had occurred in that day, and as she climbed down the subway stairs, all she wanted was to go home and take a long shower and rest. It was a tiring day with the excitement and the mystery of Francisco. She rummaged through her coat pocket and found a token and dropping it through the slot, pushed herself through the wooden, yellow turnstile. She turned toward the side marked 'UPTOWN' and climbed down more stairs to get to the train platform. After nearly a year in this country, the constant climbing up and down stairs to take the train still left her out of breath and constantly fearsome. She was regularly apprehensive while commuting in the evening and recalling frightening stories about assaults, muggings, rapes and stabbing that the news inundated the public. For those reasons, she regularly stood close to groups of people. It made Josefa feel safe, and she always traveled in the car where the conductor was on. There were a few riders scattered on the platform.

Along the dirty tiled wall, a young couple caressed each other while a junkie nodded on the edge of a worn bench. She walked closer to a family nearby, and stood against the wall, again another cautious behavior on her part. She heard about people being pushed into the tracks by deranged homeless nuts as trains roared into the platform, and she made sure to stay pressed against the wall until the train had come to a full stop, and its doors opened. As she waited for the train to arrive at the station, she never imagined ending in a place like Francisco's home.

She was overwhelmed at the things, the babalawo—a stranger— knew of her life. Facts that she had forgotten were dusted off by Francisco and placed in front of her where she could see them again. He had known so much about her, and that had puzzled her, yet she was willing to accept such madness, even if she still did not understand it completely if it meant to bring Eddie out of his coma. He knew the history of her son's name, something so insignificant, but according to Francisco was the beginning of her curse.

Finding a seat on one of the benches along the wall, Josefa sat down and closed her eyes. Francisco had revealed to her things and events she seemed to have forgotten—or conveniently forgotten—but now those memories were with her again, much clearer than the days they actually happened.

So vividly she could see Agapito now in her head; just like that day, rushing to town in search of the Catholic priest in order to baptize their newborn. Both she and Agapito had been raised Catholics, and their beliefs were, 'when a child dies if he is not baptized he would never become an angel who returns to heaven.'

She had been clutching her child, her nameless dying child, when Agapito returned. Agapito had leaned closer to her; his eyes were two red fire balls of exhaustion. She had no idea how long her poor husband had gone without sleep. He stroked the small pinkish head of their son and Josefa caught a brief expression on Agapito's face; it was a grimace look between pity and disgust. Their baby was bleeding—an internal bleeding that vomited out of his mouth in short splurges. The blood was rich, and the stink was foul, and it ran through his tiny lips leaving lines of exposed raw flesh under his chin and cheeks.

My God, she had shuddered. He was dying, little by little her baby boy was dying, and it showed in the fear that was displayed in Agapito's eyes.

"Did you baptize him?" Josefa asked Agapito, in a voice that was weak and troubled. "What's his name?"

Agapito touched the baby's shoulder wondering if the baby boy would survive the day. "Yes, I saw the priest, and he gave me this bottle of holy water," Agapito took a small bottle from his pocket. It was a plastic bottle with a frosted look to it, and on one side, there was a cross. "He baptized our son and he told me to make the sign of the cross on his forehead with the water," Agapito twisted the cap off the bottle and rubbed a few drops on the child's forehead. He traced a cross on his son's head with the holy water. "He's now a little angel," he kissed his son on the top of his head and squeezed Josefa's arm. "There, it's done...if he dies, he will join God in heaven."

Josefa closed her eyes, not wanting to hear those awful words from Agapito. She wrapped her arms tighter around the infant. 'My Sweet Lord, he's so tiny...so defenseless,' she said softly. She could feel his small heart beating hard. It sounded powerful, as powerful as the engine on a train. He was fighting back, and that made her stronger. "What's his name?" she asked again, while wiping the blood from her son's chapped lips and kissing his soft forehead moistened by the water blessed by God.

"His name is Eduardo," Agapito whispered. Clearing his throat loudly, he repeated the name. This time louder, the way a king's name is announced. "Our son's name is Eduardo Angel Santiago."

The first thought that ran through Josefa's mind was disappointment. She had a cousin; a distant cousin with the same name who was loud and obnoxious. She wanted to protest, to scream at Agapito and force him to run back and give the priest a better name. She wanted a name that symbolized her little precious boy with strength, perhaps a name like Miguel or Arturo. But she knew that it was too late, her baby boy's name was already registered by the church and soon would be archived in town.

She was tired, and there was no more fight left in her. It seemed she had been battling for weeks...even months. She knew her boy was getting better and it was best to save her strength, besides Doña Luz will be here soon. She was the other midwife who helped Doña Lola when the poor woman was either sick or too busy attending to other matters. Who would have known that someday Doña Luz would be taking over all duties because of the death of a great woman?

Josefa was still in shock that Doña Lola, the old woman whom she had known all her life, was dead. She had died delivering her baby boy, her little Eduardo, and it was hard to come to terms with such a big loss. Now Doña Luz was coming, and sweet Doña Lola was not among them. "Agapito," Josefa mumbled; her husband squeezed himself tightly next to her. She could hear his fatigued breathing relaxing into a slumber. He groaned and to Josefa that was enough indication, he was still awake. "Why did you name him Eduardo?" She shifted giving him more room; she was afraid that he would get too comfortable and fall asleep and then end up on the floor. "Did the priest suggest the name?"

Agapito yawned and sat along the edge of the bed. He rubbed his eyes, wiping away the spell of sleep that he wanted so much to possess. "I don't know...what? You don't like the name? The priest was in a hurry, you know how he gets sometimes. He was getting ready for mass, he said in any other situation he would have made us wait until he personally had come here to baptize him. Thank God, he realized the urgency, so he made an exception. When he asked me for the child's name, I just stared at him, my mind was blank. For a second, I thought he was going to yell at me to hurry up with the name," Agapito rubbed his chin, feeling the four-day growth of rough beard. "Then, the name popped into my head. It came to me, Eduardo Angel...just like that," he snapped his fingers to emphasize his words. "It sounded like a whisper that came into my ear and with the Father looking at me with those bushy eyes, I repeated the whispered name."

Stroking Eduardo's fine dark hair, Josefa repeated the name over and over in her head, trying to fall in love with a name she disliked. "Well, the least of our worries is a name." She looked at Agapito, and he had somehow rested his head on the headboard while still sitting on the edge of the bed. His body was contorted, yet he began to snore.

"Agapito," she tried to wake him up to tell him to move to one of the children's beds. "Agapito," she nudged the side of him and with mumbling incoherent words he leaned forward and buried his face in his hands. He kneaded his face as if he was reshaping a lump of clay. "Go and sleep in Felix's bed, if I need you, I call you."

"When is Doña Luz coming, wasn't she supposed to be here by now?" Agapito stood up as he allowed his weary steps guide him to his oldest son's bed. "Are you sure that you'll be okay?"

"Sí...don't worry, Doña Luz would be here soon, if we need you, I'll make sure to yell loud enough to wake you up."

"And we both know that you could yell pretty loud," Agapito said smiling; it was his way of lightening the mood of the past forty-eight hours. "I think even those across the island heard you last night."

Josefa smiled; amazed that she recuperated so quickly; just two days before she thought she was going to die. Only her sore throat reminded her of her pains. "Go, go and rest," she pushed him to the other room with her words.

"How is he doing?" Agapito stopped and gently rubbed the soft head of his little Eduardo. He wanted to kiss the infant, but could not get over the smell of the blood that was on the child's raw lips.

"He's doing better," Josefa answered him, relieved that the baby was asleep. "I feel every second his little body getting stronger. He'll be okay...you'll see, in no time this child will be chasing the stray cats outside."

Agapito began to say something, but kept his thoughts to himself. He hoped that when the child dies, it won't be too hard on his wife. He was prepared for the baby not to pull through; he just hoped that God would hurry up, the longer the child was alive and suffering in the arms of his wife, the harder it was going to be for her. He heard the dogs bark, and he went through the doorway and peeked outside. Doña Luz was approaching, and he felt relieved; the woman would know what to do if the baby dies. She had taken charge of the dead body of Doña Lola when he rushed Josefa and Eduardo to the hospital; the woman would know what to do. It was amazing how poor people accepted death with such a quickness and wasted no time at all. They saw life as borrowed time from God and there should be no qualms about it when it's time to return it.

Agapito greeted the woman, who was perhaps his age, but looked much older. Some even whispered that she was into witchcraft and for that reason; she always gave him the creeps. She walked past him; her sizeable cloth bag hung like a huge tumor growing on her back, and the scent of herbs seeped through her pores. She smiled with strong white teeth; she reminded him of a Taino Indian woman mixed with African roots. At times she smelled like earth and trees after a heavy downpour. He turned around and left them, there was nothing he could do now.

The menacing roar of the train thrusting into the station pulled Josefa back into reality, removing her memories at once. The powerful gust rushing through the tunnel threatening to pull her wool cap off her head as old newspaper's headlines whirled like dirty confetti onto the rat-infested tracks. The train thundered into the station, as the platform shook and the loud metallic screech ripped through everyone's eardrums.

Josefa rushed inside the train, hurrying toward a vacant seat like a seasoned New Yorker. Josefa plopped down and placed her bag in front of her, before someone beat her to it. There were only four stops before she had to get off, but even a mere five to ten minutes of sitting down was a blessing.

She began to think of her past, and she found it amusing how much had been blocked until today. It had been a long time since she recalled her childhood. Her memories always left her feeling inferior, and she didn't wish to relive them. Her upbringing was difficult, dictated by her family's customs and beliefs. She was a smart student who easily absorbed knowledge, but she was born at the wrong time and the wrong sex. Girls were not supposed to outshine the boys. Intelligence was not something required of a girl, soon to be a woman, and an education was seen as something wasted on a girl. It would be the adult boy who would someday become the breadwinner.

The education to a woman in those days was taught inside a kitchen, not in schools and books. Her vocation for the future was cooking without burning the beans and ironing shirts with a sharp crease. Those were the ideologies of Josefa's mother and especially of her father. You only need to master domestic chores in order to become someone's wife. With memories as sour as these, she had no desire to return to her past. No wonder it took Francisco's magic to jolt her memory, to remember how she felt after hearing the name Agapito gave their son on that long-ago day in Puerto Rico—'Eduardo Angel'—the same name of an infatuated boy.

It was not like Eduardo had been a lover; the poor young man wasn't even a friend. Yet to this day, here in the cavernous gray city of New York, she could still imagine his pale, sickly face hiding just to steal a glimpse of her. Those recollections sent shivers throughout her body. Francisco had really spooked her, not only with the accuracy of details about her life, but also the details of surreal events that were still occurring with Eddie. Her son grew stronger, his sickness succumbing to the herbal teas that Doña Luz prepared for him and the special lotions she applied to his raw skin around his mouth.

Throughout his healing, Eduardo's spirit was right there next to him. At night, he stood by Eddie's side like a guardian guard. When Eddie was finally well, the doctors proclaimed it a miracle. The same doctors who were ready to sign the death certificate of the child just a few days prior to his recovery, examined Eddie with amazement in their eyes, mumbling to themselves marveling at the recovery the young boy made.

During the lengthy consultation, Francisco implied that perhaps Eduardo was the one who assisted with Eddie's recovery. Seeing as his plan to become the child failed, he did what he felt was the next-best thing. He became Eddie's spirit guardian. As he infused his entity with the young boy, Eduardo ensured that he would be able to shadow every movement, every experience, feel every emotion that he could not experience himself.

The train screeched to a dead stop in the middle of the tunnel. The lights flickered, and the entire car went dark and Josefa nearly jumped out of her seat not expecting such an abrupt awakening from her trance-like state. Then slowly it jerked back on its bumpy ride. Finally it came to a rumbling stop in the station of Ninety-Sixth Street, and Josefa was glad that her stop was next. She gathered her pocketbook and the shopping bag with Eddie's dirty pajamas and underclothes.

The Number Six local opened its doors at One-Hundred and Third Street, and Josefa exited quickly going through the turnstile and sprinting up the stairs where the night chill awaited her. It was almost nine in the evening, and she hoped that the girls had taken the initiative to cook something. Usually she left dinner already cooked before heading out to the hospital, but with today's additional appointment with Francisco, cooking had been the furthest thing from her mind. She crossed Park Avenue scanning the elevated Metro-North tracks and tried to look closely at the underpass, making sure there were no surprises lurking in. *God…how I hate that underpass,* that distrust though crossed her mind, as it always does, whenever she came to that spot. She took a deep breath and began to say a little prayer for protection and wishing to be home soon to jump into bed for a lengthy sleep. She thought about Eddie and of Francisco's words, which still held a frightening cloud above her. According to the old babalawo, Eduardo refused to leave her son alone and join the afterworld.

It was eerie to remember all those nights that she heard the boisterous laughter coming from Eddie's crib hours after she fed him and put him to sleep. At times, she would find Eddie staring at nothing, but the ceiling, and laughing out loud. It used to take a few minutes before Eddie stopped his hysterical laughter and acknowledged her presence. He would then babble his baby talk, and in seconds was asleep again. Other times, in the silence during the night she would hear Eddie talking to someone. It would frighten her to the point that she would sit-up on the bed and strain her ears to listen, and she would stay in that position until her baby would finally fall asleep again. Those moments were strange, and although they were a cause for concern then, now that she knew the reason for Eddie's behavior; it terrified her.

"Your son can see the dead," Francisco declared in a matter-of-fact tone, the information shaking Josefa to her core. There is no comfort in knowing that your child can see the faces of those who aren't with us anymore, spirits that are supposed to move from this world, but stay wanting to be a part of God's paradise.

Josefa walked past the tall housing projects on Madison Avenue, and entered her street. The first thing that she saw were three police cars parked crookedly in front of her building. Revolving lights bathing the neighborhood in an eerie glow of blue and red. She straightened out her neck, trying to see what was going on. In the midst of the crowd of familiar faces, she saw Agapito running after the cops who were dragging someone to one of the patrol cars. She could hear Agapito's angry voice, yelling curses in his broken English. "Moda foka, das mai son. Sonnamenbishes leaf mai son alón!"

After hearing her husband yell as he tried to fight the officers, Josefa strained her eyes a bit more and saw who the person was the cops were dragging towards the patrol car. It was Felix! And seeing her son handcuffed broke the little pieces her heart had left. She ran as fast as her legs could move, and as she came closer to the scene, she could see her daughters behind Agapito; all three of them screaming and crying. Josefa's entire world was exploding. She could clearly see Felix now, his arms held together behind his back, fasten by shiny silver handcuffs. His eyes were puffy and teary, and his heavy walk seemed to lead him into the bowels of hell.

She slammed her hands against the hood on the car where the two cops were pushing Felix into, and before she could touch Felix, another cop came from behind her and wrapped his strong arms around her waist. She screamed, with a long 'NOOOOOOOOO!' Wanting it all to be a bad dream, she hoped that, as soon as she woke up, she would hear the loud snoring coming from Eddie's room. She was going to wake up and find

Agapito slipping out of the apartment to start his first job. She wanted so bad to wake up from this horrible nightmare, to have things back to the way they were, but this wasn't a nightmare. This was the hard reality her family's life had come to be.

One son was in a coma in the hospital while her other son was being taken away in handcuffs like some two-bit criminal. Josefa screamed into the night; screams tearing from her insides, haunting every person that was witnessing the scene. Clenching her fist in the air, Josefa cursed Eduardo, knowing that this was his doing. Knowing he was enjoying the pain she was going through. She cursed his existence, cursed his name, cursed his obsession, and cursed him with every molecule in her being. She wanted him to be gone from her life, from her family's life. Now she was ready to fight!

Chapter Sixteen

Eduardo's face twisted sideways with a blow that felt like a slap; overwhelming him with a pain. He heard the tendon on his neck snapping in a sickening crunching sound. He felt a numbness coat the side of his face. His body jerked, thrashing violently on the rocking chair. He was afraid he would break his mother's prize possession, so he stopped. He couldn't quite understand why he was awake from a long afternoon nap, then again, he wondered if he had really fallen asleep.

Perhaps, I am dreaming? Then again, he could have been making the painful trip toward the land of the living. *Do the dead sleep and dream?* Eduardo wondered, knowing that was a legit question to ask. Didn't he eat and drink whenever the desire for such earthly things consumed him? Although, it was quite amusing that he couldn't remember seeing his mother move much around the kitchen the same way she used to when they were still alive. There were not even the familiar aromas when dinner was simmering in the early afternoon.

But wait, Eduardo thought. *Aren't we still breathing…so aren't we still alive?* He was beginning to finally understand that their lives had been altered quite a bit. He could travel to his earthly place; able to roam among those who are still living, yet they were not able to see him, unless he allowed them…so what was he? Alive? Dead? He might be part of the ultimate stage of life where humans are able to travel from both worlds, crossing an invisible bridge across the sky. Perhaps this is another phase in the ever-changing evolution of man where there are no gods…or just one God.

Eduardo smirked, *maybe all humans are our individual gods…our private universe, and we could control our particular suns and moons, and we could even rotate around our own galaxies at whatever speed we desired.* In his cloudy mind, he heard a loud hateful shriek—which pierced savagely through his brain. It shook him, and he blinked furiously as if trying to remove something from his eyes that was irritating him. At first, he tried to dismiss it as being just another illusion, yet there was something gnawing him, assuring him that what he heard was an actual creation spawned from the other side of his world. There were screams—accusing screams—and he knew it had to be from Josefa. He was certain of that, obviously his presence was finally unearthed, and now he and Josefa will battle for Eddie. Eduardo felt a small twinge of doubt, but that soon passed, and he now twisted his pale lips into a sinister smirk. His long wait was over and there was no time for hesitation.

Yes, the wait was a long one, since the day he saw himself dressed in a suit for the first time in his life—his own funeral—and very strategically he plotted his revenge. Surely, anyone in his position would have been angry and confused as well, gazing at your own rigid body inside an open casket in the middle of his parents' living room. It was pathetic at how he saw the arrangements inside the only home he knew. The few pieces of old furniture were pushed against the walls, while the funeral parlor's metal folding chairs were gathered in front of the coffin. He could still remember the scent of flowers and burning candles that surrounded him.

On that day, he became aware of how offensive the smell of death was. He could distinguish the strange aromas escaping from his own pores, foreign smells of chemicals and the fabric of a new suit. He could see his parents together in front of his casket, hunched like identical bundles of rags staring past his lifeless body. Eduardo remembered screaming at them, struggling to snap out of the rigor mortis that had settled over him. If they were quick enough they could help him out of the ill-fitting brown suit and take it back to the store for a refund. He was certain the suit had cost more than his parents could afford. Throughout the day, family members and neighbors offered prayers to him, and whispered words of encouragement to his parents' ears.

As the night grew shadows, low murmur of the Rosary was heard, serenaded by old women clad in black dresses and lace mantillas, and more candles were lit and faces bathed in sweat took on shiny looks. The mourners, many in their Sunday's best, drank coffee and ate buttered crackers and small sandwiches cut in triangles. Children, oblivious of the morbid event, ran and played and bruised their knees and ruined pants that could no longer be worn for Sunday Mass. He spied on the men assembled on the lower steps of the porch drinking rum and telling off-color jokes that made them roar with the abandon of mischievous boys. However, throughout the night and until early morning, there was only one person he had sought out, but never saw, Josefa—and he always felt anger towards her for that reason, but the anger was soon replaced by the love he felt for her. On that night, Eduardo knew he would never rest in peace until he possessed her love and heart.

But now, as he rubbed his face and rocked slowly on the rocking chair, Eduardo shook his head paying attention to his mother's prophecy. He must be careful. His mother had warned him, even scolded him as if he was a child, about his lack of attention to other matters. There was a man, she revealed to him, a very dangerous man who could cause trouble if he acted too hastily. This man was from the land of the living, and very powerful and knowledgeable about the afterworld. His mother felt very strong and predicted the interference of this man would upset their makeshift paradise. Even so, Eduardo refused to worry; for all he cared about was hearing the sound of Josefa's voice. He was sure it was her scream that had come across the rivers and mountains and hidden skies, which separated both of their worlds. It had come through with stinging power, and that he was sure was the slap that woke him up. Eduardo grinned and smoothed the side of his face with his long bony fingers. He stopped the swaying of the rocking chair and shielding his eyes with his hand, he scanned the area for any sign of Eddie. He smiled, Eddie was Josefa's shining spirit that now he possessed.

Eduardo was certain that the child would soon come back; he had no other choice. Besides, how long can a small frightened boy stay out there all alone? Eduardo stood up and shuffled to the edge of the porch. Feeling the hot sun on his brow, all he wanted was to climb down the three short steps and walk along the ground. He was forbidden by his mother not to venture on the reddish little path that snaked into the wilderness that surrounded the house. He was afraid, held back by his mother's warning that walking on that path would be the death of him. He could not understand why his mother worried so much about him dying when—wasn't he already dead?

Yes, he knew he was dead, and now, more than ever, he was convinced that he was deceased, because a living being could not create a vision of his former home in Puerto Rico. A living person could never travel through dimensions and portals that placed him into the homes of those he wished to visit. He had the power to either allow the living souls to see him or stay invisible or haunt them by moving objects, making noises or removing the bed sheets from unsuspecting victims. He mostly enjoyed haunting his sisters, didn't they made his life a living hell when he was alive? He gave them a taste of their own medicine, until his mother commanded him to stop. He was a mamma's boy, always was and always will be and his mother's words were like scriptures to him, and of course, he never dared to question her commands.

There was just one time when Eduardo defied his mother's attempt in making him forget Josefa. His saintly mother tried to take him to the place where his father and other family members had gathered in the afterlife, but he rejected her plans. In turn his mother refused to abandon him, and knowing very well what the consequences were, she ignored the prayers, and the candles lit in her memory by those she left behind, and decided to follow Eduardo's path, and that path was this abomination he created all on his own. A paradise of lies and deceit in which any twisted spirit was welcomed, as long as they abide by Eduardo's rules.

Eduardo wasn't a fool; he was aware that this place was not Puerto Rico, but didn't he create it to resemble such a place? He never was a religious person when he was alive, but he had heard about places like purgatory, the afterlife, and the fabled tunnel bathed in white lights. Yet this dimension resembled none of those places. Was this place like some stepping stone you were allowed to stay until you fulfill your mission? Was there a mission he had to complete? He was forbidden to reincarnate in the body of the child. He was told that such an act was an abomination, against the laws that governed them after the crossover. But who were *they*? That was all he wanted to know. He don't ever recall seen *them*, and he never heard *their* voices, yet he felt *their* ominous presence.

As a boy, Eduardo heard the old wives' tales, spoken in silent whispers about dead souls that lingered in space after their departure. Some spirits needed the help of prayers and the illumination of candles to usher them into their new world. But he knew that there were others like him, who chose to ignore such offerings and had turned away from the precious light that the candles and prayers brought. There were other souls like him; feeling that there were matters pending in the land of the living and until those situations were fulfilled, they would remain in limbo between life and death. Those were the souls that were made to suffer when living, and now with all this newfound freedom, they were supposed to forget the bad memories. Eduardo shook his head; it was not that simple—vengeance does not distinguish between the lights of life or the darkness of death.

He looked around; his eyes combing slowly through the green vegetation that surrounded the house. If he had the powers to travel between the living and the dead, then why was he forbidden to walk on the earth that bordered him? Eduardo looked down at the first step, while he balanced his body on the edge of the porch. What harm could befall him if he stepped down to the ground? He gingerly touched the first step with the top of his scuffed boot. He left the tip of the toes on the rung for a second, his heart racing hard, expecting something bad to happen. What could possibly happen, an electric shock to run throughout his body? Impossible, just like there was no electricity in his home when he was alive, why there should be some in the land of the dead?

Eduardo chuckled over the humorous thought. He put one foot

firmly on the top step while his hands held on tightly to the top of the porch. Nothing happened. He let go and distributed all his weight to one leg. He waited, and again; nothing occurred to make him abandon his test. Slowly, he placed both feet on the stair. He was overcome with joy, and he smiled at his diminutive triumph. He shot a quick glance over his shoulder anticipating his mother's appearance and long arm to pull him back. However, there was no one there, just the empty rocking chair moving back and forth, fueled by the wind. Eduardo was delighted; thrilled that he conquered a nightmarish fear.

He lowered his left foot and touched the second step. He wanted to tap-dance as he bent both knees. He stared hungrily at the dirt path, and he could see worms wiggling in and out from underneath the scattered rocks. He lifted his right foot amazed that such a simple act could be so much fun. Now he stood on the last wooden step just six inches from the dirt. The sun was beating on him, and he felt the strong rays searing the heat through his pores. He prepared to leap into the dirt.

"Eduardo!"

He nearly went flying into the ground, face first, but his mother's quick reflexes grabbed the back of his shirt preventing him from swallowing a mouthful of dirt and worms. She hit him hard on the top of his head, and he cowered beneath her slaps as she dragged him onto the porch. "What are you doing?" she pulled him by the hair and pushed him into the house. "You are no worse than that snot-nosed brat you brought into my home."

*****

Across the other side of the makeshift island, Eddie heard the commotion that came from that awful house. It sounded evil, and he covered his ears attempting to block the shrieks and yells. Under the safety of the huge mango tree, he heard the nasal voice of the old woman. To Eddie, that voice was the most horrible thing he had ever heard in his life. She claimed she was his grandmother, but he knew better, both his grandmothers were dead. He refused to be fooled by her. And, what about Eduardo? How could Eduardo fool him like this? For as long as Eddie could remember, Eduardo pretended to be his friend, yet he turned out to be a slimy, disgusting snake with a twisted forked tongue full of venom.

Even so, there was a hint of sadness that Eddie felt for Eduardo. He was once a decent man, a good friend. Could there be a reason why Eduardo turned so bad? From the protection of the giant mango tree, Eddie observed his so-called friend stepping gingerly on the three crooked rungs, and he found this to be strange and quite sad. Could there be something beyond the porch that made Eduardo uneasy and unsure? Even by the old woman's agitated performance, when Eduardo attempted to leap on the ground, seemed to be peculiar.

There was something at the bottom of that porch that frightened them. But what were they afraid of? Eddie had no clue, but he could sense there was something odd going on in this strange place, and that made Eddie feel a bit safer and a little courageous. Eddie knew that even the most maniacal villains from his comic books, they still had their weaknesses. Isn't that how Superman, Spiderman, Batman, and all the great super-powered heroes defeat them? Eddie smiled and felt hopeful. Eddie pumped his fist into the air, imagining that he was Superman ready to leap into space and defeat the mad alien monster trying to devour

Metropolis. That was it; Eduardo and his mother were trapped inside that doomed ancient house! He almost shouted that revelation to his gladdened heart.

Things were becoming clearer, and he began to see the light finally illuminating the dark road in front of him. Ever since he found shelter beneath the mango tree, he felt the presence of someone reaching out to take him to the place where he belonged. This place was brimming with rambling spirits and dead souls, which refused to go where they were expected to go. Eddie could see them all, but he also knew that there were other phantoms lurking like shadowy birds, willingly to help him return to his own home. These kindly shadows recognized that Eddie was not one of them. "What the hell is this place?" Eddie shouted, hoping that one of those spirits would stop and reveal to him the secrets of this place.

"This is the crossover where spirits make their final journey."

Eddie turned around baffled at where this voice came from. It was a voice inside his head that just whispered.

Eddie stepped away from the mango tree and strolled down a few feet toward the direction of Eduardo's house. Glancing up at the sky, he shielded his eyes from a fiery ball that seemed to appear from nowhere and now follow him. Shielding his eyes, Eddie scrutinized the entire panorama before him. Even with its familiarity of the Puerto Rico's countryside, the place was very different. Putting aside the hot sun, the mango trees, and purple mountains along the horizon; there were no other similarities to the island where he was born and spent the first nine years of his life.

This was an excellent replica, but not the real thing. For one thing, Eddie noticed that the bright orange ball across the sky only radiated with one level of extreme heat. And the rain, despite the first day outside the porch where he felt quick raindrops, there was no other existence of rain. He remembered the way the rain exploded with fury and thunder in Puerto Rico. He was beginning to observe how the birds in their frequent flight appeared sluggish, and the insects seemed to flutter more like an illusion rather than reality. There were not even mosquitoes feasting on his arms. Eddie scrutinized Eduardo's house paying close attention to the empty porch, wondering if from within the shadows around the house; Eduardo was matching his gaze.

"Eduardo has a knack for that."

Eddie jumped and turned quickly around. There was no one there, and he wondered how that strange voice popped into his head. It was a voice; he was sure of that, perhaps it was an unseen entity that decided to help him, but was too shy to show itself.

"Must be your guardian angel," the voice whispered and Eddie smiled. He felt like Billy Batson, the little boy who was Captain Marvel's alter ego in the comic books, waiting patiently for the famous yell of 'Shazam!' to transform him into a muscle-bound, flying superhero.

Dismissing the voice as an over-taxed mind playing trick, Eddie decided to hike around the grounds, amazed that no matter how far he went away from Eduardo's house, the shack always loomed in the background, like a sentinel keeping watch on his every single move. He stopped and looked down over the edge of a cliff, where twenty feet below a clear stream gurgled in lazy hypnotizing ripples. The water was so clear and pure, Eddie could see right through it. And in its depth, he spotted pebbles that shone like diamonds littering the bottom of the stream.

With a lovely azure sky above him, Eddie followed the stream. He walked cautiously along the edge of the grass in search for a path that would lead him to the enticing water. He could hear lullabies rising from the current, and the lyrics seemed to invite him to bathe in its coolness. *Somewhere there must be a path,* Eddie reasoned. He knelt down and calculated the drop. It was too high of a jump, and as he could judge, the stream was not deep enough for him to dive into. Besides, even if it was deep enough he didn't know how to swim. Even so, it was not swimming that he wanted to do, but only to soak his entire body in it. It was getting tiresome walking and looking down at what seemed to be a cruel of a joke. "Hey Captain Marvel," Eddie said out loud, not knowing why he was calling the voice Captain Marvel. "How can I reach the water?"

Eddie cocked his head, and only silence greeted his action. And except for the wind whistling through the tall grass, and swaying trees, just the stillness of the day spoke. He felt the heat penetrating his back. It made him hunched over with fatigue, and just when he was about to give up, he saw a man standing next to a fishing boat. Startled by the apparition, Eddie threw himself hard on his stomach. He was afraid to be seen. He parted the grass blades and peeked at the man. The man wore a pair of jeans rolled up two inches above his calf. His bare feet were submerged in the water, and a yellow shirt billowed around him. The man held on to a long crooked shaft, which Eddie figured was used as an oar. Eddie looked behind him and he could still see Eduardo's house, in the distance, under the orange sun. It resembled a dirty neglected dollhouse discarded by a bored child.

Eddie dug his elbows into the soft earth, dragging his body silently. He came into an opening where the grass no longer grew, exposing a patch of red dirt. If it was not for the man on the shore, Eddie would have jumped with the thrill that he finally found the illusive path he had been searching for. He lifted his head slowly and studied the man and his boat. From this distance, he could see that the narrow crystallized stream had now spilled into a large body of water. An incredible ocean roared and splashed onto the shoreline laced with wet black rocks instead of sand. There were millions of glistening rocks. *'Who is he waiting for?'* Eddie wondered as fear began to rise within him. Eddie began to retreat. He just wanted to get up and run, run as fast as his short legs would allow him.

The boatman spotted him and leaped on top of one of the rocks. "Hey," the man called out, as Eddie froze afraid to look back and too petrified to run away. "Hello son, where are you going so fast?"

Gradually, Eddie turned in slow motion, and he didn't stop until he was facing the man and his bobbing boat. From somewhere up above, he heard the cry of a bird and the flapping of its wings.

"Hi'ya son," the man waved; his smile filled his face with teeth. "Where are you heading to? Can I offer you a ride? Today is a beautiful day for sailing."

"Do not go there."

Eddie heard the voice again in his head. Captain Marvel has returned and Eddie smiled, his renewed strength empowering him.

The boatman walked a few feet closer to Eddie using the wooden shaft to keep his balance on the wet, black, rocks. He bowed and with his free hand, he swept the air between his chest and the rocks. It was his cordial invitation for Eddie to come and join him on his boat.

"No! Do not go in there," Captain Marvel warned. *"You do not belong there."*

Eddie remained still, his mouth half-way opened, and mesmerized by the friendly concerned look on the boatman's face. Eddie took one step forward, and once again, the man motioned with his hand, his smile bright and white.

"Turn around and just walk away. He cannot follow you or force you to go with him," Captain Marvel commanded.

"Hey son," the boatman jumped from one rock to another cutting the distance between him and Eddie. "You could trust me. If it's the boat that you are worried about, it might look old, but it's a strong fine little vessel. It has been doing its job for centuries and more centuries to come." The man shot a glance at the boat to ensure Eddie of the safety and dependability of his boat. Eddie followed the man's glance, and he admired the boat that rocked silently on the crashing waves of the bluish waters. He had never been on a boat before. What kind of harm would come to him if he accepted the invitation? It was just a quick little trip across the island. The man looked friendly enough; even his smile seemed genuine and hospitable.

Eddie went through the tall grass and stepped onto the narrow path, which led to the rocks where the man was standing waiting patiently for Eddie to join him. The ground was mushy, and a stink rose from it. It had the bad odor of rotten seaweed, and Eddie was sure that if he dug in the dirt with his fingers, he would find something putrid and dead. Eddie stared down and noticed that embedded onto the path were footprints, millions and millions of footprints. No wonder the grass didn't grow anymore, obviously those millions of steps had stomped the life out of anything that had tried to sprout. A gentle breeze came forth from the ocean inviting Eddie, and wanting to lift him off his feet and position him nicely and comfortably into the boat. Eddie took another step and the boatman—his smile widening—stretched out his long crooked shaft. "Go on son, don't be bashful, take a hold of my stick, and we'll be soon on our way."

"Eddie! Stop!" Captain Marvel screamed. That was the first time the voice ever shouted at Eddie. *"You do not belong, now turn around and go home. Everyone is worried about you."*

Eddie jumped as the man's smile broadened. Yet regardless of the voice's uproar, Eddie slid down the slope of the beaten path, reaching out towards the staff of the boatman. The man raised his hand, and Eddie wanted so much to grasp the stick and go for that ride on that old sweet boat, which the man assured him was fine and strong.

"Eddie!" Captain Marvel shouted again. *"You don't belong on that boat. If you get on that boat, you will be forever lost and remain in limbo. Come on child, close your eyes and listen; listen closely to the voice of your mother. Don't you hear her reading to you the daring tales of Superman? Come on Eddie take a good taste on your lips. That is the sweet taste of cherry, the cherry lollipop your mother is placing on your lips."*

Deep in his subconscious, Eddie heard a faraway voice. It was less than a whisper. He struggled to understand the faint words, and he was sure that what he was hearing was actually the voice of his mother. He strained harder, concentrating while a dull pain burrowed right above the bridge of his nose. And suddenly he could hear crystal clear the sweet gentle voice of his dear mother and tears of homesickness gathered around his eyes. To his delight, she was saying out loud the name of one of his favorite heroes; she was shouting 'Superman'. He passed his tongue through his lips, and the sweetness of cherry exploded in his mouth. Eddie looked up, startled at such revelation. He pulled his hand away from the shaft and he back-pedaled gaining his distance from the man, who currently stared at Eddie in shock. The boatman's bright toothy smile was now a twisted grimace of disappointment.

Eddie turned around and ran up the slope of the worn-out path and into the safety of the tall green grass. When he reached a secure distance, he stopped, his breathing coming out in fearful gasps. He looked back at the rocky shore and to his amazement; the man was no longer there. Eddie squint his eyes and gazed towards the sea where the ancient boat bopped in the middle of the deep-blue waters. It was navigated by a figure wrapped in a black hooded robe. Eddie stared at the great open sea as the hooded figure turned towards him. The thing smiled. It was the bony yellowish smirk of a chalky-white skull.

Chapter Seventeen

Sirens, loud screeching sirens in the night, in most places are received with apprehension. It took Josefa a while to get used to those menacing sounds when she first arrived from Puerto Rico. Now, like every Spanish Harlem resident, a screaming siren rushing past their window was another intrusion during the night. Normally, the sirens only put Josefa to sleep, but not tonight. Tonight, she was following those shrieking sounds from a livery cab Agapito had hailed to go after the squad car. She bounced around in the back seat listening to Agapito's curses while the bright neon lights of Gotham flashed before their eyes.

"Where are they taking him?" she asked Agapito over and over until he stopped responding. He had a knack for tuning out, which was something he has done lately, more since Eddie's attack.

There's no way, Josefa tried to convince herself, *of course there must be some misunderstanding, there's no way my first baby is a criminal.* She rubbed her forehead, feeling the coldness that seeped through her skin. Agapito held on to the handle on the cab door as the car rushed and swished through the traffic. They were heading downtown that much she knew by the way the neighborhood took a different, safer and brighter look. This was the guarded, expensive world that she only saw from an envious distance.

This was the world of the Americans—los blancos—where there were no bodegas with men littering the storefronts sipping beer from brown paper bags. Here the stock boys in supermarkets wore ties and starched aprons, and the cashiers wore colorful smocks with the name of the store nicely embroidered on the left pocket. *What kind of land is this?* Josefa shook her head. *What kind of land is this that makes little boys go into a coma and other boys into cold-blooded criminals?* She felt a pain, a dull pain in her heart. It can't be; there is no way her son became is a villain, not at all.

It was him, Josefa knew. *This is Eduardo's doing.* She just knew that all this was his doing—his doing—because he was not man enough to tell her how he felt when he was living. He had always been comfortable in his childish hideaways when he was alive, all those yesterdays ago, hiding behind late-afternoon shadows, and hiding inside darkened thresholds. Now he was hiding behind the innocence of her sons. *Damn you, Eduardo, may your damn soul burn in hell!* Francisco was right; Eduardo would fight to the end. *Well, you are messing with the wrong woman, Eduardo...I'll fight back even if I have to go straight to hell myself and burn your soul on a stake.*

The cab screeched to a stop, the sudden motion sending them both flying forward into the back of the front seat. Josefa jumped out and ran toward the steps where she had watched the cops take her baby. She felt a strong pull yanked her back, hurting her, and she felt her flesh already turning into an ugly, black and blue. It was Agapito, and she turned around and faced him, her eyes questioning at what the hell he was doing? Their son was being dragged inside like some animal, and here he was holding her back, keeping her away.

"¿Que te pasa?" Josefa pulled her arm from his hold. "What's the matter with you? Our son is not supposed to be in there. They made a mistake; they took the wrong child...do you understand? Damn cops made a mistake; to them all Puerto Ricans are the same."

"Wait one second," Agapito threw his arm around her shoulders and tried to keep her under his control. It didn't work, as she twisted her body and avoided his arm. "They have a warrant."

"So...a warrant is another piece of paper of lies; my son is not a criminal. We did not raise him like that!" Josefa continued her hurried toward the steps.

Agapito let out a long pissed-off breath as they climbed the steps to the precinct. He pushed the door open, and he was aghast; it was like walking into a mad room. The only thing missing were padded walls and inmates lying naked on the floor. The phones were ringing continuously, there were cops; uniformed and plain-clothes scrambling through the soiled tiled floor. They came through glass-paneled doors and slammed themselves away into rooms or just hurried through darkened staircases. There were long, wooden benches against a far-away wall. Uniformed officers guarded these benches, which were occupied by men with weary and defiant expressions, and they all looked up as Agapito and Josefa hurried in. All eyes looked away except one pair of watery eyes, Felix's eyes. He looked so small; a boy among men and Josefa ran to him until her path was quickly blocked by one of the officers.

"You have to stay back, ma'am," a young officer told her. He couldn't have been more than seventeen; he looked as old as Felix with the fuzz framing his upper lip trying to pass as a mustache. "Please see the sergeant at the desk. You are not allowed in this area."

"Pero ese es mi hijo," Josefa pleaded pointing at Félix. Her Spanish words falling in ears that had no clue at what she was saying. She looked at the cop, her eyes bubbling with tears, and she struggled with her bad halting English. "Das is me son, pleez das is me son. El is gud boy... ken me see me son?"

Agapito came from behind her. "Come on Josefa, we are not

going to accomplish anything with this guy here. He's just a baby-sitter for those guys. Let's go and speak to someone in command."

She allowed herself to be led away by Agapito, but her eyes never lost sight of her baby. She threw him a kiss and mouthed not to worry; everything was going to be okay; everything was going to be okay.

They approached a large desk littered with official-looking forms, paper coffee cups from Greek diners and the latest edition of the New York Post. Behind the desk, a bespectacled thin man spoke softly on the phone, despite the chaos surrounding him. He looked up through the top of his eyeglasses and held one finger up as he continued his conversation. Then without haste, he placed the phone on its cradle with ease and nodded to Josefa and Agapito.

"What can I do for you?"

Agapito cleared his throat; he looked at Josefa and threw a quick glanced towards where Felix was sitting. "Eh... me sun... eh overdeer..." he pointed at Felix. "Eh... no ingli... eh sorry... me sun arresti... no gud... he gud boy." Agapito felt embarrassment at not being able to express to this son-of-a-bitch that his son did not belong here. But all Agapito was only able to do was to grunt like an illiterate idiot, damn; he wished they were all back in Puerto Rico.

"Mi hijo," Josefa began to speak and that infuriated Agapito even more. He was the man of the house; it was not her goddamn business to do his job. He tried to stop her, but it was too late. She walked passed him and was now leaning over the desk practically knocking down the coffee cup adorned with symbols of Olympus.

The sergeant pushed his glasses up and looked at Josefa and then at Agapito. "One second," he raised a finger in front of him. "I'm sorry

I don't understand. Let me get someone who speaks Spanish."

Josefa nodded and attempted to smile. At least now with an interpreter this entire matter could be resolved, and Felix would be able to return home. She backed away from the desk and stood closer to Agapito as the sergeant scanned the floor and raising his neck towards the front door where two cops were entering. "Hey Jimmy," he called to one of them. "Come here will'ya...I need you to translate for these good people."

The sergeant smiled at Josefa and leaned forward, moving the coffee cup closer to him. After taking a peek inside, he deposited the cup in a wastebasket by his side. Jimmy came over removing his hat; there was a look of exhaustion in his eyes. He stopped between Josefa and Agapito and gave a go-ahead signal to the sergeant with his head. "This here is Officer Velez," the sergeant said. "Now tell him your problem and let's see what we can do for you."

Agapito turned sideways and nodded at the cop relieved that finally he would be able to tell his side of the story without sounding like a grunting ape. "My son was arrested this evening—"

"It was a mistake," Josefa intervened.

"Josefa, por favor," Agapito shot a look at her then faced the officer again. "There must be some mistake. He's been accused of killing a man, but he's not brave enough to even kill a mouse."

"He's just a boy...not a killer. There must be a mistake," Josefa added her eyes watery and red.

Officer Velez translated their words and waited as the sergeant glanced through the paper work in front of him. He pushed his glasses up, but they kept falling down the bridge of his nose. He mumbled to himself in small grunts and after turning a few more pages he looked up, his bushy eyebrows two perfect arches above the glasses. "Damn Jimmy, these are some serious charges brought against their son; I'm afraid that there's not much I could do. This would be handled by the detectives, but tell them, Jimmy, tell them that they are going to need a lawyer."

He related the message to Josefa and Agapito as best as his Spanglish allowed him to. However, hearing the deep sighs of both parents, he knew that the sergeant's message had been understood. After, Officer Velez looked toward the floor, and slowly lifted his eye up, meeting those of Josefa. How much he wished he was looking into the eyes of Agapito instead. It was harder to tell a mother that their innocent baby was not as guiltless as she wanted to believe. He saw Josefa's body sway nearly crumbling onto the floor, and he felt her shake as he supported her. He felt uneasy holding a woman while her husband stood there paralyzed. Finally, he came toward her, as the poor woman wailed a long-suffering cry. There was not much they could do now, but speak with a lawyer, because their son was in a very serious mess.

"I don't understand," Josefa pleaded in Spanish to the cop in front of her.

"I'm sorry señora," Officer Velez said. "But they also have in custody the other kids, and all of them are sticking to the same story. Your son killed a custodian while they were robbing a school."

Josefa heard the accusations and no matter how many times she rolled those awful words through her mind; they kept coming back like sharp daggers. She held on to Agapito's arm, her body slipping from his support and down to the floor. She knew she was screaming now in long, loud shrieks. It was hard to believe the screams were coming from her. Agapito struggled to keep her from falling. Yet Josefa still fell down to the floor in slow motion, while the cop's eyes looked vulnerable and sad.

The floor was cold and grainy. She hit the floor hard, her head bouncing from one of the dirty tiles to the leather shoe of the cop. The room was spinning fast, and Josefa closed her eyes to shut the nightmare away from her and for a few seconds, she found peace and solace. Visions of Eddie and Felix came crashing through, blinking images to her mind, and she mumbled their names hoping to catch their faces and take them home among the palm trees and soothing breezes of her Puerto Rico. Quick glimpses of Agapito's face appeared in front of her and then disappeared. The cop's face also flashed in her confused mind. She felt rough, sweaty hands grope her, making her feel cheap and unclean. She heard herself scream curses that she had never uttered in her life, but now were coming out of her mouth without shame. And then blackness and silence engulfed her, and she passed out.

Josefa's breathing was shallow and there was tightness across her chest. She glanced around feeling disoriented and stranded in the middle of nowhere. There were people in front of her and as hard as she tried to focus; all she could distinguish were faded silhouettes. Her eyes were open, that much she knew, and she could detect voices that slowly began to surface above her consciousness. She blinked hard and something was blocking the movement of her eyelashes, and she became alarmed. Josefa raised her arms in desperation brushing her face with her hands. A warm, wet towel covered her face, and she threw it across the room.

"Tranquila," Agapito placed his hands on her shoulders trying to push her back on the cot. "Are you okay?" he asked, releasing the pressure from her as she slowly sat up. "You gave everyone quite a scare," he added and Josefa knew that what he really meant was that she humiliated him.

She stared at her husband; her eyes blinking with sluggishness.

"Señora," Officer Velez said, as he stood a few inches behind Agapito, his thinning hair adding five extra years to his youthful face. The officer looked tired. "Stay there and rest...there's an ambulance on its way."

Josefa looked up, the words spoken around her sounding more like unsolved puzzles rather than statements. She tried to concentrate and slowly the phrases began to shed some light into her scattered brain. She had passed out, that much she knew, but it shouldn't be the reason enough for an ambulance. She threw a quick glance at the other man with them. It was another cop, and she wondered if his hands were also the ones that she felt around her when she fainted, and that thought once again brought her shame.

There was nothing more than she wanted to do, but to get out of this room and take care of Felix. She didn't need an ambulance; she had enough of sirens and alcohol-smelling hospitals to last her a lifetime. She brushed away Agapito's attempt to keep her down on the cot. She wondered who the last person was to drool on the cot before her. Abruptly, she straightened her back and swung her legs firmly onto the floor. The room spun for a light-headed second, and she closed her eyes praying to God for the spinning to stop. She had to get up, had to be strong for her son; her sweet Felix was out there, and he needed her. There was not much she could do for him by laying here like some lame-brained Sleeping Beauty while three men stood around twiddling their thumbs.

"I'm okay," she said, tiredness accenting her words. "I'm just exhausted...it has been a long day, but I feel better now. I don't need an ambulance...I just want to take my son back home." Josefa stared at

Agapito and then her eyes trailed to towards the closed door. "I don't need a doctor," she added. "What we need is a lawyer to prove that my son is not what they make him out to be, a killer."

She stood up welcoming the support from Agapito, yet feeling withdrawn towards him. For the first time in her life, she realized that her husband was a defeated man. Whatever happened to the strong man, she fell in love with? Perhaps Francisco was right about everything he had said and now more than ever all the facts were becoming clearer. Eduardo had really put a terrible curse on every male in her life, and she could not shake the feeling that things were not going to improve. Her poor Eddie was in the threshold of death. Felix was now accused of killing a man and could easily be put behind bars for the rest of his life. While Agapito, her once proud husband, was becoming a shadow of himself, a man whom she slowly was beginning to detest.

She felt awful, yet she pulled away from her husband realizing that she didn't need his support after all. What has happened? They were once strong and proud in Puerto Rico and Agapito was young, ambitious and full of dreams. He had a grocery store back then; a small little place sandwiched between a school supplies store, and a run-down place where they sold fabric by the yard. The store gave him a sense of fulfillment and the pride of a self-made man. Josefa remembered fondly how Eddie used to love waiting up for Agapito to come home at night with a wrinkled brown paper bag filled with coins; the dimes, nickels, quarters and pennies that the poor country folk used to purchase rice, beans and all-purpose flour scooped out of large wooden barrels.

Those were good days that began each morning with blue skies filled with great expectations. Nevertheless, just like everything in her life, no sooner that there was happiness, it all ended abruptly. Agapito lost everything, the store, the bit of money he had saved, and most of all he lost his pride. His once gallant stride was replaced with slouched shoulders, a weary shuffle and downcast eyes. His drinking increased and every step he took seemed to push him back more steps than he took forward.

Josefa sighed, walking slowly, wondering when this nightmare would was going to end. She had to do something, anything; Eduardo had gone too far.

They both marched behind the officers out of the room, and into the large area where they had entered earlier. Josefa panicked when she didn't see Felix on the bench. Her heart sank. "Where's my son?" she grabbed Agapito's coat sleeve. "Agapito, where's Felix?"

Agapito's stare went from the bench to the two officers, to Josefa, and then he sighed, looking lost. They both stood in the middle of the chaotic space looking at the back of Officer Velez as he walked to the front desk. After a second, Josefa followed him and Agapito followed as well.

The officer exchanged a few words with the desk sergeant and then escorted them to another room where the stench of stale cigarettes was overbearing. Josefa sat on a chair and closed her eyes; she was tired of all these little rooms smelling like street gutters. All she wanted were answers and her son in her protective arms. The cop, who somehow became their own private guide, left again promising that he would return with the detective leading the investigation.

'Investigation', to Josefa, the word had an awful sound. She squeezed her eyes pinching away a headache that was pounding in the middle of her forehead. Josefa had never been inside a police station, and finding herself in the midst of criminals, gun and filth; she came to realize that up close the cops and the thugs smelled the same way. And that stink was corrupted, dangerous and overwhelming frightening. She turned towards Agapito, and among all the men inside the precinct with their scowls and rugged, tight-jawed faces; he looked small and puny. Scolding herself for having those ill feelings toward the man she married, Josefa pushed those thoughts deep into a corner of her mind; there was no time for that now. Right now, her only concern is Felix, not even Eddie was in her thoughts.

The door squeaked as it was pushed open, and both Josefa and Agapito looked up. It was Officer Velez and another man in a crumbled sport jacket and a badly knotted tie. He defied every image of the savvy detective portrayed on television. The detective mumbled his name and for the next half-hour, the three-way conversation faded into monotonous accusations. There were fingerprints, shoe prints, and signed statements from Felix's cohorts. Everything was nicely arranged and dropped into Felix's lap.

Josefa found herself in shock; she was numb, and she struggled to get her mind back on track. She was bewildered, lost, angry, and sad. She stared blankly at the wall even after the detective had walked out leaving her and Agapito sitting in silence. There was nothing more to do, but wait until the next morning. A court-appointed lawyer will help them sort through their private hell. Officer Velez remained with them and then politely escorted them to the door and into the dark, bitter night.

Josefa didn't remember how she arrived home. She wasn't even sure if they had taken a cab, the subway or just walked through the black cold streets of the city. All she knew was that the city was cursed. A damn city where demon-like gargoyles were perched upon the top of buildings like pagan deities admiring their subordinates, and anything colorful and bright was swallowed by its cemented blocks. Josefa allowed herself to be lured into this city, and led to believe the sidewalks were paved with golden opportunities. However, Josefa found only sorrows and horror to see her sons fall victims to its cold grasp.

She was sitting on the edge of her bed sipping a cup of tea. And it seems all her surroundings lost all sense of reality. She was living in a world where she had no solid existence; she was currently in a world of crude shadows. She placed the cup of tea on the night table and rested her head on the pillows propped against the headboard. As she looked up at the cracked ceiling, she was reminded of this pit she lived in what they called home. Through the bedroom door, she could see Agapito's shoes as he sat in front of the television watching a blank screen.

To her consolation, her daughters were around her, and she realized that since the terrible ordeal with Eddie and now this latest catastrophe with Felix, she had neglected them. Migdalia was sitting close to her while Norma fidgeted at the edge of the bed by her feet and Gisela stood against the wall, her big brown eyes wide with fear. At least, Eduardo spared them from his evilness, and for that she was grateful. It was only the males whom the monster from her childhood was after, wanting to destroy them, to make them feel deprived of her love as he felt he had been deprived.

Josefa placed her hand over eyes hiding them from the world. She recalled the Puerto Rican cop translating from the indifferent detective. There was nothing they could do about bringing Felix home. Not even a lawyer with the best record would be able to find a loophole to free her son. There was just too much evidence stacked against him. The best a good lawyer might be able to do was get a minimum sentence. However, excellent lawyers were not cheap, and were not on the city's payroll. By tomorrow morning, she knew what to expect from their city appointed lawyer, who would probably be a baby-faced college grad looking for a few cases to place under his belt before embarking in a lucrative private practice.

She rolled onto her side, not wanting her daughters to see her hopelessness. She wished Agapito would take control, and carry the weight of this problem they were facing. But, Agapito's reaction now was the same reaction he had at the precinct, nothing but blank stares. Josefa trembled in agony while her daughters massaged her neck and then pulled a blanket over her. She shut her eyes tight and suppressed the scream in her throat. She felt battered, fatigued with no strength left in her, but still, she fought back the tears. And at the end Josefa cried, and liked a hungry child; she cried herself to sleep.

Chapter Eighteen

He felt the anger boiling up ever so slowly. 'Where did it all go wrong? Where?' Agapito thirsted for a cold frosty one; even better, a strong stiff shot that would immediately rip the inner lining of his throat. He could hear his daughters inside the room fussing all over Josefa; they went in and out of the room like obedient servants. He declined Gisela's offer of tea by turning away from her without saying anything. He leaned forward with the intention of getting up and turning on the television, to do something rather than sit by himself in the living room staring at the blank television screen.

He should never have opened that door when the cops arrived. He had rights...didn't he? If only he had known the trouble that Felix was in, he would have pushed Felix onto the fire escape before opening the door. Agapito was convinced that they were all racist bastards who took pleasure in handcuffing Puerto Rican kids for the entire neighborhood to see. *Why my son and not one of those neighborhood drug dealers who slapped each other five and laughed out loud when Felix was pushed into the patrol car?* Agapito cursed under his breath.

He kept hearing Josefa's moans. She needed him, but all he had were selfish thoughts. He wanted to just run all the way back to Puerto Rico or just escape to the nearest bar and get drunk. He felt useless.

"Come back in the morning," that was the best answer the surly detective was willing to give them when Josefa demanded to see Felix. He was ashamed for the way he behaved at the precinct. Instead of acting like a man, he just hid behind his wife. They transported Felix to a jail in Queens; some place called Riker's Island, and nothing could be done until tomorrow morning. "Tomorrow is another day, just go home and get a good night sleep," that was how the unsympathetic detective ended their meeting.

Agapito was convinced that if that was the detective's son or some other white wealthy kid; things would have been handled differently. Affluent kids with daddies' large bank accounts don't get hassled. However, ghetto kids are quickly labeled juvenile delinquents and are rapidly strapped to the electric chair.

Agapito wondered where Felix was now and for the first time in a long time, he felt love for his oldest son, a love he never bothered to show before. He pushed himself off the couch and looked toward the direction of the bedrooms. Everything was quiet and except for the light in the living room, the entire apartment was dark. He glanced toward the wall clock and was surprised that he had sat on the couch for over four hours. Everyone went to sleep. He walked into the entrance of his bedroom and peeked inside. He could make the outline of Josefa's body; the blanket spread in bunches around her revealing that she was still wearing the clothes she had worn all day.

Agapito stared at the empty space next to her, and its symbolism startled him and made him feel ashamed. How ironic that the woman he vowed to take care and protect, was now alone and feeling as empty as that side on the bed. He craved to go to her, lay next to her and take her in his arms, but he couldn't...then again, it had been a long time since he did. It was not that his desires were not there, but for some weird reason he just could not. He could feel unseen walls between them, walls that would become mountains, and a fortress, which, will forever keep them apart. Agapito experienced a chill run through his body. He stared lovingly at Josefa for another minute, and then slowly went back to the couch.

Chapter Nineteen

SLAM! SLAM! SLAM! Each slam was louder, more menacing, and it shook him to the point that he was losing every sense of reality. Each bang of metal doors and screeching locking bolts engaging, suffocated him with fear. Felix felt the cold horror that snatched his sense of security and rammed the terror down his throat. His lungs swell up, and his heart raced in a furious dash that made him wince with pain. He was thrown into a cell with unnecessary brutality, and after the guards left, he dared to look around.

It was like a deranged dream, but everything was as real as the sour smelling sweat that rose from underneath his pores. He was inside a goddamn jail cell; his mind registered the fact in panic. He always imagined them as small claustrophobic cubes of cemented gray blocks with a steel slab for a bed and a toilet bowl without a seat. He glimpsed at his surroundings, and this cell was not the grainy Hollywood version, but it was a goddamn fucking jail cell nevertheless.

He could hear faint sounds from other men, and Felix began to shake. *What have I done?* He thought. *I took the life of a man who came out to be worth not more than a lousy fifty bucks.* His stupid actions cost him his freedom, his life. Worse, he brought shame to his parents. Felix buried his face into his hands and sobbed trying to remove the guilt, wondering what was going to happen to him? Would he be released on bail, or are they just going to do what the laughable cliché dictates?

Throw away the key.

Somewhere inside the bowels of his dreadful confinement, he heard another booming slam of steel meeting steel. It shattered his eardrums. *Did they have to be so loud and menacing?* Felix wanted to shout as he looked up and gulped the thick saliva that coated his throat. He needed to relax, to think more clearly. *I'm still a minor,* Felix dwelled on that revelation that eased his mind. There must be some type of leniency. He was not a criminal with a rap sheet dating back to the day he was born.

Damn, he slapped his thigh twice with anger. He shut his eyes tight, clenching his teeth with enough force that made his jaw hurt. *What the hell can I do?* He could not believe how selfish he had been, knowing what his family had been going through with his little brother. Goddamn it, this was the last thing his parents needed. His father, Sweet Jesus, he had never seen that side of his old man. His father had snatched the warrant that the police shoved into his face, pretending to read its content, when he knew he couldn't read English.

Felix knew that his father had tried to delay the process, perhaps giving him time to escape. But escape to where? Hide in the closet? Wasn't that the first place they always looked? The fire escape was on the other side of the apartment, past the living room where the two huge cops were standing, dwarfing the apartment. Felix remembered how he jumped out of bed, and his first instinct was to measure the space underneath his bed, noticing with exasperation barely three inches separated the bed frame and the floor.

He could still hear his father's voice; it was an alien voice, one that Felix did not recognize. His father sounded uneducated, like an imbecile trying to speak English and what actually came out was butchered Spanish dialogue and twisted English gibberish. However, the thing that surfaced from this nightmare was his father had shown that he cared, something Felix was not used to. At that moment, Felix realized that his father loved him.

Felix rubbed his eyes; they were dry and irritated. He let his parents down. His parents sacrificed every day without any complain, and this was how he repaid them? Felix pressed his hands to the side of his head, scolding himself for his stupidity and ingratitude. Why didn't he run out of that school, warn the other clowns and forget about making a career out of breaking into schools during Christmas holidays? However, something came over him on that night. He was possessed by the devil. He was a marionette, and someone was pulling the strings. Sweet, Loving Jesus, if only he could undo what he has done.

Felix bit down hard, trying to stop an annoying twitch at the corner of his bottom lip. He had known fear before, and fear was something he could control. Those fears he could have easily conquered, but not this fear. This fear had its personal mind and its individual heart. If Felix could see its face, he knew that it had the horrible pale face of Death, and it looked exactly like the dying face of the janitor.

He figured that at least ten hours had passed since his arrest, but it felt if he had been incarcerated for years. There was no way out of this nightmare. Felix ran his fingers through his hair and angrily dug his nails deep into his scalp. He wanted to taste the same pain his parents were now feeling. His heart shattered the second his mother came to the precinct, followed by his father. Felix sadly noted how all this trauma had visibly aged his mother. Felix wanted to run to her and hug her. He could still see the raw pain in his mother's eyes, those beautiful caring eyes that have always been there for him. He could hear the desperation in her voice, her futile attempt to go passed the cops and into his arms. She called out to him, yelling to him 'my baby', and 'my son'.

The image of her screaming and trying to release herself from the officers will be embedded in his mind forever. She crumbled onto the floor, and her body became limp. Felix tried to run to her aid, but the two officers guarding him shoved him down onto the hard wooden bench and swiftly handcuffed his legs to the frame of the bench. He felt his tears burning his cheeks and blinding his eyes, and he did not care if the prisoners around him saw his tears or quivering lips. They all had mothers, and no matter how hard or how tough they appear to be; the sight of your own mother in pain would make anyone cry.

They carried her into a room, and the door closed as soon as everyone was inside. He continued to watch, shouting like a banshee for the cops to let him go; his mother needed him, "YOU FUCKING BASTARDS, LET ME GO!" His throat was hoarse, and his heart wanted to explode. He felt tormented and craved the simple touch and warmth of his mother's love. Felix continued shouting, cursing in his hard-to-understand broken English. Then, they yanked the handcuffs from the bench and dragged him into a waiting squad car and drove him away. He did not stop screaming until a cop smacked him hard on his chest and pointed with glee at the place that would be Felix's home for the rest of his life.

Inside the bowels of Riker's Island correction facility, Felix quickly learned that when you become the property of the New York City Corrections Department, you lose all rights as a human being. You go where they take you; you strip when they tell you and spread in the most humiliating position with no questions asked or answers given. The moment you become a burden to society; you relinquish your basic human rights. You become an animal that needs to be tamed.

Now, Felix had time to wonder, what was it that clouded his judgment that fateful Christmas Eve? Was it lacked of sleep or delirium? Was it that gravelly voice he had sworn he heard murmuring in his ears? He remembered the irritating voice. It had not been audible enough to, but Felix knew it was a voice; there was no mistake about it. *I must be going mad*, Felix shook his head, convinced that he was not. It must be his imagination. Felix tried to relax as he walked back to the cot and stretched out.

"Psssst... what are you going to do now?"

Felix jumped up and grabbed the steel bars of the cell. Someone or something spoke as clearly as if a person was standing next to him. "Shit," Felix hissed, there must be another inmate playing games with him. He waited patiently for the inmate to speak again. Felix held his breath waiting in anticipation and after a few minutes of silence, he shook his head feeling stupid.

He walked back to the cot and sat on the edge, trying to persuade himself that it was his own exhaustion breaking him down.

"Yes it is nene; it's all in your head," the voice floated through his ears and this time Felix didn't bother to look around. For now, he was convinced that the voice actually came from the inside of his head.

There was calmness that came over him, and he couldn't help but picturing the inside of his head. In his mind, he was navigating through valleys of raw flesh, which dipped and rose through pulsating nerves. His inner vision kept prodding deeper into the secret place where every thought and every detail about his life was stored and catalogued. It was his private file cabinet. Felix was in a trance. He had enjoyed zoning out when he was a boy; it was his way of escaping reality.

Finally, he was calm, and that encouraged Felix to continue with his meditation. He was searching, rummaging through his mind where he knew he would find the hiding place where the voice dwells. He took a deep breath and then exhaled slowly. Can this be a sign that he was losing his mind, searching for alien voices in his head? Perhaps he was already crazy, and that would explain the actions he took on that snowy night. That night, he should have been home with his family instead in the company of losers bashing a man's head in until he died.

Shaking his head violently, Felix tried to remove the image of the dead janitor from his mind. There was no reason to go on a safari inside his brain in search of the bogeyman that kept leaving him voice messages. He stood up and yawned. He was tired, but not sleepy. He walked back to the bars and pressed his face against the steel cage attempting to see more than just the corridor and the wall in front of him. "Maybe I should get a mirror," Felix smiled as images of a movie's prisoner holding mirror through the bars of their cells crossed his mind.

"They might as well hang a sign with your name and your natural habitat," the voice smoothly passed through his ears.

Felix was no longer fazed; he was more amused at the weirdness of it all.

"When is feeding time?" Felix heard the creepy voice in his ear. *"They should have school trips for the kiddies to ogle at the big bad killer. He is deadlier than a lion, and a tiger combined, more vicious than a crocodile in the muddy swamps of Florida. Don't feed the animal or you would be prosecuted to the extent of the law."*

Felix strolled back to the cot and sat with his back pressed against the wall.

"Psssst...What are you planning to do? You can't stay here and become somebody's bitch," the voice continued with a raspy laugh. *"You have to do something for yourself...it's about time, don't you think? All your life you have been a slave to everyone's whims. When are you going to do something about it?"* the voice hammered its message, and Felix listened. *"Do you really believe that someone is going to free you?"* the voice kept on. *"Why? They have a bigger fish to fry now. Your little brother is dying, so the cute one gets the nod. My boy, the last thing they need is to save the life of a selfish brat like you. That's how they are thinking now. You know you always came last...there's no denying it. Remember all those missed birthdays and the many Christmases with no presents with your name on it. You were even the last one to receive a lousy quarter for an allowance, if there was one left. Remember when you constantly had to understand because you were the oldest one. Enough reason for them to push you to the side and let the little ones, the cute ones to have the spotlight."*

Felix held his head and squeezed hard, trying to extract the voice out. But it kept on, reminding him about all the things that he thought of once in a while. He had to be strong. Those were words of self-pity, nothing more. Of course, his parents were going to come back, there was no way they were going to abandon him like a dog gone mad.

There were far away footsteps approaching his cell and Felix tensed up. For some reason, a scene from a James Cagney movie popped into his mind. It was the scene where the officers came to escort Cagney to the electric chair. Felix lowered his head and closed his eyes praying that those steps were just guards passing by for a routine check. The steps came to a halt, and he could sense piercing eyes staring at him, and Felix could not help feeling like an animal at a zoo.

"Hey kid," a strong voice addressed him, and Felix quickly raised his head to look at them. There were two Correction Officers on the other side of the bars and Felix immediately thought that they looked like two robotic giants. Both were over six feet tall with necks the size of concrete sewer cylinders. Felix could not believe that there were ties big enough to go around those tree trunk necks. The officer closer to the cell removed a ring of keys and unlocked the door, and both officers walked in.

"You didn't eat," one officer pointed to the tray with the untouched food sitting at the end of the cot. Felix glanced at the tray trying to remember when it was delivered. Maybe it had been there before he came into the cell. "Stand up," the guard instructed, it seemed he was the talker. While his partner was just there to intimidate and to stomp away any dumb ideas that prisoners might have about escaping.

Felix saw the handcuffs on the other officer's hands. Not knowing what to do, he just stared at the metal cuffs. His chest started to hurt. He swore he could hear the banging of his heart right through his shirt, and he wondered if the cops heard it too. His mouth was dry and his lower lip twitched, and he felt that any second now his teeth were going to start chattering.

"Turn around, kid," the guard with the cuffs finally spoke. Both voices reeked with authority and an air of supremacy. "We're going for a walk."

"Where?" Felix asked, with a voice that was a shadow of his real one.

"You'll find out when we get there," the officer with the cuffs said. "Now just do as you're told and turn around."

Felix turned around; his legs were trembling, and he felt his bladder opening up. He squeezed his stomach muscles to avoid embarrassment. The cuffs were cold on his flesh, and when they clicked around his wrist, he felt less than a human being. He felt dirty, useless and he wanted so much to be able to tell these two cops that he was not what they thought of him. He was not the typical juvenile asshole; he wanted to shout in his poor English. Tell them that he was a good kid. He was raised to respect his elders, to say, thank you and please. He wanted to tell them he was an honor student in Puerto Rico and when he read a passage from a book, his teachers used to always mention it sounded liked poetry. He was supposed to be a scholar, a great Puerto Rican orator with distinguishing diplomas and medals acknowledging his intelligence. He would be the next Ramon Emeterio Betances or Pedro Albizu Campos. He felt like crying because he knew, that at this moment, these two cops thought he was just another greasy-good-for-nothing-spic.

He walked, and the two officers clutched his arms with their meaty hands. If he stopped walking, then they could easily lift him up or drag him without missing a step. He passed other occupied cells, and his ears were filled with the catcalls and the cruel laughter that came at him from those faceless men from within. He wondered how long it takes until you become complacent in a place like this. How long does it take when you become a number rather than a human being? He felt the first tear streaking down to his chin and by the time that tear rolled down his neck; he was crying in nervous hiccups.

From one of the gray cells, an inmate threw him a kiss and sarcastically motioned with a gesture of masturbating. Felix kept his teary eyes down avoiding the cells where convicts stood with their hands wrapped around the bars welcoming the new meat. Then the voice came again, and its words were comforting; caring and somehow Felix found strength in them.

"Don't worry...I'll show you the way to escape."

Felix straightened his back and sniffed all the tears out of his nose. He looked defiantly at the first grinning prisoner whom he passed. "Dumb stupid maricon," Felix spat inside the cell and he felt fearless again. As courageous as when he bashed the head of the janitor with the killing blow. *I'll get out of here.* He felt a new power within, and the voice will show him how to get the hell out.

As the two correction officers led him, Felix smiled, for in his head, he heard the voice laugh out loud.

Chapter Twenty

With an uncontrollable laughter, Eduardo roared in a delightful fit. He stomped his boots down heavily on the wooden floor of the porch. He howled with a sadistic laugh that he had waited so long to let out. He never imagined that it was going to sound as rich and enjoyable as it did now. Even his mother would be pleased at his twisted happiness.

His original plan was never supposed to be like this. It was only the child he wanted. Yet the second Josefa decided to play with fire, what did she expected…not to burn? He did tweak a bit with her husband's success from the very beginning, enough to make Josefa wonder what type of a marriage she fell into. But being the loyal wife and martyr, she decided to stand by her husband—the failure—when everything went sour. Therefore, she accepted her fate by putting all her trust in her faith. Yes, the stupid ignorant faith the living are madly enamored with. If only all Christians knew the truth about life and death, would they be so ready and willing to ignore that nobody controls their destiny, but themselves, even after they're buried six feet under.

Eduardo stood up and stepped away from the rocking chair. He paced back and forth proud of his recent accomplishment, and the latest torment he created in Josefa's life. Let her precious babalawo, her lawyers and all the doctors in the world come to her aid. Let them all take a crack at his masterful plan of vengeance. Let them all try to, yet fail to correct what he sabotaged. He glanced around the grounds around the house, still wondering Eddie's whereabouts, but he wasn't too concerned. Eventually, the boy will return. Where else could the child go? For now, Eduardo would devote his time on Josefa's other son, and on the mission to destroy the little love she still possessed toward her husband and their marriage.

"Eduardo," he heard his mother's voice beckon from the darkness inside the house, and he obediently went to her.

Inside her room, Eduardo spotted her small body in bed as thick curtains covered the window, blocking the bright yellow sun from coming in. He sat on the chair she kept next to the bed. It was a habit from her previous existence. In the old days, she would sit for hours looking out the window before settling down to sleep. Now, she just kept the chair as a reminder from her past life. His mother moved slowly, shifting her body towards Eduardo, and he noticed her transformation ever since the boy's arrival. She was a different person now. He could sense an uneasy feeling and noticed the quiet pauses whenever she spoke. She was afraid of something, as if an awful incident was about to happen. Through the black shadows, he stared at her wrinkled face; her dark freckles glowing like shiny pebbles. He couldn't help feeling sad for her.

At times like this; he wondered if he was doing the right thing. His mother made the ultimate sacrifice in staying by his side, even if she was not completely sure what was going to happen to them. *Oh, you poor woman,* Eduardo thought as he placed his hand on the edge of the bed. He wanted to touch her, but at the last second decided against it. Strangely ever since they called this place home, he had not aged. Yet he noticed that his mother aged since she departed the other world to join him. He could hear the fatigue and the weariness in her breathing, and he knew it was all because of him and his tireless obsession.

"Muchacho, you woke me up with your loud laughter," she said in a weak, raspy voice. "You are playing with fate…you know that?"

Eduardo looked away, once again feeling like a five-year-old. He tucked his feet under the chair, and hunched forward. He could see her head resting on the headboard, her loose gray hair tumbling down to her shoulders like brittle old wire. He could feel her stare, sharp and strong. He kept silent for this conversation was becoming old, especially when their world and Josefa's world were drawing closer.

"Did the boy return?" the old woman asked, but her question was just a formality. They both knew that he was still out there. And the longer the boy was by himself the more dangerous their little charade became. "I see that you're trying to ruin all the males in her life, well Eduardo you are succeeding."

Eduardo kept quiet; there was nothing his mother was not aware of. It was her vocation to keep things in perspective, regardless of how strange their lives had become.

"What are you planning to do? All this could turn out to be a disaster," she lifted herself so her back was now resting against the headboard. "This child does not belong here and now that he refuses to come back…what will be next? I forbid you to continue with this crazy experiment of yours…¿me entiendes?"

"It's too late now," Eduardo said in a low voice.

"It's never too late to turn away from a path that leads to unhappiness," the old woman sighed, squeezing her eyes with her thumb and forefinger. "Mira hijo, your father still waits patiently for us. Don't you hear his calling? Shhhhh," she placed her finger on her lips and raised her ear in the direction of the window. "I could hear his calling some nights. I'm sure you do too, but you are just ignoring them, the same way you disregard my prayers when you—when you left us."

Eduardo stared at the covered window. Almost every night he heard his father calling their names. It was a continuous voice that never ceased to stop and unlike his mother who claimed to only hear his calling some nights, Eduardo heard it all the time.

"Listen to me, Eduardo…por favor muchacho, listen to this old woman's pleas. Your actions would be forgiven. They will be cast aside, waved away as just foolishness of a child who confused infatuation with love. We could all be a family once more…the three of us once again."

"Please mother," Eduardo said with annoyance. "It's not an infatuation; don't treat me like a child. I have lived long enough to tell the difference."

The old woman exhaled noisily; she wanted her stubborn son to see her frustration. He was making a terrible mistake and all she could do was stand by his side and hope that her prophecy would reach his ears. She didn't want any part of this world; this world was his only—of his own making. But did she have any other choice? How can a mother abandon her child during the time he needed her the most?

So, here she remained with only two choices, follow the call to the boat that awaits all souls or stay at the side with Eduardo defying the rules. She knew that very soon her husband's voice would no longer be heard, therefore, unable to usher them to their rightful world. But how could she convince Eduardo otherwise? How could she make him see that this place was a place created with lies? It was a dreadful spot born of his confused mind.

"This child, he will die if you intervene in his wishes. You are fooling with his confused emotions. You understand the consequences, the punishments that will fall upon you? Son, I think it's time for us to go and let this matter rest once and for all."

"No mother," Eduardo stood up and pushed the curtain away from the window. A bright streak of yellow exploded through the room forcing his mother to shield her eyes. "The time has come for my retribution to take shape. For too many years I was the butt of everyone's joke. Not this time, finally the time for everyone else to be the butt of the joke has arrived."

"And you expect this…this behavior…this vendetta is going to bring you into that woman's heart?"

Eduardo looked down at his mother and noticed the sunlight accenting her wrinkles. She looked as ancient as the sun-baked mud from outside. "Maybe knowing that no man would ever receive her love would be my satisfaction."

The old woman shook her head. Again, she squeezed her eyes with her thumb and forefinger. She let go and looked up at Eduardo. Her eyes were red, yet there were no tears to moisten them. "Hijo, don't you see that the loss of her sons would make her love them even more?"

"It would be a wasted love; mother…for her sons would never feel that love again."

"Yes they will, Eduardo. Precisely like your love for her has never died even after so long of not being part of her world, her sons too, would always feel her love until the day that she joined them again. Only remember, her love will be their shield."

"Well," Eduardo closed the curtain and the room was befallen with darkness again. "Let them feel that love, let them feel her kisses. But just like me, let them feel it from afar and let her suffer until the day she dies."

Chapter Twenty-One

Loud, clattering noises surrounded Felix, fading in and out. Felix took a quick peek at the imbeciles around him. They were young boys just like him, nervously talking fast, only wanting to either be heard by someone or listen to their own voices. It was perhaps a way to convince them that they weren't afraid. But they were all afraid—how couldn't you be? Felix avoided staring at anyone for more than a second. He had witnessed already two scuffles between punks because they took offense at someone eyed them for just a quick moment. The correction officers marched around them barking orders.

Felix looked down at the tray in front of him. The sight of runny scrambled eggs and a sausage patty with two slightly burnt pieces of toast smeared with butter was nauseating. He had forgotten the last time he ate and to his surprise, he was not a bit hungry. Another fight began to his left, which consisted mostly of back and forth shoving, and the guards aborted it quickly. Felix sat with his head lowered while everyone strained their necks to see what was going on inside the prison's lunchroom.

The jail dining room resembled his school lunchroom, and it was not surprising that it sounded the same. Shrieks of kids, and kids like him talking loud. Cursing at others and complaining of the food that they were scoffing down as if the last time they had eaten anything was years ago.

Felix found himself sitting on a table with mostly newcomers who had arrived with him last night. The news about the arrival of a certified killer made its rounds pretty quickly among the offenders who probably were in there for petty crimes, which after a few days; they would be back in the streets among friends. Felix noticed that everyone kept their distance. His killer label probably intimidated them. Felix did not mind at all; it brought him peace of mind. His first thoughts of prison were the typical clichés and he was frightened, but now he had no impressions at all. Yes, he was still afraid, but being left alone was fine with him. He was not here to win any popularity contest. Besides, he was not planning on a long stay; the voice within him was already planning an escape from this miserable place.

Felix shifted his body on the hard chair. His butt was going numb. He took a spoon full of eggs and put it in his mouth, and the sudden taste of raw eggs made his throat clamped up. He snatched the container of milk and swallowed hard, forcing the mess in his mouth to go down and quickly pushed the tray away from him.

The kid sitting next to him looked at Felix and nodded at his own tray. "It takes time to get used to this shit," the kid said while shoving a spoonful of eggs and biting half of the toast. Breadcrumbs fell all over the table. "Don't worry bro', a few days here and this fuckin' crap is gonna taste like rice and beans."

Felix nodded and took another sip of milk. Even the milk tasted warm and sour. Another scuffle began and ended within seconds as two bulky correction officers pushed each combatant away from each other. "It happens all the time," the kid said with the ability to talk and shove the smelly eggs down his throat simultaneously. He glanced at Felix's untouched tray, and Felix wondered how long before the kid took the tray and ate his food too. "If they keep that shit up," the kid pointed with his spoon toward the two fighters. "The fuckin' CO's are going to lock us back in our cells for the whole fuckin' day."

Felix's eyes took a quick survey of the correction officers who roamed around and then at the kid next to him. The kid was maybe a year younger than him. But by his mannerisms, he gave the impression that he was an old pro inside the jail's walls.

"I'm Izzy," the kid introduced himself extending his hand like a grown man. "I know this dump very well; I've been coming here for the last two fuckin' years. Half of these pricks with the sticks already know me by name."

"I'm Felix," Felix said giving a quick shake to Izzy's hand and dropping it fast. He felt odd shaking hands with someone his own age.

"I'll be out in maybe a week or two," Izzy boasted pushing his empty tray away. Yet he still looked hungry as he eyeballed Felix's tray.

A parade of prisoners marched around them, carrying empty trays to the back of the lunchroom as groups began to gather around the tables and along the walls. Felix scanned the lunchroom feeling as if he wasn't part of the scene. He felt invisible, except for Izzy. Izzy waved at guys who strolled by, yet his eyes never left Felix. Finally, he pointed to the tray.

"Yo' you have to eat that."

"I'm not hungry," Felix struggled in his bad English.

"It's not a question of being hungry. The CO's will make you go back and keep you there until you eat some of it, even if you puke," Izzy explained in butchered Spanish. He spoke the type of Spanish, New York

Puerto Ricans spoke or Nuyoricans, as they called themselves. It was a combination of Spanish-sounding words made up with English words, Spanglish as it was called out in the streets.

Felix shrugged and looked at the guards walking around. "What are they going to do if I don't eat this? It's not like I'm going anywhere."

Izzy nodded in agreement. "True, but you see it's not much, but the sooner you finish you get to be out in the yard."

Felix looked up at the wired windows; the sky was battleship gray, and it had snowed last night. "Who the hell wants to go out there in the cold?"

"Bro', everybody! When you are locked up for such a long time…shit bro', even when it rains nothing beats going outside and dreaming of a little freedom," Izzy said still eyeing Felix's tray. "Yo', you're going to eat that?" he finally pointed to the food.

Felix pushed the tray to him and turned around to look out the window. "What do you do in the yard besides freeze your ass?"

"Shit man, you do a lot. You have your smokes, play some football, and jog around to keep from getting cold. Man anything you fuckin' want that you can't do inside the box we live in," Izzy responded between spoonful of eggs and sausages. "Plus the best shit of all, you get to air out the fuckin' smell of this goddamn shitty place."

"Freedom, nene, freedom."

Felix straightened up at the sudden message in his head. The voice came back. He looked at Izzy, and the kid was wolfing down his breakfast oblivious of the voice in Felix's head. He wanted now more than ever to go out to the yard, and he glanced around noticing that the doors into the yard were still guarded by two officers.

"When do they let you out?" Felix asked anxiously. He was now desperate to go outside.

Izzy looked up from the plate that was now as clean as the first one. He glanced toward the doorway. "Whenever those fuckin' pricks feel like it. That's one thing bro' that you gonna have to get used to. All fuckin' hours are controlled by those motherfuckers…we can't even take a shit without asking permission."

Felix stood up and walked to the windows. He wrapped his fingers around the metal mesh that covered the glass. What he could see, the yard resembled a typical schoolyard from any school from the inner city. They were all constructed the same; asphalt on lopsided ground and tall fences. The only difference was that on this fence, there were no openings. Here the fence was a strong metal fortress with armed guards making sure their deadly presence was noticeable.

Felix felt someone's presence. When he turned around it was Izzy standing with the two empty trays. "Yo' bro, if I take both trays with me the CO's might get suspicious. With bad weather like this, especially the cold they are pretty pissed that they have to go outside to make sure we behave. So anything that you do out of the normal bullshit, they are ready to put their shiny fucking boots up our ass."

Felix took one tray from Izzy, and he noticed the kid was smaller than he appeared when he was sitting down. He was surprised to see that Izzy was all bones considering the way he was eating. He followed Izzy to the large garbage cans and emptied the bit that Izzy left and placed the tray on a pile with the rest. The juvenile delinquents who filled the lunchroom were beginning to march outside. When he and Izzy walked through the doors, a cold bitter wind swooped down on them.

"Who's your little friend?" the voice teased inside Felix ears.

Stopping quickly, Felix looked around expecting to see someone. He could see the quick stares he was getting from the others as he walked toward a bench pushed against a brick wall. Izzy was not far behind, and he wondered why the sudden camaraderie from the kid.

"Well nene, everybody wants to be with a killer."

He sat down and leaned against the wall and closed his eyes, somehow the cold was no longer a factor. Felix could feel the wind rushing through him, and he tried to remember the warmth, the wonderful Caribbean heat from Puerto Rico. He could sense Izzy standing next to him. Perhaps he was afraid to break some jail code by sitting down on the same bench. Felix wished that the kid would go away.

Finally, Felix opened his eyes and stared directly at the fence. He saw the barbed wire on top, which resembled steel tumbleweed. He turned from side to side acknowledging the guards in the yard and those above them with rifles held to their waist. Then the voice within him spoke again.

"Nene, you could climb that fence quicker than a cat. I'll give you the powers to gain your freedom. You don't belong here. We both know that."

Felix turned to Izzy and stared at the kid. It made the kid uneasy and sensing that, Felix dropped his stare to the ground. "Tell me…have you ever seen anybody escape from here?"

Izzy looked at Felix incredulously, and after two seconds, he finally asked. "Escape?"

"Si, do you know if anyone escaped?"

"No," Izzy shook his head, no longer the savvy prisoner he tried to be in the lunchroom. Felix now saw the kid for what he really was; a scared punk which would probably end up dead in less than two years. "I mean bro', I have heard of dudes trying, but where the fuck can you go to a place like this."

"What about jumping the fence?"

"The fence? That fence?" Izzy shot a quick glance at the fence. "Are you crazy? Man they would shoot your ass the second they see you try."

"They can't shoot people in the back," Felix added. Convinced that regardless of what the guards would try to do, the voice will find a way for him to escape.

Izzy shook his head again. He would remember the look in Felix's eyes, and it would haunt him the rest of his life. Izzy thought that look was the scariest thing he had ever seen. "Don't even think about it, man…those maricones are not holding those rifles for anything you know. Man, let's go inside and forget about playing Superman."

Felix laughed at the mention of Superman, yet sadness consumed him. Just hearing the name of a fictional cartoon character made him think of Eddie.

"I'll make you fly like Superman, nene…up, up and away," the voice whispered.

Felix took a few steps forward, and Izzy looked puzzled. He didn't know if he should just grasp his new friend's coat and pull him back. "Hey man, where do you think you're you going?" Izzy asked, not believing that this dumb ass was trying to escape in broad daylight—right here with everyone outside and guards ready to make an example of someone. Izzy ran to catch up to Felix and pulled his arm to slow him down. Felix snatched his arm away from Izzy's grip and continued walking.

"Man, are you fuckin' crazy? Come on bro', this is fuckin' suicide."

"Sigue nene. Go ahead. Nobody could keep you here. Come on nene, up, up and away…up, up and away," the voice instigated.

The voice in Felix's head seemed to criss-cross, like a train on twisted tracks going out of control. He could hear Izzy's frantic voice telling him to stop. He could hear the alien voice assuring him of his super-human powers, and deep inside; he could hear his mother's frightened voice. He slowed down a little, but his steps still lead him in the direction of the fence. He stopped in the middle of the yard and turned around. He stared at the door by the lunchroom. There he saw the other juvenile clowns loitering around. It was true what the voice was telling him, he did not belong here. He was not a juvenile delinquent—no—he was going to be something more than just another burden to society. He was going back to his Puerto Rico and become the greatest Puerto Rican orator in the island. But how can he achieve greatness while incarcerated in a place like this with a bunch of stupid losers. He was not a loser.

"You are not a loser, nene. You are the great liberator, the great orator of the oppressed. You are more than Superman fighting for the American way. You are the Puerto Rican Super-hombre."

"Come on bro'," Izzy's voice was again in Felix's ear. "The fuckin' guards are beginning to get curious. They are staring at you, man. If you want to escape…fine, but come up with a better plan. Trying to jump a fence like that it's not a plan, but a sure way to escape right to hell."

"Nene, ¿Que pasa? Did you forget how to walk? Come on, I'll help you…it's very easy…right foot forward…left foot forward. One, two and three…up, up and away, nene."

Felix began to jog, and then escalated to a run, and soon he was in a mad dash toward the fence. Izzy stood behind, his eyes bulging out of their sockets and his lips twisted in a sour grin. Izzy heard the loud command from behind him. He heard running steps bouncing off the asphalt yard. He heard the hoarse shouts from one of the guards, "STOP!" There were screams, and nervous laughter from the inmates around him. He heard the releases of safety catches from the rifles. He could smell the fear and desperation in the air. He could see the guards above, their rifles hoisted on their shoulders poised and ready to take aim at their target. He heard himself yell. "NO!"

The guards shouted again, and Izzy heard the supplication in their voices for Felix to stop. Perhaps these guards had sons the same age as Felix. How do you shoot someone who resembles your own son? Izzy wanted to yell that information to the guards that Felix was not going anywhere, that there was no way in hell he was going to be able to jump over the fence. All they have to do is run after him, tackle him to the ground and give him a good ass whipping. Let him go until he gets tired of running. And even if he scales the fence, you just wait for his sorry ass on the other side.

Izzy heard the screams again, and the commands that Felix ignored. Then, he heard shots exploding in the yard. Quickly, his nostrils absorbed the thick smell of burning gunpowder. Bodies began to scamper away from the fence and confused cries rushed at Izzy from every direction. Thick gray smoke fogged his vision and then slowly it disappeared into the solid dark clouds. He could see Felix, still standing by the fence; his fingers wrapped tightly around the chain links. Thin lines of smoke billowed in twirling action from his back. He saw Felix look up as if he was praying to higher powers of some strange unforgiving religion. He watched Felix jump and then he just hung on the fence like a poor imitation of Spiderman.

Felix began to climb slowly and again. The shouts of guards boomed through the prison yard. Another rifle clicked and another and another until it sounded like one giant deadly click. Izzy stood frozen witnessing a firing squad execution. Then his ears were shattered by the sound of death. BOOM! BOOM! BOOM!

And Felix dropped to the ground.

Dead.

Chapter Twenty-Two

The sky exploded even before Eddie saw the light. It first appeared as a blinking dot, and gradually it grew brighter and larger until it seemed to eclipse the entire sky. It hung suspended in midair, before streaking across the sky like a blazing comet, cutting the black skies into a perfect arch. Eddie shielded his eyes from the blinding light. The enormous mango tree he sat under seemed to shudder with fear.

"That's the cavalry. It came for you and to take you to safety."

Eddie glanced quickly over his shoulder feeling a presence of the entity, he named Captain Marvel. He returned, then again, maybe he never left, but had chosen to remain quiet until there was something worth saying.

"Is that one of your friends?" Eddie asked, still not completely comfortable in talking out loud or worse at the thought that if Captain Marvel was a spirit, then why he couldn't see him?

"No, that is not another friend passing to cross the river. That's your brother, and now he's trying to right his wrongs."

Rapidly, Eddie turned to where the voice appeared to be coming from. The light was now moving smoothly across the sky. He squinted expecting to see Felix flying above him.

"That's my brother?" he said, and it came out like a question afraid of a response.

"Yes," Captain Marvel answered. *"Your brother, your big brother is running to your rescue, just like that night in the middle of Third Avenue."*

As Eddie kept looking up at the sky, he saw the light stopped and hovered directly above. Almost as if it was staring down at him, and suddenly Eddie remembered what Captain Marvel was referring to. A few months after they arrived from Puerto Rico; he was walking with Felix on Third Avenue on an errand for their mother. It was a lovely, cool evening, as they strolled through the sidewalks, mesmerized by the sights and sounds of this new, strange place. Eddie liked to always lag behind his brother. Coming out of a store, two bullies, whom he recognized from school, approached him. One of them put his open hand on Eddie's chest and held him there while the other stood behind him pulling the back of his shirt. They called him names and slapped him on the head.

Eddie was afraid, and he felt alone. In his fear, he imagined Felix was already back home leaving him to defend himself against these two thugs. He looked around desperately, searching for help among the strangers who hurried past them and dismissed them as just three young punks. There was panic in Eddie's heart and from nowhere an arm came and shoved the bully in front of him onto the ground. His partner who stood behind Eddie suddenly lost his bravery, and quickly released his grip and took a few steps back. Eddie looked up and standing next to him was Felix. In his eyes, Eddie saw an image he would never forget. Felix had the look of a lion protecting his own.

Felix chased them and like frightened vermin, the two bullies ran away not bothering to look back. Eddie stood there staring at his brother ashamed of himself for acting so afraid. Yet happy to have his brother next to him showing his strength. At present, Eddie stared up at the sphere of light above him, and the same feeling washed over him. Eddie felt safe, for now his big brother was here, and everything would be alright.

Chapter Twenty-Three

Agapito placed the phone down and stared at the living room wall. He closed his eyes and stepped away from the phone, then slowly turned and shuffled his feet to the middle of the room. A cold numbness climbed steadily throughout his body, and he gasped for air. He could feel his lungs collapsing, and he winced at a tremor deep inside his belly. Shaking him, pulling at him until all he wanted was to let gravity take control and dropped him down on the hard linoleum floor. He could feel his legs swaying first to the left, then to the right. Finally, he decided to stop moving altogether. He tilted his head up toward the ceiling, and he let out a cursed yell. An excruciating pain held him paralyzed, and he closed his eyes tight, for he refused to cry. But the emotions were too raw and horrifying, that Agapito started to heave. Empty, dried heaves that brought out a metallic taste to his mouth. His body trembled and all he could do was steady and brace himself from this inevitable, vertigo wave.

In a distant faraway place, Agapito heard moans. The moans became louder and closer until they were deafening, and then he realized why; they were his own moans. Agapito let out a scream that sounded vulgar and primitive. His knees buckled and he quickly shuffled his lead-like feet to the couch where he at last allowed himself to crumble. His son was dead. Felix was dead.

"Damn you God…my son is dead!"

Agapito buried his face in his callused hands, and allowed the tears inside them. The same hands he didn't remember when he last used them to embrace his dead son. Overpowered by a grief that rushed through him was heartbreaking. And to Agapito, those emotions were alien and not part of his persona, until now. After the tears stopped, he rubbed his face and sighed.

From outside, he heard the front door of the building getting slammed against the wall, and his ears perked up. He could hear voices chattering; he knew that it was his family returning home. Their footfalls on the wooden steps creaked loudly with crunching squeaks. Agapito jumped to his feet as he used the front of his shirt to dry his face. He wanted to run away before they came in. He needed to buy himself enough time so the redness around his eyes could disappear. His hands were shaking, and while he tried to guide his steps toward the bathroom, his legs became two useless tree trunks that refused to move.

He could hear laughter coming from one of his daughters, but he was not sure which one. 'My God,' he looked up toward the ceiling seeking the face of God. 'Have I been away from my family for so long that I cannot recognize the laughter of my own children?' The steps drew nearer and now he could hear their combined shuffle outside the apartment door. There was a body leaning against the door. *It has to be Norma, the most impatient of the bunch,* Agapito thought as he could register the muffled whining from Migdalia, and he imagined Gisela's serenity. *Damn man,* he shouted to himself with desperation. *Move toward the bathroom for Christ's sakes.*

Agapito didn't want them to find him in the middle of the living room with red eyes. He heard the keys scratching on the door lock. The familiar clicks penetrated his ears as one lock, two locks and later the third lock opened up. At last, Agapito could move as the door hinges squeaked open. Agapito took one step towards the bathroom, but not before he saw the door swung open, hitting the love seat.

"Do you have to slam the door like that?" Agapito screamed at the first person that came through; it was Josefa. Their eyes met and he quickly saw Josefa's alert eyes reading him.

"Agapito… ¿Que pasa? Agapito! ¡Dios mío! ¿Que pasa?" She charged at him as their daughters surrounded her.

They all stared at him, and Agapito cursed at himself for staying in the living room. He lowered his head and rammed his hands inside his pockets while his brain thrashed in search of the right words. Once again, he possessed knowledge that would catapult the entire family into chaos, first were the cops arresting Felix and now the announcement of his son's death. He straightened his back and looked at Josefa, her eyes two piercing balls of mistrust staring back at him.

"Someone from—" Agapito clamped up and took a deep breath, and he suddenly realized he had forgotten who had called. He did not know if it was a police officer or someone from another city department. He did recall that the caller was business-like and professional; the voice possessed authority.

"Niñas go into your room," Josefa glanced at her daughters and then back at Agapito. She was still standing in the same spot; probably afraid to move and lose the strength she knew she was going to need.

"I'm hungry, ma'," Norma headed toward the kitchen.

Josefa grabbed Norma's elbow and swung her around. "Are you deaf, young lady? The three of you go into your bedroom right now."

The girls looked at each other acknowledging that there was

something very serious in their mother's voice. Her tone made them shudder. It was a side they seldom saw and when they did, they knew it was wise to listen and obey their mother's wishes.

Agapito watched his daughters walk past him. One by one they marched to their room, and each of them took their turn to ogle the redness in his eyes. He let out a deep breath, and then turned away from Josefa, trying to walk out of the living room. However, he didn't go far; he felt Josefa's grip, hard and aggressive on his forearm. He turned around and faced her. There was no hiding the truth. There was no more time to delay the awful news that placed another heavy load on their already over-burdened shoulders. He scratched his forehead trying to find the words. He bit his lower lip with hesitation and then he sighed. He lifted his head and finally looked at his wife, and saw the face he fell in love with during a better time, which now seemed so far away.

Josefa's face and expression were stiff and rigid. "Josefa," Agapito mumbled, exhaling once again bad-tasting breath. "Felix…Felix is dead," he blurted out the words.

Even twenty years later, when Agapito would recall those difficult days in his lonely studio apartment, he couldn't remember if Josefa cried. All he could remember was how he crumbled in her arms, and he cried for her, or perhaps he cried only for himself.

Chapter Twenty-Four

Bewildered by his surroundings, Felix looked around. It looked like he was back in Puerto Rico. *But that's almost impossible;* he frowned, although he was under a gorgeous Caribbean sky. Yet that aspect didn't remove all the events that transpired in what it appeared to be just seconds. How was he transported to Puerto Rico? He didn't have any knowledge to answer that question. But at this moment, he was not too concerned how he got here; his actual inquiry was if this place was really Puerto Rico.

He felt the humidity and the sweat on his forearms, and he could hear the old nostalgic singsong of the coquis, bringing him sweet childhood memories. But was all this real? Eddie was standing before him, and that confused Felix even more. He must be dreaming; Felix tried to remember the last thing that happened to him. He was shot trying to escape from jail. That much he remembered; the pain of the scorching bullets penetrating his body was still fresh in his mind. Nevertheless, here he was, standing with no bullet holes or gushing blood. *I must be dead*, Felix thought with no indifference about it.

Once again, he looked down at Eddie. Felix placed his hands on his brother's shoulder. Although he wanted to hug his little brother tight, Felix just stood there studying Eddie's face. In contrast to Felix's actions, Eddie wrapped his arms around his big brother and gave him a strong hug and began to cry.

"We have to hurry," Captain Marvel announced.

Felix heard the voice, and he was sick of voices inside his head.

He became annoyed and pulled Eddie away from him. "Eddie, stop crying everything is going to be okay," Felix said.

"And where the hell is that voice is coming from?"

Eddie was a bit hurt when Felix pushed him away. Yet, being familiar with Felix's moodiness, he dismissed it. "That's Captain Marvel," Eddie said as he sniffed hard and rubbed his eyes. "He's helping me."

"What are you talking about Eddie? This is not a dumb story from one of your comic books," Felix snapped, but seeing new tears forming in Eddie's eyes; he moved closer to his brother and patted him on his arm. "Sorry, Eddie, but who the hell is Captain Marvel?"

"He's my friend. He's making sure that I get back home and not to go anywhere near the man on the boat by the river."

"What?" Felix frowned while shaking his head. "What are you talking about and what's this place anyway?"

Eddie shrugged and then touched the lower branches of the mango tree that moved slightly by a gentle breeze. "I don't know…it looks like Puerto Rico, but I know it's not."

"How did we get here?" Felix asked, as he turned around to take a very good look at the strange place.

"*This is the crossroad of worlds,*" Captain Marvel said solemnly.

Felix spun around at the sound of the voice, surprised that this was not like the voice he heard at the prison, this voice was around them. Eddie shrugged at his brother and smiled.

"*Do not be alarmed, Felix,*" Captain Marvel articulated. "*You are safe here for now. But we have to hurry if you want Eddie to return home.*"

Looking over his shoulder, Felix tries to follow the voice that echoed from different directions. "Eddie this is weird," Felix said as he walked away to a huge root that protruded from the reddish earth, and sat down. He leaned against the mango tree and motioned his brother to join him. "Eddie, come here," Felix patted the space on the root next to him. "What is going on?"

Eddie sat down and pointed straight in front of them. At first, Felix saw only darkness, but then his eyes adjusted, and he could see a house not far from where they were sitting. It was a typical Puerto Rican house seen all over the mountains. It had the familiar old zinc roof that crowned the shack and a wooden porch that sagged to the left. The outside walls were constructed with cheap unmatched wood and painted in a blue-green color, which was now peeling. Felix could make out a shape on the porch; it was the silhouette of a person rocking leisurely on what seemed to be a rocking chair. Through the black night, he could see the glossy shine of the mahogany chair.

"I was there at first until I didn't like the guy anymore," Eddie said getting up from the root and walking across the clearing underneath the tree. "I thought he was my friend."

"Just like the voice?" Felix asked sarcastically.

Eddie turned back, a frown wrinkling the top of his nose. Felix noticed that his little brother had aged—he was still small for his size—but there was something in his eyes that made him more mature. "You don't get it, Felix, the voice that you hear is Captain Marvel, and he is my friend, not like that spooky man out there." Eddie walked away from the safety of the tree and stood at the edge where the grass grew and the fresh dew made his toes shiver. "I don't know how I got here, but I know I can't stay here. I don't belong in this place."

Felix leaned forward and stared toward the house. "Do I belong here?"

"*Nobody belongs here,*" Captain Marvel intervened. "*This is only a crossroad; see it as the meeting point of two worlds that cannot share their existence for too long. The traveler when arriving to this point must quickly continue his journey, and that's to complete the crossover to their destination. Staying here for too long, would prolong their journey and risk their soul to be trapped in limbo forever.*"

"But aren't you here," Felix jumped to his feet. "Why haven't you made the crossing?"

"*I have things that must be attended too before my departure.*"

"How do we know you are not in a cohort with the person that dragged us here?"

Captain Marvel chuckled, and it sounded rehearsed. "*You could say that I'm here as a protector.*"

"You're the protector of what?" Felix smacked his lips, not sold to the idea that the voice was selling. He cursed under his breath and quickly Captain Marvel became silent. "Come on, we can't stay here." Felix grabbed his brother's arm. "We have to find a way out of this shit."

"There's no other place to go," Eddie squinted at the darkness around them, wondering if Captain Marvel left them because Felix's rudeness. "I have walked all over this place, from one end to the other, and we are stuck here surrounded with water."

"What about that man you saw on the boat? I'm sure he knows a way out of here. Shit, he could even take us across to the other side."

"What other side?" Eddie asked hearing the desperation in Felix's voice.

"*Eddie doesn't belong on the other side!*" Captain Marvel made his presence known. *"By Eddie getting inside that boat, he will be lost in limbo with no place ever to call home, and his rightful place in his destiny will be forever lost."*

"You don't make any sense!" Felix shouted pointing an accusing finger at the direction he heard the voice come from. Again, Felix took hold of Eddie's arm and began pulling him away from the mango tree. "Come on, let's go and have a good talk to the man aboard the boat. You could see him at least...right? I don't trust damn voices that refuse to show themselves. How the hell do you think I got here? Because I was dumb enough to listen and trusted a voice just like your friend."

"Please Felix, just listen. You are putting your brother in grave danger. Stop thinking only about yourself Felix, your brother deserves better than that. Ask yourself this question...why are you here if it is not to help your brother?"

"Let me tell you, I already have enough of your shit. For all I know, you were the damn voice that lied to me in prison. Come on, when are you going to yell 'up, up and away'? Ah, Mister Captain Marvel...shit, man you are a fucking joke."

"Enough!" Eddie screamed. "Felix, that's enough. I trust Captain Marvel, so you better trust him too."

"How can I trust someone, when I can't even see him? What makes you so sure that this voice is not another conniving spirit that wants to harm you? For all we know we both could be in a coma. And the sooner we leave together, the quicker we will wake up in some hospital in New York.

"He would have harmed me already," Eddie protested.

"Maybe he's the devil, trying to fool you, trying to deceive you."

"Or maybe he's an angel who wants to make sure we both get home," Eddie defended the voice.

"Oh Jesus!" Felix exclaimed throwing his arms up in disgust.

"We could stay here for as long as you want, Felix, the two of us locking horns for eternity. If that's what you like, very well then, we both have the time, but not Eddie," Captain Marvel said not hiding the annoyance in his voice. *"Let me explain…Eddie is here against his wishes, and unless he gets to where he belongs, he will remain in a coma for the rest of his life. His earthly body will eventually perish, but his soul will linger with no place to call home. That's the reason it is very imperative for him to leave this forsaken place, but I won't lie to you Felix—time is running out. Very soon the time that controls Eddie's life won't have too much power in this purgatory."*

Taking several steps, Felix stopped on the spot where he thought the voice was coming from. There was a presence of something that went through him. It was an entity not human that moved within him like a strong wind.

"Your mother is trying to break through," Captain Marvel whispered, and this time Felix knew the voice's message was for his ears only. *"She's trying to bring Eddie back to his home; she's fighting for him the same way she fought the day he was born and was near death. Your mother is a strong woman, and she's fighting the evil obsession that caused the entire trauma in her life and the lives of everyone. But she needs help, and that help could only come from you Felix. You are the wild card the evil spirits did not foresee. You are the unwanted ingredient of the poisonous soup that has been brewing too many years now in the mind of a sick and confused boy."*

As he stared into the empty space in front of him, Felix took a deep breath, trying to comprehend what was happening around him. There was something in the voice that made him believe. He glanced at

Eddie and again; he couldn't help to see how vulnerable his brother looked. Captain Marvel saw that too, and Felix was convinced this enigmatic voice probably came to Eddie masquerading as a superhero, for it knew that Eddie would only trust and understand that type of a person. In addition, Felix realized the voice was on their side. Felix nodded toward the voice. Ensuring it that he was willing to do whatever was necessary to take Eddie where he belonged. And that was home, back home in their crammed railroad apartment where his cheek could receive their mother's kisses.

"What can I do?" Felix asked as Eddie joined them.

"Something very simple," Captain Marvel said. *"All you have to do is write a letter home."*

Chapter Twenty-Five

She stared straight ahead, her eyes tracing the frost that gathered around the windows. It seemed like centuries had elapsed since Gisela happily adorned the windows with the Christmas decorations. She lay in bed listening to the soft snores of her sisters, Migdalia and Norma. Gisela was envious of them; she too wished to sleep that soundly and peacefully. However, her sleep was troublesome, filled with voices, and she was afraid to close her eyes.

She turned on her side, wrapping the warm blanket tightly around her. There was a fear in her and now more than ever she was petrified of the dark. She could feel the surrealistic insanity that had fallen over their lives; it felt like a bad dream. *My God*, she begged; she wanted to just be able to close her eyes and sleep, but she was not able to. Every attempt just brought her the same images of Felix hovering above her. He was a spirit now. Just two days ago he had pushed her out of the way because he couldn't wait to use the bathroom. Her big brother, with his sad eyes and quiet nature was now a lingering memory.

From outside the bedroom she could hear the low voices of her father and her uncle Enrique. Gisela could still picture both men the same way she left them, sitting around the kitchen table with a bottle of rum. Both men's eyes were red, no longer because of the tears they had shamelessly shed, but because of the rum, they both poured down their throats. In her curious, silent way, Gisela watched them. Becoming agitated at every shot they took and the way they slammed the glasses hard on the table. They were getting drunk and it was all because of Felix's death, and Gisela could not comprehend their actions. In her innocent mind, this was no way to react to such a tragic event. Then, it dawned on her; alcohol was not only reserved for celebration. It usage was also to numb you from sorrow and despair. Even her mother received a dosage of something; perhaps to accomplish the same thing the men were doing—escaping reality for a while before facing it again. Tia Sara had poured two spoonfuls of medicine inside a glass of water and after stirring it thoroughly she made Gisela's mother drink it. Gisela had no idea what it was, but it quickly calmed her mother. She remembered the way her mother sat quietly on the couch staring into the wall while mumbling solemn prayers to herself and dabbing her eyes on a handkerchief already soaked with tears.

Gisela shifted again and settled on her back as the murmuring voices outside her room soothed her. Her eyes began to close, and she put up a halfhearted fight, but finally, she succumbed to the comfort of sleep. A sensation quickly ambushed her, and she felt herself floating in mid-air. There was a feeling that overpowered her, as she danced with the freedom of a ballerina pirouetting across the silky sky. She was flying now, and she could see the rooftops of buildings. A strong whistling breeze came from her left, blowing her hair away from her forehead. It filled Gisela with an overwhelming and powerful sensation; it was euphoric. A kaleidoscope of colors and shapes blinded her and at that moment, she didn't ever want to return to her ordinary life. She was within a dimension free of worries, absent from tears from drunken men and quiet sobs from a tortured woman. There were no brothers at a death's door in something called a coma, or brothers who already crossed that threshold that separates life from death. In this world, she danced among the clouds, and the dark-blue sky was not menacing, but magical.

With an undeniable determination, Gisela flew high, desperate to reach her destination before time ran out. Below her, she marveled at the power of large bodies of water from mighty oceans where whales somersaulted in giant leaps, and deadly sharks moved swiftly upon weaker prey. She could spot islands that resembled dotted green and brown specks blemishing the roaring foaming sea. Disregarding the powerful desire to stay in flight, she began to descend. The foliage of the island was thick and wild. It was just as she imagined the Garden of Eden would look like as she hovered sixty feet from the ground. There was a strong scent of flowers that rose to meet her.

Sneezing at its intoxicating perfume, Gisela noticed it lacked the certain delicacy to which she was accustomed. It assaulted her nostrils in a way that made her suspicious of the island. She glided over bushes and crooked paths of red dirt, which resembled dried rivers of blood. There was a house, at the distance. An orange sun seemed to guard the area like a sentinel. While a soft breeze moved a rocking chair on the dilapidated porch, and she sensed danger and evil, and Gisela wanted to leave quickly. Even so, there was magnetism in the air that drew her closer to the house. To her left, she caught a glimpse of two figures running toward the blue-green painted shack. Their steps were hurried and desperate. Gisela felt the presence of another person, but she was not able to see him. Him? She frowned at that impulsive thought that appeared in her mind, why did she feel so strongly that all three individuals were males?

She followed them from above, and Gisela could see that the first one leading the pack was a young boy. Eddie's face popped into her mind, and she decided to float down closer to get a better look. Gisela gasped as a tightness wrapped around her throat, and a chill attempted to take over her soul. *My Sweet Lord,* she almost screamed at the dense air around her; the two runners were Eddie and Felix. Frantically, she called out their names, anxious to get their attention. She didn't know how, but she knew danger awaited them. Something evil was hiding—calculating the time to ambush them. She knew they must be warned—they must keep away. Gisela screamed out her brothers' names. Her throat was becoming hoarse. Her shouts were losing the volume that she so desperately needed to alert them of the graveness of their situation. "My Sweet Jesus I'm losing my voice!" Gisela hysterically shouted to herself.

A strong gush of hot air came from behind her, and it whirled her with a strength that threatened to crash her against the trees' branches. She clenched her teeth and began pumping her legs while flailing her arms wildly trying to lift herself above the powerful wind. A black fog blinded her and looking down all she saw were pitch-black clouds. She waved her hands furiously, trying to clear the clouds away, but to no avail.

Another strong breeze rushed through her, dispersing the black clouds, revealing a spotless blue sky. It was the bluest color she had ever seen. It was an ocean of ultramarine ink, and it slowly enveloped Gisela in a claustrophobic embrace. To her relief, as soon as she began to panic, the blue sky began to disperse. Once again, a strong wind came from her left, carrying her to the place she feared the most—the shack with the rocking chair on the porch.

Without warning she found herself standing inside a bare room, its walls and floor were constructed in unpainted wood. It had the distinct aroma of a recently built room. Gisela could even smell the metallic odor of nails and fresh sawdust from newly cut wood. In the middle of the floor was a composition notebook, and she ran to it. It was her notebook, and she felt embarrassed to find it out in the open, out where anyone could see it. She would've been mortified if anyone read her poems and her stories about lovely maidens waiting to be rescued by dashing young princes.

She snatched the notebook from the floor and quickly looked over her shoulder. She wanted to make sure that she was alone and there were no prying eyes to see her hiding place. Yet when she opened the notebook, Gisela noticed the penmanship was not her own. She smiled, relieved that it was not her notebook after all. It was silly of her to think that it was when she knew that her notebook was still hidden underneath her mattress.

With a frown wrinkling her forehead, she flipped through the pages, and what she saw was strange. Childish crude writing covered the entire notebook. The words were all strung together with no grammatical structure to separate the thoughts. She tried to read the words, and it felt clumsy, like singing a song out of tune. What at first seemed like rambling letters, slowly the style and the rhythm of the words began to make sense.

"This is poetry" Gisela whispered to herself.

There was pain in the words and a haunting loneliness that disturbed her. There were so many emotions that poured out from those words that had been written with a badly sharpened pencil. Even so, there was eloquence, which contradicted the childish print. Perhaps a child genius labored to write them or maybe a poorly schooled adult's attempt at scholastic achievement.

Gisela sat down on the floor and placed the notebook on her knees and continued to read. It was the story of a lost little boy with a lot of ambitions, but sadly, he never reached his goals. She read and she wept for the sadness, and loneliness was devastating. She was engrossed by the writings and compared it to her own writing, but this little boy's narrative was extraordinary and real. Gisela suddenly realized that those words could not have come from a child's imagination. They were too deep and raw, and they told a story of a broken heart.

Gisela flipped through the pages of what she was sure to be a detailed, chronological journal, written in a poetic form. She stared at the words and at the smudges where the pencil lead grazed the hands of the writer. She imagined the writer—just like herself—laboring over a blank piece of paper, searching for the right phrase to bring these emotions to life. Gisela stared at the poem, took a deep breath, moistened her lips and began to read the poem again. This time she read it aloud.

"I live in a dream world...
where nobody knows me.
I live in a shell...
of dreams and sorrows.
I fantasized about lifestyles...
of huge make believe castles.
I do not know myself...
and nobody knows my inner self.
Am I trying to fool the world?
Or trying to fool myself?
I live in a dream world...

and I'm lost and confused.

Should I climb gigantic mountains?

Or walk through soft meadows?

I don't know...

what life is all about.

I'm crestfallen and sad...

I feel like crying.

My soul has been beaten...

spit out to the hot sun.

Should I crawl under a rock?

Or just ignore everything that orbits around?

I live in a dream world...

what should I do?"

Gisela closed the notebook and held it against her chest. She cried softly and looking down she saw a yellow pencil with a broken eraser. She picked up the pencil, opened the notebook and began to write. She felt totally at ease writing in this stranger's notebook. She was deeply touched by what she had read and wanted to help the writer find the peace and love she sensed he craved. As Gisela wrote, her tears smeared the words that came from her heart. She then closed the notebook and fell asleep, not realizing that her tears also smeared the crudely written name across the front of the notebook. It read—Eduardo Angel Santiago.

Chapter Twenty-Six

It was still dark outside, and the wind rattled the old windows bringing in a cold draft into the bedroom when Norma nudged Migdalia. Migdalia turned the other way, facing the wall and mumbling her annoyance. Norma poked her again, this time harder.

"What do you want?" Migdalia said through clenched teeth.

"Shhhhh, not so loud," Norma said putting her finger in front of her lips. "You don't want to wake everybody up."

"So why are you waking me up?" Migdalia asked, as she turned to glare at Norma.

"Gisela is acting funny," Norma shook Migdalia by the shoulder. "Come on, we have to see what she's doing now."

"Maybe she's doing what everybody is doing now…sleeping."

"No," Norma shook Migdalia again, this time rougher. "You don't understand; I've been up for about one hour already, and I saw Gisela walking around. She was looking for something."

"Maybe she was looking for a quieter room," Migdalia lifted the blanket over her face. "Now can you let me go back to sleep."

"But she was walking around in the dark."

"Because she didn't want to bother anyone…she's more considerate than you. Now could you please leave me alone?"

"She was walking and then she was behaving like she was flying…you know with her hands stretched out in front of her. She was turning around like she was a plane or one of Eddie's comic book heroes."

"Well let her, at least she's not waking up the whole building, like you are. Now leave me alone before I punch you."

Norma stared at the door of their bedroom, wondering what Gisela was doing in the bathroom. For the past hour, she saw her sister's behavior turned into something very strange. Or, as she put it to Migdalia, *'weird'*. Under heavy eyes, Norma had watched Gisela toss and fuss until eventually caught her curiosity. It wasn't that hard when their room was not big enough to hold three beds, and all three sisters were practically sleeping on top of each other.

Faking her sleep, Norma witnessed when Gisela slid out from her bed, remove a notebook from underneath the mattress and went to the bathroom. Norma knew about the hidden notebook. She had even read some of the stuff her sister had written. At first, she was going to show it to Migdalia and have a good laugh at Gisela's expense, but after reading the poems and stories she had decided against it. She even felt bad about invading her sister's privacy.

She knew Gisela woke up early even on Saturdays, and wrote inside the bathroom. Maybe Migdalia was right, Gisela was very considerate about other people's feelings, and that is why she closed herself inside the bathroom. Probably, the devastating news about Felix and the anxiety over Eddie's condition prompted Gisela to put her emotions on paper.

However, something kept gnawing at Norma telling her that there was something unusual happening.

Norma looked at Migdalia and, by her snores, knew her sister was immersed in her beauty sleep. She thought about waking her up again, but decided that if something was wrong with Gisela, she had to deal with it by herself. She swung her legs from underneath the bedspread and tiptoed toward the bedroom door. She peeked inside her brother's room, where her uncle and aunt slept.

Norma heard the squeak from the bathroom door. She wanted to run back to her bed and not let Gisela see her, but she was already passed her brothers' room. The only way to avoid being seen was by running back to her bed. Even so, if she ran, not only was Gisela going to see her; she would possibly wake up the entire family.

Norma followed Gisela's silhouette, as it moved from the bathroom to their room. Her steps were precise, almost premeditated as if Gisela knew what spot would make the floor creak and therefore, must be avoided. When she went through their parent's room and inside Felix and Eddie's room, Norma held her breath. Just when she was about to tell Gisela that she was going to the bathroom, her sister walked past her with her eyes closed and tears streaming down her face. Gisela held her notebook pressed tightly against her chest; a lead pencil was sticking out from between the pages of the composition pad. Norma watched her sister pass oblivious to her presence. Gisela went into the room and stopped in front of her bed; she lifted the mattress and slid the notebook underneath. She then pulled the quilt and very quietly slipped back to bed and wrapped herself within the quilt. Her eyes remained closed, and tears flowed freely down her face.

Norma stood frozen, enveloped by fear. She didn't have any clue about Gisela's mannerism, but a creepy feeling washed over her and even though six other people inhabited the apartment, she felt completely alone. She wanted to scream. No longer wishing to be considerate—Norma wanted to scream and awake the entire city. A sudden tremble shook her, and there was an eerie feeling of something sharp going up and down her spine. A panic rose from a place way deep in her belly and like a foul vomit, it almost exploded out of her mouth. She clamped her hand over her mouth. Silencing whatever was trying to jump out of her. Her heart was no longer beating, but rather it was speeding, and she closed her eyes tight and clenching her fingers into fists she commanded herself to settle down.

She forced herself to walk, fighting her fears and the confusion over Gisela's bizarre actions. Norma stumbled inside the room and stood between her bed and Gisela's. If anyone looked at Gisela, they would have seen the perfect picture of someone soundly at sleep. However, Norma knew that through the darkness, there were glistening tears running down her sister's face. Norma heard and read things about people walking in their sleep; she even knew the special name for it, 'somnambulate', yet she had never known her sister to be one of those people. Maybe everything that was happening was the cause of Gisela's peculiar behavior. Wasn't Gisela the sensitive one? Her mother has always said that. Norma knew that Gisela was not like her. Norma was a fighter and kept her emotions locked, and Migdalia had her own mean conceited streak.

Norma forced herself to climb into bed, maybe in the morning everything would fall into its right place. The quilt felt warm and comfortable, and she shifted her body into her familiar, relaxed position.

Then Gisela moaned, and Norma's ears prickled up. Her sister was talking in a low murmur, and Norma strained to unscramble the unintelligible sounds. Gisela was repeating one word, over and over and it was difficult to determine where the first syllable began and where it ended.

There were soulful sobs that separated the words her sister kept repeating. Norma was afraid, now more than ever, and she tried to hide her face under the quilt. She needed to ignore Gisela's craziness. But how can you ignore something that's happening less than twelve inches from you? She yanked the covers from her face, lifted herself on her elbow and stared at Gisela. She wanted to shake Gisela and snap her out of the nightmare. She sat up and lifted her arm ready to smack Gisela and force her to wake up, but stopped.

She remembered that you were not supposed to shock someone in Gisela's condition. Instead, she nudged her shoulder a bit and waited to see if Gisela would at least move. Nothing. She nudged her again, this time a little stronger, and she could imagine Migdalia waking up and wondering why was she trying to wake everyone up. Damn, Norma cursed under her breath, maybe she was the one going out of her mind.

Norma slid out of bed and sat at the edge and leaned closer to Gisela. The mumbles from her sister, thank God, had stopped and even though dried tears still streaked her cheeks; she was no longer sobbing. Gisela was peacefully asleep, just like Migdalia and everyone in the apartment, just as she too should be. Norma shook her head feeling silly and stupid. She began to rationalize what had just occurred, trying to convince herself that maybe all this was the product of her overtaxed mind that desperately needed sleep.

She stopped staring at Gisela, swung herself back into the bed, and eased her head on the soft pillow, pulling the quilt up to her neck. She closed her eyes and pushed all the nonsense from her cluttered mind and came up with better things to think about. She forced herself to daydream—no—even forced herself to fall asleep. Norma felt her breathing slowing down and beginning to keep a soothing rhythm with her heartbeat.

Norma smiled; she could stay here, under her nice warm covers over her head resting comfortably on her fluffy pillow and listen to the magic of life re-creating itself. Yes, she could stay like this forever. Sleep caressed her. Norma could feel her body relax. She finally was falling asleep. Then, there were moaning sounds beginning to filter through her sleep, climbing steadily in the surrounding dark and in her mind. Norma dismissed those moans as pleasurable exclamation points of her newly found sleep, but then she realized those sounds were not her own. The moaning sounds came from Gisela.

Norma opened her eyes wide, and the sounds stopped abruptly. Then the singsong mumbles escaped from Gisela's half-closed lips. It was the same word or words she had repeated before. This time Gisela mumbled the words over and over and in between sobs, she sniffed hard. Norma shot out of bed, no longer able to control herself. She shook Migdalia not the least bit concerned if her sister screamed out in anger.

"Coño," Migdalia cursed lifting herself on her elbows and turning her head to give Norma a dirty look. "What the hell is wrong with you?"

"Migdalia, wake up," Norma nudged her sister's shoulder, shaking her hard.

"Dios mio, I'm up; I'm goddamn up thanks to you. Now what the hell is wrong with you?"

"It's not me, there's something wrong with Gisela," Norma said glancing quickly at her other sister.

Migdalia lifted her head and stared at Gisela for a while. She then turned to Norma and gave her a bewildered look. "There's nothing wrong with her, unless you have something against people sleeping."

"No," Norma said knowing that she had to explain herself because it seemed Gisela was sleeping peacefully. "She was sleep walking and crying and mumbling something that I didn't understand."

Migdalia rolled over to her back and propped her pillow higher against the headboard. She rubbed her eyes, removing the sleep still behind her eyelids. She turned and looked at Norma; her gaze seemed to be a silent accusation. "Maybe she was having a bad dream," Migdalia smacked her lips with the air of superiority.

"But she was sleep walking," Norma protested, hating the fact that Migdalia was dismissing her.

"How do you know she was sleepwalking? You can't really see her eyes in the dark; I mean she's not a cat that you could see their eyes bright and yellow."

"But I was next to her, and I spoke to her," Norma said as her words shot out rapidly trying to convince Migdalia of what she had witnessed. "You should have seen her; she just walked by me like I was not even there."

Migdalia raised her eyes to the ceiling and slid down inside her thick comforter. "Ay, Norma, what's so strange about walking in the middle of the night? Maybe she had to take a piss."

"Okay, she was coming out of the bathroom," Norma conceded. "But I tell you, her eyes were closed shut tight, just like when you're sleeping."

Migdalia sighed and shrugged. "So what, she didn't want to talk to you, maybe she finally got enough sense to ignore you...the same way I should be ignoring you."

"She was carrying a notebook," Norma blurted out, desperately trying to defend her allegation. "And without even looking at me, she put it underneath her mattress."

"Gisela likes to write," Migdalia said with a prudish smile. "She hides a notebook where she writes poems and stories."

"What?" Norma jumped into a sitting position pretending that she didn't know.

"Gisela likes to write," Migdalia repeated herself. "Didn't you know, you Miss Snoop Around?"

Norma frowned at Migdalia's enjoyment at her expense. She could not believe that she was not the only one that knew about Gisela's notebook and her secret hobby.

"You see," Migdalia continued, loving the rubbing she was giving Norma. It was her way to make sure that Norma knew her place. "You are not the only one that snoops around in other people's business. I knew about Gisela's little habit for a long time."

Norma plopped on her back and turned her eyes to Gisela. She then looked down at the spot where Gisela hid the notebook. But something was not right; she felt it in the air and no matter how self-important Migdalia felt now; Norma sensed something greater.

Outside a cold angry, wind gained strength and rattled the old windows. A chill produced goose bumps on their arms. They were both fully awake now, yet they remained silent staring at their walls plastered with pin-ups of the latest young heartthrobs from the television and recording industries. The two sisters heard the words and mumbles that came from Gisela, though her body was still and her lips parted slightly. Norma looked quickly at Migdalia questioning with her eyes if now she finally believed her. Migdalia sat up slightly and took brief glances at Norma and then at Gisela.

"What is she saying?"

"I told you," Norma said, relief coating her words. "That's what she was doing when she came back from the bathroom. It sounds like she's calling someone—"

"Shhhh," Migdalia raised her hand at Norma with authority.

"*Babalawo ikú epe a* Eduardo…*Babalawo ikú epe a* Eduardo…*Babalawo ikú epe a* Eduardo," Gisela chanted and the air became frigid.

"What the hell is that? What the hell is she saying?" Migdalia asked with fear in her voice, as she leaned over, the comforter slipping away from her shoulders. She absentmindedly shuddered in the cold.

"Now you believe me?" Norma threw the quilt away from her body and swung her legs until she was sitting at the edge of the bed.

"Wake her up," Migdalia said and again with heightened fear.

"Don't you know anything?" Norma shot a quick annoying look at Migdalia then returned her attention at Gisela. "If you wake up someone in her condition the person could go crazy," Norma added not sure if that was true, but enjoying the control she now possessed.

"Nooooooooo," Gisela moaned as tears streamed from her closed eyes. They streaked in twisting little rivers all over her face, soaking the pillow underneath her. Gisela twisted her head from side to side, then lifting her chin and dropping it down hard against her chest. Her body was twisted in painful-looking contortions, and she raised her upper torso upward and her shoulders flew almost out of their sockets. Norma and Migdalia watched in horror, yet they were frozen, unable to move or even scream to alert their parents.

"*Babalawo ikú epe a* Eduardo…*Babalawo ikú epe a* Eduardo," Gisela's chant grew louder. Many years into their adulthood, Norma and Migdalia could not understand why no one woke up on that dreadful early morning.

Gisela opened her eyes, no longer chanting or crying, but serenity seemed to cloak her. She sat up in the bed pushing the quilt away from her body and depositing it on the floor. She lightly touched the floor with the tip of her toes. With a tiny push forward, she put both feet on the floor and stood up, her eyes vacant and distant. She turned around, giving her back to her sisters, and with one robotic motion; she lifted the mattress. She removed the notebook and sat on the edge of the bed. She opened the composition pad where the pencil marked the spot and took the pencil and began to write. She never looked down at the lined pages, and she never looked at her sisters who watched her with both fascination and fright.

Gisela stared blankly at the ceiling above as her hands moved rapidly through the notebook. Despite the dim light of early dawn, she was writing in flashing motions with no hesitation or pauses.

Then her hand movement came to an abrupt stop, and the pencil broke in half. Both pieces fell upon the floor with a muted thump. The broken halves of the pencil bounced twice and rolled under the bed.

Gisela stood up, slid the notebook under the mattress and then stared out the window mesmerized by the howling wind outside.

Norma and Migdalia saw a small smile form at the corner of Gisela's mouth, and comfortably lay down on her bed. Ignoring the quilt that was on the floor, she curled her body in the middle of the bed and in seconds was fast asleep.

Gisela slept until the morning was bright, and the sky was a passive blue. And for the rest of her life, she had no recollection of the event that occurred that night.

Chapter Twenty-Seven

"Everyone has a purpose in life. The least significant one sometimes ends up with the most important task in the universe."

Felix stared toward the house looming about sixty feet in front of him. His little brother was standing a few inches from him, and he could hear Eddie's choppy, dry wheezing. Even though Felix could not see the other person, the constant sound of the voice reminded him that it was not just he and Eddie on this journey. It was still difficult to fathom what was going on, and he wondered if all this was a lucid dream. However, when reality bit hard, it assured him that this was not a dream. It was wild; there was no doubt about it, but surely, it was not a dream. It was as real as the hot sun that baked his back into blisters right through his shirt.

"Everyone has a purpose in life. The least significant one sometimes ends up with the most important task in the universe."

He was already cranky and pissed off. With disgust, Felix spat on the ground. He was tired of hearing that dumb message from the ghost or whoever the hell it was that Eddie called Captain Marvel. The closer they got to the lopsided wooden shack, the so-called cloak and dagger mission—as the voice had put it—became more laughable.

The voice had conjured up a plan, but it was still not clear what that plan would be. They were to enter the house without being seen, and then gain access to a notebook supposedly under the bed where the big bad monster slept. Eddie had taken his time to educate Felix about this horrible monster, which after Felix got a glimpse of the individual, it turned out to be some sick looking man. To Felix, this boogeyman would not even frighten a fly, and he posed no threat at all.

They remain inconspicuous, hidden by tall blades of grass that surrounded the house, waiting for something. Yet Felix had no idea what. For some reason, it seemed that Captain Marvel was the commander responsible for this mission. Felix passed his fingers through the thick grass. It had the appearance of a soft green carpet from afar, but up close the blades were hard and sharp; each blade felt rubbery and fake. He could see large brown spots along the grass, and each blade ended in brittle blackened tip that resembled smoldered candlewicks. Besides the odd texture of the grass Felix realized, there was something missing. However, he couldn't figure what it was until he snapped one of the grass blades in half. The grass didn't have that wonderful aroma, which Felix loved and always associated with the color green.

Felix snapped another blade and brought it to his nose; it had the awful odor of something rotten and foul. He spat upon the ground and wiped his hands hard on his jeans. Eddie came to him looking anxious, yet there was gladness and a sense of relief that shone through his wide eyes. Felix wondered, was Eduardo's notebook the key to their escape? He also wondered if both, he and Eddie would be going home together, though something in his gut told him otherwise. Felix needed to figure out where he was and why was he here? The one thing he was sure of was that he was dead, but his only concern now was to bring his brother home and hopefully end his family's suffering. After that, he will gladly face his destiny without fear after his task is complete, and his little brother is out of danger.

"Are you okay?" Felix asked Eddie, taking his brother's hands and squeezing hard. They were moist and cold even though they were under a suffocating hot sun.

"Yeah, I'm okay," Eddie nodded as he nervously licked his lips while looking at the house with dread in his eyes.

"I still see him on the porch," Felix pointed at the figure of a man sitting motionless on the rocking chair. "How are we supposed to enter the house with him there?"

"He has left his body," Captain Marvel announced. *"His spirit is traveling to the other world, but we have to hurry because he could return with no warning."*

"What?" Felix turned and grabbed Eddie by the shoulder, holding his brother back from the house. He fixed his eyes on the spot where the voice had come from. He felt uneasy about Eddie's situation. It was not so much that he did not trust Captain Marvel; he was mostly apprehensive because it was just a voice. Who's to say that this was not the same voice that egged him on into escaping and getting himself shot like a rabid dog? Nothing made sense since he felt his spirit erupt from his dying body as it crumbled in the cold prison yard. He had also heard a voice in that fatal Christmas night when he killed a man. Were these voices all one in the same?

Felix leaned and whispered in Eddie's ear. "Your friend Captain Marvel sure comes out as Mister-Knows-it-all. How can you trust him? He might be leading us into a trap."

"He could hear you," Eddie said gravely. "He is just trying to help us; I trust him."

Felix looked around hoping that this crazy character that Eddie had named Captain Marvel would make himself be seen. "Just kidding…I'm only kidding, Eddie. Tell him that I'm sorry to doubt him."

"*Don't worry, Felix,*" Captain Marvel said, the sound billowed in the wind. "*When you are old as me, you developed a thick skin. It takes more than just juvenile mocks to insult me.*"

There was a sudden silence between them, even the breeze became still. "*It's time to get Eddie back home,*" Captain Marvel said and Felix took a deep breath and lifted himself above the grass and followed Eddie.

They reached the side of the porch, and Felix felt an intense heat rising through his shoes from the edge to the grass, near the reddish dirt. Eddie was already climbing the steps to the porch when Felix felt a strong grip upon his arm jerking him back, before he touched the dirt under his feet.

"*You cannot walk along that path of dirt!*" Captain Marvel shouted.

Felix looked down at the reddish dirt. He was puzzled for all he could see was small black pebbles and wiggling worms burrowing in and out. He turned around in a complete circle. "Why can't I walk on this dirt?" Felix didn't hide his annoyance in his question. He was beginning to resent the constant warnings and strict commands of someone whom he couldn't see. "Eddie just did…damn you're really a pain in the ass, you know."

"*I'm just trying my best to protect you and help your brother return to his world.*"

"Who the hell made you our savior?"

"*I understand your suspicions*" Captain Marvel was now close to Felix's left ear, forcing the boy to lean away. "*But if you don't trust me, please trust your brother. For his age, he possessed incredible wisdom. He knows I'm not here to do any harm...to either one of you."*

"Okay, so why can't I follow Eddie? If I can't follow him, then how the hell am I supposed to go inside the house and get my hands on that precious notebook?"

"Stop thinking like a human," Captain Marvel said with a touch of humor in his tone.

Felix's forehead wrinkled as he shook his head, baffled now more than ever. "Stop thinking like a human? How the hell am I supposed to think... like you? A bodiless boogeyman?"

"Exactly," Captain Marvel responded ignoring Felix's mock. *"You are no longer the person you believe you are. Unlike Eddie, you have crossed both worlds. You belong here and the sooner you believe that, the sooner you can adapt yourself. You see, for everything you lost, including your life, entering this world awards you uncontested powers."*

Staring at the spot before him, Felix was convinced that in order to see this Captain Marvel, all he had to do was to stop thinking like a human. But how was that possible?

"I will tell you this Felix; I promise you that after Eddie returns to his life, I will make sure that you find the right path. There are a lot of loved ones, family members that are aware of your arrival. They wait for you patiently, to welcome you to their world...my world, and now it is also yours. It is the world that we have all known during our human existence as the Afterlife. Don't worry; your loved ones will wait for you, for there is no concept of time to this world. Time is not measured by the same formula as in the world for the living. Days, hours, minutes are not part of our vocabulary. However, in Eddie's world, even though he is here, his life is still controlled by his own time. Our only concern is Eddie's return to his previous life. If we fail

Eddie, my friend…he will be forever damned in this place. It will become his private hell through all eternity."

"Who are you?" Felix questioned with words no longer laced with anger or suspicious, but with an understanding of what was on his plate. "I know you are not Captain Marvel," Felix laughed a little, and Captain Marvel chuckled as well.

"You're right; I'm not…I didn't even know who Captain Marvel was until Eddie told me. But I sensed from your little brother that Captain Marvel was a safe image, one that he could trust. Eddie was scared and lost when I first encountered him, and I knew I had to gain his trust, so I became that symbol. He needed to follow me to avoid the deception of the angry, jealous souls trapped in this pagan world."

"But Captain Marvel? I would have guessed he would have chosen Superman instead."

"When I came to him at first, of course he was startled; he was confused. But when he heard my voice, he thought of the character of Captain Marvel. He described to me the attributes of a fearless adventurer who befriended a young boy, about his same age, also trapped in another dimension."

"So now you are a superhero?" Felix asked.

"Your brother loves to live around the fantasy world of his fascinating comic book stories. There's nothing wrong with that, on the contrary, because of his rich imagination this ordeal has been easier for him to deal with. You see Felix; your brother still believes that this is all a dream. He thinks he's dreaming and part of the ultimate comic book."

"You didn't answer my question…so are you pretending to be a superhero?"

"To satisfy your curiosity, no, I do not fancy myself an adventurer. But Eddie does. And if that's what it would take for his release from this horrible world, well,

then I can assure you that yes, I will be the superhero that Eddie believes I am."

Felix turned and saw Eddie already standing at the porch waving frantically for him to join him. It must have taken a great deal of bravery and determination for his kid brother to stand next to the man who has become the boogeyman in his world. "So okay Captain Marvel, how can I get there from here if I can't step down this dirt path?"

"Do not think like a human being."

Felix looked intently at the red dirt; it was the color of crumbled adobe bricks. He could tell that if he passed his hands through it would feel rough and hot. He ogled the ground closely, and he could see thin billows of smoke snaking out from its depth. There was something under that maggot littered soil that frightened him, and he averted his eyes. The swirling smoke had a bewitching hypnotizing effect. Felix did not want to be drawn into the smoke so instead he looked up at Eddie and closed his eyes. *Do not think like a human being,* he kept saying to himself, repeating Captain Marvel's words and believing them to be a life-saving catechism.

"Go on Felix, your brother awaits you…time is running out for him," Captain Marvel whispered and Felix felt an assuring pat on his back. The touch felt good and soothing and provided newfound strength for Felix. Now he understood; everything was clear. He was no longer human; he was currently a spirit like them. Felix felt his body lose gravity. He reached into the sky with outstretched arms. To his amazement, his entire body followed his arms. He smiled as he flew across the sky, and the reddish dirt was no longer an obstacle keeping him from the porch. Everything was possible now as he flew to where Eddie waited for him. Felix shouted with relief knowing that Eddie was going to be safe and able to go home.

"Up, up and away," Felix roared and laughed as the wind blew his hair back. He landed clumsily on the porch to Eddie's admiration. He glimpsed at the man in the rocking chair, and Felix thought he looked ill as he followed Eddie inside the house. The extreme heat inside the dark room hit Felix unexpectedly; he felt his throat close. He winced and sweat began to gather in his eyes. Eddie was already inside the tiny room. Felix watched as his brother lifted the thin mattress from a cot and pulled out an old worn composition notebook tied with rubber bands. Eddie turned around and offered the notebook to him. Felix took it and examined it closely. Behind him, he felt the presence of Captain Marvel, and all at once the room seemed to close in. This unseen presence seemed to seep through the walls filling the room with anxiety.

"We have to hurry up, Felix. Even the house does not approve of our company," Captain Marvel warned.

"It's just a house, an old pathetic little shack," Felix tried to sound tough, but his words were laced with panic.

"This house and the entire place were built by weak desperate spirits. But just like Eduardo's mother they have no power unless Eduardo is in full command. And as you could tell, Eduardo is occupied by other matters in Eddie's world."

"Where's the witch?" Eddie asked his eyes piercing at the wall in front of him trying to see through to the other side where Eduardo's mother dwelled.

"She's still there," Captain Marvel nodded toward the wall. *"But no harm will come to you, as long as we hurry."*

"Okay, so let's start," Felix began to remove the rubber bands from the notebook, each twisted band dropping toward the floor. He opened the composition pad where a pencil had held its spot. A swirling mist reached inside his nose, and he sneezed. He grabbed the pencil and took a deep breath wondering how do you begin a message that is supposed to travel to another world? He let the dull point of the pencil rest on the blank page. A slight vibration ran through his arm, and the pencil tapped into what seemed to be Morse code. After that it began to move at first in short hesitation, gradually gaining speed. Felix felt his hand move automatically, and he felt the hand of another person guide his own as it wrote. It was the hand of Captain Marvel.

The pencil moved, from left to right. Felix saw his hand traveling in quick flashes, in stages of shutter-like speed and then another hand appeared on top of his. It was an older hand, and fear surfaced and his heart beat loudly while his lips trembled. Then he remembered the message from Captain Marvel, 'do not think like a human being', and steadily he settled down. Felix wrote rapidly, the pencil moving as swiftly as a conductor's baton. When he finished, two pages were covered with lines and lines of zeroes and ones and to his surprise, he understood the message that was written in one of the oldest languages in existence. Felix let the pencil drop and when it hit the floor, it broke in half and lazily rolled underneath the cot. Felix exhaled in relief and seeing Eddie's contemplative eyes he winked at his little brother.

"You did well," Captain Marvel patted Felix on the shoulders and then gave him a smile. And for the first time, Felix saw the face of Captain Marvel. It was the face of an old man, which looked like an older version of the man on the rocking chair.

Chapter Twenty-Eight

They huddled together on the edge of the bathtub. Migdalia stared at the notebook Norma removed from under Gisela's mattress. They were both fearful; it seemed silly, even funny for them to be afraid of a simple notebook. It had taken Norma a long while to remove the notebook after both sisters decided to look and see what Gisela had written. The notebook felt warm to the touch and Norma just wanted to drop it, instead she handed it to Migdalia. Why were they acting like this? What could possibly be so important and at the same time so frightening about some silly notebook that Gisela uses to write her poems and corny fairy tales? Now as they shivered inside the bathroom, they both hesitated before opening the pad.

Migdalia bit her lips and braced herself. She felt Norma's body heat, and she took a deep breath and opened the notebook. They promptly flipped through the pages filled with Gisela's neat handwriting. They came across two blank pages, and both looked at each other, feeling like two idiots for getting all hysterical until Migdalia turned the next page, and their eyes fell upon lines and lines of zeroes and ones. Two pages were covered in those strange arrangements of zeroes and ones. They looked at each other in bewilderment.

"We should tell mami," Norma said and for the first time in her life, she was not so fearless.

"Tell her what? What is all this?" Migdalia asked flipping both pages, back and forth, feeling stupid that this nonsense caused her to be this frightened.

"I don't know what it is, but we should show it to mami," Norma kept staring at the notebook.

"What are we going to tell her?" Migdalia shut the notebook and waved it in front of Norma. "Look mom, we couldn't sleep so we decided to snoop around Gisela's things."

Norma glared at her sister, and snatched the notebook away. "Look, we both know what happened in there, maybe all these numbers mean nothing to us, but maybe it will make sense to mami."

"Ay Norma, now I feel more stupid than anything. I should have punched you in the nose when you were trying to wake me up."

Norma studied the pages, carefully scrutinizing each line, searching for some hidden meaning, something that would make Migdalia see the urgency to the situation. Two minutes ago, Migdalia was cowering like a frightened child, but now she was back to her normal obnoxious self.

"You know," Migdalia stood up and took two steps toward the direction from the door. "I'm going back to bed and leave you here by yourself. If Gisela or mami gets up, I don't want to be involved with your dumb ideas."

"They are not dumb ideas," Norma said, her eyes glued to the last page of the notebook. "What do you think about this?"

Migdalia rolled her eyes and then looked at where Norma's finger was pointing. Migdalia squinted closely and the uneasiness she felt before returned within. On the last line where the zeroes and ones ended she saw in plain writing what appeared to be a message written in haste. She knew without a doubt that it was Felix's handwriting, but how was that possible? Migdalia didn't know, but she knew Felix's penmanship.

As children in Puerto Rico, Felix had a problem learning and writing his alphabet, their mother assigned Migdalia to help him. For the next four to five years, it was her job to make sure Felix wrote his letters according to the sentence, and when to differentiate the use of capital or lower case letters. He had a bad habit of constantly using the lower-case letters even at the beginning of a sentence. Plus, being left-handed, his letters slanted to the right margin. Gisela's writing was neat. The letters were straight and carefully executed, almost the mirror image of a typewriter. It was impossible; it couldn't be, but what she and Norma were staring at was the distinct handwriting of Felix. The grim message that the slanted, all-lower-case letters spelled out convinced her that something was terribly wrong. Migdalia's hands trembled thinking that the notebook held the answers to all their questions. Migdalia read the message again, first to herself and then out loud.

"He wants him; he wants Eddie. Hurry up or Eddie will die. Babalawo, iké epe a Eduardo. Bendicion."

Then, something in the bathroom moved. There was a knock at the door and then slowly the door's lock clicked, and it swung open crashing against the wall.

Migdalia and Norma ran out of the bathroom, hurling the notebook against the wall, where it bounced off the cabinet mirror and fell on the ground with an ugly thud. They stumbled inside the dark living room. Norma crashed hard against the love seat by the front door, while Migdalia wrestled with the heavy curtain that separated the living room from their parent's bedroom. Migdalia panicked feeling giant hands fondling her and the more she turned to keep them away, the further she became tangled in the cloth.

She grabbed something that felt solid and menacing on top of her, and she pulled down, bringing the curtain and its rod to the floor with a loud boom. From behind, Norma rammed her in the middle of her back and both sisters screamed in horror. Something was attacking them—that much they knew—and now they didn't care who they woke up or who else found out about the notebook. They thrashed violently on the floor tugging wildly at the curtain and struggling desperately to get back on their feet.

Agapito jumped to his feet, from the couch where he had fallen asleep, the alcohol still fogging his mind. Confused and startled, he yanked at the curtain while lifting his arm with his cocked fist ready to strike. Josefa ran around him, grabbing his arched arm to keep it from coming down. She pulled him back, and they both fell backwards. Agapito cursed; his arms flared viciously, and he staggered to his feet.

Enrique and his wife Sara came running out from Felix and Eddie's room, their eyes swollen by sleep and their mouths shaped in perfect petrified 'O's'. Migdalia was hollering. Her screams were hoarse and inhuman as she rolled across the floor with Norma pressed hard against the frame of the threshold. Migdalia was finally able to get to her feet. With eyes wild with terror, she kicked furiously at Norma, who was still tangled inside the curtain.

"Stop it! Stop it!" Josefa yelled as she clutched Migdalia's shoulders, shaking her from side to side. "Dios mio, stop it."

Migdalia stopped and stared blankly at her mother. Her lips were cold, and they shivered and tears began to form and fall clumsily on Josefa's arms. She wanted to tell her mother everything that had occurred; from the time Norma woke her up, to Gisela's strange chanting and writing in the dark, to Felix's handwriting. 'How can that be, mami?' she wanted to scream for answers. Felix is dead. Felix is not coming back. Felix will never write his name in his funny slanted manner, with his hand twisted in a way that just by looking at him, it seemed painful. Migdalia wanted to tell her mother everything that was clouding her troubled mind, but she couldn't. Her lips moved to form words, but her tongue was held captive and all she could do was make mumbling incoherent sounds. She looked around; blinking to adjust to the light that someone turned on.

Migdalia saw her father's blood-shot eyes staring at her. Peeking above her father's shoulder was Tio Enrique, also with blood shot eyes, stifling a yawn with the back of his hand as Tia Sara kept her hand over her mouth. On the floor, Norma was beginning to get up, and finally; she was kneeling on one knee, and her hair was untamed. Migdalia could hear Norma wincing silently in pain.

Helping Norma to her feet, Josefa asked sternly "What's going on? The two of you come here," Josefa started to lead them to the living room, but Migdalia was still afraid of the notebook and of Felix's cryptic message. She felt her mother's soft hand rubbing the back of her head and then Josefa pulled her in a motherly embrace. "Come on," her mother said in her reassuring voice. "Don't be afraid, everything is okay. What happened to you two and why are you up so early fighting like animals?"

Migdalia and Norma looked at each other neither one wanting to be the first to reveal what had taken place. They stared at each other wondering how can you retell reality from what seems like a horror story. What was supposed to be their mother's reaction when awakened in such a disruptive manner?

"Gisela was acting crazy," Norma blurted out.

"Now what does Gisela have to do with you two rolling and screaming in the middle of the floor?"

Norma jumped to her feet quickly and waved her arms in front of her, understanding her mother's rage. Her mother was thinking that her, and Migdalia was fighting. "No mami, it's not what you think, we were not fighting." She wanted to laugh and actually; she did. However, it was a morbid laugh, and Norma put her hand over her mouth silencing her laughter.

"In that case, if you two were not fighting, what was all that screaming and kicking?" Josefa was now looking at her daughters, and because of Norma's insistence that they were not fighting and Migdalia's silence, she was sure that both girls were telling the truth.

They sat on the couch. Agapito dismissed the early-morning disturbance to be the nervous energy of his daughters and left Josefa and the girls alone and walked into the kitchen. Tio Enrique looked around remaining for a few seconds in the living room and after feeling awkward he mumbled something to his wife, and both retired into the room leaving Josefa and the girls by themselves.

"We were running out of the bathroom," Norma started speaking, and she was thankful that they were alone and could tell their mother everything. It was best to say what was in their mind better in private without everyone staring at them. She took a deep breath, and a quick glance at the small hallway that led from the living room to the bathroom. Feeling safe, without hesitation, Norma blurted out the early-morning events. At first, the story seemed scary and dangerous, but now in the light of a new day and standing in the safety of her surroundings; it was just plain, stupid and corny. However, the second she told the story again, the fear returned.

Norma watched her mother intensely. She was searching for any sign that told her that her mother believed her.

Josefa turned to Migdalia. "Why are you not saying anything? What's your story?"

Migdalia shrugged and stared at Norma. Josefa noticed the nonverbal communication between her daughters, and she knew that something was wrong; it was not like Migdalia to stay quiet and let anyone take control of a story.

"Where's the notebook?" Josefa asked, and once again watched the silence that went back and forth between Norma and Migdalia.

"It's still inside the bathroom; we threw it when we ran out," Migdalia said staring into the wall of the living room. She glimpsed swiftly at Norma and then looking toward the direction of the bathroom; she shuddered. It was not lost on Josefa of how afraid both girls were about returning inside the bathroom.

Josefa stood up and walked into the bathroom; she felt her daughters' eyes on her back. Entering the bathroom, she couldn't escape the cold feeling that seemed to drip from the pink-painted walls, and quickly she was reminded of her aunt's burning back on what seemed to be a long-ago afternoon. She glanced about the room and lying across the floor under the sink was the notebook. She bent down and took the notebook. It was an ordinary composition notebook with Gisela's name written neatly along the line across the front cover. She opened the notebook and glanced through the pages filled with poems. She knew about her daughter's passion for writing.

Josefa smiled, poor child; all along Gisela thought that nobody knew, when, in fact, her secret was no secret at all. She felt bad about holding this private notebook in her hands, and she wanted to walk to her daughter's room and just put it back. But what if something here linked together the family's chain of events? What if Norma and Migdalia's wild tales were not the ranting of two overly emotional girls? Josefa said a soft apology to Gisela and flipped the pages until she came to the last two. The second she saw the zeroes and ones her heart stopped, and she gasped. The writing transported her back to the time she met Francisco, the old *babalawo*. The method of writing she saw in Gisela's notebook was identical to that the priest used when he conversed with the *Santeria* gods and spirits.

Did Gisela also converse with the same deities and spirits? And if that had been possible, was the spirit Felix's? Josefa closed the notebook and exhaled, trying to vanquish the fear that clutched tightly around her heart. She went back to the living room and sat down with her daughters. For a moment, Josefa searched in her mind for the rationality of the mysterious circumstance that surrounded them. For a long while all three sat in silence, then Josefa stood up, still holding the notebook and instructed Norma and Migdalia to go back to bed. "It's still early. There's a lot to do today."

Josefa watched her daughters get up, and as they marched to their room, she called out to them. "*Niñas,* and do me a favor, keep this quiet for now. Gisela does not have to know what happened last night and this morning. I don't know what to make of this, but one thing I know, this is very serious."

Josefa opened the notebook and then shut it with a loud clap. "There's someone who will know what to make of this," she said. "Yes there's someone who will know," Josefa added, but she was no longer talking to her daughters, but talking to the aura that she felt was inside her home. She smiled, and that smile made the presence within the walls very afraid.

Chapter Twenty-Nine

The Santeria priest flipped the pages of Gisela's notebook back and forth, carefully studying them. Francisco hummed to himself, and he smiled at Josefa. And she returned his smile noticing his easy grandfatherly gesture. She was glad that she had come to him with the notebook.

The babalawo leaned forward and like a blind man reading Braille, guided his index finger slowly through the neatly written ones and zeroes. Josefa watched closely, feeling a bit guilty that at this very moment, Agapito was making arrangements to bury their eldest son, when she should have been there also. But the circumstances arise by this notebook were too important to be simply ignored. She pushed that guilt away. She knew in her heart that if she didn't want to lose another son, this was the path that she must take.

Francisco tapped on the notebook and looked up. Josefa straightened her back and leaned towards him. "There's a lot of power here," Francisco said nodding his head. "Besides your son Felix, there's another person there that is doing everything in its power to bring Eddie back. Felix mentioned him as someone by the name of Captain Marvel. Does that make any sense to you?"

Josefa thought for a moment, and just as she was about to say that she didn't know, a vision popped into her head. Yes of course she knew. It was the last comic book Eddie bought when she took him to the candy store. Their excursions to the candy store became a Sunday ritual. Eddie woke up early with her and attended Mass. He enjoyed walking with her along the quiet sleepy streets, and he carried a shopping bag filled with the empty soda bottles he collected during the week. After church, they would shop along the avenues. While Josefa bought bread, bacon and eggs to prepare breakfast, Eddie would go next door to the candy store and cash-in the empty bottles for comic books. He emerged from the store with the comics under his arm and a smile that could light up the gloomiest day.

"Si, Captain Marvel is a cartoon character from one of the comic books Eddie loves to read," Josefa said. "But I don't understand, that's just a cartoon, a silly cartoon that only exists in the funny books."

"Well to us Captain Marvel is just a silly cartoon drawing, but to your son; he might be as real as you. By this writing, by this message, Captain Marvel is a spirit. Someone who is helping him and making sure that Eddie returns to you and back to this world."

"Who sent that message?" Josefa asked even though she knew that the words written in the notebook were definitely those of Felix. "Did my son write it?" Josefa swallowed hard. It was too difficult to be sitting here asking questions about the whereabouts of her two sons as if they were safe somewhere across the street. "Could you communicate with them?" Josefa added, now sounding desperate.

Francisco rubbed his chin, and his forehead became a canvas of wrinkles. All his years practicing the old African religion, never had he encountered such forces and powers. He read the message over and over since Josefa handed him the notebook, and the message was clearly understood. Any priest with less experience than him would have been able to understand the cryptic message. Even so, it was not only the message that was fearful, but also the consequences if no action was taken.

"Mira hija," Francisco took Josefa's hand, patting them. "Oye esto, Eduardo is desperate now and desperate people do desperate things. That's what makes him at the moment more dangerous, more unpredictable."

Josefa nodded, understanding very well what the old man was telling her. She felt Eduardo's presence inside her home. God, she shivered. How long has he been inside her walls? How many years has he been manipulating her life? "So what do you see in that message?" Josefa asked bracing herself.

"I see Felix's confusion and his determination to make amends. Felix is not like Eddie. Eddie probably sees this as some comic book adventure, unlike your oldest son that understands what has happened to him, he knows the consequences. He's still confused by what he is dealing with, but this Captain Marvel is making him see the entire picture, and that is a big plus. Felix knows that Eddie's safe return is in his hands and his chances to succeed are excellent. You see; Eduardo never counted on Felix to reach what he always felt was his safe haven. He was confident that the life Felix was involved in would keep him away. Eduardo never thought that Felix entered his world. That was something that happened without his knowledge."

"So if Eduardo was not responsible for Felix, then who was to blame?"

Francisco looked up from the notebook. How can you tell a mother that sometimes their little boys grows up to be confused dangerous human beings, victims of their own stupidity?

"I don't know," he lied. "It is not clear how Felix got there, but the most important thing is that his presence in that world will make a big difference in securing Eddie's safety."

Josefa closed her eyes and combed her hair with her fingers. "Ay Dios mio," she mumbled. "I can't take this anymore, no puedo mas."

"Mira Josefa, I know that you have been through a lot, pero oye mi hija, everything is going to turn out for the best. With this message from Felix, he gave us the key to Eddie's return. We just have to act quickly and for the love of God, hija, you have to be strong—stronger than you have ever been.

Francisco returned his eyes to the opened notebook. He studied it for a while and continued talking. "It seems that Eduardo had become more arrogant about this entire ordeal. The poor soul has become intoxicated with his new powers in the spirit world and just like a man who becomes drunk and feels he's invincible the same thing has happened to Eduardo. He is no less a fool now than when he was alive, but his new abilities blind him from seeing what is right and what is wrong. His mother tried to warn him, but the poor woman allowed her love for her son to deceive her; she jumps at her son's every whim. The sad thing is that you cannot really blame her; the woman always felt responsible for her son's weakness. She is a mother and true martyr."

Josefa flinched, wondering if Francisco's words were also meant for her. Was she also trapped in that martyrdom of motherhood? Did she also feel guilty about Eddie's sickness? Was she also responsible for Felix's death? Why was she here inside this place that contradicted her Catholic upbringing? Didn't the Bible warn against the acceptance of other gods? *'Those who run after other gods will have nothing but trouble. I will not pour out offerings of blood to those gods. My lips will not speak their names.'* Were not those the words of God in Psalm 16? Wasn't Francisco a believer of many gods and rituals of the oldest religion brought to civilization from the dark jungles of Africa?

Josefa felt confused and angry. She lowered her head and closed her eyes searching for a sign to assure her that she was doing the right thing. Most of all, she wanted to know for sure that God not only approved of her decisions, but was also lighting her path. Josefa looked up at the old man and forced a brave thin smile. There was so much to ask, so much she needed to know, but the words escaped her and all she could do was sit there surrounded by visions of her two sons in a land where no human being belonged. "With Felix's message," Josefa's voice shivered. "Can we save them?"

Francisco shook his head sadly. "We could bring Eddie back. However, with Felix…his destiny has already been chosen."

Josefa let out a small cry. 'My God,' she chastised herself. 'What kind of mother sits in a room with ancient African artifacts while one son is slowly dying alone in a hospital while another son is cold inside a morgue?'

The high priest reached out and took Josefa's hand caressing her fingers and removing the coldness from them for he knew her pain. "Oye mi'ja, for the good of your sons you cannot give up. You can't blame yourself for the acts of an evil deranged man. Let me read to you what Felix wrote, and then you would see the beautiful young man you gave birth to. You should be very proud of him."

Josefa dabbed her eyes and then rubbed both cheeks, removing the tears. "Go ahead, señor, tell me what my son wrote and let's bring my little Eddie home. Go ahead, señor, there's nothing in this world that's going to keep me from them."

Francisco smiled and began to read Felix's words disguised in the numeric language of the African tradition. "Mami, if you see Eddie now you'll scream with disgust. He is covered by a layer of mango juice and barefooted. He looks like a pig—un pordiocero—the way you always call us when we are dirty and in need of a bath. I want to say I'm sorry; I feel so bad to make you, and everyone had to deal with my stupidities when your hands are already full with Eddie's sickness. Please mami, I hope you forgive me, but enough about me; I cannot be selfish, always thinking of me. I'm sure with el Señor Francisco, after we bring Eddie back, we could have our little talk then, but for now let's concentrate on Eddie. Besides time is running out, and this old fool who Eddie calls Captain Marvel is pushing me. He feels that some sickly stupid man who is snoring on a rocking chair can harm us if he wakes up and finds us inside his room writing in his smelly notebook. The notebook smells like something died inside its pages. If it were up to me, I would not even touch the damn thing, but if I don't write this, Eddie will never go back to you, that's what I know and nobody has to tell me. I'm the only one that's capable to touch this notebook, the only one that's capable to write the message your friend will be able to interpret. I understand that only a spirit untouched by the times and law of this place, can do what I am doing, so I guess that means I'm a spirit now."

Francisco stopped reading and looked up at Josefa expecting the woman to be in tears, but she was not. She was sitting upright, leaning slightly toward him. He looked down again at the pages and continued as a strong wind shook the windows, and Josefa watched the bared branches from the trees bend like thin long arms.

"This man wants to hurt you, yet I feel sorry for him; we all should feel sorry for him for he is very confused. Maybe a few prayers and some candles would lighten his black soul. But still he must be defeated. He has ruined not only your life, but also every male who gets close to you, and that includes papi. And sadly after this is over, so will your marriage. I'm sorry to tell you this, but I have no choice, I must tell you everything that's coming into my mind. If I don't write this, Eddie will be worse than dead, he will stay in that coma forever. Not like me, I'm part of this world, and Captain Marvel promised me that he would make sure to put me on the path where I will join everyone in our family that is here. Hope grandma' does not pinch my cheek the way she used to always do."

Josefa smiled and shook her head; she felt Felix close to her. She could not recall the last time she hugged Felix or simply sat next to him and talk to him about everything important in his life. She exhaled loudly. Part of her wanted to tell the old priest to stop reading for it was too painful, and she no longer wanted to feel that hurt, but another part of her wanted Francisco to continue. She already lost one son to this demon from her past; she was not going to let him take another one. "Siga señor, please go on. Do not let my tears stop you, for these tears are not of pain anymore, but anger and if Felix has a way to beat this—to beat Eduardo in his own game—then let's do it. So go ahead señor, keep reading the words of my child."

Francisco nodded and started to read again. "Our time is very precious now, Captain Marvel keeps pushing me, and Eddie is just looking at me, the way he always looked when he knew the answer of a question. Here is what you must do. Eddie must be cleansed of Eduardo's touches, if not, it doesn't matter what you and Señor Francisco do; Eduardo will always be in control. Captain Marvel tells me to prepare. Eduardo is going to know the second the cleansing begins. He's going to feel it, and he will fight; he will fight with everything he has to prevent losing Eddie, which in turn will make him lose you, you mami, forever. You have to remember this is not about Eddie or me, but you; that's all he has ever wanted, the people around you, are just pawns for him to use and discard as he pleases. But no matter what mami, no matter what, you must not give in, not even if my soul is used to bargain for Eddie's life. Mami you cannot worry about me anymore; I'm no longer part of your world, but Eddie is. He is the one that must be removed from this Godforsaken place."

Francisco paused; he was exhausted and a trembling inside his body made him feel uneasy. There was evil surrounding them, and he felt his orisha, his Santeria god, settle within him to protect him. He tried to be inconspicuous while he cleared his throat, but even that did not fool Josefa. She noticed the slight change in his demeanor, and she could sense the nervousness in his gestures. Francisco smiled at Josefa, again trying to give her the assurance and the strength she needed. From this moment on, Eddie's survival depended on their combined strength and faith.

Josefa stared at him and he looked back, his eyes penetrating hers. Francisco saw strength in the depth of her brown eyes that he only saw just a few times in his life. It was the powerful strength of a mother. Francisco heard Josefa's husky whisper for him to continue.

"Just keep him busy; keep Eduardo busy," Francisco continued reading Felix's words. "He will be angry and that's good; it will be his downfall. The longer he's in your world, the more time we'll have to help Eddie get back to you. He wants him; he wants Eddie. Hurry up or Eddie will be lost forever in this world."

Francisco closed the notebook and slid it across the table to Josefa. He didn't have to read the last thing that was written on the book for Josefa already knew the last word. Felix wrote in his slanted penmanship just one word asking for her blessing, 'Bendicion'.

Josefa slipped the notebook inside her bag and with her lips tight in a single line nodded to Francisco. "So Eduardo is here," Josefa said.

"I sensed his presence very quickly, but he won't dare come here," Francisco acknowledged.

"Will he be at the hospital with Eddie?" Josefa asked.

"No he won't be around Eddie's human form for now. Eduardo is sure that having Eddie's soul in his hold is enough, but you are the one he always wanted. I could sense his evilness waiting for you outside."

"So, he will follow me to the hospital?" Josefa was becoming worried, and she grasped both hands to keep them from trembling.

"No he won't, as long as I'm with you, the orishas will keep him from following us. We will be hidden from his eyes and when he decides to go back to his world, Eddie will already be cleansed and Eduardo's powers will be gone...gone forever."

Josefa stood up and looked at her watch, outside the day had converted into the night even though it was only a little past four. She watched Francisco walk toward a small closet and retrieve a bag. He went around gathering things from the shelves of the closet and then zipped the bag and turned to Josefa. "Esto se acaba hoy," the old santero said, and after looking around the room, he repeated himself again. "Today this evil will come to an end."

"Señor," Josefa took a few steps and then turned around. "What were those other words at the end of the message?"

"Babalawo iké epe a Eduardo? Iké means death, and epe means curse...that message was for me from Felix—Babalawo, bring death to Eduardo's curse."

Chapter Thirty

Eduardo shifted, and for a second Captain Marvel and the two brothers held their breath. They watched him closely, trashing from side to side in the rocking chair. They feared he would wake up, but instead Eduardo released a loud snore and continued sleeping.

"Never thought that spirit needed to sleep," Felix shook his head and nudged Eddie on his side pointing at Eduardo.

"He's not what you see as sleeping," Captain Marvel said looking down at Eduardo. *"He's traveling throughout the world of the living. When that happens, the body which is just an empty vessel, stays behind."*

Felix looked up, in the distance; he noticed quick flashes in the sky. Captain Marvel also looked up. *"Those are the new arriving spirits, those with no extra baggage to keep them guessing where they are supposed to go. They are like animals with natural instincts knowing exactly when and where to go."*

"And that's where?" Felix asked.

"To the place we were led to believe; the afterlife. Where all humans belong after our time is completed here on earth."

"I thought this was the afterlife," Felix said spreading his arms around him.

Captain Marvel chuckled. *"No, these are just the gutters of losers and those that are discontent with their destiny. This is the place where confused spirits that are still trying to find a way to return to a world that is no longer theirs."*

"So why are we here then? Are we also losers?"

"No, we are not losers; we are here for a reason, except for Eddie. He is here as a prisoner," Captain Marvel responded.

"What about me, am I a prisoner as well?" Felix asked, still holding the notebook.

"No you are not, you are here as a protector to your brother. When the time is right you too will join the flight of spirits," he pointed to the blue hot skies. *"That journey will carry you across the waters that divide the lands and bring you to your place of rest and peace."*

"So who brought me here if I'm not a prisoner of that clown on the rocking chair?"

Captain Marvel turned and stared at Felix's questioning eyes. He began to speak and then became silent. There was no need for him to elaborate, sometimes the best things said are those left unsaid. *"Your destiny brought you here,"* Captain Marvel finally said, hoping to sound convincing.

"My destiny? Was it my destiny to die like a dog?" Captain Marvel could not look at the boy, so he walked to the other side on the porch and leaned against the ledge. He resembled a grandfather enjoying time with his two grandsons.

There was a slow smirk burrowing dimples on each side of Felix's mouth as he nodded. "Wait…wait one minute," he walked across the porch and stood in front of Captain Marvel. Under the sunlight, he could see Captain Marvel much clearer, and there was a strong resemblance to the man in the rocking chair. Felix glanced at Eduardo for a moment, then turned and glared at Captain Marvel. "You look just like him or should I say he looks like you. Why do you look like him?"

Captain Marvel released a defensive smile, which seemed to accuse him more than Felix's questions.

Standing behind Felix, Eddie had a perfect view of Captain Marvel. He took a peek at Eduardo, and he studied the old man. For the first time, he realized that they could have been the same person in different eras. Now everything became clearer. Captain Marvel made himself look like the superhero from his comic books, yet all along; he was someone who could easily have been related to Eduardo.

"I'm his father," Captain Marvel said and his face no longer held a smile, but a look of pain and deep sadness.

Felix started to say something, but Eddie spoke first. "If that's your son, why are you trying to hurt him?"

"I'm not trying to hurt him; I'm trying to bring him home."

They all stood in their own private silence as the sun became brighter and hotter and the earth beneath the porch seemed to simmer with an unseen fire. Then, Eduardo moved. He opened his eyes and leaped to his feet with a ghastly scream ripping from his throat.

Chapter Thirty-One

"I know what troubles you, but don't worry, all your doubts have no merit. If you trusted me this far, then trust me to the end," Francisco said as he and Josefa boarded a livery cab and instructed the driver to take them to the Children's Hospital in Manhattan. At first, the driver disapproved the long ride from the Bronx to the city. However, after Francisco agreed to pay the exaggerated fare, the cabby put the car in gear and drove.

"We are only heading toward the hospital now because of the faith and trust I have in you," Josefa said as she looked out the window as the cab made a right turn towards the Triboro Bridge.

Francisco pressed hard against the back of the seat and braced himself; he had a phobia about cars, especially taxis. He watched Josefa closely, and he knew her ordeal well; the poor woman was confused. She had many questions, and her apprehensiveness was understandable. He turned his body in angle to face her. "You're Catholic, right?"

Josefa turned away from the window and peeked at Francisco before returning her eyes to the dim crowded Manhattan skyline. From the height of the bridge, the city across the river looked like ominous tall shadows with millions of yellow eyes. "Si, I was raised in a Catholic household. The last time I went to Mass was with Eddie. That was when he bought the Captain Marvel comic book. He particularly enjoyed that comic book because he related to the little boy who becomes a big, powerful hero. I could still hear him, 'Shazzam!' That's what he kept shouting through the streets." She smiled, and she was surprised that no tears were shed. "Why do you ask if I'm a Catholic?"

"Because I see the struggle in your eyes about what you are doing. To tell you the truth, that's normal, many times religious people that are raised by the words of the Bible find it very hard to accept another belief. I know that the average person, not familiar with the Santeria religion, tends to see it as black magic, rather than something that respects and worships the same God."

Josefa nodded in agreement with Francisco. Yes, she was hesitant about consulting Francisco; he represented an unfamiliar world, but she did feel comfortable with him. Josefa closed her eyes and lowered her head and rested on the cab's window. "To think that I was always the first one to look down at those that ran to the local spiritualist for anything. I used to laugh at my aunt because to her, a simple cold was the result of an evil eye or voodoo spell." Josefa laughed, then the thought of Eddie and Felix brought tears to her eyes, and she sniffed hard to keep them at bay. This was not the time for tears; this was time to do something about her sons. She turned and looked at Francisco trying to believe in him.

"Let me explain something to you," Francisco said in his easy manner. He would have made an impeccable teacher, a perfect doctor, perhaps he was that and many other things. "I'm also a practicing Catholic. I was baptized, received my communion, and I kneel down and do my share of 'Our Father's and 'Holy Mary's'. The same way people pray to different saints; I also pray for the saints, the orishas of Santeria; they are all under the protection of the Almighty."

Josefa was surprised to hear that, yet the guilt was still there. While Agapito and Enrique were taking care of the funeral arrangements for her son, she was on some wild adventure battling a spirit. *My Sweet Lord,* she allowed herself to pray, *am I doing the right thing? Are You approving this madness?*

She felt Francisco's hands take hers and squeezed lightly. "There is truth that many people see Santeria as the magic resolution for every problem that crossed their path. For every person that comes to me with a serious problem and needs the help of the orishas, there are at least four or five that just come for no other reason, but to look for things, a simple aspirin and a day's rest won't cure. Hey, I get sick too, but I don't see it as an evil spell. Sickness is just part of human nature. However, Josefa, there are also occurrences in this world that come from another world, and they bring with them suffering and harm."

Francisco let go off Josefa's hand and braced himself against the back of the seat; he couldn't wait to reach the hospital. He watched nervously as the cab exited the bridge and swung towards the F.D.R. Drive. "I understand your confusion about what's going on in your life. And I do understand very well your feelings about God and Santeria. I know in this day and age people have been tainted by television and movies. Anything that shows demonic possession or spirits is always associated with black magic. Just try to understand that Santeria, like any other religion is an extension of God, the heavens and the saints. The Catholic Church understands there's evil around us; it understands the sinful deeds that come from demons, which are why the church allows exorcisms. Even the Bible recounts how Jesus exorcised demons from those possessed. There are also prophetic ministry leaders among the Pentecostal church that have what they call a spiritual gift, which allows them to hear God's messages through the Holy Spirit. Now, do you consider them some type of black magic controlled by demons or Satan himself?"

Francisco removed two vials from his jacket and puts them inside Josefa's hand. "This is holy water I get from the church every time I attend Mass. In the religious stores throughout the city, the botanicas; they sell bottled holy water supplied to them by Catholic churches and priests. We use it to clean those that are in need of it, like your son Eddie. Mira nena, to believe and practice the Santeria religion does not mean that you won't be able to also practice Catholicism. What you feel now is confusion, perhaps the same confusion I felt the day I realized I was born with a gift. I also questioned my loyalty to God and the church, until I learned more about it from my padrino—my Santeria godfather—and the man who initiated me into the mysteries of the orishas. Let me tell you this, and hopefully it will serve to answer those questions. Santeria initiates should be baptized Catholics, remember there's evil and there's good. Some use Santeria for evil and some use it for good. There are good parents like you and there are others that should not be around children. It's the oldest paradox in the world, how can evil exist on the grounds of goodness? I could perhaps tell you stories about evil men disguised in the cloth of Jesus. Santeria is an extension of God and the teachings of love and helping your neighbor."

"If it's an extension of God, then why is the religion masked in such secrecy?"

"Sadly the religion is not openly accepted or approved. Maybe the politics of the world do not allow the church, especially the Catholic Church to come out and give Santeria the support that would make it more acceptable within the community. I personally know priests and doctors that have directed troubled people to seek my help. Have you ever wondered why modern medicine turns their nose at old proven remedies to alleviate sickness? It's all politics my dear Josefa. You should remember that it took herbs, teas and the knowledge of a simple, so-called uneducated woman to do what the great science could not do, and that was to save your son's life," Francisco chuckled. "Sometimes I feel like the ancestors of Santeria, the Yoruba tribes of Africa of how they had to hide their beliefs from the Christian masters. Now that's hypocrisy. The Christian masters didn't follow the teachings of God about love among another human being. Where were their loving beliefs when they put kings and queens in chains?"

The cab steered out of the F.D.R. traffic and then took Second Avenue towards downtown. The stores along the avenue were still adorned with bright colorful Christmas decorations even though the holidays were almost over. Josefa couldn't believe how time was flying. She realized that New Year's Day was next week, and she was saddened by it. That had always been one of her favorite celebrations; it was the only time she felt a sense of renewal and hope. Now for as long as she lived, the holidays would be a time of mourning the death of her oldest son. If this man was going to help her Eddie, she was willing to believe and accept the consequences.

The cab pulled alongside the curb, and they climbed out of the car.

Battle for a Soul

There was a cold wind that came from the East River and to her surprise, she was sweating. She took a deep breath and stared at the hospital building. She felt like she was staring at the bowels of hell. "May God be with us, Francisco," she said.

"He is, nena, He is," Francisco repeated, and then closed his eyes for a second. He felt the stirring of the orishas ready to assist him in the battle for Eddie's soul.

Chapter Thirty-Two

Eduardo blinked hard, and his eyes focus on the three figures in front of him with savage hate. The figures stared back still shaken by Eduardo's sudden outburst, as the rocking chair moved back and forth. Eduardo's head turned slowly and glared at everyone, registering each face and form. He gazed at his father with disappointment; the old man should have left him alone. Then, he switched his eyes on the stranger and found a familiarity in his youthful face. He resembled Eddie, and Eduardo considered this like a difficult math problem.

What type of trick was his father playing now? Eduardo took a few steps and came around the rocking chair, and he fixed his stare on Eddie. He couldn't let the child go—not now—not ever. He had to seize Eddie away from them so nothing would be lost, but he had to act fast. He could feel strange energy coming from the living world, and that perception told him that he must take them by surprise.

With his hands hooked like the talons of a hawk, Eduardo lunged at Eddie. However, the child was too fast. Eduardo recoiled and attacked again, but this time the stranger jumped in front of Eddie and with one hand, brushed Eduardo's attempt with ease. Eduardo was surprised; it was impossible for a mere youth to brush him away like that. He always felt that he was invincible. Out of frustration, he screamed and the sound seemed to echo inside his throat. He attacked again with blinded rage. His hands closed around Eddie's arm, and he pulled the child towards him.

Felix jumped between them and swung his fist. The punch landed hard on the side of Eduardo's face, and Eduardo felt the strength behind it. It was a solid punch, and it rocked him as he let go of Eddie and tumbled backwards, flipping over the rocking chair in a clownish somersault.

Eduardo staggered to his feet. His breathing was shallow and there was a rotten smell of fear inside his mouth. Locking his angry eyes with those of his father, he screamed. "Why are you doing this father?" All this was his father's doing; he just knew it. His own flesh and blood was the culprit sabotaging his life. The two men guarded Eddie like bodyguards, and the sudden realization of the stranger's identity made Eduardo gasp with alarm. The stranger was Eddie's oldest brother. Eduardo chastised himself for not paying more attention to Felix's whereabouts. His mother foretold the danger of bringing Felix here, and Eduardo had heeded her wishes. It seemed obvious that his own father took it upon himself to bring the boy instead.

"Eduardito, por favor let's go where we truly belong," Eduardo heard his father's voice. His father sounded tired and weak as he begged. The old man came forward and stood between his son and the child. *"Gather your mother and let's leave together and allow these two brothers to follow their own destiny. Please son, please…enough is enough. It's time to stop this foolishness; you are no longer part of her world."*

Eduardo grimaced with repulsion as he glared at his father. "Foolishness? I never asked you to stay here, surrounded by what you call foolishness. If you chose to stay here and now you want to leave, that's your problem, go on leave nobody is keeping you from your destiny. I don't remember ever inviting you here. Look for the man in the boat by the river of the souls as he waits to take passengers to the other side,"

Eduardo pointed toward the river. "He'll be more than glad to take you there; I'll even give you the coins that you need for your fare. For me, I instead have chosen this place as my home. And your wife—my dear mother—has chosen to be here with me, to help me achieve my dream. I guess she has more loyalty than you. However, don't worry, I know in your own selfish way you want the best for me, too—well that's what I'm doing; waiting to claim what's good for me. I will make Josefa mine."

"She was never yours, my son...it was all an illusion that you try making real, but all along it was just an illusion, a cruel one. Come on my son, it's time to let go. There has been enough suffering for this family that didn't deserve such fate."

"What about my fate, father? Ah...what about my fate? What about my desires and hopes?"

"They all perished the day you died my son. We are part of a world now that doesn't think or live like the world we left, don't you understand? What happened in our other existence was for a reason, we cannot play gods." Eduardo's father came closer. *"These two boys do not owe you anything. Don't you see that they are frightened? They don't belong here...one already lost his life because of all this...this foolishness. At least let the other boy return to his world, to the world for the living."*

"Again you called it foolishness; I see it as my predestination. But if it pleases you, father, the boy will return when I'm also able to return with him. I will possess his soul." Eduardo bowed before his father in a mocking way. "There's nothing here for you to do, father," Eduardo smiled, his pale white complexion accentuating his yellowish teeth. He slowly moved to the side, keeping a good distance from his father while concentrating on the two brothers.

His father was wrong, Eduardo couldn't see any fear in their eyes, but instead what he saw was a fearless determination to defeat him.

Eduardo concentrated on Eddie, and he didn't look like the same confused child when he first arrived, and that angered him.

"Oye muchacho," Eduardo addressed Eddie, dismissing his father. "What kind of manners did your parent teach you? Eh? I opened my home to you, and you insult me by going to this old fool, to listen and believe the diarrhea that comes out of his mouth." Eduardo shook his head and sucked his lips making an annoying slurping sound. "Now come here, I don't have time for games anymore."

"Eddie stay here," Felix glared at Eduardo, and with his hand, he held the notebook, he guided Eddie to stand behind him. He then turned and looked at Eduardo with defiance. "The only place he's going is back home."

Eduardo laughed, but the laughter was forced and all it did was confirm that he feared Felix. Then, he saw the notebook, and coldness invaded his heart. He squinted at the notebook that was his life, his soul, the only connection to his very own existence. He watched Felix switch the notebook from one hand to the other, the way you taunt a cat with a ball of yarn. Eduardo turned and smirked at his father, attempting to hide his apprehension of seeing his notebook in the hands of the enemy. Again, he bowed before his father; it was a custom his father brought from fighting Japanese in some American war. Now his father's silly custom that amused Eduardo as a child, he was currently using to mock him.

His father must have known that the notebook was his soul, and that thought made Eduardo hate his father even more. His old man knew that only a recent arrival into the world of the dead could write and send a message to the living. Now everything was becoming clearer to him. His father brought Eddie's brother here for that purpose alone, to do what he wasn't able to do. What an old fool, his father was, with the pathetic notion that families should always stay together. Eduardo shifted his body again circling the rocking chair, planning his confrontation.

"Well father, again you betray me. The most sacred thing, which we hold dearly in this horrible land—our soul—you sold it to the highest bidder."

Balancing his weary body on the ball of his feet, the old man looked around. He could feel the heat rising through the cracks of the wooden floor; it felt like thin fingers trying to pull him into its depth.

"What happened with my son?" Captain Marvel asked while he moistened his lips, a human gesture, and ventured closer to the center of the porch. *"You have become a stranger in this old man's eyes."*

"Correction father, I hate to be such an ungrateful son. Yet the real question is…what happened with my father? Because the man standing in front of me, deceiving me is a stranger, he is an enemy that seeks my destruction rather than my survival."

Eduardo's father glanced at the two boys. He peeked at the reddish ground that beckoned him, and he straightened his back and raised his voice above the strong winds that ripped through the branches of the tall mango tree. *"I have failed you, son; I have failed you and for that I beg your forgiveness,"* he said raising his arms and opening them as a symbol of defeat. *"But your obsession with the life of a woman who didn't even notice you when you were alive must come to a stop now. Too many lives have been ruined already, but it doesn't have to continue. Come on son, it's time to let the dead rest and allow the living to live."*

Eduardo studied his father and the old man almost made a believer out of him. Even so, at the end, all his father represented was bitter memories of a haunted past. "Father, for the last time go away and let me be."

"No! This charade has lasted far too long. It ends here, NOW!"

"But father how can it end when you yourself brought more people to what was supposed to be an intimate little gathering?" Eduardo smiled and pointed at Felix; it was time to expose his father's lies. "Does this boy know how he came to our little party? Tell me father, does he know? Should I tell him or would you rather do the honors and tell him how you manipulated him?"

Felix's eyebrows arched in anger. "You son-of-a-bitch! What sick game are you assholes playing?"

Captain Marvel turned slowly and faced Felix's rage. He lowered his head and then raised it back up and threw his shoulders out like a proud soldier facing a fierce adversary. *"You are mistaken. I am not playing any game you can be sure of that. I'm here with one purpose only, and that's to take my son back to where he belongs and in the process return your brother to his own place."*

"And me?" Felix asked forcefully. "What about me? Who the hell brought me here? I'm beginning to doubt it was him," Felix shouted pointing angrily at Eduardo.

"You are right," Captain Marvel agreed as he took a deep breath and then slowly exhaled. *"I brought you here…it was my voice that you heard in your mind all along. The voice that came at you in the school on that night when you became a killer…I was the hand who directed your actions. I was the voice in the prison that gave you the extra push and convinced you that you could fly and escape. I was the voice in your dreams telling you how to be your own man. I deceived you and for that I will pay dearly, but if you ask me if I'm sorry, I would be lying to you if I tell you that I am."*

Felix took two steps back; his mind was twisting and circling in a mad spin at what he was hearing. His life didn't have to turn out as it did. All along his life was controlled and manipulated by some…some bastard of a ghost that oppressed him. "You took my life, even before I had time to discover it."

Captain Marvel stared at Felix and lifted his arms to his chest in a gesture that he was not hiding anything. *"You were destined to die anyway. I just accelerated the process in order to help another life grow…your brother's."*

"There wasn't a goddamn thing wrong with my brother until your bastard of a son came into his life; maybe my own life wouldn't have been so fucked up either if it wasn't for him and you!" Felix spat with hatred over the porch rail.

"You are right," the old man said in a voice that pleaded understanding. *"You are right, Felix; my son was responsible for your brother's sickness, and maybe for your sufferings too; that's why I made it my duty as a father to right my son's wrongs."*

"And the duties of a father gave you the right to take my life as well?"

"That wasn't a choice…it was your destiny to die in order for your brother to live," Captain Marvel walked closer to the two boys, yet keeping Eduardo at bay. *"If I sat and done nothing, not only would your brother remain in a coma forever; your mother would have probably gone insane; your father would have been destroyed, and you would have died in vain. You were destined to die in a botched robbery, gunned down like some stray mad dog. You would have brought shame to your family, but instead you are giving them their lives back. You are bringing your mother's son, your brother, back to her. With your death, you have given life to so many."*

"Bullshit! I already brought shame to my family and all because of you," Felix looked at Eduardo's father wanting just to swing with all his might and pound the old man. He took a few steps forward, his anger boiling until he could not think rationally. He clenched his hands into fists and began to raise them. Then he felt Eddie's gentle touch on his arm and all the anger he carried defused into the hot, dense air.

"I believe him," Eddie said looking at Felix. "If it was not for Captain Marvel, I would probably be dead by now or whatever it's called in this place. Maybe everything that's happening now was already written on the book of life and death. Felix, this man saved me from Eduardo and his sick ideas. You see; I have known Eduardo, even before I was born; he was inside our mother's womb trying desperately to be reincarnated through my soul. I've known Eduardo longer than I know you and because of that, Felix, I believe in Captain Marvel for he knew his son's obsession. He is a father and that's his son," Eddie pointed with his chin at the direction of where Eduardo stood.

"And no matter what sons and daughters do, they will forever be their little babies, the tiny angels who God placed under their care. Remember how papi tried to protect you from the police, how mami denied your actions and how at this very moment, she's doing things she never imagined just to save me. Don't ask me how I know, but in this world the impossible becomes possible. So you see, Felix, that's what parents do who love their children, they sacrifice themselves, and they will battle until their last breath, to protect their children. Captain Marvel is only a poor father trying to erase the mistakes of his troubled son. But I believe in him Felix, and with his help all this will come to an end, I don't know how, but it will end….it will end."

Eduardo started to clap and threw his head back and began to laugh amusingly. "Come around everyone and hear the philosophy of a child with the mind of a wise old man. Eddie, remember to thank me some day for the intelligence I have provided you with. But don't worry; when we return to your mother's world, I will give you more powers than any of your heroes in your comic books."

"You won't do such a thing," Felix took a few steps towards Eduardo. "I could beat you. You are afraid of me, you sick bastard. You should listen to your father and go with him, to wherever demons like you belong and let my brother return in peace."

"*Listen to the boy, my son,*" Captain Marvel said. "*Call your mother and let's leave this lie.*"

Eduardo kept his eyes on his father; he knew he couldn't be trusted. His father moved nonchalantly. Eduardo played the possum game, but from the corner of his eye, he also kept vigil on the two boys. His father was about to do something, what exactly he didn't know, but whatever it was; Eduardo made sure that Eddie was part of the plan. From behind him, Eduardo heard a sound and by the reactions of the others, he was not the only one that heard it. It was the silent movement of his mother, and soon the odds were going to be tilted in his favor.

Captain Marvel felt the shifting of the ground and this disturbance assured him that time was running out. His arrivals in Eduardo's makeshift world provoke upheaval and soon Eduardo's entire twisted paradise would be swallowed up into the bowels of the underworld. At all costs, he must prevent Eddie from falling into his son's grasp. The child must leave this world before it's too late. He hoped now that what he told Eddie all along would finally make sense. The old man took a deep breath, again a gesture from a lifetime that no longer had any importance in this slice of the afterlife, and then he leaped.

He felt his fingers brush against Eduardo's hair as he pulled his son down and they both fell heavily on the rotten planks of the porch. He now wished he was this Captain Marvel the kid spoke so much about as he felt himself struggling against the strength of his son. He felt pain, but that was impossible, in the land for the dead; pain was just an empty emotion from the human past. Nevertheless, he felt pain as he crumbled weakly on the porch as his son staggered to his feet a few feet away from the brothers.

Eduardo gasped; his breathing was heavy and there was a taste of medicine in his mouth. He could see that in the commotion, the boys were no longer paying attention to the whereabouts of his mother, who waited patiently behind the entrance to the house. He moved slowly toward the boys, his smile crooked and sinister. He had to guide the boys towards his mother without revealing his strategy. Eduardo saw how Felix kept Eddie behind him, protecting the child from him.

"I'm not a weak old man like your father," Felix challenged Eduardo. "The devil is waiting for your soul, and I won't make him wait any longer."

Eduardo took the challenge as he leaped and put his hands around Felix's neck. The momentum carried them to the floor. Felix was strong and Eduardo felt the warmth of the boy's human life still in his hold. With panic and desperation, Eduardo bellowed at his mother. "Take the child now, mother, while I feed this parasite to the unholy ground." He felt Felix twisting his body sideways and without any difficulty, Felix slapped Eduardo's hands away from his neck and smacked him hard. The punch landed on top of Eduardo's nose, and he felt the pain travel through his eyes. Eduardo tried to struggle from underneath Felix's tough youthful body, and he wondered how long could he keep up the fight. The boy was too damn strong. He wanted to see if his mother had the child, but it was impossible when Felix's fists continuously pummeled him.

Eddie tumbled upon the floor, his ankle twisting at the weight of Eduardo and Felix. He scuffled to his feet while looking at his brother swing his fists wildly at Eduardo. He felt some pity for his captor. Even though Eduardo wanted to harm his family, Eddie still had a soft spot for him. This sick man was not really bad; he was not the evil person he was portrayed to be; he was just a confused infatuated man who fell in love with a woman who God did not create for him.

Eddie stepped back looking down at the fight in front of him; he was confused at what he should do. Across from him Captain Marvel was feebly stammering to his feet, and Eddie could see the old man was saying something. He was yelling, but between the grunts and the punches of Felix, it was impossible to comprehend what Eduardo's father was saying. He was pointing frantically and when Eddie finally understood, it was too late. Captain Marvel was warning him about the old witch behind him. Eddie felt the long hooked nails of the aged woman clasp around his arms, and her stench of death suffocated him as she pulled him into the darkness inside the house. He tried to free himself, but the old woman was strong and then the walls around him exploded.

It was a loud boom that deafened his ears and shook the foundation of the dilapidated house. It sent Eddie sprawling. Surrounding him were old evil spirits with sunken eyes and sneers that hid the maggots in their mouth. They all came to him with outstretched hands and malicious laughter. Eddie screamed and for the first time in his life, he was afraid of ghosts.

Chapter Thirty-Three

Josefa entered the room, and Francisco followed behind her. There was a foul smell in the room, like dead carnations in a funeral home. Eddie's hospital room was at the furthest corridor, curving away from the nurse's station. At first, Josefa wondered if that was the sign when a patient had no chance of surviving, therefore there was no need to place him close by. Perhaps that was a blessing in disguise; hopefully, the Eddie's cleansing could be performed by the babalawo without any interruptions. How could she explain to a doctor or a nurse the chanting of an old man in an obscure African language? How could she make them understand what they were dealing with was something not from this world?

She was grateful the desk nurses always dismissed her with a quick glance from their paperwork. Coming here every day she became a fixture of the hospital, as common as the guy who brings the lunch or picks up the garbage, another faceless person. Even the guards in the lobby with their matter-of-fact nods probably didn't notice Francisco.

She went to Eddie and his forehead was perspiring even though the room was cool. She placed a kiss on his forehead and unwrapped the cherry lollipop from her pocketbook and passed it over his lips. She then took the comic book also from her pocketbook, the one with Captain Marvel, and gently placed it on his chest. His tiny chest rose and lowered in such a tranquil sleepy way.

Josefa smiled and touched Francisco's arm. "I'm going to call my family. I won't be long."

"Yes, go on make that call. Your family must be around Eddie as quickly as possible. I will start the preparation of the cleansing. Time is running out; we must hurry."

Again, Josefa lowered her head and kissed her child and then went out to the public telephone by the elevators.

Francisco placed the bag on the nightstand next to Eddie's hospital bed and began quickly to rummage inside the bag. He could feel the tension in Eddie's aura. He could sense the battle in the room, and he also could feel the spirits around them waiting, for the moment, to grasp Eddie's soul. He hurried, and his hands were shaking. He took a deep breath and willed them to be still. He hoped Josefa's family could get there fast; Eddie needed his family close to him; otherwise, nothing in Francisco's powers could bring Eddie back.

Francisco removed a green and yellow beaded bracelet from the bag and quickly tied it around the child's left wrist. The bracelet was called an idé and it belonged to Orúnla, the old babalawo's patron saint and the orisha of Francisco's devotion. The idé was to be worn only on the left wrist, which is the symbol of life as the right hand symbolizes death. This was to symbolize the pact between the orisha Orúnla and Death where no one can die in a room when someone is wearing the green and yellow beaded bracelet. Francisco knew that Eduardo was desperate now and planning Eddie's death.

It was then that Eduardo could easily exchange the child's soul for the powers to regain his entrance in the world for the living. For that insight, Francisco knew that the idé would keep Death from claiming the child's life. Eduardo had to be defeated; the man's perplexed soul must be thrown on the path of judgment and let God or the Devil himself decides Eduardo's fate. "May God protect your soul," Francisco prayed.

Josefa came back to the room and stood next to the bed. She held her son's hand and noticed the beaded bracelet, and just when she was going to ask Francisco about it, she panicked. Eddie's hand was cold when not too long ago he was perspiring, and her first thought was that her little boy was dead and Francisco was giving her child his last rites. She gasped, and her knees buckled under her.

"Josefa are you okay?" Francisco asked as he helped her to a chair next to the bed.

"Mi hijo, please señor don't tell me it's too late." Josefa's voice was weak as her teary eyes stared in agony at her comatose son.

"Your son is okay, please control yourself; we don't want to bring the attention from the nurses or doctors. We don't have much time. Hija, we must hurry. Is your family on their way?"

Josefa nodded, and her lips trembled uncontrollably. She was on the brink of screaming and losing her mind completely and to add anguish to her dilemma her conversation with Agapito had been a battle in itself. He was angry; demanding her whereabouts and questioning what kind of mother she was to be missing all day when her son was dead in the city morgue. At least, he agreed to come, but not before stressing the fact that things were going to change. Maybe Felix's message was right; their marriage was over and perhaps Agapito knew it too.

She passed her hand over Eddie's hair and then caressed his face. Again, she looked at the beaded bracelet on Eddie's left wrist and wondered why Francisco placed it there. She kept the question to herself and placed her trust in Francisco. "Hi'jito, wake up," she kissed him again. "Shazzam," Josefa whispered into his ear not knowing exactly why, but it felt right, so she repeated the word of her son's hero again, "Shazzam."

Chapter Thirty-Four

Shazzam! Eddie heard the word, not sure where it came from, but he heard it again, *Shazzam!* The spirits were around him ready to attack him, when suddenly they kept away as if a wall shielded him from them. The fear he felt before quickly disappeared. Eduardo's mother stood in front of him, her hands clutching his arms and where her fingers pressed against his skin, he felt a burning sensation. Outside as far as he could see, Felix and Eduardo were still wrestling on the floor and with blinding the sun coming through the entrance of the shack, all Eddie could see were their silhouettes. He couldn't make out the body of Captain Marvel, but he knew that he was still out there.

There was a feeling on his left wrist and with newfound strength; he yanked his arms from the restraints of the old woman. He ran outside, ahead of the clumsy shuffles of Eduardo's mother, and the spirits that now stood like bewildered creatures. Eddie shook his head with disbelief, to think that a few seconds ago they had frightened him. He knew that something was happening; something was invading this awful place. Eddie touched his left wrist, and he felt a pulse, a slight twitch, and he absentmindedly scratched his wrist. It felt good to scratch; it brought him comfort and now all he wanted was to keep scratching until he could remove the strange pulse that vibrated on his left wrist.

"Stop scratching!"

Eddie jumped and he saw Captain Marvel standing in front of him, pushing him out toward the porch.

"Stop scratching! That's your life that you feel on your left wrist, if you keep scratching you are going to scratch your life away."

Eddie was puzzled; everything was coming at him too fast. He could sense the hesitation of the spirits that kept protruding from out of the walls. And throughout the shack the walls seemed to disappear and vaporize into thin air and in their place, an army of creepy spirits appeared crowding the inside of the rooms.

Eddie and Captain Marvel rushed onto the porch, and the first thing that Eddie saw was Felix standing over Eduardo. Slowly, Eduardo struggled onto his feet and a sheet of blood masked his once pale face. Eddie started to walk towards Eduardo determined to help him, until Captain Marvel grasped Eddie's arm and pulled him away.

"Stay here child; this battle is between my son and your brother. We cannot interfere; destiny is taking its course," Captain Marvel said, and Eddie saw the seriousness and sadness in the old man's eyes.

Eduardo felt blood running down his face, and his body shouted in pain. But how can that be? How can that be possible? He looked up, through blinded eyes, and he coughed, spitting blood onto the planks of the porch. He could feel the heat from the red dirt beneath the porch rising and felt the burning vapor clog his nose. He could see the notebook where it had landed when he fought with Felix and now Eduardo understood why he hurt and bled like a human again. He watched helplessly as Felix bent down scooping the notebook and winking at him triumphantly. The boy held his soul and with that possession, he also held onto his physical weakness as well. He was surrounded, and Eduardo fixed his sunken eyes on all three of his enemies that stood in a semi-circle while he labored to rise again. This fight was not over yet; he tried to convince himself. Eduardo stumbled over his feet, wincing from the pain that covered the right side of his body. He supported himself with the porch banister wondering where his mother was. Why can't the spirit fight? Why can't Death come and claim Eddie's life?

"You wretched demons from hell, come and claim what belongs to your master!" Eduardo shouted over the edge of the porch. "I am offering you the soul of a child, come send your demons, your best demons and take my gift to the Dark One and let the master of hell reward me for my deed."

"The only soul that the demons will claim will be your own," Felix said. "Mira pendejo," Felix waved the notebook high over his head. "Here is your black soul; the evil, shit of a soul that hell has been missing."

Eduardo scowled, and he could feel a void in the cavity of his chest. It dawned on him; a body with no soul is just a carcass of nonexistence. At the moment, he understood the reason why he couldn't possess or control his creations in this corrupted corner of his twisted mind. The energy of his soul was missing and without it, all he had created were no longer at his command. He needed his soul, and his notebook was where his soul resided.

"Okay boy," Eduardo spoke; his words trembled as each syllable tumbled out of his mouth. "Very well, you have defeated a sick man. I accept my defeat like a man. Now go ahead, take your brother home and then follow my father—my traitor—to where the two of you belong. I have no more quarrels with you or your brother, just go and let me stay here in my self-appointed hell. Go ahead, boy, go before I change my mind, and I let all my spirits, my warriors, rip you limb by limb." Eduardo waved his hands dismissive. "Go, just give me what belongs to me and let me decide the fate of my own soul. Let me have my dignity, for you have already taken my life."

"You want your soul?" Felix stretched the notebook in front of Eduardo, taunting him. "No wonder this notebook is your soul. It's dirty and it smells like shit, just like its owner."

"If it amuses you to mock me, go ahead boy, amuse yourself. Anyone can beat a sick, weak man like me, especially with the help from a witch doctor. Your parents will be proud because for once in your pathetic loser of a life you have done well. Now give me my notebook and get the hell out of my world." Eduardo shouted. "Now give me back my goddamn soul!"

Felix walked over to the front of the porch and peeked down at the reddish dirt; it seemed to bubble like boiling mud inside a cauldron. What did that dirt represent? Why was it forbidden for those that were dead to set foot on its surface? He turned around and stared at Eduardo, and he saw a fear in the man's face. "You know you have been the cause of many years of suffering to a woman whose only mistake was her beauty and kindness. You had no right to make her life a living hell because you fell in love with her. You fell in love with an image, an idea, not with a real person, yet you decided to curse this woman and every male around her. You are a dumb fool; don't you know that everyone will fall in love with someone who will not return the love? Just ask yourself; did you ever present yourself to her? Did she know of your intentions? Did my mother ever hear the love you had for her come from your lips? Did my mother deserve the life you shit on?"

Felix came closer to Eduardo. He felt the emotion building up in his words and to Felix those were the emotions that he held all his life. He was angry at himself for making that sweet woman cry for him. He wanted to blame Eduardo for all that, but he too had to share the blame. However, there was no way in hell he was going to forgive this monster for what he did not only to his mother, but to Eddie and everyone in his family. Felix shook his head, slowly from side to side, removing the blame that he was pinning on himself. Eduardo had been the cause of everything, and now he had to pay.

"You really want your soul back?" Felix asked holding the notebook over the edge of the porch. He could feel the dirt move with some ghoulish anticipation.

Eduardo shrieked at the sight of his precious notebook being held above the reddish dirt. Something in there represented danger, something in that maggot infected hot earth was what gave dead souls nightmare in their sleep.

"Please give me my soul, and forever I'll be your slave," Eduardo pleaded. "I will make your mother rich; she will be a queen among royalty. Please boy, give me my soul."

"You really want your soul?" Felix shouted. "Well then go and take your fucking soul!"

Eduardo watched in horror as Felix flung the notebook in the air. The notebook went straight up into the hot blue sky and slowly came back down. He ran to it with desperate outstretched hands as he attempted to catch it before it could land on the reddish dirt. The notebook touched his fingertips ever so slightly, and then it flipped away from his reach. Eduardo screamed as the notebook, pulled by an intense gravity, plummeted into the crimson dirt. Eduardo's eyes opened wide in dreadful terror. He ran down the crooked wooden steps and on the last rung, he stopped.

He wanted to leap into the folds of the dirt and grab his soul, but there was a fear and hesitation in his moves. He looked up and his baleful eyes fixed on Felix, and he saw the boy's triumphant smile. Then, Eduardo looked at his father and felt hatred against the man that gave him life. I hate you father, Eduardo wanted to tell him, but now hate and love were not important. Only his soul mattered, and he begged God to stretch His holy hand and save him from hell. He felt tears clouding his vision, and he looked at Eddie and for the first time realized that this child had been his only friend. Could anyone blame him? The only thing he ever wanted was just the simple thing that all humans have and take for granted, to be loved and be able to love.

He glanced at his surroundings; the place that had been his safe heaven, the place he thought he could play God, but now he realized there's only one God. Eduardo turned his face from everyone and stared at the notebook that lay on the ground. "I'm sorry Josefa," Eduardo screamed as he leaped into the red burning dirt in search of his soul.

With a thunderous groan, the earth erupted and from its depth, a ghastly shriek ripped through the air. Powerful explosions rocked underneath the house. Tremors uprooted mango and avocado trees effortlessly. The tangled remains tumbled into the opened ditch.

Amidst the destruction of the angry earth, Eduardo stood between the foundation of the porch and his notebook. He reached out, and he felt the pages from his notebook tickle the tips of his fingers. Eduardo smiled and then he laughed as he stood firmly on the reddish dirt. Nothing was going to keep him from grasping and embracing his soul again. Perhaps all the stories and warnings about the forbidden earth were just lies of the bored spirits wanting to entertain themselves at the expense of the gullible newcomers.

Eduardo sneered at the onlookers on the porch, and he jumped with glee. He roared with delirious laughter as the shrieks from underneath the earth chased the millions of maggots out from their subterranean homes. Then the rumbles stopped, and the earth became silent and still. It was calm and above Eduardo, the sky was blue and peaceful.

He walked on the crimson, hot earth, which had terrified him since the first day of his death. "There was nothing to fear," Eduardo shouted. "There's nothing to be afraid of." He pointed to his father and then waved at everyone who stood upon the porch. His three enemies will pay.

Eduardo turned and went to where the notebook was. He bent down and brushed away the hundreds of maggots with a look of disgust. He snatched the notebook and with it in his possession, he felt something bloom within. It was his soul settling where it belonged, and Eduardo smiled for he knew nothing was going to stop him from finishing the battle. He took a few steps towards the steps and underneath his feet, the earth burped. There was something moving; he could feel the vibration, coming from somewhere deep within the bowels of the glowing earth. It was surfacing with a destructive speed. He could hear the sound of stones and earth shattering beneath his feet. The earth buckled, and Eduardo stood in fright as he lost his balance and the shifting ground hurled him into the ground. He landed hard and clumsily and a crunchy sickening sound informed him that both of his knees were shattered in the fall.

He tried to get up—he had to get up—but it was impossible to get up, instead he crawled on his belly. Desperately, he dug his fingers into the scorching earth; dragging his broken body towards the dilapidated steps. Finally, Eduardo comprehended, and with that understanding, he panicked. There was a truth about the reddish forbidden earth; the demon was coming to claim him. The monster waited until Eduardo regained possession of his soul, for a soulless body is only an empty carcass and of no use for the master of hell.

The earth exploded with a diabolical screech, and a thick gray vapor rose from the gaping hole, as it swallowed half of Eduardo's body. He screamed, loud and dreadful as the soul searcher came forth. Sharp, long twisted fangs ripped into Eduardo's legs, and he began convulsing. He felt the tendons of his legs been shredded into fleshy ribbons. He heard the sound of bones crunching as the force of the fangs opened and closed around them.

Eduardo never ever imagined the real death of someone already dead could be so excruciatingly painful. Desperate, Eduardo looked down at the yawning hole where the soul searcher was buried and between swallows of dirt and scurrying maggots he gawked in nightmarish horror as hundreds of steel-like teeth fed from his body. With useless punches, Eduardo walloped his devourer in futile actions. He saw his own dark; maroon blood stained the earth, and now he understood why the earth was a scarlet color. The earth was dyed by thousands and thousands of gallons of putrid blood spilled by sinners like him.

The soul searcher jumped out; his top torso was a picture of abomination spawned only from the fires of hell. The creature was large; it eclipsed the blue sky, and its shadow darkened the porch. Its size mocked the huge trees that were now falling into the cracked terrain. Its large deadly jaws chomp down, and Eduardo swung helplessly from them. Eduardo no longer screamed for his mouth was filled with blood as he gurgled a sickening, choking sound. Eduardo's body trembled, and his face contorted and his screams were heard for the last time. It was the sound of a soul snatched by the devil himself. Eduardo's eyes popped from their sockets and then in a giant chomp Eduardo was gone, into the belly and into the fires of hell.

There was a soulful scream that came from inside the shack. It was Eduardo's mother, and she ran out screaming hysterically for her son. She knocked her husband, Captain Marvel, out of the way sending him sprawling head-first into the rocking chair. Felix turned around, transfixed at the madness that was unfolding before him. He was not able to react and all he saw was a blur of raggedy clothes and the body of an old woman. He tried to jump in front of Eddie, but everything was happening too fast, and he watched in terror as the old woman wrapped her arms around Eddie and leaped into the still hungry reddish earth, where the soul searcher waited for more souls; its hunger not satisfied yet.

Chapter Thirty-Five

Francisco felt a jolt, and he grabbed Eddie's bed headboard to keep from falling. They were losing Eddie; he could feel the child's soul submerging into evil and darkness. There was a foul smell that thrust violently up into his nostrils, and Francisco knew exactly what the smell was; it was the burning of flesh and the suffering of souls. Josefa felt the jolt too, and her eyes widened in disbelief and shock.

"Where's your family?" Francisco asked with urgency.

Josefa looked toward the doorway wishing her family would materialize before her. She could feel a feverish heat seeping from Eddie's body. "My God," Josefa gasped. "My little boy is burning." She wanted to run out of the room and scream for the nurses and doctors to come in quickly, but hesitated. Why did she trust this African voodoo instead of trusting science?

Francisco read her movements, and he placed his hand on her shoulders to make her listen to him. "Please Josefa, if you call the attention from the doctors you'll be pushing Eddie to his death. Por favor, we must trust and have faith in what we are doing. My orisha, my saint Orúnla sensed your disturbance and your indecisiveness. If you insult him, the pact with Death will not protect your son. The beaded bracelet on his left wrist will have no meaning or power."

Josefa closed her eyes, placing her hand over her heart. "My sweet Lord, who can I trust?"

"Listen…" Francisco shook her as she looked at him with weakness in her eyes. "We can no longer wait for your family; your faith and motherly love are enough to bring Eddie back. Please, you have to trust me, just like you trusted Doña Lola's friend in bringing Eddie back from the dead when he was born. Now you have to trust me too. Today will not be the first time Eddie was saved by the powers of Santeria. That woman slaved day and night to bring Eddie back from Eduardo's clutches was a santera, a priestess of the Santeria religion. Her name was Luz; she was an omo-Changó, a daughter of the saint Changó and one of the most powerful of the orishas. She along with Doña Lola is among the spirits in this room waiting to help us, but you must give them the okay. Just like you gave your trust to Doña Lola and Doña Luz ten years ago, they are asking you now to do the same."

Josefa turned away from Francisco and went to her son; she took the lollipop and rubbed it against his lips. She pinched his puffy cheeks and removed his wet hair from his hot forehead. She lowered her face and placed it against his, wanting to transfer the pain and the sickness from him and to herself.

"What can I do Señor Francisco? What can I do to bring my baby home?"

"Take the holy water and pour it into that glass," Francisco instructed as he closed his eyes and began a chant. His chants asked the orishas, his Santeria saints to bless the room and to guide him. There was a movement around the room, and a sense of empathy surrounded them. The two midwives appeared before them once more to help bring another beautiful soul into this world.

Chapter Thirty-Six

Thunder rumbled within the black bloated clouds, darkening the sky. Felix ran past Captain Marvel and distraught watched his brother thrash violently, fighting the clutches of Eduardo's mother. Felix hurried down the steps and reached out for his little brother, but the distance was too great. Holding onto the frame of the porch, he extended himself as far as he could without risking falling into the feeding grounds of the monster. The old woman was screaming, and the sound made Felix's blood freeze with fear. He wanted to shout at her to stop, until he realized that he was screaming too.

The beast leaped out, twisting in the midair, its body a mass of mangled muscles covered with raised burning scales. Its mouth was huge and lined with crooked, cracked teeth and long rows of fangs. In one quick motion, it crunched down on the old woman's lower torso. Felix jumped back, afraid, and he looked around searching for something to battle the creature with and save Eddie. Captain Marvel appeared behind him, and the old man's eyes were wild and in shock.

Felix could see Eddie's head bopping up and down, and his brother resembled a frightened puppy in the jaws of a bulldog. Felix focused on the monster as it slithered awkwardly circling the house, and its body seemed endless. It was an enormous, hulking thing. Arrow-shaped scales covered each side of the creature, and they opened and closed akin to tiny suckling mouths gasping for air. There was something liquid that oozed out from under the scales; polluting the air with a stench that reminded Felix of rotten meat. Dark slanted eyes without pupils blinked stupidly at Felix while the old woman hung repulsively from the side of its huge half-closed mouth. The beast seemed to be grinning. No longer biting on the struggling body of Eduardo's mother, the monster sniffed towards the direction of the porch.

Even in her comatose stage, the old woman still held Eddie tightly in her grasp. Even so, seeing how Eddie kept fighting to free himself; it made Felix proud of his little brother. However, he wanted to tell him to stop his thrashing. He was afraid that, with one giant gulp, the monster would swallow the old woman and Eddie as well.

"*It's confused,*" Captain Marvel said from behind Felix's shoulder. "*It could smell our souls, but as long as we stay here it cannot attack us. It knows that we are nearby, but it can't see us; the creature is blind.*"

"But it's looking straight at us," Felix said, his voice cracking with panic. "What the hell is that thing?"

"*The creature is an extension from hell. I supposed it's rewarded by the demons for its tireless service. It feeds upon the flesh from the dead. Its only purpose is to devour the sinners after their souls are taken to their judgments. It will stay here until it can no longer smell the scent of our dead souls.*"

"But my brother is not dead."

"*That's what is causing confusion to the monster; it smells our dead souls, but it also smells something alien. It has never smelled the soul of the living.*"

"So it means that Eddie will be saved then," Felix exclaimed, a hint of hope lighting his mind.

"*No, it just means that it will take a while for its unintelligent brain to register that even though it's a new smell, it's still another soul."*

"We have to help him then," Felix said, but more to himself than to the old man behind him.

Felix went slowly down the porch steps. He could feel the heat rising around his ankles. It felt like hundreds of mosquitoes biting on them, and absentmindedly he scratched them, and then he straightened and stared at the monster.

The monster rolled and then it jerked forward, its lazy, dumb eyes blinking constantly. Its large flat snout moved from side to side, sniffing the air and for a second, Felix thought that the creature was going to lunge at him. Felix climbed up one rung as his breathing came in halting hiccups. He could feel Captain Marvel on the top step, and Felix shot a quick glance at the old man. He returned his attention to Eddie and motioned him to stay still, afraid to call out to him.

"You could speak to your brother. The monster is as smart as the maggots that caress its trunk," Captain Marvel informed, and Felix nodded with approval.

"Eddie," Felix cupped his hands as he yelled. "Eddie, don't move."

Eddie looked up, and Felix was surprised there was no fear in his eyes. He waved at Felix just like he always waved whenever he rode on the Merry-go-Round. Felix smiled and somehow he knew that everything was going to be okay. Felix waved back.

"Stop punching her and try to pry her fingers open," Felix yelled, and the monster twitched its head forward and Eddie's body went crashing against the lower lip of the thing. The monster groaned and moved closer to the porch, and Felix moved up another rung bumping against Captain

Marvel. The old man didn't move.

"Shit," Felix complained. "You're going to make me fall right inside the monster's mouth. Go up, goddammit! Will you fucking go up?"

The old man looked sharply at Felix, ready to complain about the young man's language. Instead, he turned and watched Eddie trying his best to do what his big brother told him to do. The poor boy's legs dangled as he fought hard to pull free from the clutches of the woman. But her arms were wrapped too tightly around his waist. Captain Marvel could see Eddie pulling her fingers apart and just touching her dried wrinkled fingers made the kid shudder. From the safety of the porch, Captain Marvel could hear her low moans. There was a glazed look in her eyes as she stared upward.

Eddie turned his head away from those dead eyes and struggled to break her grip. He caught a glimpse of Felix standing on the porch steps, and Eddie felt that if he stretched his hands to Felix as far as possible and if his brother did the same. Then, with their combined strength, he could free himself from the woman's hold. He kicked with his legs to get momentum and reached out. Felix also stretched out, but because he was still standing on the top rung, the distance was too far.

Virtually reading his brother's thoughts, Felix climbed down the steps until he was on the last rung. Again, he felt the hot stinging vapor burning his ankles. Felix extended his hand as far as he could, yet there were still at least two feet separating them. The monster began to move, and Felix could hear the rumbles of a roar slowly building inside the belly of the creature. If the monster roared like before there was no doubt that it would take Eddie to his death. The snake-like beast thrust forward and with the abrupt movement, droplets of the green ooze from its scales flew above Felix and Captain Marvel. The ooze landed on the far end of the porch and the second it hit the wooden planks it bursts into flames.

The creature wobbled and then belched taking Eduardo's mother a bit more inside its jaws. Eddie screamed at the sudden shuffle. Felix reached out, and his fingers found Eddie's and each brother curled their fingers together. Felix pulled hard and the monster sensing the disturbance rose a few inches from the ground. An awful shriek spewed out from the depth of the beast's gargantuan mouth. With stupid eyes that closed and opened into slits, the creature leaped into the air aroused by the closeness of Felix's soul. Felix jerked towards the thing, yet he refused to let go. He could not let go; he would not let go as he found himself airborne with both his hands now clamped tightly around Eddie's arms. His body slammed hard against the body of the monster. It was like hitting a wall. He nearly passed out as dots of pain traveled inside his head.

Paralyzed by the unexpected movement, Captain Marvel stood at the top of the steps following the flight of the beast. The monster somersaulted through the air, and the huge serpent-liked body twisted with surprising agility as it pivoted and dove downward. Captain Marvel could see the two dangling bodies of the two brothers holding to each other. In unison, the boys screamed. Then, to his horror: the grip of his dead wife finally came loose and Felix and Eddie were no longer attached to the beast. The monster plunged, and so did the brothers. Captain Marvel could now see the entire mass of the creature. It was the hybrid of a snake and a giant maggot. Captain Marvel whistled with awe and fear. *"My Lord, this thing is the flesh-eating worm of our final resting place."*

The gigantic worm burrowed into the red earth with boisterous sounds of pulverizing rocks and uprooted trees. The earth shook, buckling the ground and lifting the shack from its foundation. Thrown onto the porch, Captain Marvel tumbled with great force against the rocking chair, as it crashed on top of him. He pushed the chair away and scurried on all four to the edge of the porch. With wild eyes, he gasped at the huge hole in front of him. Foul smelling vapors rose and intruded his nostrils with a burning sensation.

The old man shielded his face and frantically searched for the two boys while praying for their survival. He jumped onto his feet and ran from one corner of the porch to the other. Squinting through the thick smoke, he searched and finally spotted them. They were slumped on top of the trunk of the massive mango tree. The same tree where Eddie found refuge on the day an old man became a colorful comic book hero to a frightened little boy. They had to get out of there; that much Captain Marvel knew. He could hear an apparent rumbling from beneath the earth announcing the return of the beast.

A bestial growl came forth as the giant maggot bursts out in an explosion of shattered boulders and red dirt. Its body settled with a thunderous boom and with amazing speed, its snout began to sniff the air. It slinked towards the porch, stopped and slowly turned its repulsive body as its empty eyes sensed the boys. The nose once again pointed at the sky inhaling the smell in the air, fascinated by Eddie's soul; a clean, pure soul. It began to slide and as the scales expanded, the dark-green ooze marked its path. A high pitch shriek bellowed out of that hideous mouth, perhaps announcing to his master below the arrival of new souls.

Captain Marvel saw Felix move, and his motions aroused the worm. *"Get up!"* the old man shouted. *"Felix, get up!"*

Felix lifted his shoulders and craned his neck; he felt sluggish and sore. He reached out and touched Eddie and shook him to make sure his kid brother was alive. Eddie opened his eyes and Felix squeezed him again, relieved that Eddie was okay. They had fallen from a great distance, and Felix was amazed that they both survived the fall. Perhaps in this crazy land of monsters and spirits you could not die, especially if someone was already dead. He brushed his brother's forehead; Eddie was in a daze, and Felix wondered if it were possible that Eddie would die here if he still belonged in the world for the living. He shook his head not knowing what was feasible in this place; perhaps nobody knew the rules in this hell. "Are you okay?" Felix asked Eddie.

"Yeah," Eddie mumbled in a whispering voice.

Felix glimpsed around them, there were thick clouds of smoke billowing above the craters. He knelt, stood up and then helped Eddie to his feet. They were on a tree trunk larger than the deck of a boat and when a strong wind blew away some of the smoke, across from them, Captain Marvel appeared. The old man was running wildly from one corner of the porch to the other. In any other circumstance, he would have looked comical. He was shouting something, but the creature's howls drowned his screams.

Captain Marvel observed the hulking beast slither forward with alarming speed, its gigantic snout jerking from the porch to the fallen mango tree. Captain Marvel slapped his thigh in annoyance; damn, Felix was still thinking like a damn living person. The old man stomped his feet on the porch in a child-like tantrum. His agitated actions caught the attention of the monster. The creature was puzzled and to his delight, Captain Marvel saw it glide in hesitant motion. It seemed to surrender its deadly speed, yet its nose sniffed in the direction of the boys.

"Felix!" Captain Marvel yelled, cupping his hands over his mouth. *"Stop thinking like the living. You are dead, boy, do you hear me? You are dead. Save your brother."*

In desperation, the old man watched as Felix cocked his head trying to capture his words.

"Get up!" Captain Marvel screamed, and he felt his voice grow tight and hoarse. The creature again dismissed him and returned his attention to the boys. *"Felix!"* he felt helpless now. *"Dammit kid, get up, you are no longer human. Come on boy, you can fly! You are a spirit now!"*

The old man held his breath and watched eagerly as Felix began to pull Eddie. As they held onto each other, they ran along the tree trunk while the monster increased its speed. *"Up, Felix!"* Captain Marvel screamed waving his hands up. *"Felix! Up, up! Up, up and away, Felix! Up, up and away!"* the old man's voice trembled; his screams burned his throat. He saw Felix stop abruptly and stare at him and to his panic, the colossal worm jumped.

Frozen on the rotted planks of the burning porch, Captain Marvel paused. He witnessed the worm dive onto the fallen mango tree. He heard the crunching of the tree trunk snapping in half and the wild roar of the creature. It was a combination of a terrifying loudness, and he didn't know if the monster's howl was a triumphant one. There was a brown-reddish cloud that rose into the sky as the creature rammed into the earth taking with it the huge mango tree.

The old man screamed and then cried with jubilation when he saw Felix and Eddie rise up and climb the gray clouds. He jumped with excitement and shook his fist with joy. Both boys were flying above like two real comic book superheroes.

Landing awkwardly on the porch, the boys missed falling on top of Captain Marvel by just mere inches. Felix was exhausted; he found the strength of carrying another person depleted his new-found powers. It was natural for someone still stuck with the ideas and the way of thinking of the living world to adapt in moving like a spirit. Elevated with exuberance at seeing the boys next to him, the old man jumped on top of them and hugged them as if they were his own. Now he understood his son's obsession with this family, there was something magical in their aura and that aura was the glue that kept their family together. It was obviously Josefa's unselfish love.

"Wow that was fun," Eddie exclaimed looking at his brother in awe and with a new-found respect.

With a frown wrinkling his forehead, Felix backed away from Captain Marvel. "Why were you yelling so much? Couldn't you tell it was impossible to hear you above that thing's roars? The thing almost got us because I was trying to hear what the hell you were saying. Of all the time, you invaded my head with your voice, why didn't you do it now when I would not have minded at all?"

The old man walked gingerly to the upturned rocking chair and placed it upright. It was a bit of struggle, and he leaned on it for support. Eddie looked at Captain Marvel and for the first time the old man seemed ancient and weak. He no longer resembled Captain Marvel.

"I'm sorry, Felix," the old man said, exhaustion coated his words. *"But we also have stupid rules here too. The second spirits are revealed, the power to move voices from one to the other are no longer possible. I'm sorry if I almost got your brother killed."*

"A lot of shit I better learn here, right?" Felix said.

Eddie came forward and looked up at the old man's face. He noticed the deep wrinkles that seemed to have been etched by a knife. "What's your name, besides Captain Marvel?" Eddie touched him gently on his arm, feeling the old man's fatigue and wanting to know his real name.

Captain Marvel tousled Eddie's hair and pinched the child's ear lobe. There was something about the man's tired eyes that seemed to want nothing more in the world, but a final rest. *"My name is the same as my son's…Eduardo,"* the old man answered.

Felix flinched for a second and opened his mouth to say something, but Eddie spoke first. "Hey just like me! I bet they called you Señor Eduardo."

"Actually since I came back from fighting World War II, everyone called me Eddie…just like you."

There was a serenity that circled all three of them. They were in the center of a place where perhaps God and the Devil stood to choose side and see who would be playing for each other's team. Here in a broken down, poor imitation of human life, all three stood, without touching, without embracing, yet feeling as one.

There was a grunt from the earth's core. The groan became a gargle, and the ground rumbled and hundreds of cracks criss-crossed throughout. Fissures burst out, while black smoke with flaming tongues climbed into the sky and scorched the clouds.

"Sweet Jesus!" the old Eddie shouted as the remaining walls of the shack began to tumble. Then from the back the zinc-rusted roof caved in with a mighty force.

"Felix! Felix!" the old man cried, and he swallowed hard attempting

to hide the hysteria in his voice. *"You have to get Eddie out of here."*

"How the hell can we get out of here?" Felix screamed as he stared wildly at the destruction around him.

"You have to go to the shores of the river; that's the crossroad from the world of the living and the underworld. There Eddie will be able to get home. However, you must hurry, my boy, or Eddie will be forever trapped between both worlds, in another place similar to this one. Places like this are all in abundance, created by many spirits refusing to follow the chosen path that God has put before them."

"But how can I take him there? I know that monster will come out from the earth the minute we set foot on the ground."

"Stop thinking like a human, boy, and start thinking like what you are now, a spirit."

"You mean I could fly there? It's a long way from here."

"Yes, boy, you could fly from here, but we call it transcending. All you have to do is shed your human ideas and let the instinct of the underworld carry you," the elder Eddie moved rapidly coming around and grabbing the rocking chair by the armrests, while the rage of hell was unleashed underneath and around the porch. *"You have to take this with you. This is Eddie's way to get back home."*

Felix looked at the cumbersome rocking chair, figuring out a way to carry that and Eddie across the land and to the shores. "Well, will you be coming with us? I need help. I can't carry both."

"No, my job is complete with you and Eddie. But my duty as a father and a husband is not done yet."

"What do you mean?"

The man once known to Eddie and Felix as Captain Marvel pointed at the gaping, burning hole where they could hear a thunderous sound coming forth. It was the monster coming back to finish what he was spawned to do. *"I must look for my son and wife, even in this bowel of sinners, we are still a family. Our love, even so, burns within our bickering souls."*

Felix came around to the old man and shouted into his ear. "But they are in hell now."

"Yes I know, but everyone that goes to hell, doesn't mean that they have to stay there. I'm sure God will listen to me. He will bargain with the Devil for our souls. They are not blackened like those of murderers and insane sinners. I'm counting on that as a father, as a man, I could argue for the return of our souls into God's paradise. There are many levels in hell, I'm sure I could bring us to a level in hell, which will be closer to heaven."

From beneath the porch an explosion rocked the foundation; lifting the porch from its four crooked posts. All three of them stumbled and staggered fearing that the jaws of the creature would crash through the floor. There was another explosion that shook the burning shack violently and the small fire that had sparked from the monster's dark-green pus was now a wall of flame. The fire ran across the wall covering it in ashes and sparks. When it finally turned into a loud crash, it revealed the burning room where once an old woman sat by the window listening for the cries of a lonely husband.

"You guys have to leave now. Please I could feel the tremor of the worm coming for his claims," the old man shouted pushing Felix into the rocking chair.

Felix took hold of Eddie and looked down at the chair. "What's so important about that old piece of shit?"

The elder Eddie shook his head from side to side, and he placed his hands gently on Felix's shoulders. *"Your human fire still burns in you, but I could tell you this much, it won't be for long. This rocking chair was my son's only way to relieve and calm his epileptic attacks. The rocking motion always soothed him. It was his last link between the living world and the underworld. He always associated our home, his safety, and his dreams through the chair. There on that chair,"* the old man caressed the back of the rocker. *"My son, my lovely, beautiful son would sit and dream about a normal life, not restricted by a disease that ravaged his mind and body. He would fantasize about your mother and making her his bride. He dreamt about making his own happy family, his own son, who would carry his legacy, his name into the future of many generations. All he ever dreamt on that chair was to be a man,"* the ancient man paused and exhaled while he continued.

"When my son died, he always returned to the chair. Every night when everything was quiet, I could hear the soft squeaking sounds of the chair rocking back and forth. It was like having my dear boy back. His mother took it upon herself to rock herself for hours and hours…day and night. Sitting there, it was the only way she could feel close to him, to her Eduardito. She would sing and rocked him to sleep, right there on that rocking chair, to our poor son who was dead. When my wife died from a broken heart while rocking on the rocking chair, it was like finding the door in this place. I was already dead, and I tried to welcome her to our new world and to convince Eduardo to join us. However, she joined him instead in his forbidden quest to be your mother's lover. No one knows exactly how he did it, but Eduardo brought this chair from the world of the living into this world. It is perhaps the first and last time a spirit has been capable of transporting a solid living matter to the underworld. Now it must be returned, and Eduardo will no longer be able to go back to a world that is not ours anymore. Through Eddie, the chair will be returned, and the chair will return Eddie as well."

Felix looked down at himself. He noticed he was fully dressed, even the 'Sacred Heart of Jesus' medallion was on the chain around his neck. He lifted the medallion and showed it to the older Eddie. He wanted to prove that bringing a solid matter was not impossible. The old man smiled, amused at Felix. The boy was still finding it hard to grasp the spirit world. It was going to take the boy a long time to finally believe and readjust his way of thinking.

"You are not really wearing those clothes or medal around your neck as much as I'm not wearing what you see. We are spirits, my boy; we are lights of energy. Our human eyes deceived our vision just to comfort our souls. It would take time for your mortal mind to accept such a unique concept; I know mine did. What now might seem alien to you, very soon it will be as normal as the faces of angels and the horns of demons. Don't worry, it will be strange, but an exciting world as well."

The last remaining walls of what was the old woman's room came down. It took half of the porch with its force and sent the cowering spirits into other places like this one. Flames whipped savagely around them and now the walls of the other side of the shack were ablaze. The thin mattress that once protected Eduardo's soul, rolled and burned into a crackling ball. Now the putrid floor sunk and joined the flames that reached out from the red burning earth. A beam from somewhere inside the remains of the shack came crashing right behind Eddie, and the child pushed his body into his brother.

"You two have to go now," the old Eddie said. *"Please don't you see what's happening, hell is trying to burn this place down; it smells the richness of Eddie's clean soul. Please go before the worm, the carrier of sinners returns."*

"But how can I take Eddie with the chair? In midair, I might lose control and kill my brother," Felix was desperate.

"Look there in the sky," the man once called Captain Marvel by Eddie pointed above. *"Your mother has sent you some help. Your mother will never fail you...for all mothers are the protectors of God's little ones."*

Above the inferno, two silhouettes appeared through the blackened acrid clouds. There was an aura around them, and as they descended, the flames of hell seemed to burn a bit less. They were two elderly women dressed in flowing white and light blue robes, the colors of the Holy Virgin Mary. They looked like two virgin themselves and Felix immediately recognized them as Doña Lola and Doña Luz, the two midwives of his youth. They came to rest on the smoldering porch and then each woman stood by Eddie's side. "Your mother awaits you," Doña Lola said. "It is time to go home."

Eddie watched them, and something in their faces filled him with serenity. He was going home, and that thought made him feel sad and happy. There was a void in his heart, and he wished he didn't have to go as he turned and looked at his protector, his Captain Marvel. He approached him, and he wanted to be brave; he wanted to smile, but instead he closed his eyes and cried as he buried his face into the old man's arms. Eddie did not remember his grandfathers, all he knew were faded black-and-white photographs, but embracing this old man felt like he was embracing his own grandfather. "Will you be able to come and see me?" Eddie asked, yet knowing very well the answer.

"I don't know if I am able to go back to your world, but don't worry I'll always be watching you from my own world. That my little friend is a promise," the old man half-smile with joy and sadness.

Eddie felt the gentle touch of the two elder ladies on each arm, and he knew it was time to say good-bye perhaps forever to Captain Marvel. "Thank you," the child said as his body was lifted by the two midwives.

Felix nodded towards the old man as he grabbed the rocking chair. "Well, señor I guess we might see each other around, maybe you could show me the new neighborhood."

The elderly man laughed and it felt good, as he watched them go up into the skies, while underneath him, the sounds of the worm got closer.

"Come now, beast from hell," Eddie the old man exclaimed. *"I'm ready."*

Chapter Thirty-Seven

From above the dark, smoke-bloated clouds, the two brothers and the two midwives witnessed the eruption of the red dirt below. The worm leaped out and its huge mouth twisted with a roar. They watched the beast topple out of the flames and into the sky. It spun around and twisting its mammoth body it went straight to where the old man waited with his fists poised in defiance. Eddie screamed, and Felix squinted his eyes. The monster fell as it eclipsed the last remaining wreck of the shack and through the fiery red dirt, it burrowed into the ground. It rammed into the earth in a rain of shattered rocks, snapped, uprooted trees and the last of the wooden planks of the porch. There were thunder and lighting, which shot out from the pit and into the skies blackening the horizon with the colors of the night. More spirits erupted from their hiding places that were perhaps concealed for centuries. They burst out from tree trunks and the foliage shrieking in a confused madness.

In solemn silence, the brothers and the two midwives hovered above. They watched the red earth disappear violently. In its place, a huge crater was formed, exactly where the worm-like monster had gone into and soon all that was left was the cavernous mouth of a bottomless pit. It was the entrance to a land of demons where condemned souls would suffer an eternity in the brimstones of hell.

The abyss was a gigantic valley, where nothing would ever grow, only the hopes of those captives in its stronghold. Chiseled and covered with razor-like corners, red-orange walls stood out; resembling evil sculptures created by the scorching hands of demons. From above their safe distance, the motley group of two brothers and two mid-wives looked down at horned-winged creatures. Each demon held a hard-forged pitchfork, which they used to hook and throw terrified souls into the lava-filled seas. Souls of naked men and women lifted their hands supplicating for a salvation, which perhaps was now too late to be sought. They splashed into the hot fiery river, their haunting screams like funeral songs.

In desperation, a few attempted to scale the walls like frantic reptiles, slithering upward. Yet no sooner did they touch the top of the pit that a pitchfork would hurl them back into the volcanic fire. And all those poor souls with their faces all twisted and suffering as one screamed in horror, while some even begged for God's saving hold. They shouted in unison, 'Our Father who art in Heaven, hallowed be thy name,' and tearfully chanted 'Hail Mary's', hoping their prayers would reach God's ears. And in one small corner, the two brothers and the two old women witness, three figures that knelt in front of a shadow. Beyond the thick black smoke that swirled out of the hole, they could easily make out the hunched body of Eduardo's mother; her only sin was in trying to be a good mother. They also could see for themselves the shaken defeated body of a very sick man; his sin was that he fell in love with a woman whom he could never possess. And as a protector of these two sobbing souls, a polite little old man stood up like a hero. They could hear his eloquent speech as he begged for forgiveness, understanding and salvation in Heaven.

Then from the shadow, a creature moved, not with sympathy, but with delight, basking in his powers over the newcomers. Perhaps enjoying the reality that power is the seed of arrogance, and arrogance is the seed that gives pleasure in seeing the sufferings of others. The creature was a dark silhouette with leathery flapping wings. A whip-like tail coiled around two bow-legged masses of muscles that ended in hooves. And as the demon pointed at someone below, he did it with black-nailed hands, where streams of fire shot out. It seemed to relish on its power that inflicted more pain on those poor souls, who now regretted their sinful earthly ways. Then the winged demon began to pace; royalty in the vast of hell. From the shadows, it looked up and found Felix's mesmerized eyes, as well as Eddie's and the two holy beings.

The face seemed to be etched in tarnished granite with rivers of deep wrinkles and maggot-laced hair. It was the face of evil and of centuries-old nightmares. The eyes were two fine red slits, and its nose was a protruded sharp distortion that sneered with every breath it took. The chin was a construction of an elongated point, which slightly curved at the end. The mouth was a continuous grin that did not hide the old brownish fangs, which salivated with drooling smoke. However, the most horrible aspect on the face was the snake-like tongue, and it hissed at the two boys above. It was the face of corruption and of wickedness. It was the face of a demon who tried to hide its disappointment of losing the precious innocent souls of two boys.

He nodded his head, in a saluting grace. Then, he spread his mighty wings and raising his arms the demon scream as repugnant as his foul stench, which contaminated the sky. He raised his voice loud over the clouds, and it called out Eddie's name, frightening the child.

Eddie turned his head away quickly from the sight that will become his nightmare for the rest of his life. There was an explosion, and a blazing heat rushed at them from below as it pushed them higher into the sky. The flames scorch them and blinded them for a few seconds. Eddie did not want to know the cause of such a powerful eruption. He just wanted to go home.

At last, Eddie opened his eyes. Encircling them were clouds, and as they floated upward, the sky began to change in density and shape. There was still apprehension in Eddie as he looked down, not wanting to find the horrible face of the demon, but to his content, only thick, milky clouds peeked back. It felt like a brand-new world, and he marveled at the fluffiness of the clouds. Eddie closed his eyes, and it was good and refreshing to feel the clean wind brushing his hair. The coolness of the rushing wind was cleansing him and ridding him of the foulness, which he knew would stain him for life.

He opened his eyes again to see that the clouds disappeared and in front of him was the bluest sky he had ever seen. Below them, he could see tall trees, impregnated with fruits and exotic flowers. A butterfly flew greeting him to this paradise, and it landed softly on his shoulder, and then it flew away.

All four flying figures in the sky began to descend, and Eddie watched with fascination, as the top of the tall trees grew closer. They floated down through the trees, and soon they were overwhelmed by the sweet scent of green.

They landed softly as the dew-filled grass moistened Eddie's feet and before him, soothing waves from a river rolled gently onto the shore. Upon the river, a weathered boat bobbled in and out of the waters and standing on it was the boatman. Eddie knew the boatman was waiting patiently for his brother's soul. There were happy, vibrant sounds and when Eddie looked across the river, he saw a group of people waving at them. Some were jumping exuberantly while others shielded their eyes perhaps to get a better look at the new arrival. Eddie turned toward Felix and then back to the people and felt sadness. He stared again at Felix, who was gently placing down the rocking chair on the threshold that would forever separate them.

The two midwives watched them with motherly love. Doña Lola took Felix by the hand and squeezed hard and walked with him to where the group of people still waved. They were now calling out his name. "They are waiting for you...they are your beloved family members that have made the journey, which you are making as well. That will be your world, our world, and the next level to the doctrines of God."

In silence, Felix contemplated at the other side. Then he turned trying to see through the trees and green vegetation and the hell; they escaped. "But I killed a man; I broke one of God's commandments. Why am I not there instead?"

"What you have done in your earthly stage, taking the life of a fellow brother that will be a sin you will stand trial for. Nevertheless, do not worry, mi hijo, I'm sure that what you have done all your life, the sacrifices you made and the protection you have given to your little brother will be taken into consideration. God is a very understanding Father, plus you were deceived, manipulated by others. Go to God with humbleness and with a pure heart. If you do my son, your sins will be forgiven. Go on child, go with God."

Felix blinked and in his heart, he felt something being lifted. He felt the touch of God already removing the sins that he had committed in his human world. "Before I go, I need to know what's going to happen to my brother. I'm not going anywhere with the boatman until I know Eddie is home."

"He will return to his home and never again will the sickness of a dead man ravage his body and soul," Doña Lola said, and then they were joined by Doña Luz, who quickly winked at Felix filling him with memories of her. Doña Luz spent almost three months dutifully with Felix and his family when Eddie was born. She was the one responsible for releasing Eddie from the grasp of Death. She also noticed the way Felix had withdrawn as everything orbited around the newborn's needs. From those early days, Felix became the errand boy, the one to eat last and to understand that the little ones always came first.

Because of that Doña Luz regularly sneaked a candy or two to Felix whenever she saw him feeling alone. Now as she planted a kiss upon his cheek, she reached out and placed in Felix's hand a piece of caramel. "Go my son, go on. Everything will be fine; Eddie will find his way home."

"But how will Eddie know how to get home?"

"He'll know; all he has to do is sit on the rocking chair."

"The old man mentioned that the rocking chair belonged to the world for the living. Now how will that be possible? I know that the only thing here of Eddie is his soul, his body is still in the hospital, but how can something made of wood return from this world?"

"Every matter, regardless if it's a living creature or something created by the hands of a laborer possesses energy. The chair's energy will take Eddie home and after that the chair will become another piece of dead wood in this forest. It's time to leave, not only for us, but also for you too as well. Please, your mother is waiting for Eddie now and God is waiting for you."

The two midwives smiled and walked toward the river as their flowing gowns danced in the wind. They began to ascend, and soon they were part of the trees, the flowers and the peaceful wind, which hummed a sweet song.

Felix and Eddie stared at the ladies disappearing like apparitions in a dream and then their eyes roamed through the vegetation around them. It was beautiful scenery rich in kaleidoscope colors. Both brothers could hear the soft gurgling sound from the waves hitting the shore. They could hear the haunting low whistles of the wind as it swept through the tree branches. They could hear the silky butterflies flapping their tender wings and the flight of multi-colored birds. They could both hear their hearts parting, and they stared into each other's eyes.

"Well kiddo," Felix tried to be brave. "I guess this is it, very soon you'll have your own room."

Eddie shook his head as tears spilled from his eyes. "No," he whispered sounding hoarse. "No," he repeated, his voice small and sad and the words trembled.

"Yes Eddie," Felix came to him and placed his hands on his little brother's shoulders. He swallowed hard; he did not want to cry. He had to be brave, he kept repeating to himself.

Eddie went to him and wrapped his arms around him. Felix felt the strength of his brother as a knot lodged in his throat. He could feel Eddie's tears wetting his shirt, and he could feel his little brother's heart pounding hard. Felix tried to push him away gently and into the rocking chair, but Eddie tightened his arms. "No," Felix heard Eddie's wail, and he could not control his own tears anymore. Felix felt them drip slowly down his cheek.

"You can't leave, please you can't leave," Eddie was sobbing loudly now, his red face contorted with pain and grief.

"Yes Eddie, we both have to leave."

"Why can't we leave together? There's enough room for the two of us on the chair."

"Eddie," Felix tried to pry his brother's arm from his waist, but all he could do was lift Eddie's teary face up to his. "We are now part of two different worlds. The place where I'm going, someday you will join me, but only when God decides. Now you have to return. You have to go to your own world."

Eddie sniffled hard and let go of Felix, yet standing close. "Felix," the child looked deep into his older brother's eyes. "Am I going to Heaven?"

Felix smiled as he fought to keep his composure, his bravery intact. "No kiddo—" Felix shook his head biting his trembling lower lip. "No kiddo, you are not going to Heaven, but to a better place. You are going to the embrace, to the arms of our mother."

Then Felix crumbled to the ground burying his head in his brother's small chest. He wrapped his arms around him, and he hugged him tight. He did not want to let go. He held on to Eddie, and now he was the one that did not want to go, maybe Eddie was right, maybe there was enough room on the rocker. Perhaps he didn't die; after all, maybe just like Eddie he was laying in some dark, alcohol smelling hospital waiting for his soul to return. Felix felt lost and afraid…there was a sense of homesickness that grasped his heart and made him cry even longer.

Then from across the river Felix heard his name called, and he looked up as the tears ran down his face. Eddie took his hand, and both walked toward the shore of the river where the boatman solemnly waited. Felix took a deep breath and then kneeling down took a cupped hand into the water and washed his face; his tears joining the clear serene waters of the river. He exhaled and led Eddie where the rocking chair stood as the wind rocked it back and forth.

Eddie looked toward the chair, the rocking chair that had fascinated him since the first time he met Eduardo. Now he understood the strong desire he had on that long-ago day to sit and rock back and forth in the chair. The old midwife said the energy was calling out, perhaps just like him; the rocking chair wanted to return home. Eddie sat down as his body slid all the way to the back. It was comfortable, and it felt cool; he put his hands on the armrest feeling the smoothness of the mahogany wood. He smiled at Felix, who stood in front of him and there were no more tears between them for there was no reason to be sad. They will see each other again, if not sooner maybe later. Perhaps one day when Eddie crosses the river with the boatman, Felix for sure will be the one jumping and waving hello. Both brothers' eyes locked upon each other and soon Eddie began to rock slowly, slowly and smoothly. He felt the wind rush through his hair, and his eyes began to close. It felt great and he heard, in the distance, his brave brother wishing him good-bye, and soon they'll be together again.

Eddie smiled and slowly opened his mouth, and one word came out.

"Shazzam!"

Chapter Thirty-Nine

Josefa looked down lovingly at Eddie and softly whispered the word 'Shazzam'. She touched his face, the way she checked if he had a fever, he felt cool, like he always did after taking a bath. She combed her fingers through his hair, and it felt dry and airy, not like before when it was hot and perspiring. From outside the room she could hear voices, getting closer and louder. She could hear Norma's voice among the others and the constant hush, hush from Agapito. Her family had arrived, yet something gnawed at her, perhaps a premeditation bringing bad news. Josefa stared at Francisco, and his eyes looked fatigued. There were dark bags under his eyes, and his hands trembled when he waved them frantically around Eddie during the cleansing ritual.

She saw him clutch something unseen, which he then deposited inside the glass filled with holy water. He did this many times. It was a ritual that he called a 'despojo', the removing of the bad spirit from Eddie, and now seeing her little defenseless boy still in a coma; she wondered how effective this cleansing was. Probably, God was punishing her for turning to hidden, obscured beliefs. Perhaps it was what she deserved, for believing so foolishly and trusting her sick little boy in the hands of a man, that regardless if he meant well, a senseless old man enamored with an antiquated African religion.

Josefa kept her eyes closed as she held the Captain Marvel comic book wanting to be nearer to Eddie. He still slept like an angel and Josefa lowered her lips to his puffy cheeks and kissed him. "Shazzam," Josefa whispered and then she pressed her forehead on Eddie, trying to remove the hurt as her tears began to fall gently on Eddie's peaceful face. "Shazzam," again she whispered while holding the comic book, and she felt Agapito's presence coming beside her. Her daughters' hands were upon her back, and she could distinctly tell, which were Migdalia's, Gisela's and Norma's.

Josefa sobbed quietly while caressing Eddie's face. "Shazzam," she said. "Shaz—"

"—zam," Eddie finished.

Josefa held her breath; her heart seemed to stop. She didn't dare to exhale or move. She stared down at Eddie, wondering if what she thought she heard was another cruel joke from God or was it really Eddie's voice.

She placed her face close to his, and she gasped when his eyes fluttered. She was shaking as she clutched her heart. "Baby," she whispered into his ear. There was a slight, weak moan that escaped his lips. Josefa felt her knees buckle under her weight, and she crumbled on Eddie's bed. Then slowly Eddie opened his eyes. He blinked rapidly adjusting to the light.

Josefa screamed with joy as she looked down at Eddie's face. She lifted him up into her arms, and her eyes were blinded with tears of joy. She screamed again not caring who heard her shouts of happiness. She placed wild kisses all over Eddie's face and Josefa felt her heart, her beaten heart pounding filled with energy. She rocked her little boy; feeling his thin body so weak and so tender and she rocked him not wanting to ever let go.

Nurses and doctors ran into the room, and Josefa could feel the strength, and love that were coming from the strong embrace of her family. Eddie gave her his toothy smile, something she thought she would never see again. Agapito put his arm around her, and she felt the closeness of her daughters around her too. They were crying and each trying to touch Eddie and be close to him. Together they built a wall, one that would never to be broken again.

Francisco stepped from the shadows and witnessed the euphoria, and he was pleased. Bowing his head, he gave his humble thanks to his orishas, and saved the best heart-felt thanks to God.

As he looked around, Eddie felt his family's tears raining down on him. He felt their love, yet one love was missing until an apparition manifested and joined them. It was Felix, and Eddie reached out his hand, and he felt the warmth of Felix's soul. In the dim light upon a place where many people died and where many souls embarked, Eddie saw a new beginning indeed and a love for life. Eddie felt his father's strength, and he felt the strength of his sisters, each one an individual fire. He also felt his mother's powerful strength; a strength that he would always carry with him into his future.

He felt his big brother's strength, rushing through him. Felix had kept his promise that he would make sure his little brother got home. Eddie now envisioned Felix climbing into the boat, where the boatman would take him to the arms of those waiting for him at the other side of the afterlife. And Eddie smiled and feeling the strong embrace of his mother; he realized that Felix was right. Yes, he was home, and yes it was true, to be in the arms of their mother was indeed better than Heaven.

About the Author

Manuel A. Meléndez is a Puerto Rican author born in Puerto Rico and raised in East Harlem, N.Y. He is the author of a mystery/supernatural novel "When Angels Fall", two poetry books, "Observations Through Poetry" and "Voices from my Soul" and a collection of Christmas short stories, "New York-Christmas Tales". "Battle for a Soul" was inspired by events that resulted in his own naming at birth, and these events haunted him from childhood and throughout the writing of the book. The author lives in Sunnyside, N.Y. harvesting tales from the streets of the city.

Battle for a Soul